DEATH NOTICE

Zhou Haohui was born in 1977 and lives in Yangzhou City, Jiangsu Province. His *Death Notice* trilogy is China's bestselling crime series to date. An online TV drama based on the novels has received more than 2.4 billion views, making it one of China's most popular online shows ever.

DEATH NOTICE

ZHOU HAOHUI

TRANSLATED FROM THE CHINESE BY ZAC HALUZA

First published in the UK by Head of Zeus in 2018

Originally published in China as *Si wang tong zhi dan: an hei zhe* by Beijing Times Chinese Press, Beijing, in 2014

9 7 5 3 1 2 4 6 8

A catalogue record for this book is available from the British Library.

ISBN (HB): 9781786699404
ISBN (XTPB): 9781786699411
ISBN (E): 9781786699398

Book design by Maria Carella

Printed and bound by CPI Group (UK) Ltd, Croydon, CR0 4YY

Head of Zeus Ltd
First Floor East
5–8 Hardwick Street
London EC1R 4RG
WWW.HEADOFZEUS.COM

CONTENTS

CAST OF CHARACTERS

THE 4/18 TASK FORCE

CAPTAIN HAN HAO—Chengdu Criminal Police, leader of the reinstated 4/18 team

OFFICER YIN JIAN—Assistant to Captain Han

CAPTAIN PEI TAO—Longzhou Criminal Police

CAPTAIN XIONG YUAN—Chengdu Special Police Unit (SPU)

OFFICER LIU SONG—Chengdu SPU

MU JIANYUN—Psychologist, lecturer at the Sichuan Police Academy

OFFICER ZENG RIHUA—Chengdu Criminal Police, supervisor of digital surveillance

SERGEANT ZHENG HAOMING—Chengdu Criminal Police, member of the original 1984 4/18 Task Force

DEATH NOTICE

PROLOGUE

Don't you remember me, Student 8102?

Once the overture finishes, the first act must commence.

It has been far too long since the overture faded . . . But the day has finally come.

I can barely restrain my excitement when I think of the beautiful dance about to begin. Won't you join me, my old friend? I know you've been looking forward to this for far too long.

I can see you reading this letter. You're trembling with excitement, aren't you? Your blood burns, and an unstoppable pressure is building up inside you. I feel it, too.

I smell your eagerness. Your anger. Even your fear.

Hurry. I'm waiting.

CHAPTER ONE

AN IMPENDING STORM

OCTOBER 19, 2002. 3:45 P.M.
CHENGDU, SICHUAN PROVINCE

A chill had seeped into the air during the Mid-Autumn Festival celebrations in September, and it had only deepened as the weeks passed. The last several days had seen constant rain and plummeting temperatures. A mist-laced wind whipped and howled past the city's high-rises and through its streets, spreading a cold misery through the air. It may have been a Saturday afternoon in Chengdu, but the glum weather had already stripped the provincial capital of its characteristic energy.

Zheng Haoming sprinted out of the taxi, forgetting all about the umbrella resting on the vehicle's floor. He dashed to the sidewalk and darted into a doorway marked SKYLINE CYBER CAFÉ.

Unlike the sparsely populated streets outside, the internet café was bustling. The shop had always enjoyed a steady stream of customers, as it was located within walking distance of several universities. The café's pudgy owner stood behind the front desk, flanked by two employees in their early twenties. His last check of the register had come up short, and until he finished reviewing the entire month's security footage, this red-faced man was determined to witness every transaction that took place inside his establishment. He raised an eyebrow as he noticed Zheng hurrying through the door. A middle-aged man was a rare sight here.

Zheng's clothes were soaked. His hair was tangled in knots. He placed a bag onto the counter, then fished out a slip of paper from one of its pockets and handed it to the owner. His hoarse voice betrayed a touch of fatigue.

"Look up this address," Zheng ordered. "Tell me which computer it belongs to."

The plump owner recognized the string of numbers on the slip, as they fell within the range of IP addresses used by the café's terminals. However, he regarded the piece of paper with an indifferent glance.

"Why should I?" he replied with a cold, disdainful look.

"Just be quiet, and give me the information!"

The owner shrank back from Zheng's scorching gaze. The older man's outburst startled a nearby network administrator as well; the young woman's bright black eyes swiveled toward the source of the commotion. The owner felt a raw wound where his pride once was.

Zheng appeared to be on the verge of losing his temper. He took out what appeared to be a wallet, unfolded it, and slapped it on the counter.

"I'm a police officer!" he hissed.

The owner looked down, and he immediately sucked in his breath. A badge decorated in red, blue, and gold was mounted inside the upper flap. Below it, protected by a shield of transparent plastic, was a card displaying the man's picture, name, and rank. He swallowed bitterly and handed the slip of paper to the girl beside him.

"Lin, look this up for Sergeant Zheng."

The girl compared the address with the others on the server's control monitor. "It's in the second row," she announced a moment later. "Sixth from the left."

Zheng glanced at the young man seated at that particular

computer. He appeared to be around twenty years old, and his hair was dyed red.

"How long has he been there?"

"Since noon. He's been on for almost five hours."

Zheng removed a digital camera from his bag. He pointed it at the customer and tapped the shutter button until he had taken ten photographs. Within the clamor of the café, the young man was so absorbed in his virtual world that he did not even notice the stranger taking pictures.

The digital camera beeped. The officer checked the device and saw that its memory was full.

He breathed a sigh of gentle relief, as though he had just completed an important task. Over the past two weeks, he had visited every single internet café in the city, and he had taken over three hundred photographs of the customers inside. Yet he had no idea whether any of his efforts would make any difference.

Come on, just go and see him. It's been eighteen years, Zheng thought. *It's time.*

He left the Skyline Cyber Café and trudged down the sidewalk with a new destination in mind. The wind clawed at his cheeks, and he ducked into the collar of his thin jacket. A fragrant blast of steam from a nearby wonton stall rolled over his face, providing a welcome contrast.

For the first time he realized how truly empty Chengdu's downtown streets had become over the past few weeks. He felt exposed now. Vulnerable. The feeling was as unfamiliar as it was unsettling. A few cold droplets of rain landed on his neck, and he tried, unsuccessfully, to suppress a shiver.

I'm waiting.

Those words made Zheng Haoming's blood run cold. Eighteen years ago, he thought he had escaped from this nightmare. Now he wondered if it had ever ended in the first place.

10:17 P.M.

A streetlight flickered over the neighborhood's north entrance, illuminating a ten-foot gap set between two cement walls. The wide metal gate stood open. Zheng had tried the east entrance first, but the gate there had rusted shut. He aimed his flashlight at the wall on the left. Three characters had been etched into the cement.

"Meiyuan Cun," Zheng murmured to himself.

Plum Orchard Village. It sounded pleasant enough, but Zheng, who had grown up in this city, knew this place by a different name. *Touyoupo Cao,* in the local Sichuan dialect. The Cockroach Nest.

After two minutes of navigating the development's narrow and confusing lanes, Zheng felt like a rat in a maze. Dilapidated single-story apartment buildings boxed him in on every side. A sickly glow flickered from the dim, shattered streetlamps, and an unnerving odor of mildew filled the air.

The rain continued. A layer of sludge glistened upon the pavement. Raw sewage, maybe. Possibly vomit. Ignoring the filth of his surroundings, Zheng walked up to a cramped building. He checked the address and rapped his knuckles three times against the wooden door.

"Who's there?" From inside the apartment, the weak voice rasped against Zheng's eardrums, sending pins and needles across his scalp.

After weighing his options, Zheng chose the most direct response.

"Police."

He heard soft footsteps from inside. Seconds later, the wooden door opened. In the room's faint light, a grim figure stood before him.

The officer had prepared himself for this moment, yet he still felt himself grimacing with suppressed disgust. He stood face-to-face with a human gargoyle. Of course he had come on a night like this.

Scars the color of mud marked the man's hairless scalp. As Zheng studied the craggy features of his face, he could not spot a single patch of intact skin. The man's eyes were askew, and a large chunk was missing from his nose. His upper lip was split at the center, giving him a rabbit-like appearance.

Zheng drew a deep breath. "Huang Shaoping."

The gnarled man shivered, and he stared at his visitor.

"Are you . . . Officer Zheng?" The man's voice seemed to rattle through shredded vocal cords, as though he were simultaneously gasping for breath.

Zheng raised his eyebrows. "You remember me, even after all these years."

"How could I forget?" Huang gritted his teeth. His voice made Zheng picture a rusty saw, but it didn't stop the officer from trembling with excitement.

"I have pictures to show you. New pictures." Zheng's hands trembled so fiercely that he nearly dropped his camera. He stuffed the device back into his pocket. "I haven't forgotten either. Not even for a second!"

"Come in."

Huang leaned against a walking stick. As he turned to lead Zheng deeper into his home, Zheng saw how badly time had treated his wounds. Huang's legs were twisted like burnt branches leading down from the painful-looking hump on his back. The house was small, no larger than 100 square feet. A small room had been partitioned off beside the door; peeking inside, Zheng spotted a food-encrusted pot on top of a cooking range. He moved farther inside the main room, brushing a cobweb from his face. A bed, table, and several chairs had been set up here. In the only part of the room that seemed to have any life to it, a news program blared from the old-fashioned twenty-inch television standing atop a pile of yellowed lumber.

Zheng felt a pang of pity for the man. Huang never should have ended up like this. His life had been far from luxurious before, but if not for that vile crime eighteen years earlier, at least he would be able to walk outside without drawing stares and whispers.

After leading his guest to a chair and seating himself on the edge of his bed, the hobbling man wasted no time on pleasantries.

"I don't understand. It's been so many years. I've heard nothing."

"Yes, but I've never stopped looking. I think he's back." Zheng took out his digital camera and found the pictures he had taken earlier. "Here. You must tell me if anyone stands out."

"They're all so young!" Huang leaned closer and peered at the camera's display. His head fell. "It was eighteen years ago—most of these kids hadn't even been born yet."

"Please, look again," Zheng said, scowling. "I've waited years for a lead like this. I can't leave any stone unturned. Even if it isn't the same person you saw eighteen years ago, there could still be a connection. Focus. Even if you have the slightest suspicion, don't ignore it!"

The scarred man glanced at Zheng in confusion, but he seemed to be trying. He looked carefully through the camera's pictures, focusing on each one for several seconds. Once he reached the final image, he shook his head.

"Is this all you have?" Perhaps reluctant to disappoint his visitor, Huang added, "Who are these people, anyway?"

Zheng didn't answer. If it wasn't even the same person, how was Huang Shaoping supposed to know if they were connected? Zheng's request was far from simple. In fact, it was absurd. He put the camera away and heaved a grudging sigh. Huang knew nothing. In this eighteen-year-old tragedy, he had merely played the role of victim.

As if he had read Zheng's thoughts, Huang snickered. It was hard for Zheng to tell who Huang was laughing at. The man's torn lip curled upward, revealing a row of bone-white teeth.

Zheng raised his eyebrows. "Can you see a doctor about that?" He winced as soon as the words left his mouth.

"Oh, why don't I give my plastic surgeon a call?" Huang snorted, but it sounded as though he were choking. "Take a look around this place. I'm lucky to have made it this far selling scrap and collecting welfare. Just let this old man die in peace."

"Well, you've seen the photos," Zheng said brusquely. "Get in touch with me right away if you think of anything. I might come back to ask you more questions sometime soon."

Huang leaned against his cane and rose up from his bed. His disappointment was perfectly clear. There was nothing more to say.

||||

TWO DAYS LATER: OCTOBER 21, 10:52 A.M.
CHENGDU CRIMINAL POLICE HEADQUARTERS

The tension filling the office of Captain Han Hao was thick enough to choke on. Captain Han pounded his fist against the polished oak desk and stood up from his chair. His shoulders bulged underneath his crisp blue uniform shirt.

"Tell me everything!" His voice was just below a roar.

Sitting across from him was Officer Yin Jian. Yin was by no means a tall man, but he felt absolutely minuscule under Captain Han's wide eyes. He recoiled slightly in his seat.

"We just got a call from Nancheng station," Yin said. "Sergeant Zheng Haoming has been murdered."

"Give me details!" Han's cheek twitched. His words sent chills down his subordinate's spine.

"Ten minutes ago, the station received a phone call reporting a homicide. The first officers were on-scene five minutes later. They identified the victim as one of ours and immediately notified us. That's all I have. They're still in the process of gathering more details."

"Let's move!" Throwing on his uniform jacket, Han strode out from his office.

Yin hurried after him. "Captain, there's also a rather unique situation. The man who reported the homicide is also a cop."

"From Nancheng station?"

"No. He says he's the captain of police in Longzhou."

"Longzhou?"

Han frowned. Longzhou was a backwater that was at least a two-hour drive from Chengdu. What was a small-town captain doing on his turf?

Regardless, he did not have the luxury to ponder aimless questions. On the way from his office to the parking lot outside, Han made a series of calls. He marshaled the department's best forensic scientist, their top criminal investigation expert, and their most capable search team—ordering them all to converge at the crime scene as soon as possible.

The news of Sergeant Zheng's death had sent shock waves through Chengdu's police community. The murder of any police officer was shocking, but Zheng Haoming was a legend.

Sergeant Zheng was dead at the age of forty-eight, after serving a full quarter-century on the Chengdu police force. His talent for law enforcement had been apparent from the very beginning of his career. Although he lacked the police academy education that was now standard among members of the department, which prevented him from receiving a promotion beyond sergeant, he was an icon within the force. He had been spending more time behind his desk lately, but the department was still full of officers he had personally mentored. Even the irascible Captain Han softened in his presence.

His murder was a dagger through the heart of every police officer. For Han, this blade plunged deep.

Once inside the police car, Han turned his attention to the officer waiting at the wheel.

"Step on it!"

The car became a flashing blue-and-white blur as it shot down the road, sirens blaring.

Two years prior, Zheng had moved his family out of police housing to a quiet new apartment far from the tumult of downtown Chengdu. Rather than let the aging police apartment lie idle and unused, Zheng still spent nights there whenever he worked overtime. It allowed him to keep in touch with colleagues, and helped to avoid disturbing his sleeping wife and daughter. He called it his second office.

Zheng now lay dead in his second office, virtually within spitting distance of the police station. With the help of the driver's lead foot, Captain Han reached the apartment in under ten minutes.

The apartment was located in a quieter section of the city in a cluster of small, old-fashioned brick and concrete buildings. A young officer from the police station stood watch at the street entrance. Han opened the door and jumped out before the patrol car had even come to a complete stop. In seconds, he was jogging up the stairs.

When he reached the third-floor landing, he spotted two officers standing guard outside the door to the apartment. Both recognized the captain at once. A tone of respect marked their greetings.

"Why are you both standing out here?" Han's expression was stern. "What's going on?"

The younger officers looked embarrassed. One scratched his head.

"We're not too clear about that. There's a cop in the room, and he won't let us inside. He said we had to stand guard out here."

The two officers explained that they had rushed to the apartment immediately, but the man who had called the emergency dispatch center was already inside the apartment. Both were shocked when he flashed a police badge and refused to allow them inside. Seeing no other option, they called in their report to headquarters while they waited outside.

Han gritted his teeth. Instead of questioning the officers further, he entered the apartment to see for himself.

The residence was a pure example of function over form. The living room on his left contained a sofa, a wooden coffee table, and a dark television set. He stepped into the kitchen on the right, absently taking note of the pile of empty instant-noodle packages on the counter. Then the smell hit him.

The room reeked of blood, thanks in no small part to the building's poor circulation. Zheng Haoming lay on his back on the living room floor. Judging from the large crimson pool beneath the sergeant's neck, Zheng had been dead for at least several hours. Next to the corpse was a man crouched on one knee. He was examining a cleaver on the floor.

"You're the cop from Longzhou?" Han demanded.

Yin Jian entered the apartment as Han spoke, and he took his place behind the captain.

The stranger looked at both of the officers with a gaze that could cut steel. He wore a windbreaker that hugged his thin frame, and he appeared to be around thirty.

He raised his left hand, the palm facing out toward Han and Yin. At the same time, he drew a badge holder from his chest pocket with his right hand. He tossed it toward Han, who snatched it from the air.

"Captain Pei Tao," the man said. "Longzhou Police Department."

After glancing at the man's ID, Han passed the badge to Yin. "Verify his credentials," he ordered.

Squinting, Pei sized up the two officers.

"I take it one of you is in charge of this investigation?"

Yin gestured toward his superior. "This is Captain Han Hao, Chengdu Police Department," Yin said.

Pei nodded. "Then I'm sure you've investigated plenty of crime scenes like this one. Just take care not to disturb any potential evidence around the body."

Han's face soured. He dismissed Yin with a wave of his hand. Yin left the room, shaking his head. There was an unspoken rule among the members of Chengdu's criminal police force: no one gave orders to Captain Han.

Han aimed his finger at the younger officer. "Captain Pei, why exactly are you here?"

Pei stiffened. Judging from his expression, he had just realized that his previous comments had not been well received. He promptly stood up.

"I came here on a private matter with the sergeant. I had no idea that he—"

"Since you came here due to personal matters," Han coldly interrupted, "you must leave the scene immediately. Report to Officer Yin outside. He'll record your account."

Pei fixed his eyes on the tall, athletic police captain. Han reciprocated with a steely gaze of his own. Voices filled the hallway outside; seconds later, there was a flurry of uniforms and equipment as the forensic scientist and other investigators filed into the apartment.

"Get moving," Han said. "I don't want you interfering with our work."

With a curt nod, Pei strode away from the body of the sergeant. He stopped in front of Han.

"I've already found a few leads. Perhaps we could exchange theories on how the sergeant was murdered."

"Make no mistake, Captain Pei. As a witness, and as the one who reported this crime, you're legally obligated to cooperate with our investigation. But I'm sure you already know that. You must have investigated plenty of crime scenes like this one." The faintest hint of a smirk crept over Han's lips.

Yin poked his head through the doorway. "Officer Pei, please come this way." His demeanor was a welcome contrast to Han's. Seeing a chance to extricate himself from an awkward situation, Pei nodded and left the room. As he did, Han began his inspection of the crime scene.

IIII

Yin led Pei away from the apartment and over to a quieter section of the hallway. His gaze lingered on the fist-sized patch of blood staining Pei's left pant leg.

"This is all standard operating procedure. Right now I'd like you to give me your account of what happened, starting from your arrival at the scene." Yin took out his pen and notepad.

The whine of sirens crept in from the windows, and the two men saw several police vehicles pull up outside the building. Han's reinforcements had arrived.

Pei waved his hand at Yin. "We'll have plenty of time to discuss what happened later. Right now, there's something more important. Do you have the authority to give orders to the officers who just arrived?"

Yin shook his head. "Captain Han's inside the apartment. Why would they listen to me instead of him?"

"In that case, tell the captain that you need to begin a citywide search for our killer. He's male, thin, and approximately five-foot-five. He may have a knife wound on one hand. The suspect was in this area sometime between eleven o'clock last night and two this morning." His eyes gleamed as he rattled off each detail.

Yin fidgeted slightly. "There's no way that the captain will agree to that."

"You know I'm right." There was an undeniable firmness and confidence to Pei's words.

Yin forced a smile. "No, I'm afraid you don't understand. It isn't a matter of whether or not I believe you. You need to do as the captain says, not the other way around."

Exhaustion soured Pei's features.

"Fine. Just make sure that you take all this down. The reason for my visit here was a private matter. I called Sergeant Zheng's office at 9:52 this morning. He didn't answer. I got through to one of your colleagues, who gave me his mobile number. Again, no answer. I managed to reach an aunt of his who told me he often stayed at this apartment when he was working. I arrived here at 10:37.

"I knocked. No one answered, but I could smell a strong odor coming from inside. The door was unlocked. I opened it, saw the body, and reported it to the police. Then I carried out my initial investigation of the scene. The officers from the station arrived at 10:49—ten minutes after I called. In order to preserve the scene's integrity, I didn't allow them to enter the apartment. At five minutes after eleven, you and the captain arrived."

Pei recited each piece of information with the fluency of an actor who knew his lines inside and out.

"9:52. These times are very . . . exact," Yin said, with palpable suspicion.

The man from Longzhou gave him a grim look. "The times are accurate—you can trust me on that. My watch is precise to the minute."

After double-checking everything he had jotted down in his notepad, Yin looked back up at Pei.

"Did you know Sergeant Zheng?"

To Yin's surprise, Pei shook his head. "No."

"Then why did you have private business with him?"

Pei paused. "It concerned the details of a separate case. A case that Sergeant Zheng was in charge of."

"A case?" Yin scratched the tip of his nose. This answer only confused him further. "Wouldn't that make it official business?"

Long seconds passed before Pei responded. This time he spoke much more slowly than before. "It's an eighteen-year-old case. I was one of the people involved, before I joined the force."

"That's practically ancient history. Why would you suddenly want to go digging through the past all these years later?" Yin pursed his lips. "Let's stick to the matter at hand. Now, describe the scene as you saw it."

Pei looked startled. A chill came into his voice.

"I wouldn't say that the cases are unconnected."

Yin squirmed under Pei's piercing gaze. "What is this case, exactly?"

Pei saw that the officer was nervous, unpredictable. After forcing himself to relax, he took a calming breath and asked, "How long have you been a police officer?"

"A little under two years," the man answered honestly.

"Did you graduate from the Sichuan Police Academy?" Pei asked, referring to the province's most prestigious law enforcement institution.

"That's right. I majored in criminal investigation."

"We're practically classmates, then." Pei smiled at Yin, his eyes gleaming. "I graduated from the academy in '84. Same major as you. Does Wei still teach for the department?"

"He does!" The young officer's head bobbed up and down. "I had him for a course on trace evidence."

"Wei and I attended the academy together," Pei said. He patted Yin on the shoulder. "Ask any of the old instructors in the department, and they'll probably remember me."

"Well, what do you know!" Yin made no attempt to hide his new sense of camaraderie.

Pei's features hardened. "My sincerity should be clear enough.

Am I correct in thinking that I can trust you? Because I need your help."

Yin nodded immediately. Pei's charisma was undeniable. He had swept away the young officer's suspicions with an almost brotherly tenderness.

"Excellent." Pei rubbed his jaw in satisfaction. His lips curled into a slight grin. "You don't need to ask too many questions about that old case. Not for the moment, at least. Right now I have a few questions of my own. Did Sergeant Zheng exhibit any unusual behavior over the last few days? Did he say or do anything out of the ordinary?"

Yin wrinkled his brow in concentration and glanced down at his feet. "Anything unusual? Over the past few days, he did most of his work outside the station, but that isn't strange. I'm sure you spent a lot of time on fieldwork as well."

"How many cases was he working on, exactly?"

Yin shook his head.

"None. I mean, Zheng was no spring chicken. The department stopped putting him in charge of cases a while back. His work generally revolved around analysis and supervision. Still, he was always busy. Even if he hadn't been assigned any work, he would venture outside the station fairly often. 'Feeling the city's pulse,'" Yin said. His eyes suddenly lit up. "I just remembered! I think most of his business over the last several days was about some kind of preliminary surveillance."

Pei raised his eyebrows at this last revelation. "How do you know that? Did he discuss his work with you?"

"No, the sergeant always kept to himself. He wasn't much of a people person. The only reason I'm guessing that he was doing surveillance work is because he took a digital camera with him on each of those days."

"Was it a silver Nikon?" Pei raised his eyebrows.

"That's right. All our cameras are the same model. How did you know?"

"There's a Nikon inside the apartment. It's on the living room table!"

Pei looked past Yin. A pair of stern new arrivals from the Chengdu police guarded the door. Pei's chances of entering the apartment again were now slim to none. His best option was to turn to his new comrade for help.

"I need to see that camera right now," Pei whispered. "Do you think you can get it for me?"

Yin hesitated. "Well . . . I'll give it a shot. The captain has the final say."

Pei nodded. As dissatisfied as he was, he knew Yin's hands were tied. The officer was Han's subordinate, after all.

Fortunately, Yin did not disappoint. Moments later the officer emerged from the apartment holding a dull silver camera in his newly gloved hands.

"I can show you the photos in the camera's memory, but you can't personally touch the camera. Captain's orders."

As Pei watched, Yin cycled through each of the photographs that Zheng had recently taken. Pei's eyes were glued to the camera's display. Occasionally, he frowned and asked Yin to stop on a certain image. Each time he did this, he would take out his trusted pen and notepad to scribble down a few notes. Half an hour later, Yin finally reached the last of the three hundred images stored on the camera.

Pei let out a long breath. "Okay. These photographs follow a very clear pattern. However, there are a few suspicious points worth noting. Most important, at least we have our hands on a valuable lead now."

"Let's see if I can figure out this pattern you mentioned. The photos were taken at several internet cafés. Zheng took these pictures from a concealed position, meaning that the subjects were unaware they were being photographed. I count a total of fifty-seven individuals, primarily teenagers and young adults.

However, their ages seem to be all that they have in common. I wonder what Zheng was hoping to find by taking pictures of these people?" Yin's eyes shone with an eager light. "Did I leave anything out?"

Without even realizing it, he had handed Pei the reins of the conversation.

"Your count was off by one. If you look through the photos again, you should find that Zheng photographed fifty-eight people in all." Pei twirled his pen in his fingers.

"Do you mean I miscounted?" Yin gave Pei a puzzled look.

"No, you counted correctly. The images do show fifty-seven different subjects. Did you notice that every picture has its own file name?"

Yin fiddled with the camera. "You're right. They're all numbered."

"Each picture is automatically numbered in sequence," Pei said. "Now here's the kicker—the six images that should be labeled 280 through 285 are missing."

"You're right," Yin said. Realization dawned on his features. "It seems too deliberate to be a mistake. These images could very well have contained a fifty-eighth individual."

"But who deleted them? And why?" Pei muttered to himself. "This isn't as simple as it looks."

"Are you suggesting that this is somehow related to Sergeant Zheng's murder?" Yin asked. "Was the sergeant trying to track down this fifty-eighth person? In that case, wouldn't you say we're a little late? The culprit already deleted our most important clue. I'm willing to bet that the other people in those photos don't even have anything to do with this case."

"But we still have other leads to follow. We can at least try to uncover what the sergeant was searching for in the first place."

"How do we do that?" Yin asked, unable to restrain his curiosity.

Pei pointed to one section of the notes he had taken while viewing the photographs: *Skyline Cyber Café, October 19, 3:47 p.m.*

"In the last few photos," Pei said, "the internet café's window is visible behind the subject. The decal on the window says 'Skyline Cyber Café.' The time stamp indicates this was two days ago, in the afternoon."

"I'll pass this on to the captain," Yin said, admiringly.

"Providing he's willing to listen. Right now I need to follow up on a lead of my own." Pei tore a sheet of paper from his notepad and scrawled out a phone number. "Please get in touch with me if anything happens."

After giving Yin an amiable pat on the shoulder, Pei headed down the stairs.

||||

Two hours later, the entire Chengdu criminal police force held an internal briefing with ranking officers from every station and substation throughout the city. A solemn mood had taken hold of the room. All eyes were focused on Captain Han. The man was ashen.

"As I'm sure everyone is aware, a brutal homicide took place this morning." Han's voice cracked, as he strained to control the grief and anger roiling in his heart. "Nothing further needs to be said about the victim's identity. Now, the scene of the murder."

Han's assistant, Yin, was standing at his side. He turned on the room's ceiling-mounted projector when the captain gave the signal. Photographs taken at the crime scene appeared on a large screen for all to see.

"There are three major knife wounds on the body: a stab wound to the abdomen, a cut on the right upper arm, and a slash wound across the neck. The wound to the neck was fatal. The blade sliced open the victim's carotid artery, leading to the excessive blood loss that killed him. According to our forensic evaluation, the time of death most likely occurred between midnight and two o'clock in the morning."

A series of close-up images appeared on the projector screen to accompany Han's explanation. The people in this room were no strangers to violence. However, the photographs of dark blood and the corpse of a veteran comrade sent an icy shiver down each officer's spine.

Zheng Haoming's eyes were shut, but his mouth was wide open as if he had been trying to scream. A close-up of the cruel slash across his neck. A ruler indicated that the wound was 2.75 inches in length.

"Judging from these wounds, the murderer used a small, razor-like weapon. A cleaver was also left behind at the scene. The research done by our technicians tells us the fingerprints on the handle and blade belonged to the victim. Therefore, it appears that the victim wielded the cleaver in self-defense. From these findings and other evidence, we can state with certainty that the victim was engaged in a fierce struggle with the murderer before his death."

Han gestured to Yin. A succession of photographs of the other areas of Zheng's apartment flashed upon the screen.

"This is a fresh gouge on the surface of the living room table. The mark is consistent with impact from a sharp-edged object. Possibly even Zheng's cleaver. The items inside the cabinet were in complete disorder, most likely because the cabinet was struck. There's a large amount of blood spatter here. It looks like the victim suffered his fatal wound somewhere around this area . . ."

The audience listened in silence. As Han continued his description of the scene, the others in the room pictured the struggle between Zheng and his killer.

The screen showed a close-up of the wooden floor of Zheng's apartment. Han nearly flinched when he looked at this picture.

"This photo was taken beside the victim's feet. We can see

several circular drops of blood on the floor. The blood most likely fell from a significant height. Since the victim was wearing long-sleeved pajamas, his clothes would have soaked up the blood from any wounds to his upper arm and abdomen. The blood from the large wound on his neck wouldn't have left those kinds of drops either. We can be all but certain that these bloodstains came from the killer."

He turned to his assistant.

"Yin, go back to that close-up of the cleaver you just showed. All right. Everyone, take a look at the bloodstains at the edge of the cleaver."

"Does that mean that the killer was wounded?" one of the officers asked.

Low, excited voices rippled around the room. If the killer had left blood or any other physical evidence at the scene, it would go a long way in helping them identify and track down the suspect.

"I can tell you with one-hundred-percent confidence that this is exactly what happened!" The other officers hushed as Captain Han swept his piercing gaze over the crowd. He brandished a report in his hand, holding it up for all to see. "These are the results from our lab test. The victim's blood type isn't B, but the bloodstains on the cleaver and floor are. There's no doubt about it. This is the killer's blood. Now, let's have a look at the photographs of the kitchen."

The next image on the screen showed a small wood-lattice window in a style common to older residences.

"This window overlooks the small park at the center of Zheng's development. It was opened outward when we arrived at the scene. The glass at the very bottom of the lattice had been shattered." He made another signal to Yin, and a new image replaced the previous one. "This is the kitchen cupboard. We found knife marks here as well."

He paused, giving the other officers time to process this new detail.

"It appears that the killer made his way to the third floor by scaling the drainpipe and the second-floor window along the rear of the apartment building. He then broke the glass in the window, opened it, and entered the apartment. The noise woke Zheng and he went to investigate. The two encountered one another in the kitchen and began to engage in physical combat. Zheng grabbed a cleaver to defend himself. He was forced backward as he fought, and finally succumbed to his opponent in the living room."

"Were any of the assailant's fingerprints or footprints found at the scene?" interrupted one officer.

Han shook his head. "No. The individual may have been wearing gloves and shoe covers. It would seem that this person knows a thing or two about how we conduct our investigations." He narrowed his eyes. "Even so, we have a firm grasp on several leads. I want everyone to note our projection of the killer's physical description. He's most likely a young or middle-aged male with a slim build, between five-foot-three and five-foot-seven, with a fresh knife wound on one hand."

After a brief scramble for paper and pens, the assembled officers scribbled down the details. Several moments after Han had finished giving his description, a soft murmur broke the silence hanging over the room.

"Captain?"

All eyes turned to the source. It was Yin.

"Is there something you'd like me to clarify?" Han asked, scowling.

"No, sir," Yin said, promptly shaking his head. "I'm just thinking about the officer we found in the apartment this morning. It's almost as if he read our minds."

"Are you talking about Pei Tao?"

"This morning he told me that we should launch a search for a male suspect—thin, approximately five-foot-five, and with an injury on one hand."

Han's eyes widened in surprise. Despite the brevity of the physical description he'd just announced, it had taken hours for the team of technicians to determine those details.

If one knew that the killer had silently scaled three stories and squeezed through a small window, it would be a simple matter to conclude that the individual in question was both slender and agile. Coming up with an accurate estimate of the individual's height, however, was no easy feat.

The investigators discovered that the struggle between Zheng and his killer had left the wooden sideboards in the kitchen and living room scored with knife marks. All signs suggested that the murderer had wielded a sharp knife; each strike had been a powerful stab, and so the killer inevitably would have chosen a stance most conducive to applying force. Operating under this hypothesis, they could use the locations, angles, and depths of the marks to deduce the attacker's approximate height. Doing so involved a careful process of calculation, and it was hard to imagine that brainpower and the naked eye alone could accomplish this same task.

The killer had left bloodstains on the floor of the scene. The study of blood spatter was an art in itself—the higher the point from which the blood had fallen, the larger the area of the mark it formed when it splashed onto the floor. Thus, one would be able to approximate the height from which the blood fell by contrasting these marks with those of the mock simulations performed at the scene. The final results from the department's tests indicated that the blood had fallen from a height somewhere between 2.5 and 3 feet above the floor. Considering the warmer and thicker clothing people typically wore at this time of year, the hands and face would be the only parts of the body from which blood would drip if one were wounded. After they'd determined the height from which the blood had fallen, Han's analysts concluded that one of the murderer's hands had been injured.

To Han, the idea that Pei had ascertained all these details in such a short time was inconceivable. Yet his shock quickly faded from his expression, as if masked beneath a layer of frost.

"Pei Tao's motives are still unclear. He is a key suspect in our investigation. Yin, what's the status on the surveillance I ordered?"

"I assigned Jin Youfeng to tail him. I haven't heard back from him, but I'll see if I can get in touch with him right now." Yin took out his cell phone and dialed. After several rings, he heard an answer on the other end of the line. "Officer Jin?"

As Yin listened, his features stiffened. He grunted several awkward replies before approaching Han. Handing over his cell phone, he said, "Captain, you should listen to this."

Giving his assistant a puzzled look, Han accepted the phone. "This is Han."

A baritone voice answered. "My apologies, Captain. This is Pei Tao."

"Pei Tao?" Han appeared as dumbfounded as Yin. "Where is my officer?"

"We had a slight misunderstanding. I was following up on a lead when I noticed someone following me. I found an opportunity to subdue my pursuer, and I took it. When he resisted, I simply followed my instincts. This only happened a moment ago, by the way. In fact, you called right when I found his badge. Your officer should wake up soon. Please accept my apologies when I say that this was purely an accident."

The sincerity in Pei's voice was not enough to clear Han's cloud of rage. The captain was just barely able to keep himself in check.

"Officer Pei, this is Chengdu. Not Longzhou!" Han shouted, flecks of spit flying from his lips. "You had no right to do what you just did."

"I understand your frame of mind. My reaction a few

moments ago was far too rash, without question." Pei's tone suddenly grew grave. "But you would understand my actions if you only knew just what kind of opponent you're up against."

"So you've found another lead?" Han asked.

"That's correct. I hope you're willing to hear me out this time."

Captain Han clenched his teeth. "I'll wait for you at police headquarters in half an hour. Meet me in my office."

"I'm on my way." Pei paused. "Well, I do have some good news for you. Your officer is conscious."

After several seconds, he heard Jin Youfeng's voice.

"Captain, I . . ."

"Waste of a badge," Han growled. He stabbed at the phone's keypad, ending the call.

||||

The bitter smell of nostalgia struck Pei as he entered Han's office. This pristine room, with its slick surfaces and state-of-the-art computer, was exactly the kind of office he had once imagined for himself. Life, however, had decided differently. Pei pushed these thoughts aside. Captain Han was seated behind his desk, an expectant look on his face.

"Have you made any more progress?" Pei blurted.

"I'm not obligated to report to you."

Pei pursed his lips. The captain's response was neither friendly nor hostile. It didn't take a police education to sense that he was on thin ice. Considering his interactions with the captain thus far, his best option was to yield now. He forced an awkward laugh. "You do have a point there, sir."

Han's mood seemed to improve after this small display of humility.

"We've already ascertained the suspect's physical description," Han informed Pei. "We've also set up checkpoints at strategic bus and subway stops throughout Chengdu. We are also carrying out archival investigations at every level in order to determine whether the suspect could have been involved with any cases Zheng was in charge of."

"I see your line of reasoning," Pei replied at once. "You think someone wanted revenge against the sergeant."

"There were no indications of burglary at the scene. The suspect forced his way into the building and carried a knife. This murder was clearly premeditated. Do you have any other ideas?"

Rather than answer, Pei changed the topic. "Do you know why I was at Zheng's apartment?"

"As a matter of fact, that's precisely what I'd like to know." Han stared at Pei. "What exactly was the nature of your relationship with the sergeant?"

Pei took out a folded piece of writing paper and handed it to the captain. Han unfolded the paper and began to read:

Don't you remember me, Student 8102?
Once the overture finishes, the first act must commence.
It has been far too long since the overture has faded . . .
But the day has finally come.

As Han read the entire letter, his brow furrowed in bewilderment.

"I received this letter two days ago. It was sent from within the city. 8102 was—"

"Your number at the Sichuan Police Academy," Han interrupted. "You entered the provincial academy in 1981 and graduated in '84. Your grades were extremely impressive all around. You graduated at the top of your class. In short, you were one of the most outstanding students the academy had ever seen.

"However, something happened right before graduation. A misstep that resulted in your assignment to the third-tier city of Longzhou, shattering your hopes of a posting in a top city such as . . ." Han paused here, and Pei saw the ghost of a smile. "This one. You were sent to a station in the suburbs and made a common police officer."

Pei clenched his jaw. Was Han gloating? Or was he simply trying to earn Pei's respect?

"Still, you rose through the ranks quickly," Han went on. "You were promoted to station captain in eight years. Later, you were transferred to the city's criminal police force." Smiling, Han tapped a finger against the file on his desk. "I ran a full background check on you."

An uneasy feeling overtook Pei. Several seconds passed before he spoke.

"What's that you called it? A misstep?" Pei forced a laugh. "Let's dispense with the euphemisms, Captain. It was an out-and-out disaster."

Han was surprised at Pei's sudden honesty. Up until this moment, he had chalked up the captain's behavior to arrogance. Now, however, he saw it under a different light—as an expression of overpowering sincerity. It was a shame for such an outstanding officer to have had a promising career limited just because of a few incidents. He suddenly found himself attempting to console Pei.

"You can call it what you like, but it's all in the past now. Sooner or later, some things have to be let go."

"No," Pei said with a painful shake of his head. His eyes opened so wide that Han could see veins bulging at the corners. "I can't let it go," Pei said, cold as ice. "It never ended. He's come back—he's still here!"

Pei's puzzling outburst reminded Han of something. Picking up the handwritten letter, the captain fired off questions. "Who wrote this letter? What does it have to do with Sergeant Zheng's murder?"

Pei rubbed his temples with both hands. Gradually, his emotions cooled. "When did you join the Chengdu criminal police?"

"Ten years ago. Right after I received my master's in criminal investigation at the People's Public Security University." The name of China's elite police academy rolled off Han's tongue with pride.

"So this might be new to you." Pei sighed. "I went to the Skyline Cyber Café after I left Zheng's apartment this morning. Zheng had taken pictures of a customer there two days ago, at 3:47 in the afternoon. I asked the network administrator to call up the customer's browsing history. That's where I found this page."

Pei, having regained his composure, handed Han a printout of a web page.

Despite his lack of expertise, Han immediately recognized it as a post from a message board. The original poster's username was *Eumenides*, typed in Latin script rather than Chinese characters. The subject of the post consisted of four words in a striking bold font:

A CALL FOR JUSTICE

Filthy souls inhabit this world. The law should be a tool for cleansing society, but the law is weak.
People commit crimes, but too often they fall outside the law's jurisdiction. Or the law fails to find any evidence to convict. Too often wrongdoers are able to bribe themselves out of the law's reach.
Society needs a different kind of justice.
I will deliver justice.
I will cleanse this world of evil.
The list of wrongdoers, however, is still unwritten.
You have the chance to write it.
Tell me who deserves to be on this list.
Tell me who does not deserve to live upon the earth.
Tell me who is outside the reach of the law.
Tell me their name.

Tell me what they have done.
I will judge them.
You have two weeks before I post the final version of my list.

"This could just be a prank." Han shook his head noncommittally. "You see things like this all over the internet."

"A prank?" Pei gave a bitter laugh. He leaned over Han's desk, full of indignation. "This is monstrous! This is why Sergeant Zheng lost his life. And his wasn't the first life to be sacrificed. Eighteen years ago—"

Without pausing, Han asked, "What happened eighteen years ago?"

Pei pulled himself back and shook his head. "I can't," he said.

Han slammed an open palm against his desk. He glared at Pei.

"It's classified," Pei said, his expression grave.

"And you can't tell me a single thing about it?"

"There was an investigation here in Chengdu eighteen years ago. The nature of this case was so disturbing that, in order to prevent a panic, it was classified at the highest levels. All investigative work on the case was carried out secretly, by a special group organized for that very purpose. However, their investigation was never concluded." Pei regarded Han with a grudging look. "I'm sorry, but that's all I can say at the moment."

"The case is classified, and yet you seem to know all about it."

The corners of Pei's eyes twitched. This question seemed to have touched a nerve. His voice was just above a growl.

"Don't you see? I was . . . involved. This case was what made my career fall apart! I was questioned by one of the members of the task force. By Sergeant Zheng."

The captain's eyes widened. Facts finally locked into place. Causes and effects.

Pei Tao had been part of this case from the very beginning.

Eighteen years after the initial investigation, he received a bizarre letter and returned to Chengdu. Now Zheng had been murdered. A new chapter in this tragedy had begun.

But what exactly had Zheng been investigating all those years ago?

When Han finally looked at Pei, his expression was mixed. He tried to keep his composure relaxed. "If you can't tell me any details, then why are you here?"

Pei stared unflinchingly at the captain, and he enunciated each of his words carefully. "To beg you to submit a request to your superiors right away. I'm here so you will declassify the case, and re-form the 4/18 Task Force!"

CHAPTER TWO

THE EIGHTEEN-YEAR-OLD TRAGEDY

OCTOBER 21, 4:00 P.M.
CHENGDU CRIMINAL POLICE HEADQUARTERS,
CONFERENCE ROOM

Heaving a sigh, Captain Han Hao rested his hands on the thick stack of case files on the conference table. He had visited the department archives two hours earlier with the sole purpose of declassifying these eighteen-year-old documents. Only after reading the files and familiarizing himself with the history of this case had he realized just how ruthless and fearsome a foe he was about to face.

Fortunately for the captain, he would not have to face this opponent alone. Seated around the conference room's long false-oak table were the new members of the task force, reorganized after nearly two decades.

Pei Tao sat at the opposite side of the table. Although his gaze lingered on those files for quite some time, there was a glassy look in his eyes, as if he couldn't decide which emotion was appropriate . . . guilt, anger, or fear.

He would never forget what had transpired eighteen years earlier, and he knew the only way to break free of the past was to find this bloodthirsty maniac and end the cycle of death.

Next to Han sat his assistant, Yin Jian. Yin watched Pei with intense curiosity. An air of mystique shrouded the newcomer from Longzhou, and this was precisely what intrigued Yin. His thoughts were riddled with questions: Who exactly was Pei Tao? What had happened to him all those years ago? Why had he returned to Chengdu?

Another young man sat at the table, wearing an expression that was the exact antithesis of Yin's. He looked much younger than the other officers, and was scrawny—bordering on emaciated. He wore glasses, and his head was propped up with one hand. His attention, albeit negligible, seemed focused on the pen he was spinning intricately in his fingers. He seemed utterly disinterested in any of the other people seated in the room, save for several brief instances in which he raised his head and glanced around the table. A fierce intelligence shone in his eyes, but only for seconds at a time. If not for his sky-blue uniform, the others in the conference room would never have guessed that he was a police officer.

Sitting next to the young man was a swarthy, well-built officer who appeared to be in his thirties. His posture was as straight as a steel beam, and his gaze exuded strength. The man glanced at his wristwatch. In a deadpan tone he announced, "It's time, Captain. Let's get started."

Han impatiently tapped the pile of documents with his finger. "We're still one person short," he said.

The seat between Pei and the young man twirling his pen was indeed unoccupied.

"Discipline should take precedence at a time like this," the well-built officer said with irritation. He looked at Han, and his voice rose. "How are we supposed to be any kind of a match for this killer if we can't even stay on the same page?"

"We aren't going to proceed until the entire team is in this room." A commanding tone seeped through Han's lowered voice. The muscular officer looked away and said no more.

"There's no need to wait," someone said from outside the room. "I've been here for some time already."

A slender woman strode through the door, providing a stark contrast to the room's thick aura of masculinity. Even Pei snapped out of his contemplation and looked up in surprise.

She was a true southern beauty, with large eyes and an elegant mouth and nose. The jet-black sheen of her hair offset her pale skin. While her exquisite features made it hard to guess her age, she radiated a frank, mature intelligence.

Han squinted. "And you would be Ms. Mu?" he asked.

The woman nodded. "That's right." Her lips spread into a smile, and she addressed the rest of the room. "I'm Mu Jianyun, a criminal psychology lecturer at the provincial academy."

Han smirked—*Mu Jianyun*. When his superiors at the provincial headquarters had recommended an expert in criminal psychology, he never considered that the individual they sent might be a woman.

"Why didn't you come in until now?" the muscular officer asked, as irritated as he was bewildered.

"I was watching you from there," Mu answered. She pointed to a window high in one of the room's walls. "When the captain mentioned that one member of the team hadn't arrived yet, each of you displayed different—and quite telling—reactions."

The officer exhaled slowly through his nostrils, uncomfortable at the thought of being observed.

Mu sat in the unoccupied seat between Pei and the bespectacled young man. The latter's eyes were still fixed on her; he had been watching her from the first moment she entered the room. He cleared his throat. "In that case, Ms. Mu, care to share what you learned?" he asked with a smirk.

"It doesn't take an expert to observe," Mu said, turning her attention to him, "that you are the least enthusiastic about your work. Of course, as someone who spends each day communing with an endless stream of ones and zeroes, it's completely understandable that you'd feel some measure of boredom. The loneliness of a job like yours can be suffocating at times. It could even affect one's personality. Coming across a woman you haven't met before, for instance, would give you a thrill, a sense of novelty. I sincerely hope that this feeling can inspire you to apply an appropriate amount of effort, and professionalism, toward your job. However, I want to make one thing very clear—to everyone here. Our relationship will remain professional in nature and nothing more. Even if your skills with computers have made you something of a legend in law enforcement circles, Zeng Rihua."

The young man's features twisted awkwardly. "I'm just honored that word of my reputation has reached a woman as beautiful as you."

Mu smiled. Instead of continuing this exchange with Zeng, she shifted her gaze to the muscular officer sitting on the opposite side of the table. While there was no enmity in her expression, the man squirmed under her gaze. He looked down at the table.

"Special Police Unit Captain Xiong Yuan, I presume?" Mu paused. The man did not answer. "You excel at carrying out orders, and you have a very calming influence on the people you work with."

Xiong looked up, his expression growing more cooperative.

"As for you, Captain Han . . ." Mu looked at the captain and considered her words for a moment. "You're extremely decisive, a necessary trait for a leader. Once you've made a decision, you rarely give in to others' suggestions. This has its pros and cons." She glanced at Yin. "Yet your assistant is filled with curiosity and a drive for exploration. He can help provide you with a wider range of information. In a sense, he complements you very well."

Han gave a noncommittal grunt. He was more interested in Mu's analysis of one particular member of the team. "Three down and only one to go, Ms. Mu," he reminded the lecturer.

"Captain Pei, you mean?" Mu smiled. "Something seems to be bothering him. Something tied to those documents in front of you. I see grief in his eyes. It's mixed with anger and, if you'll forgive my bluntness, an irrepressible fear."

Curiosity seized the others and their eyes immediately turned to the captain from Longzhou.

Pei could not hide his surprise. Admittedly, Mu's analyses of the other team members had been accurate, but she had obtained those results by examining their words and actions. Impressive, but not profound. However, she had read his innermost emotions through his expressions alone.

Pei kept his gaze level and steady. He stared at Mu intently, and she looked away gracefully.

"Enough," Xiong Yuan boomed. "Let's quit stalling."

Han nodded. "I'm officially commencing this meeting. You are all here because you've received orders from your superiors, so I won't waste any time on small talk. The 4/18 Task Force has been re-formed. This group consists solely of the people in this room. My role is that of group leader. Any questions so far?"

Zeng dragged his pencil through his disheveled hair and squinted at the oversized calendar on the wall with mock surprise. "Don't you mean the 10/21 Task Force?"

Xiong and Mu frowned at Han, both confused.

"Re-formed?" Xiong murmured under his breath.

Han raised his hand, and the room was silent.

"We've all been summoned to investigate Sergeant Zheng's murder. However, there's disturbing information that has just come to light. This is not the first time a police officer in this city was murdered in this manner."

Han's voice was low. He glanced at Yin, who tapped a button on his laptop.

The ceiling projector flashed, and an enlarged scan of an old color photograph of a garishly furnished room appeared on the screen. While the colors of the wallpaper and couch seemed to have faded with time, the scarlet pools of blood sent a shiver down Mu's spine. A male body lay facedown on the floor.

"This homicide occurred on April 18, 1984," Han continued. "The victim was Xue Dalin. He was male, forty-one years old.

He was also the vice commissioner of Chengdu's criminal police at the time."

Pei's expression remained deadpan under Mu's watchful eye. However, the others looked shocked. She couldn't blame them, as she felt the same way. Despite having lived in Sichuan all her life, this was the first time she had heard of this murder. Had the city actually covered up the death of one of its top law enforcement officials?

"You're currently looking at the crime scene. The victim was murdered in his own living room. Multiple knife wounds were found over his entire body. The fatal wound was here on his neck. His carotid artery had been cut. He simply bled out until he died. The victim's wife was away on business on the day of the murder. His only child, a daughter, was living at school. The victim was alone. No fingerprints or footprints were found at the scene. The investigation turned up only one lead: this piece of paper."

The projector cycled through other photographs taken at the scene. As the team members watched, an image of a scrap of paper appeared on the screen. They stared at the clean, meticulous handwriting upon it:

DEATH NOTICE

THE ACCUSED: Xue Dalin
CRIMES: Dereliction of duty, accepting bribes, collusion with organized crime
DATE OF PUNISHMENT: April 18
EXECUTIONER: Eumenides

Each character was a display of expert calligraphy. At first glance, the handwriting was indistinguishable from printed text.

"Was this—" Mu paused for a split second. "Was this left behind by the killer?"

Han, however, continued listing the details from the case file. "The officers who arrived at the scene found this piece of paper on the victim's desk. It was attached to an anonymous postcard that was delivered two days before the murder."

"The eighteenth of April," Zeng mused. "That would explain the name of this team. Why have I never heard of this case?" Zeng looked around the table as he asked the question. The others were all equally puzzled—except for Pei, who was shaking his head bitterly.

"I've only just learned of this case myself," Han said. "All information pertaining to the case was made classified almost immediately after Xue's murder. The mayor and the commissioner were afraid that the news of the vice commissioner's murder would cause a panic. At the time, the task force carried out a covert investigation. Sergeant Zheng Haoming was one of the team's members."

Again, Mu noticed that Pei's reaction was in complete contrast to the others'. The rest of the team appeared noticeably disturbed as the link between two police killings eighteen years apart became clear as day. Pei, however, remained stoic.

"They never solved this case? I guess you get what you pay for when you ask for a secret investigation," Zeng snorted. "What was the department so paranoid about?"

Han scowled at Zeng, and took a deep breath. "It isn't as simple as that," the captain said in a low voice. "There were several other victims. Yin, the projector."

A new photograph appeared on the screen. The image showed a spacious, dilapidated building that seemed to have suffered a massive fire. Every corner of the ruined area was scorched and charred. Pei, who had kept his composure throughout the entire meeting, suddenly recoiled, as if from an electric shock.

"Where's this?" asked Zeng, as loquacious as ever. "And where are the victims you mentioned, Captain?"

"The victims? They're here, and here." Han swept a laser pointer over the image. "Over here as well."

Pei clenched his fists until veins bulged from the backs of his hands. The others scrutinized the photograph, but the image was too dim for them to distinguish anything in particular.

"Go to the close-ups," Han told Yin.

Nodding, Yin clicked a button on the small remote in his hand. Close-ups of each of the areas Han had just indicated appeared upon the screen. The conference room fell silent at once. Even Zeng was holding his breath. The team finally had a clear view of the victims' remains.

"Remains" isn't the most appropriate term, thought a shaken Zeng. *"Ground meat" would be a much more accurate descriptor. Blackened, to be specific.* He could distinguish only vaguely which charred chunk of human remains was a limb and which a fragmented skull.

The butchery was sickening. Han looked away and found himself observing Pei, wondering what memories tortured him.

Yet Captain Pei's gaze did not stray from the horrifying images on the wall. He was fixated. His icy sorrow thawed, transforming into blazing anger.

Han finally broke the silence.

"What you're looking at is another scene from the same case from 1984. This used to be an abandoned warehouse for a chemical factory on the outskirts of this city. On the afternoon of April eighteenth—immediately after Vice Commissioner Xue was murdered—an explosion occurred at the warehouse. Raw chemicals stored on-site ignited and caused the deaths of two individuals, as well as severe injuries to a third. The subsequent investigation revealed that the two people killed were students at the provincial police academy. The injured party was a homeless scavenger."

Yin fiddled with the remote, and a medium shot of a handsome young man appeared upon the screen. Mu recognized the crisp blue shirt worn by students at the provincial academy, and what looked like the Distinguished Scholar medal, although the design was a bit cruder than the one currently used. The young man had a cheery expression and a confident smile.

"Yuan Zhibang, one of the deceased. He was a member of the academy's class of '84, a criminal investigation major." Han glanced at Pei as he spoke. The others, all of whom shared some familiarity with Pei's background, followed Han's gaze.

Pei drew a deep breath. "Yuan was my roommate," he said hoarsely. "And my closest friend."

"The documents I have here state as much," Han said. He motioned to Yin, who cued another image.

The next photo showed an attractive young woman in an academy uniform, with long hair tied neatly behind her head. Even in the old photograph, her eyes shone brightly.

Pei felt a tingle at the back of his throat, as though something were stuck there. An absent look filled his eyes as he stared at the girl in the photograph.

"Meng Yun, the second victim at the explosion. She was a criminal psych major at the academy and a member of the class of '84. According to our information, Meng's relationship with Captain Pei was far from casual." Han paused. "To put it bluntly, the deceased was romantically involved with Captain Pei at the time of her death."

Those words stabbed at Pei's heart. He closed his eyes, as if that could help shield him from the pain of the memory.

Suddenly, the conference room was abuzz.

Xiong did not make eye contact with the newcomer from Longzhou, seemingly out of respect, but Zeng stared with blunt curiosity. Mu glanced only briefly at Pei before returning her gaze to the projector screen. She seemed to have taken a keen interest in this young woman who had been cut down in the prime of her youth.

Growing impatient, Zeng turned to face Han.

"Well, what caused the explosion?"

"We have information on that," the captain replied, "but a good deal of it consists of notes provided by Captain Pei. Instead of reading those, I'd like to ask the man himself to give us his account. It should be clearer than my own conjectures, at the very least. Don't you agree, Captain?"

Han's last sentence may have taken the form of a question, but the command was clear.

Lacing his fingers together, Pei covered his eyes and massaged his temples with slow but forceful motions. It had taken eighteen long years, but now he finally found himself sitting before the task force once again. This time, however, he was not merely a witness. He was finally part of the investigation.

Even after so much time had passed, his memory was clear. When he lowered his hands, a spark of light returned to his eyes. He was ready to tell his story.

"Back in 1984, I was weeks away from graduating from the provincial academy with a major in criminal investigation. By then, everyone in my class had already begun training with the police here in Chengdu. We were all excited at the prospect of doing real police work, and a lot of us were eager to see the opportunities that a degree from the academy could afford us." Pei paused here and took a deep breath.

"The eighteenth of April was on a Wednesday. I was at the local precinct that afternoon working on some extra training exercises. My roommate Yuan left campus earlier that day. He told me he had a date with a pen pal. The whole thing sounded a bit quaint, but I knew how far Yuan would go to get a date. I was more concerned with the dinner that Meng and I were going to have later that day. She had a set of keys to my dorm and was supposed to come by ahead of time to wait for me. I headed back to my dorm around three. When I arrived, the entrance to the building was unlocked, and Meng was gone. She'd left a note near the door, in a place that was easy to spot."

"This note?" Han held up a small sealed plastic evidence bag containing a slip of paper. Pei nodded, and the captain read aloud: " 'Get in touch with me on the radio ASAP.' "

"Telephones weren't as common back then as they are now. And forget about pagers and cell phones," Pei went on. "I knew a bit about radios, though. I'd set up a transmitter-receiver and linked two handsets to it. The signal range maxed out at about six miles, and Meng and I typically used them as walkie-talkies to keep in touch with each other. I'd left mine at home when I was out doing fieldwork, and I was worried there was an emergency and Meng needed to talk right away. Without wasting another second, I picked up my walkie-talkie and tuned it to our frequency. But I couldn't get through to her."

"Why not?" Han asked.

Pei shook his head slowly. "The gear we were using was old, and the signal was pretty unstable. We'd run into problems every now and then—we might lose the signal or there'd be interference and someone else would be using our frequency. I didn't have much of a choice, so I sat and waited for her to reach me. That was when I spotted a second letter on the table. Someone had already opened it."

Yin pressed a button, and an enlarged photograph of the letter popped onto the screen.

"Yes, that's it."

The writing on the letter was familiar to everyone in the room. Just like the one recovered from Zheng's apartment yesterday, it consisted of several lines of perfectly composed characters.

DEATH NOTICE

THE ACCUSED: Yuan Zhibang

CRIMES: Serial philandering; emotional abuse and abandonment of an innocent woman, causing her suicide

DATE OF PUNISHMENT: April 18
EXECUTIONER: Eumenides

"Another death notice?" Zeng muttered incredulously.

"What was your reaction when you saw this letter?" Han asked. "Were you aware that Vice Commissioner Xue Dalin had been murdered that morning?"

"No. I didn't have any knowledge of the murder," Pei said, and he paused. "However, the combination of the threat and Meng's strange absence instantly gave me an ominous feeling."

"Yet you did nothing," Han remarked as he leafed through the case materials in front of him. "You sat in your room and waited until you were able to reach Meng. According to the file, you waited thirty minutes."

Pei nodded slowly.

"Thirty minutes and you reported nothing to the police. Thirty minutes, despite your supposedly 'ominous feeling.'"

"I didn't think it was worth reporting."

Pei had a point, Mu thought. If he hadn't been aware of Xue's murder, this anonymous letter might have looked like an attempt at a practical joke. A dark one, perhaps, but still a joke.

"I see," Han said. "Tell us what happened after you found the letter."

"I left the radio on and waited. After about half an hour, the signal came back. I heard her voice."

"What did Meng Yun say?"

Pei shut his eyes and furrowed his brow. He stayed quiet for several heartbeats. "She sounded anxious. She said she was with Yuan, that he was trapped inside an abandoned warehouse. He was handcuffed to the floor, with a timed explosive strapped to his chest."

Mu interrupted. "What were they doing together?"

"I believe that Meng entered my room and discovered Yuan's

anonymous death notice. She got worried, and she went to help him."

"You believe so?" This response didn't satisfy Mu. "Did Meng tell you this, or is this your own speculation?"

"My own speculation."

"What was the nature of the relationship between Meng and Yuan?" she asked.

Pei didn't answer.

"Let me be more specific. Who was closer to Yuan: you or Meng?"

"I was, of course. Yuan was my closest friend at the time. Meng only knew him through me."

"Then why did she go looking for Yuan? You both saw the same letter, yet you—Yuan's best friend, as you just emphasized—stayed in your room. That seems odd to me."

Mu held Pei's gaze and waited for his explanation. Pei stared blankly, as though this question had caught him off-guard.

"I . . . I don't know. Maybe it was intuition—she might have subconsciously picked up on whatever danger there was."

Mu's face twisted at that. "Then why didn't she report it to the police?"

"I don't know," Pei said, avoiding eye contact with Mu.

"And how did she find Yuan?"

Pei shook his head. He offered a sad, reluctant smile before giving the same reply as before. "I don't know."

"You didn't ask her? These are all very basic questions."

"Captain Pei might not have had time to ask them," Han said, breaking his silence. "According to the information we have, only three minutes were left on the bomb's timer when Meng finally got in touch with Pei. Is that correct?"

"Yes," Pei answered solemnly. "We only had enough time to discuss how to disarm the bomb."

"What kind of bomb was it?" Xiong asked. His mastery of bomb disposal was well known throughout the department.

"I didn't see it," Pei said to Xiong, "but I suppose Captain Han's files have enough detailed information pertaining to the explosion to tell you that."

After rifling through his files, Han took out a document pouch and handed it to the SPU captain. Xiong picked out several documents and began studying them.

"I was only able to get a sketchy picture of the situation from my exchange with Meng," Pei continued. "Yuan had been handcuffed to an iron pipe inside the warehouse. The explosive device was somehow wired to the handcuffs. If they tried to cut the cuffs or move the bomb, there was a good chance that it would go off."

"So their only option was to disarm the device," Xiong said, nodding. "What did Meng and Yuan know about bomb disposal?"

"Yuan and I had both taken a course in bomb disposal. By the time I was able to reach her on my walkie-talkie, Yuan had told Meng how to open the bomb's outer casing. All she needed to do was pull the trigger wire connected to the timer."

Xiong's brow creased. "It says here that the bomb had a dummy wire installed?"

"That's correct. Meng told me that there were two wires. A red and a blue, twisted around each other and leading into a sealed control box."

"Meng and Yuan would have had no way to tell the real trigger wire from the fake," Xiong said.

"Hell, why not just use all the colors of the rainbow?" Zeng chuckled, in stark contrast to the rest of the room's dour mood. "It's an intriguing dilemma, though. Like binary code. One or zero. Life or death. An impossible choice. Personally, I'd go with red. It's my favorite color. Anyone else?"

The other team members looked at the young officer in collective dismay. Han was nearly fuming. Pei's eyes were vacant, and the unforgettable hiss of static filled his ears once more.

||||

The noise was a metal file scraping against his eardrum. Her voice ebbed and flowed through the sonic chaos. It would remain forever etched in his mind.

Meng. She was stronger than anyone else Pei had ever met. Yet in that terrible moment, her voice was bizarre and sob-choked, warped by panic into a hoarse, tearful parody of itself.

"Please, Pei, tell me! Which wire? Red or blue? You need to tell me now!"

"I don't know . . ." Pei said weakly.

"There's no time!"

"There's no point asking him!" Yuan's voice, tense yet helpless, was intertwined with the static. "You have a fifty-fifty chance either way!"

"Pei, there's only one minute left!"

"Meng," Yuan cried, "forget about me! Run away while you still have a chance!"

"No, I'm not leaving," Meng said, steel returning to her voice. The sound was muffled, as though she was pressing the walkie-talkie to her lips.

"I don't care if you don't know which one it is, Pei. Just give me an answer."

Pei's voice was almost as hoarse as Meng's. "I can't."

Meng made a noise that sounded like pained laughter, and then she began counting down. "Eight . . . seven . . ." Her breathing grew short and labored.

"I'm sorry, Meng," Yuan said.

Each time she exhaled into the speaker, Pei felt a jolt in the pit of his stomach. His head was throbbing. Finally, he screamed into the walkie-talkie, "Red—Pull the red wire!"

Pei waited. His thoughts slowed to a sudden halt. His mind was blanker than a snow-covered field.

Endless hours seemed to pass. Then a sound—as quick

and sudden as a cough—whispered through the walkie-talkie's speaker.

Pei had lost the signal.

||||

"Captain Pei? Captain Pei?" Han raised his voice with each repetition, but with no success.

"Pei Tao!" Mu repeated. Her hand squeezed the captain's shoulder.

Pei shook his head and promptly snapped to attention. He forced a smile. "My apologies, everyone."

Han scowled at Pei's sudden lapse of attention. He looked at the documents in his hands. "According to our records, you used the radio to remotely instruct Meng how to disarm the bomb. She pulled the red wire at your prompting. When she severed it, she triggered the bomb. Is this correct?"

Pei shut his eyes and grimaced. He nodded.

"What grounds did you have for believing that pulling the red wire would disable the bomb?" Han asked.

Pei froze. "None," he said. "It was . . . a guess."

Mu raised her eyebrows at this.

Xiong shook his head gravely. "It's a nightmare scenario," he said. "Captain Pei was forced to rely on a hunch to make a life-and-death decision. In a situation so desperate, did he have any other choice?"

Zeng looked over to Pei. His expression shifted from cocky to sympathetic. "Let the record show that male intuition is a load of shit."

"Since you had no grounds for doing so," said Han, eyes locked on Pei, "why did you instruct Meng? If you'd let her make the decision on her own, she might have ended up choosing the right wire."

"Is that what you believe would have happened?"

"She had a fifty-fifty chance of getting it right. The same odds as you. She was at the scene. You, on the other hand, had nothing more than her description to rely on. Even if we're talking strictly about intuition, you should have trusted hers! Why did you tell her which wire to pull?"

Pei avoided the captain's furious glare. His mind was awash with a sense of panic he knew well. Which wire would Meng have chosen if the choice had been up to her? The unknown had writhed unanswered in Pei's heart for eighteen years.

"Let's analyze this from a psychological perspective," Mu said, after observing Pei with quiet intensity. "Captain Pei's decision could be considered a fight-or-flight reaction. What prompts someone to make a decision in a situation as urgent and stressful as this one? Not logic or reason, but instinct. It's simply a reaction decided by one's own personality."

The storm inside Pei's mind began to clear. The captain looked back at her gratefully, and their eyes locked. An eerie thought came to him—that her focused gaze was sharp enough to pry the secrets loose from the deepest corners of his mind.

Han nodded. "All right. Let's keep our focus on the details recorded in the case files. Statements taken from residents in the vicinity of the warehouse put the time of the explosion at precisely 4:13 p.m. The detonation's concussive force had a radius of 650 feet, causing immense damage to a nearby produce market. According to the report, the blast was even heard from a hospital located more than five miles away. The warehouse stored chemicals primarily used for making cosmetic products. They were extremely volatile, and the fire was massive. Meng Yun and Yuan Zhibang would have died instantly. The conflagration also inflicted critical burns on a third bystander."

"You mentioned this third person earlier," Pei said.

"Huang Shaoping, a scavenger in his mid-twenties. He was camped in the warehouse when the explosion went off. Huang was interviewed at length several times after he recovered, but he wasn't able to provide any information that could aid the investigation. It seems he was just in the wrong place at the wrong time."

Han rubbed the bridge of his nose. "Let's return to the present. Yin will provide you all with copies of the relevant documents and materials so that you can review them in detail after the meeting."

Han glanced at the team's technological expert. "Zeng, please tell everyone what you know about the situation."

Grinning, Zeng pushed his glasses up the bridge of his nose. "Some of you might not be familiar with me. In that case, let me introduce myself. My name is Zeng Rihua. I'm the tech supervisor of the provincial department's digital surveillance team."

Pei masked his surprise. This sarcastic individual was the last person he would have trusted with a position of leadership.

"A week ago, on October fourteenth, Sergeant Zheng came to me and asked if I could help him run some surveillance. A few strange posts had appeared online around that time, and Zheng was hoping that I could dig up some information about the poster."

A screenshot of a page from an online forum flashed onto the screen. It was the same Eumenides post Pei had tracked down in the internet café. *A Call for Justice.*

"What did you find?" Pei asked anxiously.

"The original post was made at 2:11 p.m. on the fifth of October from a computer here in Chengdu, at the Qianghui Internet Café," Zeng reported with mechanical precision. "It was posted on Chengdu's largest online message board. By the time Zheng found me, the post had already been read 25,220 times, and had received 1,525 replies from a total of 1,330 users."

Zeng looked around the room. A host of blank faces stared back. He felt like a teacher explaining calculus to a class of elementary students.

"That means a lot of people saw it," he said.

Yin tapped a button on his laptop, and a multitude of replies appeared on the projector screen. Some users derided the original poster, calling the person "deluded" or "psychotic." Others wondered if it was a practical joke. Some had even submitted names in the hope that they would fall prey to the poster's singular brand of "justice." The crimes listed in these posts ran the gamut from petty thievery to murder.

After giving the other team members a moment to read the replies on the projector screen, Zeng continued. "The individual, 'Eumenides,' submitted this post from inside an internet café. Obviously, they wanted to conceal their identity. Network administration here in Chengdu is about as airtight as an open window. If you want to find out who used a certain computer ten or so days ago, you'd have better luck going door to door. So, at Sergeant Zheng's request, I set up an online surveillance program. It would automatically detect and record the IP address of anyone viewing the thread. If that address happened to come from a café here in Chengdu, I would immediately notify Zheng; he would then go to the location to photograph any evidence."

"Zheng had the right idea," Pei murmured. "Eumenides must have checked the forum regularly for new replies. This is a cautious individual we're talking about—he wouldn't risk accessing the forum from a private computer."

"Precisely. However, Zheng kept me in the dark about the case from eighteen years ago. I had no idea that the plan would lead to such grave consequences," Zeng said.

In the wake of this new development, Mu aimed a question at Zeng.

"Could this be why Sergeant Zheng was murdered? Was he silenced after taking a picture of Eumenides?"

"The sergeant's camera was found at the crime scene," Han said calmly. "Several of the images on it had been deleted. We have reason to believe that doing so was the killer's primary objective, in addition to murdering Zheng." The captain shot Pei

Tao a deliberate look. Pei had come to the same conclusion at Zheng's apartment.

"Can we retrieve these deleted photos?" Xiong asked.

"This guy may be a professional when it comes to murder and explosives," Zeng said, snickering, "but he doesn't know jack about digital technology. It's possible to recover a deleted image as long as the space it originally occupied remains empty. Of course, this requires a bit of high-tech expertise."

"Do we have the equipment to do that?" Pei asked.

"My people are already on it. We'll have the data by tomorrow morning." Zeng thumbed his nose smugly. "Then we'll take our first look at the culprit."

Pei rapped his knuckles against the table. "Perfect!" He immediately restrained his enthusiasm, returning to a serious tone. "We need to start making preparations. Most important, we need to organize enough manpower for our investigation. This is no ordinary opponent that we're facing. We need to be ready to spring into action at any moment."

"You don't need to concern yourself with that." Han's tone was oddly strained. "Captain Xiong and I will lead this investigation. My people are handling the search for our suspect. The SPU team will focus on preparing for any special situations."

Xiong nodded, instantly understanding. Mistakes had been made eighteen years earlier—mistakes that could not be made again.

"How can I help?" Pei asked.

Han met Pei's eyes for several seconds before giving his answer.

"You're a long way from Longzhou, Captain Pei. Technically speaking, there's no need for you to get further involved. We requested you join this task force due to your unique perspective and history. With this in mind, I expect you to reflect on your memories of the 1984 murders and think outside the scope of our main investigation. Perhaps you'll turn up a few new leads.

However, I should stress that your role on this team is not a primary one."

Pei nodded grudgingly. "I see."

Han's formal tone masked a different message, and one that Pei perceived instantly: Han didn't trust him. It wasn't as if he had any choice in the matter, though.

"I believe it was you who specifically requested my presence here, Captain Han," Mu interjected, her tone all business. "What will my role be in this investigation?"

"You will work with Captain Pei. You're a gifted psychologist, after all. Help Pei search his memory for any leads we might have missed, and build a profile of this madman." Han paused, and then added, "Am I understood?"

"Yes, sir," she said, her somber gaze once again fixed upon Pei.

CHAPTER THREE

OPENING MOVES

OCTOBER 21, 6:25 P.M.

The sky was dark when Pei stepped onto the busy sidewalk outside the criminal police headquarters. Shops were still selling off their stock of the mandatory Mid-Autumn Festival delicacy, mooncakes—round pastries stuffed with fillings of red bean paste, lotus seed paste, and egg yolk. Pei sensed the post-holiday languor and calm of Chengdu's strolling citizens, and he wondered what would happen if they knew that a ruthless killer was hiding among them.

He walked quickly to the guesthouse next to headquarters. The medium-sized building was only two minutes away, and it was where every member of the task force would sleep for the foreseeable future. The younger team members kept their personal lives private, but Pei had seen Xiong on the phone immediately after the meeting. The SPU captain had repeated the same phrases again and again, trying to keep his voice calm: "It's just temporary!" "You know what this job is like!"

Pei's own accommodations provided him with all the comforts of home, which, everything considered, was not exactly much to begin with. He washed his face in the bathroom, then went to his desk to begin examining the case files.

Pei had once been a suspect in this very investigation, but

he knew almost nothing of the case's specifics. He had made two serious mistakes back then. First, he had failed to promptly notify the police after realizing that something might have happened to Meng. Second, he had blindly advised Meng while she was trying to disarm the bomb. Since then, he had imagined dozens of scenarios that might have transpired had he done things differently and reported his suspicions immediately. The police might have reached the warehouse in time. They could have found Meng before she even arrived at the warehouse. He could have saved her.

If only he had told her to pull the other wire . . .

He would never forget the sound of her panicked voice coming through the walkie-talkie.

Regret had followed Pei ever since that day, like a shadow trailing inevitably behind him. He would never think of himself as anything but a failure.

The mistakes he made that afternoon forever altered his path. His promising career was cast aside, and he was forced to return to his hometown of Longzhou, a small, cozy city where little ever changed. Before he knew it, he had idled away eighteen years of his life.

Almost as agonizing as the fact that the two lives closest to Pei had been cut short was the knowledge that he never had the chance to exact revenge against whoever had done it.

Now he did.

As Pei pored over Sergeant Zheng Haoming's journal, recovered from the late officer's apartment, he felt himself pulled back into a past he had never truly left behind.

APRIL 18, 1984

A series of murders like this is all but unheard of in modern-day China.

Xue Dalin, the vice commissioner of police, was murdered in his home this morning. Later in the afternoon, there was an explosion inside a chemical warehouse located along Chengdu's eastern outskirts, immediately killing two students from the academy. Due to the gruesome nature of this case, the city kept all details out of public view. A task force comprised of the most elite law enforcement officers in Sichuan has been covertly assembled. I have the honor of counting myself among its members.

The killer is clearly very familiar with police investigative techniques. No fingerprints have been found on the anonymous letters. These death notices, with their flawless, almost typewritten script, have stumped our efforts to identify the writer. Likewise, we have been unable to collect any fingerprints or footprints from the scene of Xue's murder. It can therefore be deduced that the killer performed a careful sweep of the scene after killing Xue. Psychologically speaking, we are dealing with a careful, levelheaded personality.

The fire at the warehouse has reduced any possible evidence to ashes. It took our technicians hours to collect the remains of the two victims. It was impossible for us to tell which parts belong to whom.

As of yet, there has been only one promising discovery: a survivor was found at the scene. However, many of his bones are broken, and severe burns cover most of his skin. He was taken to the Provincial People's Hospital for emergency treatment. His chances of survival remain uncertain.

APRIL 19, 1984

I questioned the academy student Pei Tao again this morning. He was in obvious shock. Or, to put it in colloquial terms: he was a wreck. I sympathize with him, to be honest. From everything that I've heard from his peers and instructors, Pei is a phenomenal and dedicated student. It's undeniable that he has taken it upon himself to bear a certain amount of responsibility for the bomb's detonation.

I arrived at the Provincial People's Hospital this afternoon. The lone survivor of the explosion was still unconscious. His condition was extremely critical. In the interests of this case, I hope that he regains consciousness as soon as possible. However, from a more humane point of view, death would be a kinder fate.

APRIL 20, 1984

We are approaching the investigation from multiple angles. My assignment is the man who survived the explosion.

He is still unconscious. I must confirm his identity, but his face . . . Not even his own mother would recognize him now.

No wallet or identifying documents were discovered on the man's person, but the doctors found a coiled copper wire among his remaining personal belongings before they performed surgery on him. It might be useful in determining his identity.

The copper wire is tangled up, but it's approximately six-and-a-half feet in length when stretched out. It appears to be a stripped electrical wire.

APRIL 21, 1984

I made several important discoveries today.

There was an abandoned section of cement tunnel approximately 100 yards south of the site of the explosion. The tunnel was at least seven feet wide. Some odds and ends and scavenged junk were piled up inside. It looked as if someone had been living in there.

In the middle of all that junk, I found a stripped casing for an electrical wire. Judging from the length, it could be a match for the copper wire found in the man's pockets.

Who is this man? A homeless scrap collector? I can only wait until he wakes up before I know the answer.

The doctors report that he's through the worst of it.

APRIL 25, 1984

Things are looking up today.

The man finally regained consciousness. He could barely remember a thing. Not even his own name. The doctors said that his kind of memory loss is typical for someone who's suffered severe injuries. I need a way to jump-start his memory.

I returned to the cement tunnel to take a few pictures. I'll have to wait until at least tomorrow morning before I can have them developed.

APRIL 26, 1984

I showed the man the pictures from the tunnel. He appeared confused. Understandable. Then I showed him the copper wire and told him that it had come from his pocket. I encouraged him to try his best to recall what happened.

His expression changed, and he seemed to remember something. It took a great deal of effort, but he began to speak. I leaned in close until my ear was a single hair's breadth away from his lips.

"I live . . . inside that tunnel."

I was overjoyed to get a witness account. Finally. He told me more.

Huang Shaoping grew up in a rural part of Anhui Province, over 1,000 miles away. He came to Chengdu after both his parents had passed away, in order to make a liv-

ing for himself. Unable to find a job, he had no choice but to call the tunnel his temporary home. He made his living by collecting and selling scrap. To most people here, Huang would have been just another nameless migrant worker.

I asked him again what had happened on the day of the explosion, but he shook his head and said nothing. The memories still seem to evade him.

I will bring pictures from the explosion site tomorrow.

APRIL 27, 1984

I showed Huang the pictures from the warehouse. He seemed quite startled when I told him that a man and a woman had died in the same explosion that had critically injured him. At last, he began to remember.

Huang was resting in the concrete tunnel on the afternoon of the 18th. He claims to have seen three people enter the warehouse over the course of one hour. It's far, but the mouth of the tunnel does give a direct line of sight to the warehouse entrance. He witnessed an unknown male enter the warehouse at 3 p.m., followed by a second man around thirty minutes after. Then, no more than a few minutes later, one of the men left. A third person, female, arrived about a half hour later. Huang's curiosity overpowered him when he saw the woman arrive, and he snuck inside for a closer look. The man and the woman were shouting at each other. However, before he could comprehend what was going on, he was caught in the explosion.

When I questioned him, Huang was sure it was the first man to enter the warehouse who left approximately half an hour before the arrival of the woman. If this is true, then we need to find this first individual. Huang's van-

tage point from the tunnel was far, but he swore that he could recognize him.

Pei stopped reading. His left hand was curled into a fist. If Huang Shaoping had seen the suspect, then why hadn't the task force made a composite?

According to later entries in Zheng's journal, the task force plodded ahead without any substantial progress or new leads. The gaps between entries gradually grew longer, and the sergeant's writing began to betray a sense of frustration. The investigation came to an utter standstill over the following two years. The team was disbanded, and all active investigations were closed.

However, earlier that very day, investigators had discovered a new notebook in Zheng's office at the scene of his murder. Inside were the current journal entries written in the days before his death. Pei rifled through the pile of documents he had brought back to his room until he found a black spiral notebook. He opened it eagerly.

OCTOBER 13, 2002

I had long assumed that this was over. That all those memories would remain sealed forever, just like the files. Perhaps I was wrong.

I discovered an envelope on my floor this morning. Inside the envelope were two items: an anonymous handwritten letter and a slip of paper with a web address on it. My heart was hammering as I set the envelope's contents down onto my desk.

That handwriting—I'd recognize it anywhere! Flawless calligraphy. Perfectly level characters. Every line was a scar in my memory. It was the same handwriting I studied hundreds of times, eighteen years ago.

I accessed the website. What I saw absolutely shocked

me. Has he returned? No, I shouldn't even entertain the thought. What if this is the work of someone involved with the case back then? An attempt at a prank?

I checked the envelope and its contents. No fingerprints, no stray hairs, no anything. It's as if the letter and the note sprang into existence and sealed themselves into that envelope.

The 4/18 Task Force was disbanded ages ago. I could very well be the last of the team members who still cares. What should I do? Report this to the provincial department, and continue the old investigation? That seems too rash . . . I'd be risking both my job and my reputation if I got excited about a mere scrap of evidence. Han and his people cannot get involved. Not yet. I need to deal with this under the radar.

OCTOBER 14, 2002

I got in touch with a whiz kid named Zeng Rihua at the provincial department. He agreed to help me run some online surveillance. I borrowed one of the department's digital cameras. With Zeng's help, I've already taken photographs of possible suspects. The case was classified years ago, so I can't tell anyone what I'm doing or ask anyone else to help. I hope I'm not wasting my time.

OCTOBER 19, 2002

Took lots of pictures today. Saw Huang tonight. He wasn't able to identify anyone in the photos.

That forum post has been getting a lot of views and replies. The poster has remained silent, however. Maybe this is just a sick prank.

Zeng tells me that teenagers and young adults make up the majority of users on online message boards. It would be hard to connect any of them to a case from 1984. Even so, perhaps I should investigate some of these kids. Zeng tells me that he's noticed some strange discrepancies in the provincial headquarters' computer database recently. His theory is that a hacker was poking around in the provincial system. If he's correct, it could explain how a hypothetical prankster could have found out about this old case.

That was the final entry in Zheng's journal, from the day before his murder.

If only you'd reported this to the provincial headquarters . . . Pei sighed inwardly. As absurd as it was, he could almost picture Zheng listening in from beyond the grave. "When you were struggling with your killer," Pei said aloud, "you must have realized that this was no prank. But by then it was too late, wasn't it?"

Three knocks on the door interrupted Pei's thoughts. He straightened the documents back into several neat piles and got up from his seat. When he opened the door, Mu Jianyun stood before him.

"Good evening, Captain."

"Here to talk about the case?" Pei did his best to sound friendly. "Come in and make yourself at home."

He returned to his seat, and Mu sat on the sofa opposite him. She cast a sidelong glance at the files on his desk.

"I just finished reading the case files as well. Would you mind lending me your expertise to answer a few questions?"

Pei smiled. "Don't be so polite. And I wouldn't go so far as to call myself an expert. What's on your mind?"

"Since my background is in psychology, I typically approach a case by analyzing the suspect's criminal motive and state of mind. From there, I can deduce his or her social background, life experiences, and personality traits to create a psychological profile. One thing that stands out in our case is the alias used both in the earlier anonymous letters and in the more recent online posts."

Mu picked up a pen and wrote the word *Eumenides* on a notepad. "Do you know what this name means?"

Pei didn't answer.

"It's a name given to the Furies in Greek mythology. Goddesses of retribution. The legends say that the Eumenides would track down those who had committed serious crimes. No matter where these criminals went, Eumenides would follow and fill their consciences with agony and guilt. In the end, they would make each and every one pay for their crimes."

"So our killer is classically minded. Goddesses of retribution . . ."

"In the 1984 murders, two victims received anonymous letters. Both of them were death notices signed with the name Eumenides. It seems the killer was attempting to punish both victims, albeit with a twisted sense of justice. That leads me to what I wanted to ask you: Did the two victims, Xue Dalin and Yuan Zhibang, commit the crimes listed in the letters addressed to them?"

"Did the vice commissioner neglect his job, take bribes, or collude with organized crime? I have no idea. I was just a student at the academy back then. Yuan, on the other hand—" Pei hesitated. "You could say that the 'crimes' listed in his letter were plausible."

"Captain Pei, I realize that Yuan was your closest friend, but when it comes to the specifics of this case I hope that you can give me accurate and definite answers."

"I understand," Pei said, reluctantly. "Yuan was an outstanding student at the academy. To tell you the truth, I admired him in many regards, but his weakness was women."

Mu looked again at the files spread across Pei's desk. Among them was a large photograph of Yuan. The man indeed was very handsome.

"His relationships didn't last long," Pei said. "About half a year before the explosion, he started seeing a girl majoring in administration at the academy. She was gorgeous, and Yuan definitely had feelings for her. Back then I was convinced that Yuan was actually going to settle down with her." Pei shook his head and sighed to himself. "But they broke up just a few months later."

"Why?"

"Maybe it was just the way Yuan was. Regardless of the reason, he was the one who broke it off. The girl came to the dorm looking for him later that day. Her eyes were red. Yuan made me tell her I didn't know where he was. I had my misgivings, of course, but I never expected the girl to take things as hard as she did. What I didn't know at the time was that she'd had an abortion for his sake. Then she committed suicide by jumping into a river." Pei looked down, his head heavy with shame.

"Some men are such scum," Mu snapped. She glared at Pei. "What about Yuan? Did he feel any remorse after this? Anything at all?"

Pei shook his head. "He found a new girl almost immediately, through a pen-pal exchange organized by the local paper. After writing each other for a while, they decided to start dating. They arranged a time and place for their first date. April eighteenth."

Mu nodded to herself.

"So that would make Yuan's pen pal one of the last people to have seen him before the explosion, wouldn't it?"

Pei answered with a weak shrug. "I know what you're thinking, but the answer's going to disappoint you. After the explosion, the original 4/18 Task Force came to our dorm building and collected every piece of correspondence between Yuan and his pen pal. They traced the address on the letters back to their sender, who turned out to be a girl at another college here in Chengdu.

The girl had never even heard of Yuan, much less arranged to meet with him. Her classmates all corroborated her statement—she had spent the entire day on campus."

"Could the actual sender have given Yuan a false name and address?"

"That's exactly it. If you check those files a little more closely, you'll see that the letters featured the same perfect handwriting as those death notices."

"Yuan lived on campus," Mu said, excitedly connecting the dots. "It would be almost impossible to pull off a murder in such a crowded place. So the killer tricked Yuan into going to the outskirts, where a single bomb could destroy every last shred of evidence."

Pei nodded.

"This is one meticulous son of a bitch," Mu said. She frowned, and looked up at Pei. "As sickening as the killer's methods were, I can understand why this person targeted Yuan. Womanizing, impregnating a girl and then abandoning her, finally driving her to suicide. You can't tell me that you actually condone that kind of behavior, Captain?"

Pei looked away. "Of course not. But he didn't deserve to die, strapped to a bomb in an abandoned warehouse. Yuan was my friend. As despicable as his behavior was, at his core I believe he was a good person."

"I see. Captain Pei, I'm very grateful for your help. My psychological profile of the suspect is much more fleshed out now." She offered Pei a conciliatory smile. "What's your next step?"

"I'm going to pay a visit to our lone survivor, Huang Shaoping." Pei plucked a piece of paper out from the stack of photocopies. "Zheng left us his contact information."

"Excellent. I'd like to talk to him as well. Why don't we both go see him tomorrow? Besides, Han wants both of us to stay out of his hair."

Only one of us, actually, Pei silently corrected her.

IIII

OCTOBER 22, 7:12 A.M.

On a normal day the skyline would already be bathed in morning light, but today the glum autumn drizzle had cast a dim, gray haze over the city.

Pain stirred Huang Shaoping from his slumber. The old burns had healed, but whenever rain came, every inch of his skin felt like it was on fire. Sucking air through his clenched teeth, he let the agony drag him back eighteen years.

Those five seconds stood out more clearly in his mind than any other moment in his life. She tore a wire from the bomb. A ball of flame instantly engulfed her and the man next to her. Before he could react, a wave of searing heat rushed over him and plunged him into total terror and desperation seconds before he lost consciousness.

And yet he had lived. Considering his broken bones and the third-degree burns covering 75 percent of his body, his survival was a miracle.

That one moment, however, had shifted the entire course of his life. He had clawed his way back from hell only to emerge as a pitiful wreck. To the rest of the world, he was a freak.

The explosion shattered his life. People were as afraid of seeing him as he was of seeing them. He remained solitary, like a lone desert tree. No one else could understand just how agonizing the past eighteen years had truly been.

Huang curled up on his bed. Rainwater dripped in from a crack in the wall. A spider scuttled across the ceiling. His ears twitched. He held his breath, waiting.

His chronic pain had sharpened his senses. He heard footsteps approaching. Seconds later, a knock on the door.

"Who's there?" Huang rasped, forcing the question out through his teeth.

"Police."

It was always the police. Who else would visit this dump? Huang struggled to get up from his bed, and he hobbled over to the door on his crutches. When he opened the door, a man and woman in plainclothes stood in front of him. They had nearly identical stunned expressions on their faces.

Huang was well acquainted with this look. It was impressive enough that neither officer had turned tail after seeing him. Even so, he adopted a suspicious tone. "You're both cops. What happened to Sergeant Zheng?"

"I'm Pei Tao, from the Longzhou Police Department," said the man at the door, displaying his badge. "This is Mu Jianyun, lecturer at the provincial police academy." The woman at his side forced a weak smile.

"Pei Tao . . . Pei Tao . . ." Huang mumbled to himself as he read the officer's ID. He then turned his murky gaze toward these unexpected visitors.

The burn scars on Huang's face pulled his skin taut and blended into the whites of his eyes. As the man fixated on him, Pei felt a chill creep over his flesh. Fortunately, Huang quickly turned and retreated into his home.

"Come in," he said in a low voice.

A musty smell greeted Pei and Mu as they stepped into the room. Pei had seen plenty of living spaces in his time as a police officer in Longzhou, but this apartment was wretched. Mu coughed gently into her arm.

"Shut the door behind you. It gets drafty in here otherwise."

Pei noticed that Huang wasn't wearing a jacket. The man hobbled over to the bed and wrapped himself in the filthy blanket crumpled on top of the mattress.

Mu gently closed the wooden door. Darkness swallowed the room. Both she and Pei suddenly found it harder to breathe.

"We're here to ask about a case from eighteen years ago," Pei said. "About the explosion." He had no desire to mince words, nor to remain long.

Huang rolled his eyes and let out a bitter laugh. "That's the only thing I'm good for. What about Sergeant Zheng? Why didn't he come this time?"

"He's dead," Pei answered quietly. "Zheng was killed two nights ago. We believe his death was related to the warehouse explosion. We've been tasked to identify the man who did it. The man who burned you. And we are going to catch him. That's why we're here."

"Wha—what happened? Zheng was here just a few days ago!"

"He asked you to identify some photos, didn't he? Did you recognize anyone?"

"Those pictures . . ." Huang spoke slowly, as though straining to recall something. After a moment, he shook his head. "No, that person wasn't in any of them."

"Are you positive?" Pei asked earnestly. "Sergeant Zheng was murdered in a deliberate attempt to delete those pictures."

Huang nodded. "I'm certain. The people in those photos were just kids. Most of them hadn't even been born when all that happened."

Grunting in acknowledgment, Pei decided to try a different approach.

"Let's leave the photos alone for now. I want you to tell me in detail what you really saw on the day of the explosion."

Huang frowned. "I've done that more times than I can count."

"I know, I've read the notes. I want to hear it in person." Pei's tone left no room for refusal.

"Fine." With a reluctant look, Huang licked his lips and began to speak. "Eighteen years ago, I'd just arrived from the countryside. I collected scrap to get by. More often than not, I spent my nights in an old access tunnel facing the warehouse. On the afternoon of April eighteenth, I didn't feel like going out. I curled up in the tunnel and went to sleep. I awoke a little later to see a few people come into the warehouse one at a time. At first I didn't think much of it, but when I noticed a woman show up, I decided to have a look."

Pei raised an eyebrow. "Why was that?"

Huang responded with mirthless laughter. "It was an abandoned warehouse. I saw a woman walk in after a man was already inside. What was I supposed to think?" He laughed. "To think that my libido almost got me killed."

Pei's gaze sharpened until it could have cut diamonds. Huang ceased his laughter, almost without realizing it.

"You should choose your words carefully," Mu warned Huang. "One of those two was Captain Pei's lover. The other was his closest friend."

A look of fear flickered over Huang's face. He looked up at Pei uneasily.

"You couldn't know," Pei said, his tone softening. "Let's not dwell on that. You said that you saw three people enter the warehouse?"

"That's right. Three people. Two men and one woman. The first man left the warehouse before the woman arrived."

"Can you tell me specifically when each person entered and left the warehouse?"

"I didn't have a watch." Huang shrugged. "All I can tell you is the second man arrived a little over half an hour after the first. The first man left a little while later. The woman arrived afterward."

Pei and Mu glanced at one another. Both of them were thinking the same thing—the first man had waited for Yuan, ambushed him, planted the bomb, and then left before Meng's arrival.

"The case files state that you saw what the first man looked like," Pei said. "Why didn't you provide the police with a description?"

"I only saw him from a distance. I'm not too clear about his exact appearance."

Mu cocked her head slightly to one side. "Didn't you say that if you saw him again, you'd be able to recognize him?"

Huang's lips drew back into a grin, revealing two rows of gleaming teeth. "The police have done a lot for me since the accident, you know. They covered my surgery. They put me in this wonderful apartment free of charge. I just wanted to be a good sport."

"But you said—"

"I only said that I *might* be able to. And besides, that was then. It's been almost two decades since."

Mu shook her head, her brow heavy with disappointment.

This line of questioning is a dead end, Pei thought. *We need to try another angle.*

"What did you see after you followed the woman into the warehouse?" he asked.

"The building was big. Lots of dusty containers and heavy-duty machinery for moving things around. I hid behind a broken machine near the entrance to keep out of sight. I saw a man sitting on the floor. His arm was raised at an angle that looked uncomfortable. The woman was crouched at his side, fiddling with something next to him. He kept yelling at her to leave him. I couldn't figure out what they were doing. I couldn't look away. The woman was screaming into some kind of radio, saying, 'Red wire. Blue wire.' That's all I could make out. 'Red wire. Blue wire.' There was a man's voice—"

"That's enough!" Pei snapped. His eyes were red. "I . . . I'm already familiar with this part."

"What do you want to know, then?" Huang asked uneasily.

Pei took a deep breath. "Tell me what happened at the end."

"The man on the radio said, 'Red wire.'" Huang's cheeks twitched. "There was an explosion."

"What did she look like?" Pei asked, in a whisper. "The look on her face, the way she moved. You had your eyes on her the whole time, didn't you?"

"That's right. I was watching her. It's strange, come to think of it. She looked nervous right up until the end. Then right at that last moment, a strange calm came over her. I even think she was smiling. In those last seconds, she was so beautiful . . ."

Pei's fingernails dug into the flesh of his palms. Once his anxious breathing finally steadied, he stood up.

"This room is suffocating."

Mu rushed over and opened the door. A gust of fresh air swept into the room, and Pei's lungs rejoiced. Right as he was about to step outside, Huang called out.

"Just one more minute, Officer."

Pei looked over. "What is it?"

Huang grinned through cracked lips. "The wind's chilly. I need to put on my long johns. Can you help me? As you can see, my hands aren't quite as nimble as they used to be. The pants are in the trunk next to the bed."

Pei opened the trunk, and an eye-watering odor hit him. Mildew, vinegar, and sweat all at once. Holding his breath, he fished the man's wool underwear out from inside his trunk. Mu turned away and left the room as Huang removed his pants.

Huang suddenly grasped Pei's shoulder.

"Both of you aren't here to interrogate me," he hissed into the officer's ear.

Pei gave the man a perplexed look. "Of course we are. We're both members of the task force."

Huang lowered his voice as he struggled to pull up his wool pants. "The woman didn't look at me for a single second when you were questioning me. She was observing you, studying your every look and movement. I've been around a lot of cops since the warehouse explosion. I know how they work. That woman didn't come here for me. She's watching you."

Pei felt his chest tighten, but his face remained static. He helped Huang into his clothing. "Why are you telling me this?" he asked softly.

Huang forced a snicker.

"Most people can't even bear to look at me without flinching, let alone help me put on a pair of pants."

Pei studied the man's gruesome features again, full of pity. "Thank you for your time," he said, and walked out of the apartment, closing the door behind him.

Sleet fell outside. The droplets were as thin as hairs, and ice-cold against Pei's face. Mu had been standing outside for some time already. Her wary gaze flitted down the street from one rusted apartment door to another, as though any of them might burst open at a moment's notice. She looked at Pei as he stepped out of Huang's apartment.

"If you could have swapped places with Meng, would you have trusted your own judgment during those final few seconds? Or would you have wanted hers instead?"

Pei was quiet for a moment. "I'd trust my own judgment."

"Then why did Meng listen to you? Where did that blind faith come from? Come to think of it, how do you even know she did listen, and it was the red wire that she pulled?"

Her flurry of questions stunned Pei. Forcing an awkward smile, he sighed softly. "Now I know why Sergeant Zheng said that death would have been kinder to the man."

Mu smiled. "I disagree, actually. Did you see the calendar on the wall?"

"I did," Pei said after a short pause. "It was nailed right next to the door."

"It's one of those daily calendars. The kind with pages you tear off after each day. I took a look at the page up there now—it's today's date."

"You're saying he still has something to live for. A bit of a stretch, isn't it?"

Mu shook her head. “His life isn’t nearly as deprived of hope as you might think.”

||||

OCTOBER 22, 7:55 A.M.
CAPTAIN HAN HAO’S OFFICE

After knocking twice on the open door, Zeng strolled into Captain Han’s office and handed him a note. His handwriting was barely legible, and the captain wondered if this was a side effect of the young officer’s reliance on computers.

“ ‘Location: Dongming Gardens, Building Twelve, Room 404. Name: Sun Chunfeng,’ ” Han read softly, and looked up at Zeng. “What’s this supposed to be?”

“That’s the guy we’re looking for, and where we’ll find him.”

Grinning, Zeng tossed several photographs onto the table. The pictures showed a young man with bleached hair. They had been taken inside an internet café.

“You recovered the deleted photos?”

Zeng scratched his ear and gave a lazy nod. “They were taken on the morning of October eighteenth, between 10:25 and 10:30 a.m.”

Han picked up the photographs and studied them one at a time. “How did you get the information written on the note?”

“Like I said yesterday, Sergeant Zheng found the internet cafés based on the information I gave him. I checked the time the photographs were taken against the records from my IP tracer, and found they were taken at the Qianghui Internet Café over by Normal University. I went to the café and checked their records. This particular kid was using the computer all morning. I grabbed the hard drive’s operating data from that window of time. Now I know the kid’s instant messaging number, two of his e-mail addresses, and the log-in information for four different online accounts," Zeng said with a chuckle. He opened his mouth for a massive yawn. In spite of his fatigue, he looked rather pleased with himself.

"So you checked the address linked to his shopping account?" Han asked impatiently.

"Bingo," Zeng said, smirking. "His default shipping address was set to the apartment in Dongming Gardens. I got in touch with the local police station. They gave me the number for his landlord. He confirmed that someone named Sun Chunfeng moved in half a year ago. The new tenant's most distinguishing trait? Bleached hair."

Han smiled. "Good work. Still, I hope you realize that you could have just contacted me when you obtained the address. My people could have taken care of the legwork."

Zeng responded with a snicker and a shake of his head. "Geez, Captain, I thought we worked for the same team now."

"Yes," Han said, "and that means that you report to me now. Remember that the next time you feel the temptation to give orders to your IT team."

"Yes, sir. I'll stay out of your hair when you follow up on this. Damn, I really have been up all night! I have to get some sleep."

Stretching, Zeng rose from his seat and walked out of the office. Han watched his retreating figure. The kid was too lax and unruly to be a proper cop, but at the same time, his investigative skills were nothing to scoff at.

The captain considered his next move. He couldn't afford to repeat the mistakes that his predecessors made eighteen years ago.

He dialed a number on his desk telephone.

Yin answered on the first ring, as usual. Han wasted no time.

"Call Captain Xiong—I want the two of you in my office ASAP!"

||||

OCTOBER 22, 8:31 A.M.
DONGMING GARDENS

Dongming Gardens was one of Chengdu's many old-fashioned residential communities. The lanes between the brick buildings were wide enough to accommodate two cars at once, although Han only spotted a handful of vehicles on his way to the apartment building. A group of men in their seventies and eighties were gathered around a long park bench, while several old men and women were exercising on the weatherproof exercise equipment set up between buildings. Han spotted a few younger tenants hurrying out of their apartment buildings, their movements a flurry of crisp white shirts, suitcases, and dark skirts. The older tenants squinted curiously at the police vehicles entering their neighborhood, while the younger ones in white-collar dress appeared too busy to notice them.

A few unfamiliar faces were outside Building Twelve, which rose to a modest height of six stories. Dressed in street clothes, they had spread out around the building. Contrary to their nonchalant manner, these people were keeping watch over all nearby roads and alleyways. They were all top-notch officers of the criminal police force and the city SPU team who had been urgently summoned for a covert raid.

Another batch of officers entered the building. Some of them dropped back along the way to keep watch. Each floor housed four separate apartments; in addition to a standard wooden door, each apartment was further protected by a grated metal door. The members of the core unit worked their way through the building's cramped stairway until they finally arrived at the door of room 404.

Once Han and Xiong's SPU officers had concealed themselves against the wall, they ordered a flustered old man, the landlord, to approach the door. He rang the doorbell, called Sun Chunfeng's name, and shouted that he was collecting the month's rent.

After an agonizing wait, however, no response had come from inside the room.

Han signaled to Yin, who escorted the landlord away. A burly SPU officer immediately stepped out from behind Xiong and crept over to the door.

Chengdu's SPU team contained specialists of almost every variety. Officer Liu Song knew his way around locks better than any burglar in the city. He tried the protective metal door first, which swung open. Smiling, Liu Song then slid a fine iron pick into the lock of the wooden door, and a soft click sounded from inside. He raised his left hand and signaled that it was open. Guns drawn, Han and the other officers waited to spring into action.

Xiong echoed Liu's signal. Nodding, Liu pushed gently against the door with both hands. The door glided open silently, and the police dashed inside.

They found themselves within an old single-bedroom apartment. The dim, cramped living room was unoccupied, save for a faux-leather sofa and a small television set. The officers fanned out through the room. One raised his hand to signal the others to stop. They listened. A faint rustling was coming from behind the door that presumably led to the bedroom.

Captain Han rushed in front of the others and charged into the room. The light coming through the open doorway hit the bed first, and Han shone his flashlight through the room. When he spotted the figure wriggling below the window, he raised his gun.

"Freeze!" he roared.

Xiong and the others rushed inside to join him.

A man with bleached blond hair was sitting below the window and leaning back against the wall. A black cloth was tied around his eyes, and thick tape covering his mouth muffled any sounds trying to escape.

Han tensed. Something was very wrong here. He holstered

his sidearm and loosened the cloth from Sun's face. The young man gaped at him, twisting in hysterical panic. He was handcuffed to the radiator.

"Don't move! We're the police!" Han yelled.

The terror in Sun's eyes gave way to hope. He shouted something against the tape covering his mouth.

Han reached out and began to tear the tape away. Liu approached from across the room. Taking out his set of iron lock picks, the officer prepared to use his talents to unlock the cuffs around the young man's hands.

"No! Don't touch them!" Sun immediately shouted as soon as the tape was gone from his mouth. "Bomb! There's a bomb!"

Xiong's nerves snapped tight. He held Liu firmly back, and crouched to study the handcuffs. Just as he had feared, two thin wires protruded from the keyhole and disappeared through the front of Sun's shirt, at chest level.

After motioning to Han and the others to move back, Xiong cautiously lifted the front of Sun's shirt. The wires ended at a square plastic box fastened to his waist.

"That's the bomb!" Overwhelming terror had turned Sun's cries into hysterical sobbing. "It activated when you opened the door. The timer was set for ten minutes!"

Xiong spotted the box's electronic display screen. Red numbers counted down, and his blood turned to ice. Fewer than eight minutes remained.

Xiong glanced at Han. "Evacuate the building," he said.

Without another word, Han rushed his men out from the room. Urgent cries echoed through the building's narrow corridors.

"There's a bomb on the fourth floor!"

"Evacuate all residents!"

Xiong turned to Liu. "Go and assist with the evacuation. There's nothing you can do here."

Liu looked back at his superior, his expression a mix of shock and shame. If he had touched that lock . . . But Liu had his orders. Captain Xiong had to focus all of his attention on studying the bomb.

The sounds of footsteps and yelling reverberated from outside the apartment.

Sun was a quivering wreck. His panicked eyes jittered from Xiong's face to the bomb's display screen and back again.

"Be still." Unexpectedly flashing a smile, Xiong patted the young man's shoulder. "I'm going to disarm the bomb," he explained.

In that instant, Sun ceased shivering. A sliver of hope began to shine in his eyes.

Xiong grabbed for his multifunctional utility knife, using it to open the bomb's casing. The screws dropped one by one, and the case came loose in his hands. Holding his breath, Xiong gently pulled on the casing's plastic tab. Just as he was about to pull the casing away, he sensed something resisting his movements. He froze.

There was a wire connected to the casing. Despite his caution, the damage was already done. The device emitted a low beep, and the numbers on the digital display suddenly became a blur. He understood that he now had less than a minute to disarm the bomb.

Sun let out a long moan. He twisted and struggled against the ropes binding his legs.

Xiong ignored the sweat pouring down his forehead. With nothing left to lose, he tore the casing away from the bomb.

The countdown on the display screen reached zero.

A small puff of smoke burst from inside. Tiny pieces of silicon clattered to the floor. A faint but lively melody filled Xiong's ears. He gasped as he saw a piece of paper slowly emerging from inside the shattered casing.

It had never been a bomb at all, he realized. Just a music box with a switch.

The SPU captain took in a deep breath, and felt a great weight had been lifted. Then he caught a whiff of a peculiar odor. As he looked for the source of the smell, he noticed a damp patch at the crotch of Sun's pants. With a wry grimace, Xiong grabbed the slip of paper that had been spit out from the bomb's casing. He glanced at its contents and dashed into the corridor. Han and the other officers were still busy coordinating the evacuation, and it took him a moment to get their attention.

Once everyone had learned the truth about the false bomb, Liu returned to the apartment and helped Sun out of the handcuffs. It took some time for the young man to regain his nerves. Eventually the scene calmed, and he began to stutter through his account of the previous few hours.

||||

The evening after Sergeant Zheng's murder, Sun Chunfeng had been pulling an all-nighter at the café. It was dawn by the time he returned to his apartment, and he was asleep as soon as he collapsed into bed. When he awoke, he discovered that he was unable to move—his hands and legs were bound, and he had been blindfolded and gagged.

An unfamiliar man's voice explained that Sun was handcuffed to the radiator, and that a bomb had been attached to his body. The bomb's fuse wire was connected to the keyhole in his handcuffs. If anyone opened the door, they would trigger a remote control, and the bomb's timer would begin a ten-minute countdown. If anyone tried to unlock the handcuffs, they would trigger the bomb.

Sun then heard departing footsteps. He was left with no other option but to wait in fear and darkness until someone arrived.

||||

Han was furious. Sun's account had seemingly confirmed that their suspect was indeed male, but with the exception of that detail, their investigation had made essentially zero progress.

"We've been set up. The day after he murdered Zheng, he came here and set this trap for us."

"You're saying that those deleted photos were a deliberate trail left for us?" Xiong asked.

"Isn't it obvious? He knew we were bound to try to retrieve those images, and that doing so would bring us running right to him."

Xiong shook his head in anger. "Why go through all this effort just to give us a note?" he asked, referring to the slip of paper Han was now gripping in his hands. The captain had already read it so many times that he could recite the words with his eyes closed.

That perfect, mechanical handwriting.

DEATH NOTICE

THE ACCUSED: Ye Shaohong

CRIMES: Road rage, second-degree murder, abuse of the legal system

DATE OF PUNISHMENT: October 23

EXECUTIONER: Eumenides

Han's hands shook with rage. The killer's threat was clear.

It wasn't fear that made his hands tremble, but rather uncontrollable anger.

Eumenides was intentionally revealing the names of his targets and the dates of their murders. He was taunting the police. Trying to humiliate them. What else could be his intention?

Han was like a cocked pistol. The slightest amount of pressure, even unintentional, would be enough to set him off.

||||

A man toyed with an electric sensor. He was quiet, serene—the polar opposite of Han. He stared at the digits on the device in his hand, which displayed a series of recorded times, like a stopwatch.

"Twenty-one hours and fifty minutes to reach the apartment. Then four minutes and eleven seconds to dismantle the 'bomb,'" he murmured, amused. "Not a bad performance. This might be interesting after all."

CHAPTER FOUR

PEI'S SECRET

OCTOBER 22, 10:40 A.M.
CHENGDU CRIMINAL POLICE HEADQUARTERS,
CONFERENCE ROOM

Zeng had barely gotten two and a half hours of sleep before he was summoned back to the conference room. He was a mess; his eyes were bloodshot and swollen, his hair unkempt.

"Shit! So this guy Sun Chunfeng is a dead end?" Zeng exclaimed in dismay. "We've got nothing."

Han's response was abrupt. "We've investigated his family background, personal history, social life, and recent activity. He's just a typical high school dropout who fell into Eumenides's hand when he stumbled upon his 'call for justice' online. The whole thing was a setup. Sun had nothing to do with it."

The fruits of Zeng's labor—the entire IP-tracing scheme that he and the late Sergeant Zheng had coordinated—had come to nothing. Zeng grimaced as a cold realization came to him. "The plot thickens. I was wrong. This guy has been stringing us along the whole time. He's no Luddite. He's a hardened pro."

Yin had been taking down the minutes for this meeting, but now his pen froze on the page. Zeng's about-face in attitude was surprising.

"If the missing photographs were only part of the killer's

ploy, then it's just as likely that our original speculations regarding his motives are groundless," Han said. "So, let's go back to the beginning. Why did he murder Zheng?"

Yin returned to his minutes, trying to ignore the feeling that he was sinking deeper and deeper into darkness. There were more layers to this case than he had expected. He decided that his best chance was to listen to the other team members' analysis of the situation and do his best to absorb their expertise.

Xiong spoke up. "Actually, it isn't that difficult to figure out the killer's motive. Let's not forget that Zheng was killed after digging back into the 4/18 investigation. The most likely scenario hasn't changed: Zheng found a new lead, and he was murdered to cover it up. You're right. The real question is, why jerk us around? That's the one thing I don't understand." The SPU captain clenched his fingers into a fist.

"The killer's behavior was completely contradictory," Mu said.

Pei, who had been lost in his thoughts up until now, looked up at the academic. "What do you mean?" he asked.

"His actions demonstrate a psychological contradiction. If the motive behind Zheng's murder was to cover up something that the sergeant had discovered, then he should be avoiding police attention. However, by setting this trap for the police, he did the exact opposite."

"That's all well and good," Pei said, "but it doesn't bring us any closer to knowing why Eumenides did what he did."

"There's a new development," Han interrupted. "We discovered a transmitter while examining the device in Sun's apartment." He motioned to Yin, who tapped a button on his laptop's keyboard. A digital photograph of the transmitter appeared on the screen.

Zeng snapped to attention. "Of course! That fake bomb was another trick!"

"Do we know what kind of signal it was sending out?" Xiong asked.

"It was a simple transmitter connected to the timer of 'that fake bomb,'" Han said. "It was capable of transmitting the timer's current status to a receiving device."

Zeng burst into laughter. "What the hell was he doing? Timing us?"

Pei suddenly raised his eyebrows in a pensive look. He tapped the surface of the table with the tip of his finger. Han noticed.

"Something on your mind, Captain Pei."

"There's an issue with our line of thinking. Actually, it would be more precise to call it an issue with our collective attitude."

Pei ignored the offended looks in the room.

"We're asking ourselves the wrong questions. 'What do we already know?' 'Where has the killer slipped up?' We need to be straight about one thing first: We know absolutely nothing except what the killer wants us to know. We're his audience! He posted his manifesto online, murdered Sergeant Zheng, and left a trail of bread crumbs for us to follow. He even told us the date of his next murder and the name of the victim!" Pei narrowed his eyes. "He's been leading us by the nose."

As Pei laid out the collective failures of everyone in the room, he watched the embarrassment burn on their faces. All except for Zeng, who let out an unimpressed chuckle.

"Then what are we supposed to do now? Feel sorry for ourselves?"

"Captain Pei made an excellent point," Mu added. "The killer's goal is far larger than the murder of Sergeant Zheng. He's challenging the police. This is all a game to him."

"That's exactly it," Pei said. "It's a game—one that he's gone to painstaking lengths to put together. He has spent the last eighteen years planning it. Now it's begun, and he has his prey. Something is still missing from the game, though. And without this one thing, regardless of how masterful his plan, he won't find the thrill he craves."

Zeng let out an exaggerated sigh. "I'll bite. What's he missing?"

"A good game requires a skilled opponent," Pei said with a wry smile. "Sergeant Zheng's murder may be simpler than it actually seems. Remember, the 4/18 investigation lay forgotten for eighteen years. It was classified. Buried. Perhaps our killer wishes to start the game anew."

"You're saying that he killed Sergeant Zheng knowing that the police would re-form the task force?" Zeng asked.

"Look at what happened at Dongming Gardens," Pei said, his voice rising in excitement. "It was a test. He intentionally left a trail that led us straight to Sun Chunfeng. He even timed us."

"Incredible," Xiong muttered. "This is just unbelievable!"

"No, Captain Xiong," Pei said with confidence. "It fits the facts. And I have to wonder, did our performance meet his standards?"

"Indeed," Mu said, biting her lip. "If we analyze Eumenides's behavior from this perspective, there's no contradiction in his actions at all. On the contrary, they display a very distinct objective."

Yin wiped a layer of sweat from his brow. He didn't know whether to think or to simply take notes.

"It's as absurd as it is disturbing," Han said. It wasn't clear whether this was in response to Pei's analysis or to their now-redefined opponent. "If he wants to play, then by all means, we'll play!" His fist slammed against the table, spreading a chill throughout the room.

"Some game," Zeng said bitterly. "So when do we start round two?"

"Show everyone the death notice," Han ordered Yin.

Finally, Yin thought. This was familiar ground. Taking a

deep breath, he tapped the laptop's right arrow key, and a scan of a handwritten note replaced the image of the transmitter.

"This note," Han explained, "was found inside the bomb casing at Sun's apartment."

"October twenty-third," Zeng read. "Tomorrow."

"Yin," Han said. "What do we know about this 'Ye Shaohong'?"

Yin tapped a button, and a photograph of a woman appeared on the screen.

"Ye Shaohong. Female, thirty years old, married without children. A resident of Chengdu, she currently resides in the villa development located in the Jinding Center in the south of the city. Mrs. Ye is a businesswoman. Wealthy. She's the general manager of Duhua Imports and Exports, Limited. The company specializes in high-end clothing—the kind of stuff that costs a few months' salary when it's on sale."

Zeng suddenly interrupted. "There are plenty of women named 'Ye Shaohong' in this city. How can you be sure she's the right one?"

"She also received the death notice." Yin displayed the next image as he spoke. "These are the replies to the manifesto Eumenides posted on the forum. Ye Shaohong's name appeared in the third reply. More than seven hundred users replied to that post expressing their agreement. It's likely that this victim was selected by the forum's users."

"A true people's choice," Zeng said under his breath.

"But what exactly did she do?" Mu asked.

When she looked at Ye Shaohong's picture, she felt something like sympathy stir within her. The woman was attractive, yes, but "beautiful" was not the first word that came to mind when she saw Ye. "Disciplined" was much closer. The woman sported a short, stylish haircut, and makeup had been expertly applied to the taut skin around her jaw and cheekbones. Even if the men in the room couldn't see it, Mu recognized the tenacity that surrounded the woman like an impervious shell. It was the same way that Mu had shielded herself from the double standards and snide remarks that came part and parcel with being a professional woman in modern-day China. Something else lurked beneath the woman's toned exterior. It was pride, Mu thought.

Noticing Mu's and Pei's puzzled looks, Yin explained her crime.

||||

On the fifth of April two years earlier, while on her way to work, Ye Shaohong drove her brand-new red BMW into a roadside vegetable stand owned by a farmer surnamed Wang. The stand had overturned, and a dispute had then broken out between the two. Wang demanded that Ye compensate him for the damage she had caused. Ye, on the other hand, insisted that Wang's stand had been blocking the road—although a dozen other fruit and noodle vendors had also lined the downtown street right alongside Wang—and she refused to discuss the matter any further.

To stop Ye from driving away from the scene, Wang planted himself in front of her car. According to witnesses, Ye's BMW suddenly shot forward and struck Wang. The man was taken to the hospital, where he later died from his injuries.

There was no shortage of witnesses to the incident, and news of what had happened quickly spread both online and by word-of-mouth. Despite the local government's recent crackdown against outdoor vendors, many people sided with Wang, and a narrative was quickly spun: a wealthy, privileged businesswoman had killed a poor street vendor in cold blood. Ye explained that she had intended to shift the car into reverse and drive around Wang, but her nerves, exacerbated by her argument with the merchant, kept her from shifting to the proper gear. It was all a terrible and unfortunate accident, she insisted, and she was in fact a victim herself. The subsequent judicial process accepted her explanation, and she was set free after paying a hefty fine. This slap on the wrist stirred up a tidal wave of controversy; cries of blame and condemnation soon filled the media. People accused Ye's husband, a prominent diplomat based in Europe, of using his influence to make this case go away.

"In the end," Yin concluded, "Ye returned to work at Duhua, where she was quickly promoted from assistant manager to her current position of general manager."

Xiong shook his head in sharp disapproval. Similar emotions appeared on the other team members' faces.

"Now I remember hearing about this," Zeng said, raising his index finger. "So Ye was behind the wheel of that car. Yeah, I heard that the driver was extremely well-connected."

"I also believe it was intentional," Yin said, finally injecting his own opinion into the conversation. "Witnesses at the scene stated that Mrs. Ye had verbally assaulted Wang before starting the car, even threatening to run him over if he did not step away. If you ask me, her excuse that she accidentally put the car into the wrong gear isn't very convincing."

Han cleared his throat. "The law says that everyone is innocent until proven guilty. If you want to convict someone of second-degree murder, you need legitimate evidence to back it up." He shot Yin a stern look. "Heated words said during a dispute are not enough."

"So if I go out and run someone over with my car, am I innocent too?" Zeng retorted. "We're the police. Why are we trying to keep this quiet? Look, if you want to know why they let her off so lightly, there are only two explanations: either the size of her bank account, or her husband!"

Pei glanced at Zeng with increased respect.

Xiong cleared his throat. "Back to the matter at hand. What's our next step?"

Everyone's eyes darted to the head of the team. Fortunately for them, the captain had already formulated a plan.

"Eumenides claims he'll deliver his so-called justice upon Mrs. Ye tomorrow. Seeing as he's already presented us with such a blatant challenge, our best option is to spread a wide net and lie in wait."

"Have we contacted her husband?" Pei asked.

Han grimaced. "It took us a while, but we finally managed to get in touch with his personal secretary, who told us that he's currently on a three-day ski trip in the Swiss Alps. She promised that she would leave a message with his hotel, but I don't think we can count on a quick response. In the meantime, we need to take action."

That was Yin's cue. As the captain continued, Yin clicked through a series of locations that displayed on the screen.

"Since Eumenides has already revealed his planned time and victim to us, he must be anticipating that she'll be under police protection. That leads us to conclude that he'll try to carry out his assassination attempt in a well-populated area. Somewhere with complicated geography, where it'll be hard for us to be aware of everything that's going on at every moment. We think he's going to try to slip in and out under our noses."

A new image appeared on the screen—an imposing building made out of industrial glass and steel.

"Mrs. Ye's office is located in the Deye Building downtown. She leaves her house every day at nine to drive to work. The Deye Building is an older building, and it isn't equipped with an underground parking garage. This means that Mrs. Ye has to park her car at the nearby Citizen Square before walking to her office. At approximately four in the afternoon, she punches out for the day and goes home."

Now the team members were looking at what seemed to be a small mansion. Spilling out from it was an elaborate lawn ornamented with trees, hedges, and a miniature fountain.

"The villa where she lives is well maintained. It's under video surveillance twenty-four hours a day. Security at the Deye Building is also very tight. All entrances and exits are well guarded. It's very unlikely that the attempt will happen at either location."

Han paused and made sure that he had everyone's undivided attention. He pointed to the screen, which was showing a large square plaza that appeared to be several hundred feet across.

"Here," he said. "This is Citizen Square. It's a wide-open public space with heavy foot traffic and immediate access to each of the nearby main roads. It will be relatively easy for our guy to hide in plain sight, and it will be just as easy to flee. This is where he will try. Our top priority tomorrow is to secure the square."

Han glanced at Xiong. "Naturally," he added, "we still need to take precautions against any unconventional methods that may be used to commit the murder. Gas, an armed attack from long range, a hit-and-run, or an explosion. Captain Xiong, you're going to handle this side of things."

Xiong disapproved. "You're saying that we're supposed to guard Mrs. Ye for the entire day, then move in to capture the suspect when he attempts to carry out the murder?"

Han nodded. "Precisely," he said, his voice rising. "I refuse to believe that anyone is capable of committing a murder in plain sight of the police."

Xiong took a moment to collect his thoughts. "This is not the right approach. If there's one thing we can be sure about after today, it's that Eumenides is no idiot. He has to know that a public execution of Mrs. Ye is suicide for him. He's baiting us. Don't you see? This is all part of the game. We should restrict Mrs. Ye's activities tomorrow and prevent her from leaving her home. That would give us the best chance of guaranteeing her personal safety."

"And then what? Do you really believe we can keep her holed up in her house forever? Let's suppose Eumenides can't strike tomorrow. Do you think he'll just give up? What if he attacks Ye some other day when we're not around? How can we pass up our best chance to catch this killer?"

"I don't believe that Eumenides is going to show himself while Ye's home is full of police officers. He's going to wait until we're moving. When we're starting to get tired," Pei said.

Xiong scrunched his forehead. "I cannot approve of a plan that uses the person we're supposed to be protecting as bait."

Frustrated, Han mulled it over for several seconds. Rather than let the others think that their leader had reached an impasse, he decided to put it to a vote.

"Majority rule. We'll take a vote to decide which plan to use."

Xiong nodded. "I can accept that."

Zeng raised his hand first. "I'm siding with Captain Han. Besides, Ye's no model citizen. Why should she deserve such special treatment?" With a sly glance at Mu, he adopted a mocking tone. "Although, it would be a shame to let such a gorgeous woman die."

Mu met Zeng's gaze. "She's not beautiful enough to affect my judgment. Captain Xiong is right. Protecting Ye Shaohong's life is more important than anything else."

"That makes it two against two," Han said. "Captain Pei?"

All eyes darted to Pei.

"I vote for Han's plan."

"That's settled." Flashing a pleased smile, Han made a sweeping gesture to include everyone in the room. "Now let's talk strategy."

IIIII

By two in the afternoon, they had formulated a plan to protect Ye Shaohong. The crack officers in Han's criminal police squad and Xiong's SPU team would provide the manpower to secure the square, and keep Ye under constant protection.

Pei was not surprised when Han told him that he had been

relegated to a peripheral role. In theory, he would help monitor the police who were carrying out surveillance of Citizen Square. However, Han had no qualms about informing Pei that he would be an observer only. He did not complain.

They only had one day to prepare, so Han and Xiong immediately got to work. Zeng rushed back to his own room in the guesthouse in hopes of catching up on sleep. This left Pei and Mu, who had both been assigned "monitoring" duties, as the last team members remaining in the conference room. Even with Captain Han gone, Mu was still not willing to let go of her objections to the team's current plan.

"Captain, you realize that when we voted just now, your decision went against every one of the principles a police officer is expected to abide by. You're supposed to prevent crimes from happening, not bait a killer to act first."

"Do you honestly think Eumenides has a chance of succeeding under such tight police surveillance? Han's right. There's something else going on here."

Mu refused to be deterred. "To be honest, I don't give a damn about what happens tomorrow. My concern is what goes on in people's minds. Xiong and I are the only ones here who have upheld our professional and moral duty. Han is too eager to capture this killer, or perhaps is driven by his need to avenge Sergeant Zheng. Or maybe this is a manifestation of an overzealous love for his work. Zeng lacks both experience and the maturity that comes with it. Whatever the case, their reasons are compatible with their personalities. But what about you? You seem more levelheaded than Han, and you certainly aren't as shallow as Zeng. Why did you choose to put Ye in harm's way?"

Pei shook his head. "I don't know."

"Everyone's aware of their own thoughts to some degree or another," Mu said with a wry grin. "You're just unwilling to confront them. Today you pinpointed Eumenides's motive for killing Sergeant Zheng. Your theory was bold and piercing. While your explanation was quite rational, it followed an unconventional line of thinking. How did you get there?"

"Simple," Pei said. "I looked at the problem from another perspective."

Mu shook her head. "From the killer's perspective, you mean? That's the kind of thing they teach in basic classes at the academy. But you thought of something that none of us could. What does this mean?"

Pei squinted at Mu, waiting for her to finish.

She laughed again. "Out of all of us, your mindset is closest to the killer's. The two of you are very similar, in a way."

Pei stiffened in his seat. "I suppose I can't really refute that."

"The idea of matching wits with him appeals to you, doesn't it?" Mu's eyes twinkled. "Both of you crave the thrill of the game."

Pei paused, and then chuckled. Now that Mu had presented him with such a clear version of his thought process, he felt a kind of relief. "They say that to be a great cop, you need to be a great criminal."

"Professor Yang used to say that in his criminal investigation classes, didn't he? He said that a good police officer and a good criminal share quite a few common traits—a sharp mind, a meticulous nature, a natural inclination toward risk-taking, a craving for knowledge. Two sides of the same coin, in other words. What they both desire the most, and what is hardest for them to achieve, is to see the world through the other's eyes."

"Indeed. I owe a great deal to Professor Yang."

Mu observed Pei closely. "It's lucky for us that you ended up on the right side of that coin. If you'd chosen the path of a criminal, it would be a terrifying thing."

Pei shook his head. "I can think of at least one thing more terrifying."

"What's that?" Mu asked, raising her eyebrows.

"A female psychologist."

Mu froze. "So you can crack jokes, too?" she said with a scowl. "For the record, I still haven't changed my opinion about men. You really can be scum."

||||

OCTOBER 22, 6:23 P.M.
CAPTAIN HAN HAO'S OFFICE

"Well, I can forget about getting any shut-eye today." Zeng stifled a yawn. His bloodshot eyes were wide with excitement.

"What've you found?" Han asked curiously.

"The bastard posted Ye Shaohong's death notice online about half an hour ago."

Han turned his attention to the computer. Just as Zeng said, a post titled "Death Notice," authored by a user named Eumenides, was currently the subject of heated debate on the forum.

The post was identical to the letter they had found in Sun's apartment. Han scanned the replies, which already numbered in the dozens.

OP is bonkers, said one.

His eyes went to the comment below it. *Why'd he choose Ye Shaohong? Why not my wife?*

You might call him insane, another user had posted, *but he's just doing what everyone else is too afraid to.*

"Have you pinpointed the IP address he posted this from?" Han asked. "If you can, we might be able to track him down."

"He's an arrogant bastard, all right. He knew that we'd be monitoring the internet, and still he went ahead and posted this. He's using a proxy server, but we traced his actual IP address without much difficulty. It's assigned to a commercial user—a public relations company. Here's the business's registered location."

Zeng handed Han a slip of paper. Han ignored the stream of numbers that made up the IP address, instead fixing his eyes on the physical address printed below: *Haizheng Building, Yingbin Street, Office 901.*

As Han read the address, Zeng noticed a framed photograph on the captain's desk. Its faded colors showed two young officers standing next to each other with nearly identical grins. He recognized one of them—it was a more youthful-looking Han.

The captain cleared his throat, and Zeng jerked his head up. There was a stern gleam in Han's eyes.

"Go find Yin. We're heading out now," the captain said.

FIFTEEN MINUTES LATER
HAIZHENG BUILDING

Office 901 was home to a small company called White Lodge Media. There were no more than a dozen staff members, making the space feel cavernous. The receptionist directed Han, Zeng, and Yin into a meeting room, and soon the company's head manager, a sweaty middle-aged man surnamed Li, stood before them, followed by the company's network administrator.

The officers' initial round of questioning verified that no one except the company's own employees had entered the office since two o'clock that afternoon, and that no employees had left during that time. Han ordered Yin to keep watch over the entrance. They were currently on the building's ninth floor. As long as they kept anyone from entering or exiting the office, it would be impossible for anyone to leave the scene.

Zeng showed the note to the network administrator. "We need to know which computer this IP address corresponds to," he said.

"I . . . um . . . I'll have to go check."

The administrator was a young man with slicked hair, and he

was also a nervous wreck. It must be his first encounter with the police, Zeng thought.

The manager turned to the stuttering young man. "You don't know this already? What the hell do I pay you for?"

The young employee's face was beet-red as he earnestly tried to explain himself. His stuttering was even more severe now. "We use dynamic IP addressing here, Mr. Li. This IP address is definitely somewhere inside the office. As for which computer, though, I'll have to . . . I'll have to verify."

"I've said it time and time again," the manager snarled. "Young people have no idea what it means to take pride in their work! When I was—"

"It's fine. This isn't his fault," Zeng interrupted. Brushing the man's hand away, he comforted the younger employee. "Go ahead and check."

The administrator took the note with him.

"So what exactly is the problem here, officers?" Li asked. "Was someone watching porn? Don't bother looking any further. It's that sleazeball Kang, no question about it. He'll be off the payroll by tomorrow!"

Han was already eager to end this conversation. "How many people work at this company?"

"Twelve, including me. This is a small business. We specialize in analyzing new media trends, and we're just getting off the ground." He plucked a business card holder from his pocket and held it out. "Here's my card."

Zeng took a card and twirled it between his fingers with faint interest. Han simply continued his questioning.

"Are all your employees present today?"

"Yes, yes, they are," the manager answered. "Every single employee is working in that room right now."

Han patted Zeng's shoulder. "Let's have a look around."

Stuffing the card in his pocket, Zeng followed Han into the

large office. The floor space was divided among ten cubicles. Inquisitive faces poked out from each one to examine the unexpected guests.

Han examined the room. Eight of the ten employees were female. Besides the network administrator they had just met, the only other male was a short young man built like an eggplant. There wasn't much here to connect any of them to a brutal, lethal criminal.

Zeng slammed his hand against his forehead. He shook his head, wincing. "Your internet is wireless, isn't it?"

"That's right. We were the first wireless clients in the entire city when we started out a few years ago," Li told Zeng excitedly. "This might look like a small company to you, but our office setup is first-rate."

Zeng raised his eyebrows. Wireless internet was becoming more common in Chengdu now, and it was certainly more widespread in more developed cities like Beijing and Shanghai, but this fact had caught his attention. Meanwhile, Li turned again to the network administrator.

"What's going on? Have you finished checking yet?"

The nervous employee crept out from his cubicle. "It's, um, a little strange. I've checked all the computers here in the office. None of them have been assigned that particular IP address."

"What does he mean? Is there some mistake here?" Han whispered to Zeng.

"The office network definitely assigned this address to a user, and, um, a computer definitely logged in with it sometime around three this afternoon," the administrator stuttered. "But the strange thing is that it wasn't one of ours." He glanced anxiously at his boss.

Li's eyes widened. "Not one of our computers? If it isn't one of ours, then how could it have accessed our network?"

Sweat began to pour down the administrator's forehead.

"I . . . I was planning to set up a password by the end of the week . . ."

"Well, there goes our lead," Zeng told Han glumly. "Anyone with a laptop could have logged in to their system. They didn't even need to be inside this office!"

Han's face fell. Their lead had crumbled to dust.

"You didn't set up a password?" Li shouted. "Why don't you just post our door key-code out front while you're at it?"

The administrator hung his head, silently enduring his boss's rage.

Zeng patted Li's shoulder. "There's no point yelling at him."

"Why not?" A vein bulged from the manager's forehead.

"Even if he'd set up triple-layer security on your network, the man we're looking for would have cracked it in a matter of minutes."

Han waved his hand. "We're finished here," he said, a tone of disgust in his voice.

IIIII

As he drove the police cruiser back to headquarters, Yin couldn't help but speak his mind.

"I knew that today would be a waste of time. The killer's too smart to leave a trail online. Why else would he have the guts to challenge us with these death notices?"

Han coldly stared at his assistant. "Our opponent is already prepared for tomorrow. Are you?"

"That . . . That's not what I meant, Captain," Yin said sheepishly.

"Just pipe down, will you two?" Zeng grumbled. "Both hands on the wheel, Yin. I want to catch up on my beauty sleep."

Yin stayed quiet for the rest of the ride back.

They reached headquarters approximately ten minutes later.

Zeng got out and walked alone. In spite of his exhaustion, he went to Mu's room instead of returning to his own quarters for sleep. He entered without knocking. Mu, busy preparing food, had left her door open.

Zeng walked right in, only to be greeted by a scowling Mu. They were both civilian officers, but due to her status as a lecturer at the provincial academy, Mu viewed herself as slightly above Zeng. She was not at all happy at his attempts to ingratiate himself as a peer.

"Why are you here?"

"To discuss the case with my esteemed colleague, of course. Why else did you think I'd come here?" Grinning, Zeng seated himself on the sofa. He inhaled through his nostrils, milking the moment. "Ah, even your room smells wonderful. Beauty is as beauty does."

"If you wanted to talk about the case, then why did you shut the door behind you?"

"Don't you usually close the door when you're meeting with the captain?" Zeng asked with a mischievous grin.

As shameless as Zeng's words may have sounded, Mu didn't view him as anything but harmless. Besides, his attitude was contagious. "Tell me what you really want to talk about," she asked. "After all, you've come all the way here. Why waste time beating around the bush?"

"Han assigned you a special task," he said in a low voice. Mu was surprised at how quickly his jocular tone had evaporated. "You're investigating Pei."

Mu tilted her head slightly to the right. "That's an interesting theory, Zeng."

The man smirked with apparent satisfaction. "As far as the case is concerned, Captain Pei Tao is as suspicious as they come. He was very close to both victims at the warehouse fire eighteen years ago—in love with one and best friends with the other. He was also the first one to call it in to the police. His behavior before the explosion was erratic, to say the least. Fast-forward to three days ago, and again he was first on the scene at Sergeant Zheng's murder. Quite a series of coincidences. All things considered, Han would be crazy *not* to have Pei under surveillance."

"Your logic is surprisingly sound," Mu said, taking a seat across from Zeng. "Is this where I'm supposed to wonder whether I've underestimated you?"

Zeng waggled his eyebrows. In his mind, it might have been a flirtatious gesture; in reality, it only made him look even goofier.

"And you assumed I was just another by-the-book macho cop! I have more information on the 4/18 case than any of you do. Han wanted me to run computer analyses on the bulk of the data."

"Oh?" Mu raised her eyebrows. "Any discoveries so far?"

"There were several internal disciplinary investigations at the academy before the 4/18 case occurred. They were all linked, too."

Mu shook her head. "The case file didn't mention any of this."

"Better put on a helmet," Zeng said smugly, "because I'm about to blow your mind. Over the course of six months before the 4/18 murders, so-called 'discipline notices' were found at the police academy."

"A 'discipline notice'?" Suddenly Mu sucked in her breath. "Are you telling me—"

"I'm getting to that," Zeng interrupted. "There were four of these notices, and each one was secretly given to a different student at the academy who had committed some kind of minor infraction. Each student was disciplined—ostensibly by the mysterious individual who had written the notes—according to the gravity of his or her respective violation. The punishments were . . . embarrassing, but none of them were felonies, naturally, and were handled by the provincial academy."

Mu sensed that Zeng was holding back intentionally. This time she refused to bite.

"Okay, okay. I'll tell you the best part. Each notice was signed . . ." He paused deliberately.

Mu rolled her eyes. "Come on, Zeng."

"'Eumenides'!" the young officer said with relish. "And it gets better. The style of handwriting was very similar to that of the later death notices."

"My god," Mu replied. She was stunned.

"There's something else I should mention," Zeng added, nonchalantly. "Each of the four discipline notices was found *after* the punishment had taken place."

"They had no warning?" Mu asked with excitement. "Tell me the details."

"My files list a total of four cases involving discipline notices. The first notice appeared in late 1983. It accused the target of cheating on an exam, and it was delivered on the day the academy announced the students' exam scores. This particular pupil wound up with a big, fat goose egg.

"The subsequent academy investigation revealed that all the answers this student claimed to have written in his test papers had mysteriously disappeared. He demanded an explanation from the course instructor, but the name and exam number written on his test papers were his handwriting beyond any doubt. The student was expelled without any further argument.

"After the 4/18 murders, though, the task force tracked this student down. He was working as a waiter in a hot-pot restaurant owned by his father. After the team members convinced him that they weren't trying to drum up charges for a lawsuit, the kid admitted that he actually did cheat on that test. However, he insisted that he had absolutely no idea as to how his test papers had become blank."

"What about the other cases?"

"The second discipline notice targeted a female student for stealing cash and personal belongings from several young women in her dorm. One day, the girl emerged from the showers to discover the clothes inside her locker had vanished into thin air. The locker was still locked tight. Only one key could have opened the lock, and it had been dangling from her wrist the entire time she was showering. It was beyond anyone how this 'Eumenides' could have snatched the clothes from her locker."

Mu stayed quiet as she tried to unravel the puzzle of Eumenides's methods.

"The third mark was a male student with a bad reputation for spying on others and then making their secrets public. One day at midnight, the campus-wide PA system crackled to life blaring out extremely private entries from his journal. Later they discovered that someone had broken into the broadcasting room and played a prerecorded message from a cassette tape." Zeng grinned before finishing the story. "Now here's the kicker—the student's journal was on his person at all times. No one was able to come up with any explanation as to how this Eumenides character was aware of the journal's contents."

He laced his fingers behind his head. Mu could tell that he was enjoying this, but she was enthralled all the same.

"The final target was another male student. His crime was . . . I guess you could say he loved too much. One girl too many, to be specific. The student went to a dance in the campus ballroom. Both of the girls he was dating were waiting for him, thus exposing his two-timing tendencies. Later, both girls claimed to have received handwritten notes from the student inviting them to the dance. Now, this kid might not have been the sharpest tool in the shed, but he clearly wouldn't have done something that stupid. This was Eumenides's work, without a doubt."

Mu's mind was racing. "What about the cassette?" she asked. "The one that was broadcast over the campus PA during the third case? Eumenides's voice was recorded on it. It's not too difficult to mimic someone else's handwriting, but transforming your own voice is a whole other matter altogether."

"You cut right to the center, like a hot knife through butter.

A woman after my own heart!" Beaming, Zeng took out an MP3 player from his pocket. "I've got the recording from the cassette right here. Would you like to listen?"

Mu grabbed the headphones, and she heard a low and muffled male voice speaking into her ears. "What's wrong with his voice?" she asked.

"That's an easy one. He was holding his nose," Zeng said, pinching his own nose as he spoke. The odd timbre sounded similar to the one in the recording.

"Can we manipulate it?"

"Eighteen years ago, the answer would probably be no. Things are different now," Zeng snickered. "Today's software can do things you couldn't even imagine. We can modify the audio to simulate what this person might sound like when speaking in a normal tone of voice."

Zeng tapped a button on the MP3 player. Now the recorded voice sounded far more normal. It also sounded oddly familiar, although Mu couldn't quite place the source.

"He sounds young now, doesn't he? That tells us that he was probably in his late teens or early twenties eighteen years ago. Now, if we make a few more tweaks with our software, we can simulate what he would sound like eighteen years later."

An eerie smile crept over Zeng's lips as he skipped to the next track on the MP3 player. The voice in the headphones was deeper now. Mu's eyes widened.

"Captain Pei!"

Zeng felt a swell of pride. He rocked his head from side to side in a playful manner. "I'm guessing you realize how important your assignment is."

Mu removed the headphones. "Does Han know about this?"

"Nope," Zeng said, shaking his head nonchalantly.

Mu stared at the young man for a long moment. "Then why are you telling me?" she asked coldly. "This is the kind of thing you should be reporting to the captain."

Zeng grinned again. "Can you blame a guy for finding an excuse to talk to a beautiful woman?"

His eyes darted slyly around the room. He didn't see any photographs or keepsakes that would suggest a boyfriend, or any family at all, for that matter. The room's only distinguishing characteristic was a small stack of books by Nietzsche, B. F. Skinner, and Cai Yuanpei—all names he barely recognized. Mu didn't appear to be the social sort, to say the least.

"Are you finished?" Mu gave a disdainful snort. "I'm calling Han and telling him to come over right now."

Seeing that Mu was about to grab the room's telephone, Zeng quickly reached for her hand. "Hey, just a minute, now. Are you trying to sell me out?"

"Maybe," she said. "Tell me what's going on, right now."

"Fine, fine, I'll tell you the truth. I haven't spent too much time around Pei Tao, but I'm positive that he isn't a murderer."

"We have his voice as evidence for these disciplinary notices," Mu said. "Even if we don't have solid proof that he's behind the death notices that followed, we have enough evidence to suspect him. He got a student kicked out of the academy, remember?"

"But those were pranks, *and* that student admitted that he was cheating. Look, at the very least, do you honestly think Pei was faking his reaction when Han told us about the explosion?"

Mu frowned at him.

"Besides, I've got a gut feeling about him," Zeng added. "A lot better than my feeling about Han. That's why I want to get to the bottom of this with an expert psychologist like yourself."

Mu murmured to herself for a moment, and then nodded. "All right, on one condition. I want all the files in your possession."

"Deal," Zeng said without hesitation. "I'll make copies for you."

||||

OCTOBER 22, 11:55 P.M.

Five years ago, Ye Shaohong had done something that made her the subject of countless conversations. She had married into a wealthy, influential family. One of her husband's relatives was a senior official in the province. Her husband had not done badly for himself either, having secured a position as a diplomat to Germany, where he now spent most of his time. His first six months away in Europe had been torture for their marriage, particularly when she had flown to meet him in Berlin only to discover half a dozen compromising photographs on his cell phone. In the end, they had come to an agreement—neither would ask questions about the other's activities during their time apart. Now, business at Mrs. Ye's clothing enterprise was booming, thanks in no small part to the vast connections at her disposal. She lived in a villa worth millions of U.S. dollars, drove a 2003 BMW shipped from Germany at great cost, and had made a name for herself among Chengdu's upper crust. All that by the age of twenty-nine.

Mrs. Ye liked to think of herself as a woman of taste and refinement. She was typically in bed by eleven every night, always with a nightcap of red wine. Tonight was different, however. Instead of drifting off into peaceful slumber, she tossed and turned in her soft bed, fruitlessly attempting to stifle the anxiety making her heart race.

She hadn't given the bizarre "death notice" much thought at first. Reporting the anonymous letter to the police had been more a formality than anything else. She'd received several similar threats ever since word of the distasteful incident with the fruit vendor had spread. The threats had made her nervous at first, but by now she was fairly inured to them. She even started to find their misplaced anger and quaint sense of morality somewhat amusing.

Tonight was different, and it was ruining her sleep.

A group of police officers had arrived at her door barely an hour after she reported the letter. They asked her question after question about what had happened and what she had seen. Reinforcements had come later in the afternoon to provide her, they explained, with increased protection. One of them—a stoic and muscular officer who was handsome in his own, serious way—introduced himself as SPU Captain Xiong Yuan. How in the world was she supposed to stay calm if the police were taking this silly letter so seriously?

Her bedside telephone rang, and she jolted out of bed. Was it her husband again? She'd tried to reassure him the first time, telling him that the police were simply being thorough and there was no real threat. Judging from her ringing phone, he wasn't convinced. After switching on the light, Ye reached for the receiver.

"Hello?"

The earpiece was silent. A chill spread from her fingers to her toes. This was not her husband.

"Hello?" She spoke a little louder, yet very timidly.

Still no one answered.

Ye flung the receiver down and sprinted out of her bedroom. Only when she saw the officers inside her living room did she feel safe.

Xiong rushed over to her. "Who was that?"

"I picked up, but I didn't hear anyone on the other end."

Ye was nearly hyperventilating. Xiong signaled to his men. An SPU officer was already listening on the living room extension, where the police had installed a monitoring device. The officer pressed a button, and the audio from the phone was routed through a separate speaker for all to hear.

They heard only silence. There was a long beep after ten seconds, and the call was immediately cut off.

Xiong turned to another officer. "Get me the caller's information right away," he snapped. Then he turned to Mrs. Ye and adopted a comforting, almost paternal style. "We'll take care of this. You can go back to bed."

"No. I can't sleep. I'm going to stay here in the living room with all of you." Mrs. Ye's porcelain skin had turned whiter than ash.

"You're safe here. That I can promise," Xiong said, smiling. "We have the entire house covered from top to bottom. No one's getting past us. My colleagues are standing guard right on the other side of your bedroom wall. If even so much as a squirrel passes by your window tonight, they'll see it right away."

"Really?" Mrs. Ye didn't sound very convinced.

"Didn't you see the white sedan parked outside your window? My friends from the police are sitting inside. One of them is Han Hao. You met him earlier. He's the one in charge of this entire operation."

Ye consented to return to her bedroom. All the same, she cracked the door open an inch or two before returning to bed.

The results from the trace came in. The call had come from a mobile number that was registered anonymously. It would be impossible to pinpoint the user. Xiong took out his own mobile phone and updated Han.

"He didn't say anything?" Han asked from the sedan's passenger seat. He continued to stare at the villa's rear window.

"Not a word," Xiong answered.

After a long silence, Han let out a long exhale.

"No. He's telling us this round has just begun."

CHAPTER FIVE

CUT THROAT

OCTOBER 23, 7:15 A.M.

Ye Shaohong opened her eyes and waited for the haze of last night's slumber to clear. She had dreamed about the police—that they were staying in her house to protect her from a killer. And then the killer had called her—

Someone knocked at her door. "Mrs. Ye? Are you awake yet?"

"Who's there?" she croaked.

"Officer Yin. Whenever you're ready to leave, we're waiting for you."

Reality rushed back to her in an instant. She reached for the glass of water at her bedside and took a long sip. The liquid was cool and soothing against her throat.

"Give me five minutes," she told the officer at the door.

When she finally walked into the living room, she saw that Han had returned. He was sitting on the large leather sofa at the center of the living room. His eyes were shut. All of the other officers had been replaced by fresh, rested faces. They were crowded together on the sofa along with Han. Laptops and notebooks lay scattered on the broad coffee table, and beside them sat the platter of peaches and a plate of sunflower seeds that Ye had placed there hours earlier. The fruit was nearly untouched, but the plate of seeds had been reduced to a pile of shredded shells.

"Captain Han," she said, "I can't do it. I think I'd be better off staying home."

The captain opened his eyes, and he straightened up slightly against the sofa. Spotting a stray piece of shell on his sleeve, he picked it off and dropped it onto the plate on the table.

"I won't force you to do anything you aren't comfortable with," he said. He sounded alert, as if he had not been sleeping but merely waiting. "We can stay here for the rest of the day and protect you. However, you need to know that our resources are limited. For obvious reasons, the police department can't accompany you like this day after day. This man is dangerous, and he isn't going to give up."

Ye grew even paler. "What can I do?"

"You can't keep hiding forever. He'll just keep waiting, no matter how long it takes. That's where we come in. We've already laid out a net for the criminal. All you have to do is go about your life and your job while we wait for him to fall into it. After that, you'll never see him again."

"Are you positive that you can guarantee my safety?" Ye asked Han anxiously.

Han nodded. "One hour ago, SPU officers performed a detailed security check of your vehicle as well as your route to work. Captain Xiong himself will personally drive you to work, and we'll have escort vehicles in front of you and behind you. We'll be on the lookout for anything out of the ordinary."

Han paused here. Ye's eyes were wide, her cheeks drawn taught. The early morning light cast a skeletal shade across her toned, slim frame. She was listening.

"After you and your police escort arrive at work, Captain Xiong will remain at your side at every step. He's an expert marksman and a black belt in Krav Maga. We'll have plainclothes officers spread throughout the square. You won't see them, but they will be there. Their sole purpose is your protection. Not a single suspicious individual will be allowed to approach you.

There will also be plainclothes officers inside your office building; they'll be dressed as security, property management staff, even your own employees. Anyone delivering food or beverages to your office during these hours will be searched by our men. We have the strictest security protocols in place. Yes, I can guarantee your safety."

Ye stared at Han, her eyes wide and unblinking. She tried to process the information that Han was relaying to her, but it was too much. The captain's words floated around her, suffocating her like a boa constrictor wrapping itself around its prey. Only one clear and undeniable fact loomed before her: she had no choice but to go along with Han's plan.

"Oh," Ye said softly.

"Just go about your day. Don't leave Captain Xiong's side, and do exactly as we say. As long as you do that, I promise that by the end of today, this will only be a memory. The kind of story you'll tell your friends over drinks."

Slowly the woman nodded. Her uneasiness was slowly replaced by a fragile hope.

"Good, and there's one final thing. It's best if I tell you this now."

"Tell me what?" she asked. The drowning sensation returned.

"Your would-be assailant is most likely a young or middle-aged male. He's about five-foot-five, with a thin build and a fresh knife wound on one hand. What this means is that you need to take care at all times not to approach any man matching this description. My officers are all at least six-foot-two, and every single one of them will be wearing either a brown or black felt cap during the operation. No matter what happens, you need to stay by Captain Xiong's side, and you need to stay in sight of our officers. Do you understand?"

Ye, who had listened closely to every single detail, nodded resolutely.

"Good," Han said, checking his watch. "Go on and get ready.

You and Captain Xiong will leave for work at your usual time. I'll take position at Citizen Square now so I can start coordinating with my people. We'll be with you at all times."

Ye started to turn around. She stopped.

"Captain Han?"

"Yes?" the captain asked.

"The crimes listed on that death notice," she said, a quaver coming into her voice. "Do you believe that they're true?"

Han was stone-faced. "It's not my job to ask those questions. The courts have already done that."

Ye lowered her eyes to the polished floor. This wasn't the answer she had hoped for.

"I'm starting to think they are," she said. She glanced at Yin, who was watching her from the sofa. Her cheeks turned pink. She walked back to her bedroom, where she began putting on her makeup.

Yin gazed at the door to the woman's bedroom. Regardless of what the other team members thought, he pitied her. Sighing, he forced himself to keep his mind on the task at hand. During yesterday's briefing, he had suggested that Xiong drive directly to the entrance of Ye's workplace. Han had rejected that proposal, however.

There's going to be a lot of people in Citizen Square, he'd said. *There'll be a high risk factor, but it's also the perfect location for our plainclothes officers to lie in wait. Our net is cast for tomorrow. If we close it tight before we even begin, how's the killer going to find his way inside? We need to leave him an opening, but I'm going to hold the drawstring. The square is this opening! We can keep her safe. And if we can't, the only option would be to lock her in a safe.*

They were supposed to be protecting this woman, but as far as Yin could tell, she was merely the cheese in the captain's mousetrap.

IIIII

TWENTY MINUTES LATER

Citizen Square was the beating heart of Chengdu. Streets and clusters of skyscrapers blossomed outward like arteries of glass and concrete. The buildings that rimmed Citizen Square housed some of the city's most prominent businesses. Among these was the Deye Building, in the southeast corner. The task force had commandeered a large room on the sixth floor of the Sky Peak Hotel, a towering building on the northwestern edge.

The window of their on-site control center provided a clear view of both Citizen Square and the exterior of the Deye Building. A row of six computer monitors stood on a long table set perpendicular to the window, and technicians buzzed around the room, fidgeting with radios and other surveillance equipment.

Han and Yin entered to discover that Pei and Mu had already arrived. Pei was helping a technician adjust the positioning of their surveillance equipment. As soon as he noticed them, he approached. "What's the situation?"

"Ye Shaohong received an anonymous call ten minutes after midnight. The caller said nothing, and hung up a minute later. Other than that, all quiet." Han kept his explanation as succinct as possible.

Mu looked at Pei. "Just like you said—nothing significant would happen at the house."

"I slept well last night," Pei said, and he looked at Han. "Too bad you and Captain Xiong didn't have that luxury."

Han narrowed his eyes at Pei, and walked over to the window. "Has all the equipment been tested?" he asked.

"Yes, it has," answered the team's technician. He handed Han a wireless radio as well as an earpiece and microphone.

Han raised the microphone up to his mouth. "This is Lima One. Lima Two, please respond."

A booming male voice answered at once: "Lima Two, in position!"

"Lima Three, please respond."

"Lima Three, in position!"

||||

It was Mu's first time witnessing a police operation as it unfolded. Wide-eyed, she approached the six surveillance monitors. Each screen displayed a separate portion of Citizen Square. As Han had explained, the feed for each monitor came from one of six high-resolution cameras that Zeng's people had installed on buildings around the square's perimeter only fifteen minutes earlier. There was a gap between the third and fourth monitors. This clustered arrangement gave Mu, a habitual visitor of art museums and galleries, the unshakeable feeling that she was watching a pair of moving triptychs.

"Are all the plainclothes officers in position? I can't see them," she said.

It was currently rush hour, and the area around the square bustled with vehicles and pedestrians alike. As hard as she tried, Mu couldn't spot any particularly conspicuous figures in the area.

Pei smiled. "Look: the man selling newspapers next to the building, the cab driver waiting for passengers next to the intersection, the sanitation employee busy sweeping, the man in the east corner keeping an eye on those bikes, the middle-aged man relaxing by the fountain, the one smoking at the entrance to that small shop, the couple sitting on the bench over on the west side, and the sketchy-looking fellow peddling bootleg movies to the people walking by. They're all ours. I see thirteen of our people in the square at the moment."

Mu looked at the captain, her surprise plain as day. Neither she nor Pei had attended the detailed briefing beforehand, nor were they familiar with any of the officers that Han might have chosen for this operation.

"The sweeper gave it away," Pei said. He sounded faintly proud, as if he had just remembered the answer to an obscure trivia question. "He's doing his job too well. If he keeps at it like that, he'll throw his back out in just a day or two. Now, look at those real cleaners. They spend most of their time standing around and resting, not bent over working."

Having overheard this, Han surveyed his subordinates in the square below and frowned. He spoke into his microphone again. "This is Lima One. Lima Five, please respond."

"Lima Five here. Lima One, please advise."

"Don't look so goddamned enthusiastic about your work. From now on, I want you to rest two minutes for every minute of sweeping!"

"Lima Five, understood!"

Mu had grown even more curious. "What about the others? Are there any holes in their disguises?"

Pei shook his head.

"We're only as strong as our weakest link. The cleaner stood out, and I was able to use his position to estimate where the other plainclothes officers should be. There's a real science to positioning plainclothes officers when you're dealing with a space as open as this. They need to monitor every inch of the square and at the same time keep an eye on each street and intersection. It's hard to describe the beauty of it in words. The academy had a whole course dedicated to the topic when I was studying."

"Even if you could determine their positions, surely you couldn't pick out every single person. There could be a thousand people walking around the square!" Mu said with clear astonishment. "The newspaper seller, for instance. There's at least ten other people selling papers in that corner of the square alone. How can you tell which one of them is really ours?"

"When running surveillance, plainclothes officers usually wear some kind of identifying clothing. It keeps them oriented if things erupt into chaos. These articles of clothing won't stand out among a large group of people, but they're easy to find if you look for them within a specific area. Today our friends are all wearing brown and black felt caps—isn't that correct, Captain?"

Pei had directed this last question at Han. The captain remained silent, but his expression said enough.

Han checked his watch. "Get in touch with Xiong and see where he is," he ordered Yin.

"They've just left Ye's villa and are en route," Yin reported after he had finished his call. "They'll be here in about half an hour."

Han switched on his microphone. "This is Lima One. All units be advised: the target will arrive in thirty minutes. Carry out the operation as planned, beginning now. There's no need to respond."

The three members of the investigation team watched the monitors. From their view inside the tiny command room, the square appeared calm. The sweeper was even leaning against his broom and puffing on a cigarette.

The red BMW entered the parking lot in front of the Deye Building at 9:25, just as Han had specified. Captain Xiong, dressed as Ye's driver, parked the car in an empty space between a white van and a black Volkswagen. Both of these vehicles were equipped with bulletproof glass windows.

Xiong exited Ye's car first. Soon two men in black felt caps exited the van and the Volkswagen and stood guard beside the BMW. Xiong then walked around the car and opened the passenger door for Ye.

The two felt-capped men stood about thirty feet away from each other, one in front and one behind. Xiong stood in the middle, with Ye close behind him. Together the four of them walked briskly toward the entrance of the Deye Building.

Other plainclothes officers stationed at the square assumed their assigned positions around Ye and her escorts. Five of them appeared to be casually walking, each with their own distinct destination in mind, yet as Ye moved, she was always flanked by at least two officers fifteen feet away.

Three officers remained fixed in their original positions around the square. Each position was a central point for foot traffic. These officers glanced in every direction, paying careful attention to any unusual activity in the square.

Inside the command room on the hotel's sixth floor, Han and the others supervised the operation from above. With every step Ye took, they could feel her feet treading upon their own hearts.

The square bustled with pedestrians. Mothers pushed strollers across the stone pavement, past elderly people carrying overstuffed bags of produce. A group of middle-aged and elderly women at the southern edge danced to the music pumping from a large black speaker on the ground. As Ye and Xiong advanced, a steady stream of pedestrian traffic passed through the protective circle of plainclothes officers. None of these civilians seemed to notice that anything was out of the ordinary.

SPU Captain Xiong finally escorted Ye into the Deye Building. The officers in front of them halted in the lobby, where they would keep watch. It was at that moment that the elevator reached the ground floor. The security guard standing by the elevator door barely glanced at Xiong. Any more than that, and both men would have risked blowing their covers.

Xiong allowed himself to exhale. His SPU officers had been assigned security duty for the building's interior. The knowledge that his own men were present eased the pressure on Xiong's nerves. He allowed himself a moment to shut his eyes and exhale. The first stage of the operation was behind them.

||||

"What's your next move?" Mu asked Pei.

Pei blinked at her for a moment. "What do you mean?"

"You've already put yourself in his shoes, haven't you? I see your eyes darting back and forth. You've barely looked at Ye. You're looking for holes in the operation. You're trying to get inside his mind."

Pei felt all eyes in the hotel room turn to him.

"You're right. I am looking for flaws. That way I'll be able to figure out what action the killer might take," he said. He turned his attention to Han. "You're running a very tight operation, Captain. I didn't notice a weak link. I don't have any idea how to pull off Ye's murder. Unless . . ."

Han's eyes narrowed at once. "Unless what?"

"We're missing something crucial. It would be almost impossible to slip past Xiong and his officers' defenses, and even if he did, he'd have no chance of escape. He'd be swarmed by more than a dozen officers immediately. No matter how many times I play the situation out in my head, the best result he can hope to achieve is annihilation. If he touches Ye, it's suicide. It ends as a defeat for everyone."

"A defeat for us?" Han growled. "As long as we beat Eumenides, I can almost stomach the loss. Besides, if you'd ever seen Captain Xiong in action, you'd be begging Eumenides to try something."

Mu cocked her head. "Couldn't he just kill her from a distance? You know, with a long-range rifle?"

"A sniper rifle?" Yin squinted. "Where do you think we are, Washington, DC? Not even our department has that kind of equipment."

Han shook his head. "Very unlikely, Mu. There's never been a homicide case like that in the history of China."

|||||

INSIDE A LUXURY SUITE

"A sniper rifle? How ridiculous."

The man's lips spread into a frigid grin. A handful of users on the forum were excitedly debating how Eumenides might carry out his sentence against Ye Shaohong. One of the more popular suggestions had involved a long-distance attack.

Unless he had some very unique connections, it would have been all but impossible for him to get hold of a sniper rifle. Likewise, if he had opted for a more common firearm, such as a pistol, he would be mobbed by police officers the second he unholstered it in public. It was beside the point. Using a gun was never an option.

He rose and walked to the bathroom.

The face that stared back at him in the mirror was as familiar as it was alien. He rubbed his cheek. The stubble felt prickly against his skin, despite the white bandages on both his hands. He picked up a razor and carefully shaved the stubble away, then carefully wiped down the sink.

Relaxed, he shut his eyes and rubbed his smooth jaw.

He remembered.

What's a killer's weapon of choice? A gun? You could not be more wrong.

Mark my words: Never use a gun. When you grow accustomed to using a gun, you are already standing on the brink of your own destruction. First, you'll have to risk everything to find one. And you'd have to find one you can trust. Then you'll have to work out a way to carry it. And what are you going to do with it when you're done? These questions will slow you down. They will make you a slave to the gun, just as they will leave a trail for the police to follow.

The best weapons are those that can be found anywhere. Use what you can get anytime, carry freely, and dispose of whenever you wish. Your weapons will become your most intimate partners in the coming days. You must find a reliable partner, one that will never betray you.

The man opened his eyes, and he carefully disassembled the razor in his hands. A thin blade gleamed in the mirror.

||||

OCTOBER 23, 4:00 P.M.

Afternoon rush hour had arrived. The streets around Citizen Square were choked with cars and buses, and even the shoulders were crammed full of anxious cyclists. Taxis were lining up around the square; their drivers flipped through newspapers and smoked cigarettes, at peace with the commuter chaos around them.

Even though the day was quiet and uneventful, Ye Shaohong had been fidgeting for the past seven hours. She liked to think of herself as an occasional coffee drinker at best, generally preferring tea, but the five crumpled espresso-stained cups in her wastebasket said otherwise.

Even within the climate-controlled safety of Ye's spacious offices in the Deye Building, Xiong remained stoic and vigilant. Now that they were inside, the chances of Eumenides striking during this time window were slim to none. Their most dangerous trial would come when it was time to escort Ye back across the square to the car.

The plainclothes officers had been in position around the square for some time. So far, no one had reported any suspicious individuals, or seen a match to the suspect's physical profile.

Back in the Sky Peak Hotel, Pei peered tensely at the monitors. He wanted Ye to make it back to her car without incident, but at the same time, he also yearned to catch his first glimpse of Eumenides. He remembered Mu's comment in the conference room the previous day, about how his vote of agreement with Han's plan went against every one of the principles a police officer was meant to uphold.

Han studied the square through the window. "This is it," he announced. "Ye and Xiong are leaving the building!"

The room itself seemed to hold its breath in anticipation. As Ye and Xiong exited the Deye Building on the first monitor, the other screens showed the thirteen plainclothes officers dispersing throughout the square. Within moments they had formed a secure perimeter.

As Pei studied the monitor, he noticed a taxi parked at the square's southeast corner. A figure appeared to be moving in the passenger seat.

"Something's wrong," he announced.

"Show me," Han said, rushing over.

Pei strode over to the window and pointed toward the vehicle he had seen in the monitor. "The red taxi in the southeast corner has been parked there for over ten minutes, but look closely. There's someone in the passenger seat."

The taxi in question was outside the officers' perimeter, but it was still within a manageable distance from the hotel. Han could just make out the shape of a silhouette inside.

He switched his microphone on. "This is Lima One. Lima Seven, eyes on the red taxi one hundred feet southeast of your position."

A bike-mounted officer posted on the eastern side casually turned his head to focus on the taxi. The passenger-side door opened, and a man exited.

Despite their distance from the ground, Pei and the others had a clear view through the monitors. The man was short and thin as a rake, and he was holding an opaque plastic bag in his right hand. He glanced around the square, and his gaze quickly locked onto Ye Shaohong. He began to walk toward her with brisk steps, his left arm swinging back and forth as he walked. The officers in the command center could see something white covering his left hand.

It's a bandage, Pei thought.

Han's heart thumped against his ribs. "Lima Seven, move to intercept. He's a match!" he yelled into the microphone.

Lima Seven was already moving. He flew off his bike and pounced on the man like a wild tiger. Before the man had moved five feet from the taxi, Lima Seven tackled and pinned him to the ground. The man struggled with all his might to get up, but he could only twist and squirm pathetically on the ground.

Confusion quickly replaced Han's initial excitement. How could someone this frail possibly have killed Sergeant Zheng?

As Lima Seven cuffed the suspect, Han saw a man exit a black taxi at the eastern edge of the square. He was short, thin, and he carried a plastic bag in his right hand. A white bandage was wrapped around his left. As soon as he stepped outside the taxi, he took off in a sprint toward Ye.

Suddenly there were more than a dozen scrawny men, all with nearly identical features, streaming from taxis parked all around the square. Every one of them was making a mad dash directly at Ye and Xiong.

Han's perimeter unit sprang into action. Each officer instinctively chose a different angle to intercept the incoming men. The thin men were no match for the officers in hand-to-hand combat. One by one, they were forced to the ground. Some were quickly handcuffed, while those who attempted to resist got a taste of the Chengdu Police Department's elite combat training.

Han's expression remained grim as he observed the action from six floors above. Almost twenty men had simultaneously stormed from taxis—far outnumbering his thirteen officers. Police hidden inside the white van and the Volkswagen also joined the fray, but there were just too many of the strangely similar men. Two of them had already slipped past the protective perimeter and were only a couple of yards away from Ye.

However, neither individual so much as touched her. Xiong had left Ye's side to dash toward them. He showed no mercy. His fist struck the first man's ribs like a sledgehammer, and then did the same to the second one's jaw. Before they could even begin to wheeze in pain, the two had already collapsed to the ground. Their knives fell from their hands, but something didn't feel right to Xiong. It was the way the weapons hit the pavement, he thought. However, he had no time to dwell on this observation. He was already standing face-to-face with three more men.

These men had been right at the heels of the first pair. However, they froze in their tracks as they watched their comrades fall. Their faces were marked with blank incomprehension.

The SPU captain made no move to strike. Instead he returned to Ye's side, keeping his eyes on the three men, his fists waiting. He would not leave her side. If it came down to it, he would not hesitate to kill anyone who made a wrong move.

All of this occurred within seconds. The civilians in the plaza were only just beginning to react. A pair of university students fled screaming, while a group of elderly dancers stood gaping at the brawl that had broken out. After first backing away, some of the bystanders gradually drew closer again until they could watch from a safe distance.

Xiong turned and saw Ye behind him. She was trembling. He pointed to her BMW, which was now only fifty feet away. "Run for the car!" he yelled. "I'll meet you once I've taken care of these three!" He turned back to face the knife-wielding trio. This was Eumenides's doing. Of that he was certain.

Han surveyed the scene, bile rising in his throat. The plainclothes officers were closing around these new arrivals, and while it appeared that the situation would soon be under control, this did not change the fact that their entire plan had been thrown off balance. They needed to get Ye into her car now.

As if he could read Han's mind, a tall officer with a black felt cap was already approaching Ye Shaohong, who was only ten yards from the BMW. The tall officer waved to her.

Ye sprinted toward the officer without hesitation. Her momentum and fear sent her sprawling, and he caught her firmly. The officer put an arm around her shoulder, and together they dashed to the BMW.

"Quick, open the door!" he yelled.

Her fingers shook as she fished out her keys from her purse. After several attempts, she opened the door, and the officer helped her into the passenger's seat. With Ye now inside the car, he took the keys. Two beeps sounded and the door was locked again.

As Han watched this scene unfold from above, he finally permitted himself to breathe a sigh of relief. Even if any more of those strange men appeared, Ye was safe.

The plainclothes officers subdued their targets one by one, and then rushed to the middle of the perimeter for support. The three assailants standing dumbfounded at the center of the ring quickly dropped to the ground. Now Xiong turned and ran to the BMW.

Another thin man emerged from a taxi at the edge of the plaza, not far from Ye's car. He simply stood beside the taxi's door with a blank stare on his face.

The officer who had just helped Ye into the BMW immediately began rushing toward this newest arrival.

"Police! Get down on your knees!" he yelled.

With a yelp, the man bolted. The officer chased after the suspect, and within ten seconds he had already shortened the distance between them. His legs pumped with smooth, mechanical precision.

Curious, Han turned his head toward Yin. "Who's that? He's a real sprinter."

"Not a clue," Yin said, shaking his head.

Many of the plainclothes officers had already changed their clothing before returning to their posts in the afternoon, in order to avoid arousing the killer's suspicion. A knit hat alone wasn't enough to identify the officer from this distance.

Pei's eyes also followed the officer. He watched on the monitors until the man had chased the suspect beyond the cameras' field of vision, and then he returned his attention to the square. After surveying the area, his eyes grew wide with surprise.

"Wait—he wasn't one of the men you assigned to the square?"

"What do you mean?" asked Han.

"Your thirteen officers are still inside Citizen Square, so who's that?" Pei's tone had become tense.

Han's jaw dropped. "This is Lima One," he cried into his microphone. "Check the sparrow's condition! Check the sparrow's condition, now!"

Xiong, who was already standing in front of the BMW, knocked on the door. No response came from inside. His stomach churned. He pressed his face to the window and peered inside. A low moan escaped his lips.

Ye Shaohong's head was slumped to one side, as though in peaceful slumber. The stream of blood that oozed from her neck, and had already dyed the right side of her blouse a deep crimson, implied otherwise. Her left hand hung limp at her side, directing the flow of fresh blood toward the leather gearshift, a dazzling shade of red replacing the original eggshell white.

Because the other officer had run off with the BMW's keys, the police had no choice but to break the car door's window. A medical examiner was immediately rushed to the scene. He pronounced the woman dead on the spot.

The gash across Ye's throat was three inches long and one third of an inch deep. Extremely level, it had most likely been made with a sharp razor blade.

Both her windpipe and carotid arteries had been cut. The

wound had caused her to go into shock from acute blood loss, resulting in death.

IIIII

The surveillance video from the scene had recorded everything that afternoon. During the task force's meeting several hours after the incident, each member was given a transcript of all key events that had occurred from the moment of the culprit's arrival at the square to the moment he vanished from the cameras' field of view after the murder:

16:02:23—Ye Shaohong and SPU Captain Xiong Yuan emerge from Deye Building.

16:02:33—First suspect exits taxi. Two seconds later, Lima Seven tackles suspect to the ground.

16:02:35–16:02:38—Numerous suspects mob Citizen Square, overwhelming the plainclothes officers at the scene.

16:02:39—Man in black felt cap enters the scene from the lot south of the square. As the other officers devote their full attention to the suspects sprinting toward Ye Shaohong, his appearance goes unnoticed.

16:02:46—Having subdued two suspects, Xiong is locked in a standoff with three other suspects.

16:02:49—Man in black felt cap walks behind Xiong and motions to Ye. Noticeably panicking, Ye immediately runs toward him.

16:02:56—Man in black felt cap escorts Ye to BMW.

16:03:08—Man in black cap helps Ye into the passenger's seat of BMW. Only the driver's side of the vehicle is visible at this point.

16:03:10—Plainclothes officers assist Xiong in subdu-

ing the final three suspects in the square. Xiong begins running toward BMW.

16:03:11—Unidentified male subject with his left hand bandaged and carrying a plastic bag emerges from another taxi on the east edge of the square. The man in the black cap immediately charges him as if in pursuit.

16:03:19—Man in black cap jumps parking lot railing. Camera feed loses subject.

According to everyone who had laid eyes upon Ye's killer, the man had kept his black felt cap pulled very tightly over his eyes and his jacket collar popped high. Not a single witness could provide an accurate description of his face.

The captain was not in a good mood. The other members, Xiong in particular, all felt the weight of today's tragedy upon their hearts. Both the criminal police squad and the SPU team had invested dozens of officers in the afternoon's operation. Not only that—both groups' leaders had even been on the scene to coordinate the proceedings. Their impenetrable net had done nothing to stop the killer from fulfilling his original threat. Rather than capture Eumenides, they had arrested eighteen "suspects" who seemed utterly unaware of a single detail surrounding the case.

The first man the police interrogated was named Ai Yuncan, a twenty-five-year-old migrant laborer who had been working a low-paying job in a local restaurant ever since his arrival in Chengdu. Approximately two weeks earlier, he had spotted a flyer posted on the street. A massive entertainment center was seeking what they referred to as "PR gentlemen." The advertisement promised good pay and benefits, including a monthly salary exceeding 10,000 yuan. On top of that, the physical requirements for job applicants described him perfectly: *Applicants must be approximately five-foot-five and slight of frame.*

He called the number on the advertisement, and the man who

answered told him that the "PR gentlemen" were expected to provide sexual services for wealthy female clients. The physical requirements specified on the flyer had been made by a new client who was looking for several men to engage in BDSM activities. Ai hesitated, but the employer sent him a picture of the female customer. To his shock, she was drop-dead gorgeous. His most primitive desires set aflame, he followed the employer's instructions and replied to the email with a photograph of himself. The employer was satisfied upon receiving the photograph, and immediately transferred a thousand yuan to Ai's bank account, calling it a "preparation fee."

After receiving this transfer, Ai had no more misgivings. He followed the strange instructions to the letter. Later that day he purchased several items: bandages, a leather whip, and a rubber knife. Purchases in hand, he waited anxiously for his beautiful client to summon him. The call finally came yesterday afternoon. He was told that because of the illegal nature of this kind of transaction and the distinguished status of the client, both parties needed to agree on a covert rendezvous method. The man sent Ai a picture of the client's BMW and told him that the client would emerge from the Deye Building around four o'clock. At that time, Ai was to be waiting near Citizen Square and stay within sight of the building. Once the woman left the Deye Building, he would need to promptly follow the client and get into the car with her. Ai would not be the only applicant with these instructions, however. The successful applicant would ultimately be determined by the client's decision.

In order to ensure a fair competition, all applicants were required to wait inside taxis at designated locations. They were only allowed to leave the vehicle and meet the client once they had received an order via text message. Furthermore, they were to put the accessories they had previously purchased into a black plastic bag that they would carry with their right hand; they would wrap the bandage around their left hand in order to satisfy one of the client's special predilections.

All of the other men gave accounts strikingly similar to Ai's. A grim sense of shame filled Han and the interrogating officers as they realized the truth behind that day's events. These men had been intended as an elaborate distraction, nothing more. And the police had been hopeless to resist, like moths to a flame.

CHAPTER SIX

TWO MINUTES

OCTOBER 23, 8:15 P.M.
CHENGDU CRIMINAL POLICE HEADQUARTERS,
CONFERENCE ROOM

The conference room was bathed in cold, artificial light. The last time the 4/18 Task Force had gathered around the table, the room had buzzed with anxious energy. Now, the room was more fit for a funeral.

The investigators had analyzed every possible route the killer could have taken from his last known position, and Han had organized a ten-block-wide police sweep of the surrounding area. They found nothing. Had he concealed himself somewhere in the vicinity of the square? Had he slipped away in a vehicle? Had he disguised himself and blended into the crowd? Did he have an accomplice? There were too many unanswered questions.

The team watched and rewatched the footage recorded at the square. Using a series of geometric algorithms, Zeng mapped the locations from which each of the eighteen decoys had emerged relative to the strategic positioning of the plainclothes officers, the precise times the decoys charged the square, and the paths they took to Ye. The results were alarming. The strategy seemed deliberately orchestrated to create instantaneous chaos. Their arrival had forced the police's protective perimeter to collapse like a house of cards in a windstorm.

The final decoy broke through the perimeter northeast of Xiong, at an angle that made it only natural for Ye Shaohong to hide behind the captain. At the same time the killer, wearing the same pattern of outfit as the other plainclothes officers, entered the square from the opposite direction. The decoys herded Ye straight to him. Xiong was subduing the two suspects to his north, and could not stop her. It was exactly the kind of distraction the killer would have needed and planned.

Zeng had traced the text messages received by each of the decoys to a prepaid number linked to a forged ID card. Another dead end.

Han paced alongside the table, his hands clasped behind his back. "Yin, can you repeat the description of the killer as written in the report for Sergeant Zheng's murder?"

"Five-foot five," Yin recited, "with an injury on one hand."

Han picked up a folder that held the report on Zheng's murder. "That's right. That's exactly right."

He turned on the room's projector. As the machine warmed up, a black-and-white image slowly formed on the screen. The others recognized the angle at once. It was a still from one of the surveillance cameras around Citizen Square. Xiong shivered as he recognized the figure standing next to the BMW.

"Xiong, how tall would you say the killer was?" Han asked.

The SPU captain shifted uncomfortably. "I can't say for certain. I didn't get a good look at him."

"But if you had to guess?" Han pressed.

Xiong paused, and a bead of sweat trickled down his brow. "Just under six feet."

"Exactly!" Han picked up the report folder again. "Does someone want to tell me how our killer had a six-inch growth spurt overnight? More important, does someone want to tell me why we told Ye Shaohong and everyone involved in today's operation to be on the lookout for someone who was the wrong height?"

Yin shifted in his seat. "Maybe Eumenides is working with someone else—"

Han flung the folder against the wall. It hit the wood paneling and exploded into a flurry of paper and photographs.

"We don't have a single piece of evidence to support that! The man we saw in the square yesterday has dictated every single one of our actions. We've been his puppets from the start!" The hard truth had stripped away the captain's confidence. He looked around the room. "Do any of you have anything to add?"

Xiong broke the silence. "I failed. I should have realized what was going on. I knew something was wrong with those knives when the first two decoys dropped them. They didn't hit the ground like real knives, but I didn't even stop to ask myself why. Ye is dead because I was too foolish to stay at her side."

"You were protecting Ye! Those *men* posed a real threat. In the heat of the moment, it was impossible to figure out what was happening based on how a knife hit the ground. And you couldn't be expected to identify each one of the plainclothes officers on the scene. None of us did. That's precisely how this bastard slipped through our defenses." Han gritted his teeth. "I'm at fault for improperly planning this operation."

"The guy knows exactly what he's doing. More important, he knows exactly what *we* are doing," Zeng said, pinching the bridge of his nose. "What he doesn't realize is that he's already given himself away."

"Speak clearly, Zeng," Han spat. Zeng had an infuriating habit of intentionally keeping his listeners in suspense, and Han was sick of it.

Still composed, Zeng licked his lips and shook his head. "Do you really think someone like Eumenides can come from out of nowhere? He must have had formal training, and there has to be some kind of record on him. We can start by investigating any relevant officers one by one. I can access databases containing records for every single officer who's received police or military training over the last two decades."

Pei, who had been quiet until that point, turned to Zeng. "It looks like you've already started," he said coldly.

"What is that supposed to mean?" the young officer asked, forcing a laugh.

"What were you doing in my room?"

"I have no idea what you're talking about."

"You weren't present during the operation today," he stated. "You were digging through my things."

Zeng tried to hide his surprise. He had indeed slipped into Pei's room while the others were away, and he had done so on Han's orders. He had certainly not done a sloppy job of it. In fact, Zeng was positive that he hadn't left any traces behind. He had worn gloves—and even a hair net. How did Pei know?

"Nothing gets past you, Captain. Why the stern look? Hiding anything you don't want us to see?"

"This afternoon, Longzhou's network monitors detected a breach in the city's telecommunications database. Someone accessed my phone records from the past month. My trusted colleagues in Longzhou were able to trace the hack to its source. Another one of your jokes, Officer Zeng?"

Zeng was uncharacteristically embarrassed. He said nothing.

After a moment of reflection, Han tried to smooth things over. "This could all be a misunderstanding. I suggest a private conversation, Pei. Let's not bring this up in an official meeting."

"No." Pei turned to Han, and his expression hardened. "This is no misunderstanding. You told Mu to investigate me too, didn't you? How can I still be a suspect? There's a murderer out there killing at will, and you're sending two of our team members off on a wild goose chase. We need to stop Eumenides, not carry out internal investigations. A meeting like this one is exactly the time to bring it up."

"Captain Pei, you're right about one thing. I did order Officer Zeng and Officer Mu to investigate you," Han said diplomatically. "Sergeant Zheng is murdered, and we find you kneeling right next to the body. Then we learn that you were inextricably linked to the tragedies that occurred eighteen years ago. I'd be a fool if I didn't investigate you."

"I'm supposed to believe that's the whole story?" Pei was now seething with anger. "Or was it that I questioned your authority and humiliated the man you sent to tail me? Tell me, Captain Han, what exactly has your investigation into me turned up so far?"

Han paused. The entire team was watching. He couldn't afford to show as much as a shred of weakness.

"Let's begin at the beginning. You were the first to suggest that the suspect was around five-foot-five and that he had an injured hand. It was an audacious deduction, especially since you came to this conclusion before even leaving Zheng's apartment. It was also wrong, and now we've paid dearly for it."

Pei was tempted to remind Han that his own analysts had come up with the exact same physical profile, but instinct told him to hold his tongue.

"Now we come to the fiasco at the Deye Building. With the exception of the officers taking part in the operation, not a single person was aware of our surveillance arrangement. Yet as soon as you walked into that monitoring room, the very first thing you did was pick out every one of our plainclothes officers. Just showing off, Captain Pei?"

Both officers glowered at one another. The room felt as stable as a propane tank in a burning building.

"Captain Han, Captain Pei—get a grip on yourselves!"

Xiong's reprimand left the team members' ears ringing. Pei felt as if he had been slapped in the face. He realized that he had overstepped his bounds. Considering the evidence, Han actually was in the right here. Pei was lucky that Han had even kept him on the team in the first place. As a tense silence filled the room, he tried his best to regain control of his emotions.

Zeng cleared his throat.

"I was there when Captain Pei spotted the surveillance team in Citizen Square. For what it's worth, I could tell he was using observation and good training to put the pieces together. Here's the question I'm more concerned about: How did Eumenides do the same thing?"

His question hung over the team like a darkening cloud.

Pei snapped his fingers. "The hotel!" he blurted.

All heads in the room promptly turned to him.

"What do you mean?" the captain demanded.

"If someone wanted a clear picture of how the police were carrying out their surveillance, they'd need access to a full, panoramic view of the square. He'd need to find high ground, just like we did. So where would you go if you were looking for a tall, concealed observation point near the square?"

"He was at the hotel too," Xiong hissed.

OCTOBER 23, 11:09 P.M.
SKY PEAK HOTEL

The task force returned to the towering structure opposite the Deye Building, the Sky Peak Hotel. Flanked by the rest of the team, Han marched to the front desk and demanded the security footage from the past several days.

At around 10:00 p.m. the previous night, a male had checked into room 714. He remained in the room overnight and left shortly after 3:00 p.m.—an hour before the murder—without returning, and he never checked out. The footage showed a male figure matching the height, build, and gait of the killer from Citizen Square. None of the cameras had captured a clear shot of his face.

The seventh floor provided an excellent view of the plaza, literally just above their base of operations. Pei was about to point this out to Han, but judging from the look of rage on the captain's features, they had both reached the same conclusion.

Han promptly ordered the hotel staff to provide him with information from the ID card the suspect used when checking in. Within two minutes, Zeng verified that the card was a forgery. It wasn't the same fake ID that Zeng had tracked down earlier that day, but it was more than enough to strengthen the team's suspicions. When Han asked for the man's distinguishing features, the receptionist who had been working at the time in question told him that the individual had sported sunglasses and a thick beard.

"A beard?" Yin scribbled in his notepad. The other team members seemed indifferent, however. "Captain, should we notify the lead investigators to focus on men with beards?"

Han shook his head. "The beard's fake."

Yin stared at the security monitor in confusion.

"The killer's no idiot," Pei explained. "He wouldn't have anything as conspicuous as a beard. Both the beard and the sunglasses were tools for disguising his features. Nothing more."

Yin grimaced. He tore the page from his notepad and crumpled it up.

Han was already focused on another part of the video. "Look! He had a suitcase when he checked in, but not when he left. We can't rule out the possibility that he'll come back."

Xiong understood. "I'll position my people nearby."

"Right. We need to assign people to the lobby as well. Yin, you coordinate with Captain Xiong." Han looked at each of the other team members. All of them appeared eager to move, but Pei seemed particularly anxious. His pupils were wide with excitement. "Okay," Han said. "Let's have a look at his room first."

One of the staff members grabbed a keycard and led them to the door of room 714. The red backlit words DO NOT DISTURB glowed on the LED display below the doorbell. According to the employee, no one else had entered the room since the man had checked in.

Pei's heart pounded like a jackhammer. If the man who stayed in room 714 was the killer they had seen in the plaza yesterday, they were finally closing in.

Han ordered the hotel employee to open the door.

The door swung back and a distinctive odor seeped into the dim hall that sent chills down Pei's spine. Images of decaying flesh and exposed organs flashed through his mind. He saw Mu pinch her nose, and the poor hotel employee looked like he was going to vomit.

"What is that awful smell?" he exclaimed.

Han entered the room first and slid the keycard into the wall slot. The lights switched on, scattering the darkness and revealing a well-kept hotel suite. A suitcase lay open on the king-sized bed. Pei sniffed, and quickly realized that this was the source of the odor.

The team cautiously gathered around the noxious suitcase, and peered inside together.

The suitcase held about a dozen neatly arranged glass jars. Each jar, roughly the size of two fists stacked on top of each other, was filled to the brim with a briny liquid. Now Pei recognized the smell. Formaldehyde, an embalming agent. A grotesquely shaped object floated inside each jar.

"Excuse me," the hotel employee said, covering his mouth with one hand and pushing past Mu and Zeng with the other. The man rushed out into the hall.

Shivering, Mu stepped closer to her male colleagues. "What . . . What is this?" she asked in a hushed voice.

No one answered. Han donned a pair of white cotton gloves, plucked one of the jars from the case, and examined it against the light.

When Zeng recognized the object soaking inside the formaldehyde, he let out a rather undignified shriek. "It's a scalp! Fuck—it's a human scalp!"

Indeed, several strands of hair still clung to the object. The scalp drifted gently through the liquid as the bottle shook, like a nightmarish jellyfish startled by movement.

Mu had seen enough for one day. She dashed out of the room, gasping for fresh air.

Pei's gaze lingered on the piece of scalp. He then switched his focus to the label stuck to the bottle's surface. On closer look, it was covered with a good deal of handwriting. Han noticed the writing on the jar at the same time. His eyes widened as he turned the jar and read the strip of paper:

DEATH NOTICE

THE ACCUSED: Lin Gang
CRIME: Rape at Baijia Temple Village
DATE OF PUNISHMENT: March 18
EXECUTIONER: Eumenides

The same perfect handwriting. A heavy red checkmark had been drawn through the characters for *Lin Gang*. Several team members were familiar with judicial notices, and they knew full well what red marks signified.

"The rape at Baijia Temple?" Pei asked in astonishment.

"It's one of the province's most brutal unsolved cases," Zeng told Pei. "It happened last year. I'm actually the one who sent the assistance dispatch out to the public security network. The culprit had one distinguishing feature: a five-centimeter-long scar from a knife wound on the left side of his forehead."

As if in response to Zeng's words, the chunk of scalp inside the bottle began to uncurl, revealing a long and distinct scar.

Pei grunted a noise that could have been a laugh or a sigh. "He did more than crack the case for you. He even footed the bill for the court and held his own trial."

Han felt his heart sink. As the captain stared at the red checkmark, it seemed to morph into a mouth leering at him. Veins bulged along his wrist. Han placed the bottle back inside the suitcase and raised another. Floating inside was a ragged piece of skin with a steel-gray tattoo of a bat.

Another notice was attached to this jar, with a checkmark just like the others:

DEATH NOTICE

THE ACCUSED: Zhao Erdong
CRIMES: East Elm robbery and murder
DATE OF PUNISHMENT: May 11
EXECUTIONER: Eumenides

East Elm. The name of that upper-class neighborhood sent long-forgotten images surging through Han's mind. Rows of tall, pristinc apartment buildings. A trail of red across a hardwood floor, leading to a dead man slumped against a bloodstained wall. Han had led his own officers through a marathon of sleepless nights in search of the owner of a bat-shaped tattoo. Now that it was right in front of his eyes, he wasn't sure quite what to feel. Should he be pleased? Sorrowful? Angry?

Silence spread through the room as Han, Zeng, and Pei removed the formaldehyde-filled bottles from the case one at a time and set them down onto the bed. Mu returned to the room, wiping her mouth with her sleeve. Additional human body parts of various shapes and sizes occupied the containers, one per bottle—a finger, an ear, a nose, and more. Located on each "sample" was a distinguishing feature of a subject of a police search. A red checkmark adorned the death notice attached to each bottle—that is, except for the final one.

Half a tongue floated inside the jar. Several lines of script had been written upon the piece of paper stuck to the glass.

DEATH NOTICE

THE ACCUSED: Peng Guangfu
CRIME: Mount Twin Deer Park police slaying
DATE OF PUNISHMENT: October 25
EXECUTIONER: Eumenides

"There's no checkmark," Pei noted. The others nodded. This was the only unfulfilled death notice.

Han looked dumbstruck. Yin and Zeng exchanged wide-eyed looks.

Pei noticed his fellow teammates' odd behavior, and he shot Zeng a questioning look. Suddenly Mu touched Pei's arm. He looked at her, but she shook her head.

Not now, her lips said soundlessly.

Han slowly set the last jar back inside the case. After a concerted effort to keep his emotions under control, he picked up his mobile phone and called Yin.

"Tell the officers standing by that they're dismissed. He isn't coming back."

Pei knew Han was right. Eumenides had wanted the police to come, and he had led them here like rats in a maze. The room wouldn't contain a single worthwhile lead except for whatever the killer had deliberately chosen to leave out on display.

The follow-up investigation would only verify Pei and Han's conclusion. Not a single fingerprint or strand of hair to be found—only the suitcase and its gruesome contents.

There were thirteen jars. Each bore an individual death notice. Twelve of the sentences described on the notices had red checkmarks, with only the sentence for Peng Guangfu unmarked.

Hiding in plain sight among the macabre display of jars were two items: an external hard drive and what appeared to be a signal receiver.

"Looks like I've got work to do," Zeng said, eyeing the hardware.

||||

Clustered in the conference room, the task force viewed a video on the projector screen. A short, stocky man kneeled in front of a dreary stone wall. He faced the camera. His arms and legs were bound, and his features were distorted with terror. The team members could faintly discern a scar on the left side of his forehead.

Pei could not place the location. The texture of the wall was too rough to have been inside an apartment or a warehouse. It might have been a cellar. The lighting was too dim and the angle too limited for him to make a confident guess.

After several seconds, they heard the voice of a man outside the frame.

"What is your name?"

"Lin . . . Gang," the stout man stuttered.

"How were you involved in the rape that occurred on the third of August last year in Baijia Temple Village?"

Lin Gang lowered his head. "I . . . I'm the one who did it."

The other man spoke in a low rasp. For Lin, the effect must have been terrifying; however, Pei recognized the man's motivation behind doing so. He had disguised his voice for his intended audience—for the police officers who would eventually view this recording.

"The woman you raped. What did she look like?"

"She was . . . thin. Her hair was short, cropped to—"

"No. Tell me something that only you saw. Something that the public doesn't know."

"I don't understand . . ."

"If you don't tell me, I can cut you and let you bleed out slowly. It'll take half an hour, maybe forty-five minutes. It's your choice."

"There was—there was a mole. On her breast. About as wide as the end of a chopstick."

"Good."

A shadow flickered past the lens, and the other man walked behind Lin Gang and untied the ropes binding him.

Lin rubbed his bleeding wrists. His head turned; there was a vacant look in his eyes, and he grew pale.

A hand entered the frame. Glinting between two fingers was a plain razor blade.

"I'll give you one more chance." The man's words were even more piercing than the blade. "Stand up and face me."

Lin shook his head in desperation, and he began to sob and tremble. "No . . ."

"Stand up."

He shivered. Rather than rise, he curled into a quivering ball.

There was a disdainful snort, and the blade flashed before the camera. Terrified, Lin raised his arms as if to protect himself, but before he had completed this motion, he crumpled to the floor stiff as a board. Dark blood pooled from his neck. A dark figure crouched next to Lin. He worked the blade with quick, surgical strokes.

Pei held his breath in anticipation as the killer's head came into the frame, but he quickly let it out. Of course. The man was wearing a ski mask.

"Eumenides," Xiong growled. "It's him."

Han held a finger up to his lips and glared at Xiong.

They heard a soft squishing noise, like the sound of noodles being stirred in a bowl. The man rose, and he held something thin and flat in front of the camera. The team members gasped as they recognized the object they had seen inside the first jar. A human scalp.

"So? Was it true?" Zeng asked.

Han furrowed his brow. "Was what true?"

"The mole. Was it really there?"

The captain pursed his lips, as if thinking to himself. Finally, he nodded. "Yes. Only a handful of people would have known that detail."

"Could Eumenides have gotten into the archives and found the file for that case?" Pei asked. "He could have found someone who fit Lin Gang's description and fed him that line. All of this might have been a show for us."

"It's unlikely," Han said, shaking his head. "Very unlikely. We would have heard if there had been a break-in."

The man who had just executed Lin was evidently just as well-informed of the details behind the other unsolved cases mentioned on the other jars. There were twelve videos after this one, and each documented a similar "trial" performed by the masked man. Each began with a brief interrogation, with questions touching upon very specific details relating to the case. The background of each video was the same—the same stone wall, the same unrevealing angle.

"They can't all be telling the truth," Zeng whispered in disbelief. "He has to be feeding them lines, just like Pei said."

Pei knew true terror when he saw it. It was the kind of terror that would make truth pour out of whomever it seized.

Once each victim had confirmed their identity, the man untied the rope binding them. He said the same line near the end of each recording: *I'll give you one more chance*. Yet none of the victims in his little performances seized the opportunity to challenge their captor. They didn't seem to have the slightest desire to do so. Once their hands and feet had been freed, each and every one of them curled into a ball and awaited the man's fatal blow like a petrified rat.

These hardened rapists, thieves, and murderers had stood face-to-face with this strange man, yet somehow couldn't even beg for their lives.

The final video may well have been what Eumenides had most wanted the police to see. It had been filmed in the same dim, dilapidated environment as the others. A man in his thirties or forties knelt upon the ground. The camera lens was pointed toward his face, making his features clearly visible.

"State your name."

"Peng Guangfu."

"How were you involved with the armed robbery that occurred at the Sunset Hotel on the evening of October twenty-fifth last year?"

"I hit the place. Me and Zhou Ming."

"Stealing twenty-four thousand yuan in cash altogether. What happened after you fled the Sunset Hotel?"

"It was late. We ran into some cops."

"How many?"

"Two."

"Then what happened?"

"They chased us, so we ran into Mount Twin Deer Park. There are rocks and little caves all over the park. We hid inside one of the caves."

"Did the police find you?"

"Yes."

"What happened after that?"

"Everyone started shooting."

"One officer was killed, and the other injured. Your partner, Zhou Ming, also died in the firefight. Is that correct?"

Peng slowly nodded.

The man asked, "Do you know the names of those two officers?"

"I found out later. I saw them in the papers."

"Tell me their names."

"The cop who died was Zou Xu. The injured one was Han Hao."

Pei jumped at the mention of Han's name. He turned and looked at the captain in incredulity. Han's jaw was clenched tight. Beads of sweat had already formed on his forehead.

Pei thought back to the captain's reaction when they had discovered that jar in the hotel room. The others had exchanged glances. And then there was Mu's silent warning. They knew. They had kept him in the dark this entire time.

"Very good." This seemed to indicate that the man off-screen had finished his questioning. Finally, he said it again. "I'll give you one more chance."

Peng lifted his head and looked at the man with blank eyes.

The anonymous hand entered the frame. Contrary to the team members' expectations, his fingers did not hold a gleaming blade but rather a button-sized metal disk. The hand placed the disk inside Peng's shirt pocket.

"This is a location transmitter. I'm going to give the receiver to the police."

Peng's eyes widened. Pei noted the irony here: the mention of law enforcement gave this criminal hope.

"The game begins when I turn on the transmitter. It will lead you where you need to be. There is a catch, however. Your team must consist of four members—no more, no fewer. You must arrive here by midnight of October twenty-fourth. I'll know if you aren't playing by the rules," he said, and he turned his masked face toward the camera. "So don't try to be clever." Now he turned back to Peng. "If they play by these rules and are also successful, you may leave here with your life intact."

Han picked up the receiver that the police had found inside the suitcase. They had already attempted to turn the device on, but it was clear from the video that it would work only after Eumenides turned on the transmitter.

The video continued, addressing Peng. "There's one more issue. I wouldn't want you to let any secrets slip prematurely. We need to think of a way to prevent that."

Peng's face filled with horror. The man's hand appeared before the camera. An icy gleam flickered from the blade between his fingers.

"No, no!" Peng pleaded in desperation. "I won't say anything—I won't say anything at all!"

He had no choice in the matter. The faceless man's other hand entered the frame and pinched the sides of Peng's jaw, forcing his mouth wide open and turning his pleas into unintelligible moans.

The blade darted into Peng's mouth. Peng struggled desperately, but the killer's grip was like a vise. There was an awful shriek. A stream of blood flowed from Peng's mouth and down the man's hand. Several seconds later, the man dropped Peng, who immediately curled up in inarticulate pain. Still standing out of frame, the anonymous man wagged a bloody slice of Peng's tongue before the camera.

"I'm giving you an opportunity. I only hope you can make the most of it."

The recording concluded with this bloody scene. The team members exhaled a collective sigh of relief as the video ended.

Han shook his head, as though waking from a dream. "Closing the Mount Twin Deer Park case isn't the purpose of this team, but Peng Guangfu might be able to point us to Eumenides. We must ensure Peng's safety. If it means we can prevent more murders, then I'll play along. We'll send four people into the lion's den, just like he said."

Pei shook his head. The team had six members. There would

be two redundant individuals, and he was sure he'd be the first one out.

"How will Eumenides know if we're playing by his rules? Will he be there watching us?" Zeng asked.

"Your guess is as good as mine," Han answered. "If yesterday taught us anything, it's that Eumenides is an expert at defying our expectations. What do you think, Mu?"

The psychologist laced her fingers together. "If there's one thing we can expect of Eumenides, it's that he doesn't bluff. He might be at the location he gives you. Or he might be watching from a safe distance. Regardless, he'll keep a close eye on you either way."

IIIII

OCTOBER 24, 11:05 A.M.
POLICE HEADQUARTERS, GUESTHOUSE CAFETERIA

The cafeteria was in a small room adjacent to the lobby on the first floor of the guesthouse. Around ten people were seated at the tables spread throughout the room; judging from the stacks of paper that most of them were glancing at between bites, Pei guessed they were visiting law enforcement experts hired to hold lectures and workshops for the various branches of criminal police housed at headquarters. With nothing else to do, Pei had ordered mapo tofu, rice, and a bottle of beer for lunch.

They had less than thirteen hours before Peng's death notice would be carried out, critical moments for the task force. Han saw to it that Pei had already been removed.

"Enjoying yourself, Captain?"

Mu set her dining tray on the opposite side of the table.

"I should be thanking you," Pei said in a rather unfriendly tone. "For all this free time."

Mu smiled. "You wouldn't happen to be implying that I had anything to do with that? I'm sitting this out too, you know."

"That's because you have a more important task."

Mu stiffened. "I'm not following you," she said with a touch of frustration.

Pei took a sip of his beer. His expression stayed neutral, but it did not brighten.

"Fine," Mu said. "I admit that Zeng and I did investigate you earlier, but that was just because we were ordered to. We're all police officers here. I can tell you with certainty that neither Zeng nor I believe that you're the killer."

Pei stabbed a chunk of tofu. "How magnanimous of you."

"Listen to this," Mu said. She took out Zeng's MP3 player and selected the track he had played for her earlier.

Pei froze as soon as the original Eumenides recording began to play. The last time he heard these words, they had been playing over the police academy's PA system. His eyelids fluttered shut; he was enveloped in the past. Finally, as though waking up from a dream, he removed the headphones.

"It's me, of course. I was the one behind that incident," Pei said, his eyes watering.

"As I'm sure you know," said Mu, "4/18 wasn't the first time the name Eumenides was used in connection with the academy. Four known academy students were punished by this Eumenides. There was a male student who cheated on an exam and was subsequently expelled, a female student with a tendency toward theft, a male student who liked revealing other people's personal secrets, and another who was unfaithful in his relationships.

"I know you didn't kill anyone. I was sure of that from the first moment I met you. The grief and hatred in your eyes were real. Yet somehow, you are tied to these events. What are you hiding?"

"There's no need to be so polite. You already have enough evidence to have me taken into custody and commence a formal interrogation."

"Zeng did an independent analysis of the recording before giving it to me. Han doesn't know anything about this. The two of us believe you. Can't you believe us? I merely want to hear what you have to say."

Pei's defensive shell cracked. He decided to tell her something that he had never revealed to anyone else.

"I'm responsible for the first and third of the four events you just described. Meng did the others."

Mu gasped. "Both of you! That explains how the person who stole the girl's clothes wasn't caught. Why were you teaming up to carry out these schemes?"

"We weren't teaming up," the captain corrected her. "It was . . . a competition."

"A game?"

Pei winced at the accusatory bite in Mu's voice. The killer himself had taunted the police with the same word while he tortured Peng Guangfu.

"It might be hard for you to comprehend the kind of relationship Meng and I had. The deeper we fell in love, the stronger our rivalry grew. We both admired and respected one another, but neither of us could tame the other." He shook his head, as though waking from a reverie. "It's a strange feeling. You wouldn't understand it."

Mu's smile suggested otherwise. "I do."

"Really?" Pei raised an eyebrow.

"You're both Scorpios. When two Scorpios get too close to one another, the encounter always ends in victory for one side. And only for one."

Pei shot her a look of bewilderment.

"I may be a psychologist," she snapped. "But I keep an open mind."

"Maybe you're right about the two of us," he said. "We were always trying to control each other. Neither of us was ever quite willing to give way."

"We don't need to talk about these things right now," Mu said, poking at her steamed fish. "It would be better if you told me about what actually happened back at the academy, from beginning to end."

"The whole thing was my fault." Pei bowed his head. "A group of classmates had organized a mystery story competition in their spare time. The idea gained steam, and soon enough our entire class was talking about it. Meng had a real creative side to her. One night she told me a story about a woman who punished criminals the law couldn't touch. She gave her hero a name from Greek mythology: Eumenides.

"Meng asked for my feedback," Pei went on. "I didn't agree with her choice to make the protagonist a woman. Call me old-fashioned if you will, but I just thought it would be a little more realistic if a male were at the center of that kind of story. Things escalated into a fight. She called me sexist and patriarchal. Eventually, we made a bet. We would test the story in real life and see who would prove more successful, a male or female Eumenides."

Mu's face lit up. "The competition."

"I suppose we're all a bit ridiculous when we're young. We decided that we'd take turns playing Eumenides, and the other would assume the role of an investigator. If the latter could figure out how Eumenides had done it, they would win the bet. I was one of the top criminal investigation majors back then, and Meng was a psychology student. I didn't think it would take much effort to beat her, but after two rounds, we were tied."

"How did you manage to pull off those two escapades of yours?" Mu asked. "You might not have been able to figure out Meng's methods, but Zeng and I are just as clueless about yours. How did you do it?"

"That's between me and Meng." Pei smiled. "She's the only one I would tell."

For the briefest of moments, Mu felt a flash of jealousy.

"I never had the chance to tell her . . . ," Pei said. "But I needed to beat her. I was actually planning a fifth round—one that would catch her by surprise. It was supposed to take place on the same day she went to the warehouse in search of Yuan."

An idea came to Mu. There was another interpretation of what happened at the warehouse—a possibility no one had raised. Certainly not Pei.

"When you saw the death notice for Yuan, you thought it was Meng's handiwork."

Pei winced as if he had been slapped. "That's right. Meng had already punished a womanizer. And on several occasions she had told me point-blank that she detested the way Yuan treated women. My first thought was that Meng had done something to him to get back at me for staying friends with Yuan."

"That's why you didn't notify the police." Mu nodded. "You did everything you could to get in touch with Meng yourself."

"Meng hated Yuan's behavior, but I've never believed for a second that she carried out the death notice on Yuan. At most, I thought she might have tied him up to humiliate him—that she was just going to teach him a lesson and force me to admit defeat in our competition."

"When Mu saw that death notice, she could have thought the same thing. That you wanted to make a move against Yuan!"

"That's what I assumed later on. It explains why she didn't call the police either, and why she set out alone to search for Yuan." Pei let out a bitter laugh. His eyes were tinged red. "A few days ago you asked why Meng put so much faith in me when she was dismantling the bomb. My greatest fear is that she believed me because she thought I'd made the bomb!"

Mu nodded grimly to herself. Finally, she offered a conclusion of her own.

"What you're telling me is that the real killer copied the idea for this Eumenides character in order to carry out his crime?"

"He must have," Pei said. "He wanted to make a statement. He was the true Eumenides, not us."

"But why wait eighteen years to make his next move?"

"He must have his reasons, but I'm not sure what they are." Pei took a swig of beer and squinted at Mu. "You know, there's another thing that's been bothering me. Maybe you can help."

"What is it?"

"Meng and I always posted our notices after we had already finished punishing our targets. If we served as his inspiration, then why did he deliver his death notices *before* committing the murders? And why is he doing the same thing now? And why does he kill?"

"The killer's intentions are not yours. He adopted your and Meng's model, then constructed a game that would give him the thrill he seeks. Perhaps your way wasn't exciting enough for him. Now his game is evolving. In addition to Zheng and Ye, he's already brutally executed twelve suspects involved in twelve unsolved cases, and without giving us any warning. He attached those death notices to the macabre trophies in the suitcase only after it was too late to stop him. While this may seem to violate his original MO, it seems that doing so was merely a setup to announce his primary victim in the next round. Peng Guangfu."

"I don't think it's that simple. I've read about cases in other countries where serial killers played games with the police, but they never revealed their victim's identities before committing the murder. If it's the thrill he's seeking, then that would be the process he'd carry out. To alert the police *before* committing a murder? That's a steep learning curve. Plus, consider those videos he showed us. Not only was he able to track down suspects that had evaded the Chengdu police—he was able to murder them in complete secrecy. Mu, we're dealing with someone immensely skilled."

"So where does that leave us?"

"I need you to get me access to all the relevant files for the 4/18 case. Including anything that you or Zeng might have been keeping for yourselves."

"Absolutely," Mu answered without hesitation. "Let's go back to my room."

||||

Pei was struck by the sparse tidiness of Mu's room. A book titled *Beyond Freedom and Dignity* lay on the side of her reading desk, next to a neat stack of folders.

After removing her shoes, Mu sat down cross-legged on her bed. "Bring that chair over," she said, motioning toward the chair at the desk. "And those files."

Pei did just that, and Mu spread the contents of the folders across the bed. The documents were filled with information Pei had never seen before, including written records and analyses concerning his involvement in the case.

The more he read, the lower his mood sank. Once he felt he had already hit an emotional bottom, he shut his eyes and began rubbing his cheeks, gradually working his way to the back of his head. To Mu, it looked as if he were trying to squeeze something out from inside his brain. Or perhaps trying to keep something in.

He turned back to the files, slowly flipping through them. When he reached a certain page, he stopped. A look of astonishment spread across his face.

"What is it?" Mu asked, the hair on the back of her neck prickling.

"Unbelievable. It's unbelievable!" His eyes were gaping wide. "How could they ignore such an important discrepancy?"

"What discrepancy?"

"The time! The time is wrong!" Pei pointed to the time

stamp on one page. "Look right here. The file records the time of the warehouse explosion as 4:13 in the afternoon. No. I clearly remember telling the police that the explosion happened at 4:15! It even says so here in my statement!"

"It's only two minutes. But still . . ."

Mu cut herself off with a gentle shake of her head. She, too, had noted the differing times, but it had not seemed important enough to consider as a significant clue. The police recorded the explosion at 4:13 p.m., based on data recorded by the city's environmental department. The accuracy of this information was beyond question. Pei's testimony was off by two minutes; what was so strange about that?

"No, you can't doubt me here!" Pei said vehemently, as if anticipating what Mu was already thinking. "I was watching the clock on my wall the whole time I was talking to Meng. When the explosion cut the signal, the time was 4:15. I can tell you everything about that moment—the two birds chirping outside my window, the empty Coke bottle on my desk, the crackle from my radio. And the clock said 4:15. That was the time, right down to the second!"

"So your clock was fast."

"I used to wind that clock every single night. I'd double-check it against the time announced on the radio. It was a habit of mine; as long as I was staying in my dorm, I never broke it. That clock was extremely precise. It would keep perfect time for up to two weeks at a time."

"For argument's sake, let's say you are right about the time." Mu decided to try and accept Pei's explanation, if only temporarily. But she was still skeptical. "Then how could this have happened? Maybe . . . there were two explosions?"

Pei shook his head slowly. "That's impossible. I was talking to Meng on the walkie-talkie until 4:15. How could the police have recorded the explosion as already happening at 4:13? Unless . . ."

"Unless that conversation was staged," Mu said, continuing Pei's train of thought. "And if that were true, what would it mean?"

"Yes, what would it mean?" Pei murmured. An unbelievable hypothesis had already begun forming in his mind, one that he hoped against all hope wasn't true. He told himself to stay calm, but blood was already surging to his head.

In a calm tone, Mu answered Pei's question. "It means that Meng was still alive after the explosion."

Shock seized Pei's nerves. With a shudder, he stared dumbfounded at Mu. Finally, he spoke.

"Is that possible?"

"If this time discrepancy you're talking about really happened, then we have no choice but to consider that option."

"So you're saying that my conversation with Meng took place *after* the explosion?"

"That's right. And if we continue with this line of thought, we'll inevitably end up with two conclusions.

"The first is that your conversation with Meng over the walkie-talkie was merely a diversion she had prepared in order to make you believe that she'd perished in the explosion. The second explains why you were unable to reach her before she contacted you from the warehouse."

Pei blinked at Mu in disbelief.

"Meng simply switched off her walkie-talkie at 4:13, at the actual time of the explosion. Then she turned it on again afterward. At 4:15 she turned it off again to make you think that the explosion had actually occurred then."

Pei drew in a quick breath. "You're saying that Meng . . . that she's Eumenides? But our suspect is male!"

"Perhaps she found an accomplice." A new idea came to Mu. She rifled through the documents containing the written records. "You were able to hear Yuan's voice through your walkie-talkie, right? That gives us two possibilities. Either Yuan's voice was prerecorded—or he didn't die either."

Pei understood where Mu was going with this. Could Meng and Yuan have been conspiring together? While it would have posed little difficulty for two ace academy students to find corpses they could use to stage the aftermath of an explosion, it did bring up some serious questions. Why would Yuan and Meng do this to him? One had been his closest friend, and the other had been even closer. It was impossible for Pei to accept.

"Hold on." Mu was still examining the records. "There is no evidence for Yuan's survival. In your account, you told us that you never interacted with him during your conversation on the walkie-talkie. That means that Yuan's voice might have been prerecorded."

"So in other words, Meng had already used the bomb to kill Yuan, and she'd invented an elaborate cover-up to go along with it."

But why would she do that? Just because of a grudge? Or had she truly been unable to tolerate Yuan's treatment of his previous girlfriend—and burned his body to a crisp? If she was still alive, then where had she been for the past eighteen years? Why hadn't she tried to contact him? Question after question assaulted his mind.

"Pei, I need you to do your best to remember something. You were closer to him than anyone else. Is it at all possible that Yuan was Ye Shaohong's murderer?"

"I've watched the footage from Citizen Square a hundred times. Nothing about the man who killed her reminds me of Yuan. Or of Meng, for that matter. The killer didn't look or act like Yuan. The voice on the videos wasn't him either," Pei said, shaking his head.

"Who can he be? If Meng really was Eumenides and originally staged the explosion, then where did this new killer come from?"

Suddenly, Mu burst into a bitter laugh. Oddly enough, her expression was one of relief.

"What is it?" Pei asked delicately.

"Everything that we've just discussed is all based on one presumption that's impossible to prove—that there's an error in the time of the explosion listed in the records. Now we've even gone so far as to suspect Meng! Tell me, Pei—did Meng seem like the type of person who'd go off and commit a series of murders?"

Pei immediately shook his head.

"That's why I feel the most likely answer is that you simply reported the wrong time," Mu said bluntly. "This cannot be nearly as complicated as we're making it out to be. We are hunting a cold-blooded killer. Is a discrepancy of two minutes really worth our attention? Besides, the original investigation team was full of experienced members of the police force, and none of them fussed over this particular detail."

"No." Pei's tone remained firm. "There's something wrong here! Precision is essential to my life. I wouldn't have been wrong about the time."

Mu smiled. "Actually, I've just thought of the person we need to see."

Pei realized whom she meant. He rose from his seat.

"Huang has been lying to us," she said. "Shall we pay him another visit?"

OCTOBER 24, 2:18 P.M.
HUANG'S APARTMENT

It was the hottest hour of the afternoon. Pei and Mu felt the sun pound down as they approached Huang's raggedy home.

"It's unlocked," Huang said. They walked in and stepped into a stifling, otherworldly gloom.

The apartment had barely changed since their last visit. Huang was busy sorting through a pile of cans and bottles, presumably for resale. He stomped each empty bottle and can one at a time before tying them into bundles. This was intense work for Huang. The explosion had mangled his hands and feet—in fact, not a single part of his entire body had been left intact.

Pei observed the scene with pity. Why would a man like this feel the need to lie? What was he hiding?

Huang stopped what he was doing and greeted his guests. "You two . . . ," he rasped. "Turn the light on. The switch is right next to your hand."

Mu pulled the chain, and a cracked bulb hanging from the ceiling flickered to life. In terms of illumination, it wasn't much, but the light brought some life into the room.

"I'm too stingy to use the power for myself. I only turn it on when I have guests over," Huang explained glumly.

Mu felt guilty. It almost bordered on cruelty to suspect him of being involved in the crime.

Pei took a seat on a lopsided stool. "It's time you told us the truth," he said.

"Huh?" Huang was taken aback.

"Eighteen years ago, you said you saw the girl talking to me over her walkie-talkie. You were even able to describe our conversation. That was a lie! The conversation actually took place several minutes *after* the explosion. At that time, you should have been barely clinging to the edge of life. How could you know what had happened two minutes after the explosion?" Pei leveled his finger at the man, shaking with barely constrained rage.

Huang stared blankly. It wasn't the reaction Pei was expecting.

"Give me the truth. What really happened that day?" the officer demanded.

Huang was still gawking at Pei as if in a daze. Mu shot Pei a disapproving glance. What secrets could they expect a pitiful man like this to be hiding? Pei was acting like a bully, and nothing more.

A moment later, however, a painful sound forced its way out from Huang's throat.

"You're right. I did lie."

"What really happened?" Pei asked.

"I don't know."

"You don't know?"

"I was right next to the main door to the warehouse. At first, I couldn't see anything at all. Then the bomb went off. I . . . I really have no idea what was going on then."

"You're still lying! If that were true, how would you know what Meng and I talked about in our conversation?"

"Because you're the one who told me."

Pei looked at the man, dumbfounded. His hand subconsciously went to his sidearm.

"After I woke up at the hospital, Sergeant Zheng questioned me for days. I didn't know anything. Then one day, he left a notebook by my bed while he went to the restroom. It hurt like hell just to move my arms, but I managed to flip through the notebook. I was just starting to read someone's description of a radio conversation they'd had with the girl right before the explosion happened." Huang chuckled sourly to himself. "During your last visit, I finally learned that this person was you."

"You used my statement to lie to the police?" Pei wasn't prepared to give up so easily. "If you didn't know what happened, why would you fabricate a story about that night?"

"Look at me! How am I supposed to live? I was a junk collector without a coin to my name. Why would the doctors at the hospital want to help me? Even an uneducated guy like me knew the real reason. The police thought I was useful. They even set me up in this beautiful place. They were hoping that I could give them leads that could help them solve the case. If I was honest with the police and told them I didn't know anything, then what value would I have? Why would the doctors keep treating me?

And most important, why would the cops pay for my new apartment?" Huang's voice grew feeble, as if the air was leaking from his lungs.

Pei sat down, disappointment written across his face. As far as he was concerned, Huang was a dead end. He had simply exploited the system for his own gains. The thought of further questioning Huang filled Pei with shame.

Noticing Pei's silence, Huang returned to his own work. After he moved the bundles of bottles and cans over to the other side of the room, he went back to the officer and asked imploringly, "Officer Pei, can you help me?"

"With what?"

"Bring that hemp bag inside. I may be around your age, but the years haven't been kind to me. Seems my body gets weaker every day."

Pei felt a pang of pity for Huang. The files on the man had revealed him to be in his mid-thirties, but Huang's appearance suggested that he was at least a decade older. Pei got up and approached the door.

"There's a heap of bottles next to the bag. I'd appreciate it if you could bring them in as well," Huang added in his raspy voice. Pei left the apartment, and when Huang saw that Mu was about to go out and help him, he reached out to stop her. "Ms. Mu, could you hand me that cup of water?"

Mu obligingly picked up the cup from the side table and handed it to Huang.

"Thanks."

As Huang took the cup from her, he gripped her wrist tightly. Mu's eyes widened in shock.

"I know more," Huang said quietly, with eyes on the doorway. "But I'm afraid. You're the only person I can tell—in private."

Mu's heart was pounding. Huang wanted to keep something from Pei.

The man leaned forward until his ragged features were almost pressed against Mu's face. "Come back tonight. Whatever you do, don't let him find out."

Footsteps sounded at the door, and Pei walked back inside the apartment dragging a large bag. Huang let go of Mu's hand. She took several steps back, making as strong an effort as possible to mask her astonishment. Pei was calm. He didn't seem to notice anything unusual.

The two officers remained silent after leaving Huang's home. Pei assumed that the visit had been a failure for both of them, particularly for Mu in trying to use Huang's testimony to refute the captain's "missing time" hypothesis.

After walking side by side for some time, Mu spoke up. "So what do we do now?"

"There's definitely something strange about the time of the explosion," Pei answered. "And there might still be a way to prove it."

"How?"

"We go straight to the evidence. If my earlier guess is correct, Meng didn't die in the explosion. The female body they found at the scene wasn't her."

"How can we know?" Mu shrugged. "It's been eighteen years. They cremated the bodies long ago, and we didn't have the technology to identify DNA back then. There can't be anything of value left behind."

"We'll go to the archives in the forensic center," he explained. "In a situation like the warehouse explosion, there's no way the investigators would have been able to declare the victims' identities with one-hundred-percent certainty. It would have been standard practice for them to have saved dental casts for Yuan and Meng before cremating the remains."

"As far as I know, Meng and Yuan didn't leave behind any dental records before they perished. Even if we're able to get our hands on some dental casts, how will you know whether or not they came from their teeth?"

Pei paused. "I'll think of something," he said softly.

||||

They arrived at the archive room of the forensic center an hour later. After the two team members filled out the paperwork and received permission, which was no easy feat, the attendant presented the forensic evidence from the 1984 warehouse explosion. Pei soon spotted the dental casts taken from Meng and Yuan.

After briefly comparing both casts, he set down the larger of the two and examined the delicate one in his hand. Then he did something that made Mu's jaw drop. He raised the plaster up to his mouth and pressed his lips against it. Extending his tongue, he gently rubbed it against the two rows of plaster teeth.

As Pei kissed the mold, eyes shut, decades-old emotions came rushing back. He remembered every sunset and every embrace he had ever shared with Meng. The sensation of her lips against his was one that time could never erase.

Mu resisted the urge to turn away. She watched Pei pause; his fingers trembled as he held the mold against his lips. He placed the mold back onto the tray with a clacking sound and opened his eyes. Tears as thick as raindrops covered his cheeks.

"It's her," Pei said, unsuccessfully holding back a whimper. "She had a chip on the edge of one of her front teeth. I kept telling her to get it repaired, but she was adamant about keeping it. She said she wouldn't feel like herself without that chipped tooth."

Mu could sense the depth of the pain in Pei's words. "Good," she said gently. "So now we can be sure that Meng wasn't the killer. We can keep our investigation on the right path."

Pei wiped away his tears. He scowled. "'On the right path'? You still don't believe me about the time discrepancy?"

"The facts are right in front of us!" Mu shouted in reaction to Pei's stubbornness. She pointed to the mold that he had just set down. "Meng is dead. She perished in the explosion eighteen years ago! I realize you don't want to accept it, but these are the facts. I know you understand this. What are you fighting for, anyway?"

Lowering his head, Pei walked out into the hall. He said nothing.

CHAPTER SEVEN

DEATH MINE

OCTOBER 24, 8:11 P.M.

Mu remained in a corner of the cafeteria, alone with her thoughts and an emptied bowl of spicy dandan noodles. Less than four hours remained until Eumenides's deadline. The rest of the team buzzed like a hive of anxious bees, but she and Pei were left hanging. It wasn't exactly a pleasant feeling.

"Eating alone? Let me keep you company."

Zeng put down his tray and sat across from her. Mu didn't mind; she had gotten used to his cocky—and utterly tactless—advances. In their own way, these attempts were almost charming.

"Late dinner, Officer Zeng?"

"Ah, work. On the positive side, my firsthand knowledge of migraines has doubled over the past few days." Zeng tilted his head, and mixed his food with chopsticks. "We've made zero progress."

As a civilian officer, Zeng had also been excluded from the four-person squad currently preparing for their mission to rescue Peng Guangfu. Zeng's task was to scour law enforcement records for any officers who fit their profile of the killer.

He began his search with great confidence. He instructed his team to pinpoint a male suspect whose military or police training included instruction in explosives, criminal investigation techniques, combat, and computers. In order to narrow the search, he also cross-referenced each name with a list of students enrolled at the provincial academy in 1984, when Pei and Mu first created Eumenides.

So far, these results had amounted to essentially nothing.

An officer with the Sichuan provincial police had even put Zeng in touch with the Special Department of the Ministry of State Security. This time, however, the results were overwhelming. Zeng had spent hours sifting through the files on each match, checking the times they had reported in and out of work against the times that Eumenides had been active. He had found no matches so far.

The lack of progress gnawed at Zeng, but his disposition kept it from affecting his mood. To the contrary, sitting across from an attractive woman only increased his appetite. Which, considering the heap of noodles piled on his plate, was already considerable.

"Now, what about that partner of yours?" he teased between mouthfuls. "I hear you and the captain were thick as thieves this afternoon."

"We found several leads, but they might not amount to anything."

Mu went on to tell him about Pei's hypothesis regarding the time discrepancy in the files. Considering Zeng's knack for technical analysis, she hoped that he would be able to shed some new light on this conundrum. His eyes widened as he listened.

"I have to say that I agree with your opinion. This so-called time discrepancy of Pei's simply can't exist."

Mu lit up. "Would you be able to confirm that?"

"The police records leave no room for doubt. There was only one explosion, and it occurred at 4:13 in the afternoon, killing Meng and Yuan. Since both were very dead by 4:15, as Pei confirmed, he must have the time wrong. I'm also assuming he would have recognized an imposter from the dental cast. Therefore, if there really was a time discrepancy, we'd have to face the absurd conclusion that the dead can speak."

Theoretical impossibilities like this one are essential to breaking this case, Pei had said. *We need to find a rational explanation for this—because as soon as we do, we'll be close to cracking the entire investigation.*

"This reminds me of something one of my supervisors told me," Mu said. " 'When someone makes a choice that's impossible for you to understand, you shouldn't get angry at their stubbornness. Instead, you should consider whether this person is hiding something.' "

"It's simple logic," Zeng replied hastily. "I'm willing to bet Pei knows more than we do. If he's insisting there was a time difference, then you need to ask yourself if he's hiding something."

Mu raised her eyebrows. "Such as?"

"Meng. Can you be sure that he was telling the truth about how she died?"

Mu thought it over, and a chill went through her heart. Was it possible that the events from all those years ago had actually deepened the bonds of affection between them? If Meng had survived, she would be a prime suspect in the subsequent investigation. But would Pei mislead the police—and the task force—to protect the woman he loved?

Mu shivered with excitement. She thought back to the tears Pei had shed in the evidence room. The psychologist could only guess what emotions he had truly felt.

Zeng broke her train of thought. "You'd better keep a close eye on Pei. He might even be the key to breaking this case."

"That's right," Mu said, nodding. "I'm hoping for a big discovery tonight."

"Tonight?"

"Yes. I have a lead. One connected to Pei."

"What lead might that be?" Zeng's ears pricked.

Mu stood up. "I need to go."

"That's not fair!" Zeng exclaimed through a mouthful of noodles. "Tell me about this lead of yours before you go!"

"You worry about your assignment, and I'll worry about mine," she said, smirking.

||||

OCTOBER 24, 9:47 P.M.

The signal detector that Eumenides had left in the hotel room was the key to finding Peng Guangfu—and hopefully to capturing Eumenides. Zeng and his team had examined the device rigorously, stopping just short of stripping it apart, and they had not found a single tracing device or bug. As far as they could tell, it could receive signals but not send them.

Han had selected Xiong as his second-in-command for the four-person squad Eumenides had specified that they send. Both men then selected a partner to complete their team. Han chose Yin, his loyal subordinate. Xiong selected his most trusted SPU officer, Liu Song, the one who had picked the lock of Sun Chunfeng's apartment two mornings earlier. The résumé that Xiong presented to the usually picky Han left him quite pleased:

> *Liu Song. 25 years old; 1.75 meters; 70 kg. Proficient in combat, bomb disposal, sharpshooting, driving. Unrivaled at lock-picking. Awarded one Second-Class Meritorious Service Medal and two Joint Third-Class Meritorious Service Medals during four years of SPU service.*

The task force had not forgotten the fatal lesson of the previous day's operation. This time, there would be no opportunity for Eumenides to take advantage of a lack of teamwork. Every member of this four-person squad would be thoroughly acquainted with the others.

Xiong had suggested that once the device picked up Eumenides's signal, they would set out as instructed, but have a backup squad follow from a safe distance. If combat broke out, both teams would coordinate their efforts and simultaneously attack from within and without. This, he argued, would greatly increase their chances of success. Han rejected his idea out of hand.

During the disaster at Citizen Square they had controlled Ms. Ye's movements, but now they did not even know the location of the man they were supposed to rescue. They were in an unenviably passive position, as they could only face the killer if he deemed it permissible. Therefore, Han said, success would come only if they followed Eumenides's rules to the very letter, despite any misgivings that they might have about doing so.

The execution date on Peng's death notice was no coincidence. October 25 was the tenth anniversary of the police slaying at Mount Twin Deer Park—a day that had turned Captain Han's life inside out.

The official report gave the bare bones. At 10:12 p.m. Han and his partner, Zou Xu, had come across a robbery in progress at a convenience store at 652 Qingfeng Road, about a twenty-minute drive from police headquarters. Officers pursued on foot to the nearby Mount Twin Deer Park, where the encounter ended in a shootout. However, the report had omitted some key details:

On the night of October 25, 1992, Han and Zou Xu had first stumbled out from a restaurant called the Jade Garden, reeking of liquor.

Although Chengdu's criminal police department ostensibly maintained a ban on alcohol for officers in uniform, Han and Zou had always celebrated the closing of each case the same way. They would go straight from headquarters to a restaurant owned by Han's cousin, where they would then treat themselves to a meal of roast fish and mapo tofu, and as many glasses of 120-proof baijiu as they could handle. This night was no different.

Zou was Han's closest friend, as well as his partner. They

had both entered the provincial academy the same year. Their outstanding talents and police work caused their fellow officers to dub the pair "the Gemini." Around the same time, internal politics and promotions had left the position of department captain vacant. Everyone was sure that the next captain would be one of the two Gemini.

The rivalry that inevitably developed between them was an expression of their healthy rapport. Years of working together on the force had transformed their relationship into one of mutual reliance and trust. They were a rare match.

After stumbling out of the Jade Garden, the officers wandered through the fluorescent-lit streets of Chengdu, reliving the highlights of their latest case while their heads slowly cleared. The air was drenched with the greasy tang of frying meat and oil from the late-night stalls that dotted the sidewalks. On a whim, Han suggested that they purchase a last beer before they went their separate ways. *Let's not end the night just yet,* he said.

Zou spotted a convenience store on the other side of the road. As they approached, they heard a commotion coming from inside. Even in his inebriated state, Han at once recognized the two men threatening the cashier. They were both small-time criminals with a reputation among the local police: Peng Guangfu and Zhou Ming.

Neither Han nor Zou Xu felt this would be anything other than a piece of cake for two top officers like themselves.

Once Peng and Zhou Ming spotted the pair of uniformed men crossing the street, they followed their instincts. They fled the store.

Han and Zou followed in close pursuit. The criminals ran from the brightly lit shops and stalls of Fuxing Road and soon were charging into the pitch-dark grounds of nearby Mount Twin Deer Park. The officers spotted their quarry running toward the park's rock garden.

The massive stone structures forming dark, twisting corridors were famous across the entire province. At night, the passages were nothing short of labyrinthine. The officers' respective training did not fail them in their hunt. It took them only moments to ascertain the general layout of the area, and decide to split up and outflank the criminals from opposite sides.

Since Han and Zou Xu quickly blocked both exits, the thieves were essentially trapped.

Han, humming with adrenaline and alcohol, was the first to spot the two knife-wielding criminals hiding in a corner. He drew his gun from his holster and shouted for them to come out and surrender. Peng immediately tossed his knife onto the ground. Zhou Ming did the same.

What they did next took Han completely by surprise. Both thieves drew guns.

On any other day, the outcome of a firefight between two of the province's best officers and a pair of common thugs would have been a foregone conclusion, but the alcohol had slowed Han's reflexes. A crack came from Zhou Ming's sidearm and Han felt a bullet strike his left leg. His partner tried to take cover behind a rock while attempting to locate the source of the shooter, but he was just as sluggish. It was chaos.

Before the sounds of gunfire faded, Han had shot Zhou Ming dead and Peng had run off into the distance. Zou Xu lay bleeding to death.

Han could never purge that night from his memory. In that moment he had understood the meaning of total defeat.

Three months later, Han was appointed captain of the Chengdu police. Thanks to the official account of the incident at Mount Twin Deer Park, most people assumed that the night simply marked another highlight in his stellar career. Han, however, knew otherwise.

For Han to break free of the guilt he felt once and for all, he needed to apprehend Peng Guangfu. He had long searched for traces of the escaped criminal, and with mad tenacity. Within months after his appointment, this new police captain had forced countless informants to mobilize their eyes and ears to search for Peng's whereabouts. This not only threatened the informants' livelihoods; it limited the resources that the police could allocate to other investigations.

Han's personal manhunt finally came to an end when his superiors stepped in and ordered him to put an end to the wild search. He had no choice but to follow orders. All the while, feelings of pain and hatred remained buried deep within his heart, growing stronger with each passing day.

||||

Han knew why Eumenides had left Peng Guangfu alive. He burned with rage—but also with hope. As long as they did not fail tonight, he would be able to avenge Zou Xu.

The captain paced around the conference room table. He could not bear waiting, and it seemed like he had already been waiting for days. He was oblivious to the other team members. Liu Song and Yin were both napping on foldout cots, while Xiong was sitting at the table, his eyes fixed on the receiver.

Han's nerves had been wound tighter than steel cable ever since the team had seen the video. While the others had used their time to rest and conserve strength, he had remained on full alert.

The captain's red eyes and faraway stare were making Xiong anxious. Although he hesitated saying so, the SPU captain could no longer keep his thoughts to himself: "You might be better off sitting this one out, Captain. Eumenides is deliberately targeting you. He's counting on you to act with your heart, not your head."

"You expect me to back out now? Absolutely not!" Han exclaimed through clenched teeth. "I have no intention of admitting defeat."

Xiong didn't know what to say. The captain was unrelenting.

"I haven't lost sight of my priorities, Xiong. Yes, Peng needs to die—but not at the hand of Eumenides! The law will give him the punishment he deserves. As officers of the law, it's our duty to uphold justice and apprehend him alive. If we let Eumenides kill him, we'll be allowing Peng to evade his just legal punishment. I simply cannot allow that to happen!"

"And neither can I!" Xiong exclaimed, slamming his fist against the table. "We'll find Peng Guangfu. The bastard won't even leave my sight until I bring him back personally to receive his legal sentence."

The device on Han's desk began beeping. Xiong and Han looked at each other, their expressions all but identical.

"Liu! Yin! Time to move out!" Han shouted.

The two younger officers sprang out of their cots.

IIIII

It was almost 11:00 p.m. With only an hour until Eumenides's midnight deadline, the four-man squad set off to rescue Peng Guangfu.

Liu Song took the wheel, while the three other men monitored the signal detector. Using the device, they discovered, required almost no technological skill. Concentric circles had appeared on the monitor as soon as it was activated. The circles formed a digital map of their surroundings; the distance between two adjacent circles indicated an actual distance of about five kilometers. A solid circle indicating the device's current position remained fixed at the center of the screen. Four lines radiated from it, one toward each compass point. The transmitter's signal manifested itself as a flashing red blip on the monitor, and its coordinates appeared in a corner of the screen. To find Peng, they simply needed to follow the blip.

The initial signal indicated that their objective was located twenty-three degrees east-northeast, about fifty kilometers away from their current position. The signal originated in nearby Tailin County.

Forty minutes later, the team reached a village called Anfeng. The red blip on the device's display was nearly touching the center point.

Their surroundings had grown rougher and rockier over the past thirty minutes, and the harsh jolting beneath the SUV's floorboards confirmed that they were now driving over a dirt road. Anfeng was in mining country, and the terrain ahead would only grow more remote and treacherous. Liu Song made two passes over the darkly lit pavement before finding the narrow dirt road that led north. As they set off down the path, two mountain peaks pierced the veil of night and blocked the moon's glow. With the exception of the sliver of space illuminated by the SUV's police headlights, their surroundings appeared pitch black. The mountain road finally dwindled to an end.

The red dot indicated that they had arrived.

Midnight crept closer.

The moon had come out again. Off to the right, they could just make out a cave tucked into the foot of a mountain. The cave was level and clearly manmade. Among the shadows, they saw a mess of dilapidated equipment and machinery scattered in the mouth of the cave.

"We made our deadline," Han said.

None of the men was eager to step outside.

"It must be an abandoned mining tunnel," Yin said in a hushed voice.

The others murmured their support of his hypothesis. This mountain range was rich in coal, Xiong explained. Some years ago, a succession of hopeful prospectors had dug a series of illegal mining tunnels throughout Tailin County. The local government eventually cracked down, and the small mining operations were forced to shut down. The mountains were littered with abandoned tunnels.

The mine entrance bore a strong similarity to the gruesome videos they had watched earlier that day. The more they looked, the more they were certain they had arrived.

One by one, the team members turned to Han. Rather than give the order to move, he continued to gaze at the cavern. The moonlight gave everyone a clear view of the cave entrance. A man was standing there. His clothes and physical appearance were the same as in the video—Peng Guangfu was alive.

He twisted uncomfortably, but it was clear that his range of movement was severely limited. *Eumenides has bound him*, Han thought.

Xiong checked his watch. Just twenty-eight minutes shy of October 25. "Let's scout the place out first. For all we know, Eumenides could be right inside, waiting for us with a trap," he urged Han.

Han hissed through gritted teeth. His gut told him that if Eumenides was planning an ambush, he was already two steps ahead of their team.

"We can't afford to waste any time," he said, keeping his voice low. "Odds are that Eumenides already knows we're here. Let's get moving, but stay close. Unholster your weapons." Nodding firmly, Han signaled to his three teammates. He kept his voice low. "Let's move."

Liu Song pulled the key from the ignition. The four men exited the vehicle.

"Funny," Yin said after a minute. "My eyes are adjusting to the darkness really well."

Xiong snorted. "That's natural light, kid. Chengdu is miles from here, which means there's a lot less light pollution."

The SPU captain pointed up at the night sky. The autumn moon loomed high above them.

Liu had parked the SUV on the top of an incline. They advanced in a tight formation with their weapons out, each officer positioned so that the group had a collective 360-degree view of the mountainous terrain around them.

The mountain path beneath their feet vanished between two mounds. This marked the end of the path and the beginning of a rolling stretch of hills. Presumably, this area had originally been unpopulated, and the mining tunnel was the only reason for the road's existence. Nature appeared to have reclaimed the area since the tunnel was abandoned, erasing all but the slightest traces of human activity.

Han scanned his surroundings. He saw flickering shadows and haphazard patches of desolate shrubs and trees, and heard the wind whistling through the hills.

Treacherous terrain. Eumenides had chosen it for a reason.

Han swept his flashlight over the nearby trees and rocks, squinting as he tried to pick out anything moving in the shadows. The others did the same. He gave a signal, and they approached the mining tunnel in a flanking formation, with Xiong bringing up the rear.

The four men reached the entrance without incident. As they swept their flashlights over the area, they confirmed that the tunnel's opening was clear, with the exception of Peng Guangfu.

Xiong and Liu stood back-to-back with their semiautomatic pistols drawn, Xiong aiming his flashlight toward the SUV, and Liu aiming his into the tunnel's depths. As long as they maintained watch, Han whispered to Yin, there would be little chance of an ambush at the mouth of the tunnel. As the two SPU officers stood guard, Han and Yin approached the bound man.

Their flashlights lit up Peng's sunken eyes and gaunt, haggard features. He appeared to be in his twenties. His hair was disheveled and his beard, Han quickly realized, was soaked in blood.

Peng gaped at the two approaching officers. A whimper escaped his open mouth. His hands were tied together, and his right wrist was handcuffed to a scaffold built into the tunnel wall, making it impossible for him to move.

Yin shone his flashlight at Peng's mouth. The angry stump of his severed tongue quivered helplessly as he mewled. Neither officer could make out a single syllable of the gibberish he bellowed out.

Yin gritted his teeth as he thought back to the blade that Eumenides had wielded in the recording. They had Peng now, and that was all that mattered. Even without a tongue, there had to be other means of extracting the information they needed from the man.

Han's gaze was intense enough to bore holes through Peng's flesh. After all this time, he was finally face-to-face with the man who had changed the course of his life. He would have given anything for the chance to unleash all his hatred and rage upon Peng. He needed to stay in control.

Han turned to Liu. "Take a look at those handcuffs. See if there's a way we can open them." He paused, and he held his hand up. "Hold on a second, Liu. Xiong, I want you to check those cuffs first. See if they're linked to a bomb. We don't want to get cocky."

As Xiong inspected the handcuffs, Han stepped closer to Peng. The criminal had stirred at the sound of his voice. As Peng squinted at Han, he could see the recognition in Peng's eyes.

Ten years ago. A gloomy night. The firefight.

Peng's expression changed from hope to astonishment, and then to terror. He opened his mouth and his quivering tongue could only form unintelligible sounds.

Han stepped forward slowly. He reached out and seized Peng by the hair, forcing the man to look up.

"You recognize me, don't you?" Han seethed. "It's time for you to pay for your crimes."

Peng's cries were hurried, as though he was begging Han for mercy.

Xiong stood up and looked Han square in the eye. "There's no bomb, but there's something strange about these cuffs. There's no keyhole!"

"Liu, take a look," Han said.

Liu squatted and inspected the restraints. Several seconds later, the team had their answer.

"Captain, these are electric handcuffs! You can't open them with a key. We have to find the switch controlling them."

Han looked down. The cuffs were unusually bulky, like a steel athletic brace. The scaffold they were attached to was intricate in design and riveted to the wall of the tunnel. Dismantling it was out of the question.

If the group was going to leave this tunnel with Peng, they needed to unlock the handcuffs.

"You mean a remote?" asked Liu.

Xiong realized that Liu's skills wouldn't be useful at all in the case of electric cuffs.

"No, this lock is wired. The switch should be at the other end of the wire."

Liu used his flashlight to search for the wire. It was affixed to the scaffolding, where it stretched along the wall until veering off sharply at a bend in the tunnel ten meters ahead. To follow the wire beyond that point, they would need to advance into the tunnel.

"I'll go have a look," Liu said to Han, pointing toward the bend. The squad was anticipating combat at this stage in the operation. Any further actions required the approval of the superior officer.

"No one goes solo," Han said. "Xiong, you go with Liu. Yin and I will stay here and keep an eye on things."

"No," Xiong said. "We're doing this as we agreed before. Once we've located our target, his safety is top priority. You said we need to make sure Eumenides doesn't get to Peng. How do we know he isn't hiding somewhere inside this cave? Or right outside the entrance? We have to stay on top of Peng, no matter what happens!"

Han agreed reluctantly. He understood the reason for Xiong's adamant attitude. It wasn't just his desire to carry out his mission. It was shame. Shame for his abject failure to protect Ye Shaohong.

"Yin, you go with Liu," Han said, amending his last order. "Be careful. Radios on, and stay in contact."

"Understood," Yin said.

Covering each other, Yin and Liu followed the electric wire into the depths of the tunnel. In moments, they had vanished from Han's sight.

The SPU captain swept his flashlight back and forth in order to monitor a wider area. Meanwhile, Han drew out his handcuffs. He locked one end around Peng's wrist, next to the electronic cuffs, and closed the other around the scaffold. If Yin or Liu found the switch for his handcuffs, he didn't want Peng to make any unexpected moves.

Yin and Liu finally rounded the bend, only to find that the wire continued to stretch deeper within.

"How far do these tunnels go?" Yin whispered.

"Probably miles. If someone wandered in here without any equipment, I'd bet there's a good chance they'd starve to death," Liu answered with a grimace.

They cautiously felt their way ahead, advancing another hundred feet. The tunnel widened to the size of an apartment hallway. They froze.

"Oh, no," Yin whispered in horror.

Bodies dangled from the tunnel's low ceiling. They were arranged in a circle, at intervals of a few feet. Yin gripped his flashlight until he thought the casing would snap. Blackened trails of blood ran along the length of each motionless body like macabre tattoos, thickest at the gaping wounds on their necks.

Liu shone his flashlight from one body to another, moving around the circle. "Twelve," he said. "Twelve bodies."

"There were thirteen videos. Twelve victims executed. Peng is the thirteenth," Yin said, suppressing a shiver.

Liu slammed his fist into the wall. "It's a literal dead end."

"Look there!" Yin exclaimed. He pointed his flashlight at the left wall. "The wire splits."

Yin was right. One strand continued along the left wall, while another ran along the ceiling and through the cadavers. Liu noticed that another wire split off from the latter one.

"There are three separate wires," Liu said.

"But why? Where the hell do they go?"

Doing his best not to scream, Liu hugged the left wall and edged around the dangling bodies. The first wire led to a new tunnel, vanishing into darkness. He aimed his flashlight back at the main tunnel's rear and right walls. The hanging corpses blocked his view for the most part, but he was able to make out two more tunnels. One for each wire.

"Are you kidding me?" Yin asked in disbelief. He had not moved another inch closer to the bodies.

The paths in these mining tunnels had been dug according to the locations of the mineral veins within the mine, Liu explained, so it was not unusual for them to split off in this manner. Unfortunately, these paths wouldn't make their search any easier.

"For all we know, only one of these wires controls the handcuffs and the other two are dummy wires," the SPU officer said. Lifting his radio to his lips, he reported the new development and the horrific discovery of the bodies to his superiors.

Xiong ordered the team members not to split up. Instead, they were to trace each wire into its respective passage together. If they happened to find a switch in any of the tunnels, he instructed, they were to try turning it on. After all, these wires were linked to a pair of handcuffs, not a bomb.

Yin and Liu entered the left chamber first. The wires were concealed inside the scaffold's steel pipes. At the end of each section of pipe, a wire emerged and threaded back into the next section. This pattern continued uninterrupted as they walked deeper in, and the farther they walked the longer the passage seemed to stretch.

After about fifty meters, they spotted a round electronic switch mounted to the scaffold. Yin stood guard as Liu squatted and studied it.

"We've already found the switch at the end of one of the wires," Liu said into his radio. "There's a signal emitter here. Activating it should send out an electric signal tuned to a specific frequency. If it matches the handcuffs' frequency, then you should be able to open the cuffs."

"Excellent. Have you checked for any traps? Do you think it might be a setup?"

Liu shone his flashlight down the length of the pipe. "The wire's hidden inside piping all the way down. Just by looking, it's all but impossible to tell if they've been booby-trapped. I mean, these pipes could be filled with explosives. There's no way for us to tell without taking the whole place apart."

The crackly sound of an exhale came through the radio. "It's a risk we'll have to take. Push the button now, Liu."

Back at the mine's entrance, Xiong and Han saw a green light flicker on the handcuffs. The heavy cuffs remained locked.

Xiong examined the light that had just flashed, and saw three indicator lights built into the handcuffs. This seemed to confirm Liu's earlier hypothesis. Two of the three wires running into the passages were decoys.

"Locate and activate the second switch immediately!"

Without even pausing, the two officers rushed into the next cavern to follow the second wire. Deep within, they found another signal emitter set inside the end of a scaffold pipe.

Liu did not request permission to press the button. Han and Xiong watched another green light flash upon the handcuffs, but the cuffs remained shut.

"Go find the third switch!"

Despite the firmness of his order, something was troubling Xiong. Logically, the third wire should be the correct one. His instincts said otherwise.

The two officers located the final signal emitter as soon as they could. Liu activated it.

A green indicator light flashed on the cuffs. They remained locked.

Xiong and Han looked at each other, confused.

"Are all the wires duds?" Han asked. "What's Eumenides trying to achieve with this ruse?"

Liu's voice crackled through the radio. "We've been looking at this the wrong way. I don't think they're dummy wires."

"I have a feeling I'm not going to like what comes next," Xiong said, gritting his teeth.

"You said that a green light flashed every time I pushed each button. I think this means that each switch works. But if there are three wires, perhaps the handcuffs will only open once we turn on each of the switches at once and activate all three lights together."

"Of course!" Han said.

"Three switches, Captain. And four of us."

"Now I understand why Eumenides was so specific about how many people we could send."

"What do you mean?" Xiong asked.

"He wants to even the odds. Four of us came here, but only one of us will be able to defend Peng. If he's going to make his move, that would be the time."

Xiong's eyes widened. "Liu and Yin have to come back. Eumenides's goal here is too obvious. We have to regroup and request backup."

Liu's anxious voice came through the radio. "We found a slip of paper next to the signal emitter. It's signed by Eumenides."

"Well, read it!" Xiong shouted.

" 'I've placed a bomb inside the cave. You have until 1:00 a.m.,' " he read quickly.

All four members of the team checked their watches. It was already 12:45 a.m.

"I'm not willing to risk the chance that he's bluffing," Han growled into the radio. "We have fifteen minutes, men."

Even the most sophisticated knowledge of bomb disposal would mean nothing if they couldn't find the bomb. It could be anywhere—buried within the layer of dirt and coal, hidden inside the cavern's crevice-laced walls, concealed among the abandoned equipment scattered about the tunnels, or even inside any of the pipes. Fifteen hours wasn't enough time. They only had minutes.

They needed to vacate the tunnel before one o'clock—but they needed to leave with Peng Guangfu.

The tunnel was silent for an instant. As Yin and Liu awaited their next orders, Han and Xiong thought hard. Seconds later, Xiong spoke into his radio.

"The captain's going to join you in a minute. If we still can't unlock the handcuffs in ten minutes . . ." He glanced over at Peng. "Someone's going to have to lose their hand."

Peng's eyes widened in terror, and looked upon the sharp field knife hanging from Xiong's waist.

Han hesitated. Was he willingly going to play the part Eumenides had written for him? He could not afford to wait any longer. He needed to make a decision now!

He nodded at the captain. "Xiong, you go. I'll keep an eye on things here."

But the SPU captain refused to shirk his responsibility. "No. I can't lose sight of our objective. This is my duty." No matter what plans the killer had in store for them, protecting Peng Guangfu was still the team's most crucial task.

Han saw the grim determination in Xiong's eyes and nodded. "Be careful," he said.

The two words, simple and terse, steeled Xiong's resolve.

"As long as I'm here," he said, "Eumenides won't get anywhere near Peng."

||||

Han ran into the tunnel. He couldn't allow himself to pause, not even for a second, but everything was a blur. Suddenly, a mass of dangling silhouettes sprung up around him. A cry of surprise slipped from his throat.

Liu had warned him about the bodies, but Han could never have prepared himself for this.

He stood in a nightmare. A ring of bodies hung from the ceiling in two rows, like a gruesome chandelier.

Suddenly, a dark form sprung out from the closest passage. Han raised his semiautomatic pistol and shouted, "Stop!"

Yin raised his hands. "Captain, it's me!"

Han relaxed, and he lowered the gun. "What the hell are you doing, Yin?" he demanded.

"My flashlight broke." Yin held up a cigarette lighter.

Han groaned inwardly. "Where is Liu?"

"Waiting inside that cavern." Yin jerked a thumb over his shoulder. "I'll take the one in the middle. You take the one on the left."

"We'll radio once in position," Han said. "And be careful in there."

"Understood!"

The two men split up. It didn't take Han long; as soon as he got to the end of the wire he signaled that he was in position. Yin, moving without a flashlight, took longer. When all three of them were ready, it was 12:52 a.m.

Liu's voice came through the radio. "If we all hit the switches at the same time, Peng's cuffs should unlock. When I count to three, hold your button down for five seconds."

On the count of three, the officers simultaneously pressed their respective buttons.

Han thumbed the radio. "Xiong, how does everything look on your end?"

No response came.

"Xiong? Captain Xiong?"

"We're running out of time," Liu said, panicking. "Let's move out!" He had worked closely with Xiong for years, and his gut told him that something was very wrong.

One by one, they ran back to the entrance. Liu got there first, with Han right behind. A sickening scent reached their nostrils. They brandished their flashlights in search of the smell's origin.

Their beams lit up the bloody scene. The electronic handcuffs that had restrained Peng lay open, but Peng was far from free. The criminal lay crumpled below the scaffold, his right hand raised up as if in a bizarre greeting. Liu moved closer, and he saw the police-issue handcuffs chaining his wrist to the metal bars. Blood was pooling on the tunnel floor from a wound on his neck. His motionless body showed no signs of life.

They found Xiong a few meters away. The SPU captain's condition was nearly as dire as Peng's. Writhing on the tunnel floor, he clutched at his throat. Blood spurted through his fingers, pulsing with each desperate gasp for air.

"Captain!"

Liu dashed forward, his pained cry echoing through the mining tunnel. He dropped to both knees and pulled Xiong close in a tight embrace. The captain was still dimly conscious, and managed to open his eyes. A hint of comfort crept into his expression at the sight of his trusted colleague. He opened his mouth in an attempt to speak, but despite intense effort, he was unable to say a word.

Liu saw the hideous gash across Xiong's neck. The captain's throat had been cut, and the gushing blood was blocking air from reaching his vocal cords. His efforts to breathe only made more blood flow.

Han rushed over and knelt at Xiong's side. He shut his eyes bitterly, as if in disbelief. "Cap . . . Captain Xiong?" he asked, his voice trembling.

The sound of Han's voice gave Xiong a surge of energy. Using the last of his strength, he raised his head and seized Han's arms with both hands. Veins bulged from his wrists.

Han held Xiong's frantic gaze. An almost magnetic force connected their eyes. The captain leaned closer to Xiong until his ear was almost against the man's lips. "What are you trying to tell me?" he asked.

The captain could only gurgle.

Yin finally emerged from inside the tunnel, and froze in his tracks as he witnessed the scene.

"What—what happened?" he stuttered in astonishment.

"What the hell are you standing there for?" Han yelled. "Eumenides is here! You and Liu get Xiong into the SUV, now!"

"But what about you?" Yin asked, still stunned.

"Forget about me! Eumenides is mine!"

Now Yin took a step forward. His eyes narrowed. "He already killed Xiong. What makes you think you stand a chance?"

Han stared back blankly. Without another word, Yin turned and dashed toward the SUV.

"Captain!" Liu called out. "I can't carry Xiong up that incline by myself!"

Han grabbed the scaffolding with both hands and wrenched as hard as he could. The metal creaked, but it did not give. He shook the scaffolding once, then again. The handcuffs around Peng's wrist jingled. With a heaving sigh, Han turned back to Liu.

"Right. Let's get Xiong out of here."

The two of them worked together to carry their gravely injured comrade out. The SUV's blinding headlights shone from the top of the steep incline.

By the time Han and Liu reached the top, their backs were already soaked with sweat. They loaded Xiong into the rear of the vehicle and hopped in next to him. Han pulled the hatch shut behind them. Yin was at the wheel.

"Captain! What about Peng?"

Han blinked, as if stirred from a daydream. "Peng?" He shook his head. "No time. We need to leave now."

"Captain?" Yin asked, looking at Han in disbelief.

Han stared dumbly at the wounded man at his feet. Xiong had already shut his eyes. The blood around his throat was no longer flowing.

Liu placed a trembling index finger between Xiong's mouth and nose, but felt no air.

Without warning, he sprang up and howled like an enraged wolf. "That fucking son of a bitch!" Brandishing his sidearm, he reached for the handle to the SUV's rear hatch.

"Liu Song! Don't you dare move!" Han leaped. In a flash, he had pinned Liu to the floor of the rear compartment, alongside Xiong. He twisted his head to look at Yin.

"Drive! What are you waiting for? The bomb's about to go off!"

Yin checked the dashboard clock. 12:59. He jumped into action. He shifted the vehicle into gear and floored the gas pedal. In seconds, the SUV was racing along the rugged mountain path leading back to the city.

"Let me out! I'm going to find him and kill him! I'll kill him!" Liu's eyes quivered with rage. As Yin leaned into the gas pedal, Han's grip on the SPU officer remained strong. The SUV bumped along the path, and Liu stopped struggling. Eventually, his outbursts turned to sobs.

Han fell back onto the floor of the rear compartment. The

body of Captain Xiong lay motionless beside him. Han seized his own hair and let out an anguished cry.

A fierce explosion erupted from the mouth of the tunnel. The shockwave jolted the vehicle. Far behind them, a fiery tremor shook loose the rocks above the tunnel entrance, and a stream of boulders fell to block the opening. The body of Peng Guangfu, as well as all evidence from the scene inside the cave, vanished beneath tons of rock and earth.

CHAPTER EIGHT

DOUBTS UPON DOUBTS

OCTOBER 24, 9:00 P.M.
FOUR HOURS EARLIER . . .

Mu Jianyun walked along a bustling metropolitan street. Han, Yin, Xiong, and Liu Song were still at headquarters, waiting for the receiver to activate. While they sat twiddling their thumbs, she was going to find answers.

She turned a corner and entered a narrow alleyway. It was as though she had entered another world.

The buildings on both sides of the alley seemed to slant inward, looming over her as she walked. A bitter autumn wind swept through the Cockroach Nest, bringing with it an icy chill. Mu stuffed her hands into the pockets of her coat and used her elbows to press her clothes close against her body.

This is not a good place to be, she thought.

Mu arrived in front of the small apartment. The world had forgotten Huang Shaoping, and she imagined his life here as something from a nightmare. Probably worse than any nightmares she'd ever have.

She knocked, and the door opened. Huang stood in front of her. The poor lighting provided by the room's dusty bulb cloaked half his face in shadow.

"Hello," Mu said, not wishing for the man to sense her unease.

"You came."

"Yes, and I came alone," she said, forcing a smile.

Huang's shattered lips curled upward in an attempt to match her expression, yet he conveyed no sense of joy. "Have a seat," he said, scratching at the scars on his neck.

Mu moved an old wooden stool beside the filthy bed, and Huang used his walking stick to hobble over. She stepped forward in order to help him to the bed, but Huang seemed to sense her intention and made his refusal clear with a shake of his head.

Mu stiffened at this rebuff. The man had dignity after all.

The two sat. "Is there anything you'd like to tell the police?" Mu asked, with deliberate emphasis on the last word of her question. Her hand brushed something soft, and she recoiled. It was a stack of old utility bills.

"No. If I wanted to tell the police, I would have already." Huang shook his head. "I will only talk to you."

"I teach at the academy, but I am a police officer. And I've been assigned to the 4/18 Task Force."

Huang's cheek twitched. "That's why you have to promise me something before I tell you more."

"What do I have to promise?"

"That you won't share what I'm about to tell you with anyone else on the force. I'm asking you to do this by yourself."

"And why is that?"

"I've had to keep silent all these years." Huang was as sincere as Mu had ever seen. "And what I know would put your life in danger. I can't trust the police."

"Are you saying that someone inside the police is somehow involved in this case?" Mu leaned closer.

"Can you promise?"

She answered without hesitation.

"Yes, I promise."

Mu's heart raced as she awaited Huang's next words.

"A month before the explosion at the warehouse, the Chengdu

police made a major drug bust. Look into that before you take your investigation anywhere else."

Mu was startled. She had been expecting Huang to tell her something he had seen during the explosion, yet now he was talking about a different case altogether.

Huang did not seem surprised at Mu's reaction. "The 3/16 drug-trafficking case from 1984," he added. "Remember that."

"What does it have to do with the explosion?"

"Just look into it and you will find what you are looking for." He squinted. "I can't tell you everything now, because I can't guarantee that you'll be able to protect me. I have to know I can trust you."

Mu looked at him without disgust. The man's appearance was the same as it had been during her previous visits, yet there was something different about him. It was the way he was looking at her. Something about his gaze seemed familiar, as if she had known this man in another life. She couldn't explain it, but she sensed there was more to him than she previously knew.

"Who are you really, Huang?" she asked.

Huang bared his teeth and snickered. "You already know who I am."

Mu lowered her eyes. She was being too passive. She tried another approach.

"You've been hiding quite a bit of information from the police. Maybe I should bring you back to the investigative team and see what they think," she threatened.

"Then you'd be reneging on the promise you just made. I'd only have myself to blame, for being a poor judge of character." Huang shook his head as he trailed off. "I'll take my secrets to the grave, lady. You'll never have another chance at knowing what really happened eighteen years ago."

Mu grimaced. He had called her bluff. "I gave you my word," she said. "How can I be sure that you aren't just toying with me?"

"You'll understand once you look into that drug-trafficking case."

"Fine," she conceded. "I'll look into it."

"Don't mention this to anyone else," Huang stressed again. "You have no idea just how powerful a force you'll be going up against. I'm already crippled. You wouldn't have the heart to hurt me more, would you?"

Mu nodded her understanding. Though the situation was growing tenser, she could not help but ask one last question. "Why choose me, if you don't trust the police?"

Huang looked at her with fearful eyes.

"Every story has to come to an end. The very first time I saw you, I knew that you were the one who could pen the final page to my own chapter."

Mu frowned. What kind of an answer was this?

"Remember: 1984. Come back once you've made some findings of your own." Huang waved his hand at the door.

"We'll see."

Mu rose from the stool. She checked her watch. It was already 9:40. None of the other team members had contacted her since her departure. It was possible that they hadn't left yet. Or perhaps they had already received a signal, but had been in too much of a hurry to contact her. Either way, there was not much that she could do to help them. What she could do, however, was follow the lead that Huang had just given her. If she was lucky, it would move their investigation forward. And maybe, just maybe, it would tell her why this man was so interested in helping her.

She turned back toward Huang when she reached the doorway. "Thank you for trusting me," she said, and left.

Huang watched her as she shut the door. He scratched thoughtfully at the old wounds on his arms, and he smiled.

||||

Mu arrived at the police department shortly after 10:00 p.m. The four-man squad was still camped out in the conference room. Yin and Liu were getting some rest on a pair of cots set up in the corner. Xiong and Han sat at the table, their eyes glued to the signal detector as they anxiously awaited their cue from Eumenides. She thought about knocking on the door, but instead she turned away and walked toward the exit.

Zeng answered his door with a bleary look in his eyes. His face brightened when he noticed Mu.

"I knew you couldn't stay away," he said, beaming. "I'm still the one you trust the most, right?"

Mu sat on one of the room's chairs without uttering a sound. Silence was the best way to handle Zeng.

"Come on and tell me—any progress with that lead of yours? Run into any problems? Let's see if I can't point you in the right direction."

Mu wasted no time. "I need you to help me find some files."

"And which files might those be?"

"The 3/16 drug-trafficking case from 1984. I need everything you can get."

Zeng blinked at her, perplexed. "What in the hell for?"

"I'm interested," she answered nonchalantly. "And I'd like to know more."

"What the hell is going on today?" He gave a snort. "Everyone's interested in ancient cases all of a sudden."

Zeng's comment stirred Mu. "Who else?"

"Pei, but not for this drug case of yours. He came here after dinner and had me look up the files for the police slaying at Mount Twin Deer Park. The three of us have too much free time, wouldn't you say?"

Mu couldn't help being curious. "Why did Pei want those files?"

"Who knows?" Zeng paused. "Maybe he's trying to dig

up some dirt on the captain for the sake of some old-fashioned schadenfreude?"

"I need you to focus." Mu shook her head in exasperation. "Can you find the case files or not?"

Zeng got serious. "That might be a bit of a challenge. After all, it's an eighteen-year-old case . . . But a talented guy like myself thrives under pressure. For a gorgeous woman like you, I could track down anything."

"Then shut up and get to work."

"Yes, ma'am!" Zeng saluted. He sauntered over to the desk and turned on his personal laptop. His capacity as head technical supervisor of the provincial capital's online security team granted him full access to the department's database from any terminal.

The 3/16 drug-trafficking case was closed but unclassified, so Zeng was able to quickly look up all relevant files. His fingers danced over the keyboard like those of a master pianist performing a concerto. After a minute or so, he smiled at Mu.

"And that's all she wrote."

"That was quick," Mu said, surprised.

"You better hurry up. The files are already being printed out at the front desk."

Mu found the front desk, where the late-shift secretary was frantically trying to keep track of the stream of pages suddenly spitting out of the machine. "Those are mine. Would you mind stapling them for me?" she asked.

The woman shook her head in frustration. "I told the other lecturers that they couldn't print their notes here, and I'm going to tell you the same thing. You'll have to go to one of the print shops outside."

Clearing her throat, Mu showed the woman her police credentials and room card. The secretary's eyes widened slightly, and she stacked the pages into a neat pile without any further questions. She did, however, pause when she saw the last page.

"Do you want me to staple this one too?"

It was a color printout of a rose, glistening with fresh scarlet ink. As Mu took the printout, she felt a quick rush of delight at this unexpected surprise. Quickly regaining her professionalism, she handed the printed flower to the secretary. "This one doesn't need to be stapled with the rest. Think of it as a token of appreciation for your help."

She smiled warmly.

Mu couldn't help but bury her nose in the file as she walked back to her own room. On at least one occasion, she came inches from walking into a wall.

The head of the task force assigned to the 3/16 drug-trafficking case was none other than Xue Dalin. The former vice commissioner of the Chengdu police force and Eumenides's first victim, killed hours before the deaths of Meng and Yuan.

Pei Tao's presence had focused the team's attention on the warehouse explosion, but it had also distracted them from investigating the truth behind Xue's murder. The 4/18 Task Force of 1984 had also failed to link the two events. Somehow, Huang knew something none of the investigators did.

Resisting the growing urge to sit down in the middle of the empty hallway and read, Mu quickened her pace. She thought about going back to Zeng's room, but decided against it. She needed peace and quiet to digest these documents, and Zeng was not a person who would give it to her.

Once she was back inside her room, she spread the 3/16 files out on the desk. Over the next two hours, she studied every single page for the smoking gun that would crack the Eumenides murders. Her search was fruitless. She had hoped to find mention of Yuan Zhibang or Meng Yun, but there was nothing. Vice Commissioner Xue Dalin was the only clear connection. He had led the special investigation for the 3/16 drug-trafficking case, and one month later, on April eighteenth, he became Eumenides's first victim.

As vice commissioner of the city's police, Xue would have been in charge of many different investigations. How could his involvement as head of the investigation team in the 3/16 case be linked to his own death? Why would Huang have singled out this case in particular? And how would he have even known about it in the first place?

Mu's head was spinning as the deeper truth slipped further out of sight. She pulled herself out of her chair and approached the window. Pulling the curtains aside, she took a deep breath of the fresh autumn air drifting in. She shut her eyes and let her thoughts meld with the soft hum of traffic outside.

Just as the case designation indicated, the drug bust had occurred a month prior to Xue's murder on the eighteenth of April. 3/16 was merely the date the case had been closed. In fact, the investigation had begun many weeks before.

During the 1980s, Interpol had cracked down hard against transnational drug trafficking. As Asia's international drug cartels lost one hideout after another, they were left with no choice but to find new avenues for conducting business. It was precisely at this time that China, currently expanding its economy to make room for international business and trade, became a primary target for these cartels.

As a transportation hub and financial center, Chengdu was one of China's most dynamic trade cities. And now the ashes of the city's drug trade rose back to life. This boom soon became a major focus of the local police force. Xue Dalin, then Chengdu's police vice commissioner, was in charge of the city's efforts to fight back.

In 1984, Xue's anti-narcotics team obtained an invaluable piece of intelligence. A Southeast Asian drug ring was planning to make a major transaction with a domestic group inside Chengdu. The deal was planned for the sixteenth of March. In turn, the 3/16 Task Force was established.

The information came from an informant named Deng

Yulong. According to the personnel data included in the case files, Deng was twenty-five years old at the time but he had already been a police informant for seven years.

Before beginning his association with the police, the clever young man was typical of the dropout hoodlums found stirring up trouble on the streets. He was already making a name for himself among the local gangs. On his eighteenth birthday, after a few too many drinks, Deng stabbed another gang member and was arrested. While his chances of avoiding jail time appeared slim to none, one man stepped in to save him from this fate: Xue Dalin. Not yet vice commissioner at the time, Xue was merely the leader of the city's public security squad.

Xue instantly changed the course of Deng's life. He modified the police dispatch records so that the recorded time of Deng's offense was four minutes before midnight on the twenty-third of that month, rather than six minutes after midnight on the twenty-fourth. It was only a difference of ten minutes, but it meant that Deng would be tried as a minor rather than an adult. As a result, the court's punishment was much lighter, and he was only sentenced to two years of probation.

Of course, there was a catch. Once Deng was freed, he may have appeared to be an unreformed thug, but in reality he was a police informant. Specifically, he was Xue Dalin's informant.

Deng's combination of natural talent and early experience made him more than qualified for his new line of work, and his close cooperation with Xue was mutually beneficial. Conviction rates skyrocketed in Xue's jurisdiction and his career grew more promising with each passing day. Likewise, by tipping Deng off about imminent police raids and movements, Xue gave the ambitious Deng the tools to establish his reputation among the city's underbelly and win favor among the bosses of the criminal underworld.

As Chengdu's economy began to boom, the nimble thinking

and brute strength of a local crime kingpin named Liu Hong allowed him to quickly establish and develop his own brand in the region. Liu Hong had amassed a considerable fortune through his extortion schemes and protection rackets. He was hungry, and he began recruiting skilled criminals to further his empire.

It was at this time that Liu Hong noticed Deng. Hong was in need of an assistant in the organized crime scene, and he took Deng under his wing. Deng's entry into the inner ranks was a godsend to the police, who had been waiting for an opening to infiltrate Liu Hong's crime ring. Even better news was still to follow.

When Southeast Asian drug traffickers looked to extend their channels of distribution to Sichuan Province, they needed to go through Liu Hong. Now, tempted by the promise of massive profits, Liu Hong added narcotics trafficking to his repertoire, and in no time he had established a monopoly on Chengdu's opiate trade. After the successful completion of several smaller-scale transactions, both parties agreed on a date for their first truly large-scale collaboration: March 16, 1984.

The police were ecstatic. Now that their own informant had infiltrated Liu Hong's group, the possibility of a successful operation against the crime ring had increased astronomically—with a year's worth of outstanding service under Liu Hong, Deng had already become one of the crime lord's most trusted men. His presence at any deal involving overseas groups would be guaranteed.

On March sixteenth, Liu Hong—accompanied by Deng—met with three seasoned foreign narcotics traffickers at a designated location. Xue and his officers, all dressed in plainclothes, were already lying in wait nearby. As soon as Deng gave the signal, they would spring into action and surround the criminals.

And then, chaos.

When one of the Southeast Asian gangsters saw through a

nearby plainclothes officer's disguise, all six suspects scattered. When they found that more police officers had blocked their escape, the criminals opened fire.

It was the first time the Chengdu police force faced the ferocity of a foreign drug gang firsthand, but they were prepared. Within a minute, they managed to surround the suspects. The criminals, on the other hand, knew that their chances of survival were slim at best, and they fought with the savagery of cornered wolves.

Two officers were shot during the firefight, and then the young informant Deng Yulong turned the tide. Suddenly turning against Liu Hong, he dealt a critical blow to both groups of gangsters. When the firefight ended, Liu Hong and four other suspects lay dead on the ground.

The operation resulted in the seizure of 500 kilograms of heroin and over 2.5 million U.S. dollars in drug money. Liu Hong's criminal empire had been crushed in a single day.

With the successful closure of this case, the members of the 3/16 Task Force received a collective Second-Class Meritorious Service Medal. Xue Dalin was awarded a First-Class Meritorious Service Medal, and his bright future in the police force was all but assured.

One month later, the law enforcement community was stunned by Xue's brutal murder . . . as well as by the accusations of corruption that began bubbling up from among the ranks of Chengdu's police.

||||

Mu pushed the documents to the edges of her desk and pressed her hands against her head. Apart from Xue Dalin, the 3/16 file indicated that this was an entirely separate case from the Eumenides murders. What was the connection?

The ringing doorbell interrupted her thoughts. She checked

her watch. It was nearly an hour after midnight. "Who is it?" she called out.

"It's me," answered Zeng. What was he doing here at this hour?

Despite some hesitation, she got up and opened the door.

"I figured you were still awake." Zeng stood in the doorway hugging his elbows.

She let out a deep breath. "Is there something you wanted to see me about?" Despite her polite smile, Mu made no indication that Zeng was welcome. If he had simply come here to crack jokes, she wasn't in the mood.

As if reading her thoughts, Zeng laughed and said, "I see my little gift at the front desk didn't exactly cheer you up. No worries. I'm here to solve the puzzle that's been bugging you."

"What puzzle might that be?"

"There's no need to play coy with me." He casually strolled into the room and plopped down on the sofa. "Or do you expect me to believe that you made all that fuss over a two-decade-old drug bust because you were just curious? Do I look like an idiot to you?"

"What did you come here so late to tell me?"

Zeng held out two fingers and tapped them gleefully against the coffee table. "I know how the drug bust and the warehouse murders are linked."

Mu tried to read Zeng's face but his expression was impenetrable.

"There's a connection between the two cases?"

Zeng rolled his eyes in exasperation. "If you're going to keep playing dumb, I'm leaving!" He turned for the door, waving his hand in a lazy good-bye gesture.

Her heart leaping into her throat, Mu reached over and grabbed his arm.

"Okay, okay. Sit down and talk. You're right. I did find a

connection, but I don't know what it means. All I know is that Xue Dalin was involved with both investigations." She sat down on the sofa.

"That's to be expected. But the connection you're looking for isn't anywhere in the files I printed out for you." Zeng leaned close to Mu, and she could tell that he was attempting to show off. "I read through those files right after you left, and I came to the same conclusion. Only two words in those documents had any value: Xue Dalin. I ran a peripheral search for that name. And then things got interesting."

Mu was glued to her seat. She hadn't intended to bring in anyone else on her investigation of Huang's lead, but now that Zeng was involved she couldn't just turn him away.

"What did you find?"

"A woman." He lowered his voice to a suspenseful whisper.

Mu rolled her eyes in irritation.

"You still remember Yuan Zhibang's death notice, don't you? What was the first crime written on it?"

"Womanizing."

"When I checked the archives for records on students attending the provincial police academy in 1984, I found a file on a young woman who was abandoned by her boyfriend after she became pregnant. She eventually committed suicide by jumping into a river. Her name was Bai Feifei."

The name sent ripples through Mu's imagination. Gradually, the delicate silhouette of a young woman emerged in her mind's eye.

"Bai had been preparing to graduate with a major in administrative management," Zeng said. "She was interning at the city police department before her suicide. Her job was administrative secretary to Vice Commissioner Xue Dalin."

Mu was unable to hold back her surprise. Bai Feifei, whom she assumed was only a minor character on the edges of one case, just became the sole juncture between the murders of both Xue Dalin and Yuan Zhibang. Her mind raced.

"When did she die?"

"The twentieth of March." Zeng's reply was quick.

Xue's task force had successfully brought down Liu Hong's drug empire on March sixteenth. Four days later, his administrative secretary, Bai Feifei, was found dead. Xue was murdered on April eighteenth. On that same day, Yuan Zhibang, Bai's former boyfriend, and Meng Yun died in a warehouse explosion.

This is what Huang had wanted her to find—Bai Feifei connected the 3/16 drug case and the 4/18 murders. What did it signify? How had Huang known about the 3/16 case? And what had kept his lips sealed for the last eighteen years?

Questions wormed through her mind like creeping tendrils. Her thoughts were a jumble, and she was unable to form a coherent picture.

The doorbell rang. Zeng got up and opened the door.

Pei stood outside.

"Captain Pei?" Zeng asked, with more than a hint of surprise.

The captain glanced at both of them. His voice was low, almost suffocating. "Something went wrong."

OCTOBER 25, 2:08 A.M.

NO. 1 PEOPLE'S HOSPITAL

After wading through crowds of late-night patients and their anxious family members, Pei, Mu, and Zeng finally arrived at the emergency room of Chengdu's No. 1 People's Hospital. The other remaining task force members were there, but they didn't appear to notice the new arrivals.

Xiong's death sent shockwaves through the police force, even in the middle of the night. Commissioner Song of the Chengdu Police Department and Xiong's fellow SPU members had hurried to the hospital as soon as word of the captain's fate reached them.

Liu's eyes were bloodshot, and he sat silent and alone on a chair in a corner of the emergency room. The aura of smoldering grief and rage surrounding the SPU officer ensured no one dared disturb him.

Captain Han, team leader and coordinator of the operation, was nearing his breaking point. By the time he finished giving his situation report to Commissioner Song, his voice was barely more than a croak. The captain looked as though he had nothing left to give.

The commissioner looked almost queasy at the sight of the pain that Han, one of his favorite officers, was experiencing. Looking away from the captain, he said, "Go home and get some rest, Han."

Han nodded dumbly. Commissioner Song was right—he was exhausted. The events of the previous several hours haunted him, like a nightmare he could not awaken from. His pain seeped through every cell of his body.

Unable to find the words to respond to the commissioner, Han slipped out from the crowd in a trance. He spotted Pei, Mu, and Zeng, their faces ashen, but passed by without a word.

The commissioner drew a deep breath and yelled after him. "Captain Han!"

The yell drew stares from everyone. Han stopped and turned around, his eyes wide.

"The investigation team is still counting on you!" Commissioner Song's voice boomed. "Don't forget that!"

Han knew he needed to start over. There was only one way: *Find the bastard Eumenides, and crush him.* Anger turned to determination. He gritted his teeth, forced his aching back to straighten, and flexed his fists.

The commissioner nodded at Han with approval. "Get some sleep. The team will be waiting for you tomorrow."

Eumenides will also be waiting. With that thought, Han turned and walked to the door.

Yin Jian watched as the captain left the room. Unlike Liu and Han, who had both succumbed to anger and fatigue, he had not experienced any sort of extreme emotion after the incident at the mine. On the contrary, the gears in his head were spinning at blazing speed.

Pei appeared at Yin's side and patted his shoulder.

"Captain Pei . . . ," Yin said, his voice dreamlike. Pei's touch seemed to have disrupted his train of thought.

"What the hell happened out there?" Pei asked, motioning to Xiong's body.

Yin steadied his nerves and described how he and the team had entered the mine and found Peng, how they had been forced to split up so that Eumenides could kill Peng and Xiong right under their noses, and how they barely escaped with their lives. Pei listened with rapt attention, picturing each scene in detail.

Yin went on to explain that Captain Xiong Yuan had stopped breathing in the back of the police SUV, but Liu Song had insisted on driving to the hospital rather than directly to the forensic examiner. If nothing else, it gave them a small measure of comfort. The doctor on duty only needed to take one look at the gash in Xiong's neck to declare the SPU captain dead on arrival.

Just as Pei had originally feared, the game had been nothing more than another meticulously laid trap. By abiding by Eumenides's rules, the police had made themselves pawns in the killer's plan. Yet Xiong's death came as a great shock. Considering that they had dispatched four of their finest officers to the scene, Pei had assumed there would be no chance of a direct confrontation. Never would he have imagined that the killer would actually succeed in murdering the most formidable member of their team.

What's Eumenides's game? wondered Pei. Was this all just an elaborate provocation of the police? Eumenides had clearly intended for his plot to result in disaster for the task force, but what was his ultimate goal? To eliminate a player from the opposing side? But why arrange such an elaborate cat-and-mouse game, instead of simply killing Xiong like he had Sergeant Zheng?

They still hadn't found the key they needed to understand Eumenides's motives. Pei had already spent time pondering what they could be missing. By the time Yin finished his account of the night's events, he had a new hypothesis. But it was too early and too bold to say anything yet.

He needed more evidence, and more time.

Keeping his voice low, he said to Yin, "Mind if we step out for a minute? There are a few things we need to talk about in private."

Yin stiffened, but he couldn't refuse Pei's request.

Exiting the hospital, the two officers found a secluded spot by a corner of the building.

"What do you want to ask me, Pei?"

"While you were at the mine, I was reading the files on the shootings at Mount Twin Deer Park. It says you were in charge of inspecting the scene."

"Was there something you wanted to know about it?"

"I'd like to verify a few things. According to the description in the case files, Han fired three bullets in the firefight. Two of these missed their targets, but one struck Zhou Ming in the chest, killing him instantly. Before this, Zhou Ming had fired four bullets—one of which struck Han, another killed Zou Xu, and the other two missed. Zhou Ming's accomplice, Peng Guangfu, fired one bullet that missed. Han's partner was down before he even had a chance to pull the trigger of his own gun. Is that correct?"

Yin nodded. He had typed up those files himself. Even though the case was ten years old, the details were still crystal clear.

Pei grunted in affirmation. "The bullet casings were all collected from the scene. Three of them were crucial pieces of evidence—mainly, the ones that struck Captain Han, Officer Zou Xu, and Zhou Ming. The blood on each of these three casings verifies the timeline of the shootout, as established by Han's statement."

He reached into his pocket and took out a copy of one of the photographs from the case files.

"This is the bullet marked with Zou Xu's blood. The ballistics report shows that it came from Zhou Ming's gun. Can you verify this for me?"

Yin examined the picture. "The report says it came from Zhou's gun. What's your point?"

"I can tell a few things from this picture, but my understanding is hazy at best. I'd like you to try to recall what the actual casing looked like when you examined it ten years ago. Did the tip of the bullet show any signs of warping or abrasion?"

"If it did, all of those details would be inside the report."

Pei grimaced to himself. He wondered if Yin was being difficult on purpose. Then again, this hadn't exactly been an easy night for him. "There was a reflecting pool not far from the scene of the shootout. Did the blood spatter at the scene indicate that Han went into the pool?"

Yin sighed, and he slumped forward. "It did. Han ran after Peng Guangfu, despite his injury. He was too winded by the time he waded into the pool. He couldn't go any farther."

"I see. Thanks for clearing up those details," Pei said, and walked away.

Yin watched Pei walk across the parking lot. When the captain's silhouette vanished, Yin finally allowed himself to exhale.

OCTOBER 25, 4:20 A.M.

ZENG'S ROOM

"Is someone from Liu Hong's old crew out for revenge?" Mu asked Zeng point-blank.

Zeng scratched his head as he considered this possibility. Mu had provided him with two compelling arguments. First, every one of Eumenides's actions seemed to be directed at the police. Now that she had looked over the case files, it seemed that the victims he had targeted eighteen years earlier were also connected to the 3/16 drug bust.

"We can't rule out that possibility. Why don't we report this during our meeting tomorrow and start an official investigation?"

"We can't," Mu said.

"Why not?" Zeng arched his eyebrows in bewilderment.

She had not forgotten the promise she made to Huang. "I have . . . an informant who has certain reservations. If this information spreads to too many people, it could threaten his personal safety. I need to show him that I'm sincere about protecting him. That's the only way I'll get him to tell me more."

"Suit yourself." Zeng shrugged. That made himself Mu's sole collaborator, and he had no objections. "What's our next move?"

"I need to find Deng Yulong. He's our only reliable source of information on this case."

"Deng Yulong." Zeng spat out the three syllables. He dashed over to his desk, navigating through the mess of wires that covered his floor, and opened his laptop. His fingers became a blur as he searched the police department's databases. "Let's see what we have on the guy." In seconds, a file was displayed on his monitor.

Mu was already at his side. Her gaze was focused on a photograph of a middle-aged man on the side of the screen. He displayed a shrewd, confident gleam. The name next to the picture read *Deng Hua*. "It's him!" exclaimed Zeng.

"What do you mean? The name is wrong." Mu was taken aback by Zeng's excitement.

"You mean you don't recognize him?" Zeng tapped his finger against the table. "He must have changed his name!"

Mu shook her head.

"You've spent too much time cooped up in the academy," Zeng said. "Even if you've never seen him before, surely you must have heard of 'Mayor Deng'?"

That rang a bell. Mayor Deng had never held any actual political position, but his moniker was an accurate description of his status. In fact, he was probably more powerful than Chengdu's actual mayor.

People in the city primarily knew Deng as a businessman. His enterprise spanned a whole array of industries: real estate, investment, international trade, dining, and even music production. His background was a mystery, but his wealth was unrivaled by anyone in the province of Sichuan.

It was less commonly known among ordinary citizens—but widely rumored among those in the know—that Deng had a wide net of connections in both legal and illegal industries. There was even a saying among locals of the province. "When Mayor Deng shouts, city hall shakes!"

Mu never would have guessed that such an imposing figure could have emerged from such a sordid background. Nor would she have ever imagined that this same man had spent years as a common police informant. No wonder he changed his name from "Deng Yulong" to "Deng Hua"; he'd wanted to cover up a less-than-illustrious past.

It wouldn't be easy getting a figure as powerful and connected as Mayor Deng to dredge up the facts of an infamous eighteen-year-old case. That would take a bit of effort.

CHAPTER NINE

BREAKING OUT OF THE COCOON

OCTOBER 25, 8:00 A.M.
THE LONGYU BUILDING

Located a short walk from the massive Tianfu Square at the heart of downtown Chengdu, the Longyu Building towered above its neighbors like a redwood among reeds. At twenty-seven stories, its height made it remarkable enough; its rounded edges and reflective black surface made it resemble a dark, massive crystal shard. The magnificent structure was the property of the Longyu Corporation, the vast business chaired by the man known as Mayor Deng. Its address, 888 Shuncheng Street, had been chosen for its auspicious connotations, as Chinese culture prized the number 8. The official explanation was that the Longyu Corporation had secured this address after a fierce bidding war. Rumor, however, said otherwise.

Mu stood in the plaza in front of the Longyu Building. She noted the similarity to its owner's original name. Deng Yulong may have convinced the world that he was now Deng Hua, but it seemed that he wasn't completely willing to give up his past.

Within minutes of arriving, she had already witnessed Deng's trademark self-indulgence. As she climbed out from the taxi, she spotted a fleet of five luxury cars swooping into Longyu Plaza. They came to a halt at the plaza's center, and over a dozen young men in black uniforms stepped out of the four Mercedes-Benz vehicles positioned to the front and rear of a Bentley in the center. Each of the men was athletic and imposing. They jogged toward the building's entrance, forming two lines leading up to the front door. When the Bentley pulled up to the entrance, a particularly tall and thickly built man emerged from the front passenger's side and opened a rear door. The security team stood at attention as their esteemed employer stepped out.

The man's large frame suggested that he had once been muscular. Yet even though the majority of this bulk had long since turned to fat, he still carried himself with grace. He strode into the building with vigorous and forceful steps, flanked by a cadre of sleek bodyguards.

This was Deng Hua, the head of the Longyu Corporation. The person she had come to question.

Her police credentials granted her quick entrance into the building, but Mu found her path blocked when she reached the desk in the spacious first-floor lobby. The receptionist and security personnel required her to state the name of the person she intended to see, explaining that she would only be permitted to enter the building's offices after obtaining permission via telephone.

Mu had no choice but to be blunt. "I'm here to see your employer, Deng Hua," she said.

The receptionist was skeptical. "Do you have an appointment?"

Mu showed her badge again. "I need to speak to Mr. Deng immediately, concerning an active investigation."

The receptionist kept a stern face, hoping her imposing manner would work in her favor. Mu did not budge. Finally, the receptionist reached for her headset and dialed an internal number.

"Brother Hua, there's a police officer here who wants to see Mr. Deng . . . Yes, she says she's here investigating a case. She wants to ask Mr. Deng some questions . . . Okay. I understand."

The receptionist smiled apologetically at Mu. "I'm sorry," she said. "Mr. Deng requires a letter of introduction first. You can come back once he's spoken with the commissioner and arranged a proper time for a meeting."

To ask for a letter of introduction may have been reasonable, but to demand that the police commissioner personally schedule a meeting? Deng's nickname of "Mayor" had clearly gone to his head. Mu glared at the woman incredulously. Despite a cheerful smile, her resistance was firm.

If Mu had been sent here by Han, she would have pushed back. She had come here on the hunch of a man whom she wasn't even sure she could trust. One wrong move could severely affect the path of her career. Given the circumstances, she decided to return to the station and try to recoup her losses.

On her way back to the entrance, she noticed something odd about the lobby. She could see herself wherever she looked. She stopped in her tracks, and then it came to her—seamless mirrors stretched along the length of each wall. It made the lobby appear much larger than it actually was, and it also gave her the unsettling impression that she was being watched.

Setting aside this uneasiness, she wondered how she could go about meeting the commissioner. Through the academy president? Or should she set this angle aside for now and return to Huang empty-handed?

Footsteps clacked behind her.

"Excuse me, Officer."

Mu turned and saw a security guard. "Yes?" she asked.

"Mr. Deng has agreed to meet with you. Come with me, please." The guard turned and pointed beyond the reception desk.

Mu tried to mask her surprise. Over at the desk, the receptionist was watching her with the receiver pressed against her ear, and when she noticed Mu looking at her, she quickly hung up.

Mu wondered why Deng—or "Brother Hua"—had had a

sudden change of heart. She had little time to ponder, though, before she and the guard arrived at the elevators.

"Please go to the eighteenth floor, Officer. There will be someone to help you once you arrive," the guard said respectfully.

The elevator arrived at the eighteenth floor, and sure enough, another athletic man in a tailored suit was waiting for her when the doors slid open.

He stood ramrod straight and towered above Mu. Around thirty years old, he had a square face and large eyes set below thick eyebrows. Mu recognized him as the man who had emerged from the Bentley. Most likely, he was Deng's head bodyguard.

Mu extended her right hand. "My name is Mu Jianyun. I'm a lecturer at the provincial police academy and a member of the city police department's task force."

"A pleasure." The man shook her hand, and looked her over. "Please call me Hua," he said.

Mu grinned. " 'Brother Hua' fits you better."

Hua remained stone-faced. "Please follow me. Mr. Deng is waiting."

The eighteenth floor was quiet and pristine. While the walls here were not reflective, Mu spotted curved mirrors mounted high at each bend in the hallway, letting her glimpse around every corner. She did not see a single company employee as they walked down the hall, apart from Deng's fit bodyguards stationed in pairs at several points along the way. Mu concluded that this level served as Deng's exclusive office space. Brother Hua led her around a corner to a burnished metal door, with a guard on either side.

Hua entered first. An alarm beeped as Mu followed him, and the two guards immediately held out their arms to bar her way.

"My apologies. Please hand any metallic objects on your person to these two members of our staff. They'll safeguard them for you until you leave," Hua explained.

It was a metal detector, Mu realized. Since she was standing in the heart of her host's territory, she saw no option but to follow his rules. With a resigned shake of her head, she handed her purse to one of the men.

The alarm went silent. With a satisfied nod, Hua turned and pointed ahead. "Mr. Deng is in the office at the end of the hall. I'll meet you back here when you two finish your conversation."

Mu finally approached Deng's office. The door was unlocked. She knocked gently, and a deep voice answered.

"Come in."

Mu opened the door to reveal a cavernous room. Twenty meters deep, it resembled a lecture hall at the police academy more than an office. The red carpet below her feet was immaculately clean. Tables, chairs, and dressers lined the carpet neatly. Each piece of furniture was black with slight hints of red. A luxurious, European-style chandelier hung from the room's ceiling. The office's most extravagant feature was the layer of crystal glass that completely covered its walls, which reflected the room endlessly upon itself. The effect was dizzying.

"Please have a seat."

The man's speech was piercing and commanding. Mu looked, and saw the imposing executive desk at the office's end. There sat a dignified man with eyes like a tiger. She recognized him as Mayor Deng.

Even for a psychologist, this environment was unnerving. She knew she had to move forward, and she strode over to the chair facing Deng. Composing herself, she sat down and sized up the man sitting in front of her.

"Your office is truly one-of-a-kind," she said.

"I don't want so much as a single shadow to exist in my room," Deng answered calmly. Indeed, the glass covering every wall ensured that he could survey the entire room with a single glance.

"From a psychological point of view, this would seem to

imply that you're afraid of something. You're afraid to lose sight of the people and things around you, and in particular you're afraid of losing control."

"What's your name, Officer?"

"Mu Jianyun. I'm a lecturer at the provincial academy and member of the 4/18 Task Force."

"Oh, the famed '4/18 Task Force,'" Deng said, nodding. He snickered. "After eighteen years, you people are still stuck on that investigation. That's police efficiency, I suppose."

The man's frank remark left Mu nonplussed. Blinking away her hesitation, she decided to be equally blunt.

"We have several new leads that could give us a valuable edge in breaking the case. However, we need your assistance."

Deng tilted forward in his seat. "Let's hear it."

"We believe there's a hidden connection between the 3/16 drug bust in 1984, the warehouse explosion one month later, and the murder of Xue Dalin." Mu scanned his expression when she mentioned this name. She was hoping for a reaction, but she saw none. The man was harder to read than a statue. "That's why I'd like to ask you a few things about the situation surrounding the case you were personally involved in," she said.

Deng shook with scornful laughter. "Given my reputation, I don't think it'll come as a surprise that I'm quite well-informed as to the details of both cases. I might know a bit more than you, in fact. Rest assured, there's no connection between them. The 3/16 drug bust was the most successful operation of its kind in the history of the Chengdu police force. It was a proud moment for the department. The 4/18 murders, on the other hand, were the crazed actions of an abnormal, overinflated ego. The fact that the case remains unsolved to this very day is a mark of shame for the Chengdu police. How could you possibly link these two cases together?"

Mu laid it all out. "One of the victims who died in the explosion on April eighteenth was named Yuan Zhibang. His ex-lover was Bai Feifei, who was Xue Dalin's administrative secretary at the time. Not long after the narcotics seizure on March sixteenth, Ms. Bai committed suicide by jumping into a river. Don't you think the connection is worth looking into? What if Ms. Bai's death was not a suicide, but some sort of prelude to the 4/18 murders?"

A stretch of time passed before the man spoke again. Mu observed his reaction closely. While years of experience had taught him to keep his emotions buried, a sense of surprise still leaked through the filter separating mind and body.

"What else have you found?"

"I was hoping that you could tell us more. Anything you can recall concerning the narcotics seizure of March sixteenth would greatly aid our investigation."

Deng sneered. "There's no reason for me to waste my time on this. I have neither the need nor the obligation to assist you."

"And yet, here I am. You've already decided to waste your time," Mu said with a smile. "Why else would you have asked me to come to your office?"

Deng shook his head several times, as though admonishing a child. "No, no, no. That's incorrect."

Mu felt the blood rush to her cheeks.

"I didn't allow you to see me so that I could help you. I did it because of this," Deng said.

He flung a sheet of paper onto his desk. Mu leaned in to read:

DEATH NOTICE

THE ACCUSED: Deng Yulong
CRIMES: Premeditated murder, racketeering, drug dealing, extortion
DATE OF PUNISHMENT: October 25
EXECUTIONER: Eumenides

"While you were fumbling around in my lobby, my assistant received this fax. And I changed my mind."

The smile vanished from Mu's face. "The twenty-fifth—that's today!"

Deng simply watched her, a subtle smile on his lips.

"Mr. Deng, I need to make a call," Mu said. She swiftly took out her cell phone and called Han's direct line.

"Officer Mu?" the captain answered. "You aren't answering your phone. I need you back at the station immediately. We're about to have an emergency meeting."

"Yes, sir. Eumenides has revealed the name of his newest target. It's Deng Hua, the head of Longyu Corporation."

"How do you know that!?" Han exclaimed. "We've only just received the death notice minutes ago."

"I'm meeting with Deng Hua at his company headquarters at this very moment."

Mu could sense Han's astonishment on the other line. "You're with Deng Hua right now? What are you doing all the way downtown?"

She could lie to Han. But what would be the use?

"I'm following a lead. I needed to ask Deng some questions," she admitted.

Mu heard a sharp breath in her ear. She expected a barrage of reprimands from her superior. At the very least, she would be in for it when she returned to headquarters. But Han's response was calm, his tone businesslike.

"You and Deng are to stay put for the time being. And tell Deng to keep himself inside and safe. He is not to set foot outside. Am I clear? We will be there any minute."

"Understood," Mu said, and she hung up.

The knowledge that officers were on the way helped ease her nerves, and she was able to start thinking about the implications of the new death notice. It had arrived almost concurrently with her discovery of Deng's connection to the 3/16 drug-trafficking case. And the execution was scheduled for this day! It couldn't be a coincidence.

Deng focused his sharp eyes on her. "Officer Mu, if my hearing hasn't failed me, it would seem that this visit of yours wasn't authorized by the investigation team at all."

"That's correct," Mu answered. "I have a personal informant and my own leads. I do have the authority to investigate independently."

"An informant?" Deng chuckled. "I'm almost impressed."

Mu took the matter more seriously. "My colleagues will be here soon to protect you. Before they arrive, you are not to leave the building. Once our people are here, they'll provide you with a detailed security plan."

Deng appeared indifferent. "So in other words, my actions need to fall in line with your orders?"

"It's a request, but I *strongly* advise that you comply." Her eyes went again to the death notice on Deng's desk, and to the date written on it. "At least for today."

"Officer Mu, there are a few things you should understand," Deng said. "First, no one can order me around. My daily itinerary is prepared long in advance, and any changes will interfere with my subsequent plans. This is unacceptable. I'll remain in my office until this evening, at which point I'll leave for the airport and take my 8:40 flight to Beijing."

"But today is unique," she said, pointing to the death notice. "Do you understand what that is? Someone is planning to murder you. This is an extremely dangerous killer."

"Which brings me to my second point," Deng continued. "Someone trying to kill me might seem extraordinary to you, but not to me. Everything I now possess was earned with my own sweat and blood. And I could fill an encyclopedia with the names of every person in the world who has wanted me dead. Do you know how much my head is worth to certain groups? A million U.S. dollars! That's more than enough money to attract any top-notch international assassin. If I were to change my personal schedule every time someone made a threat on my life, Longyu would be in chaos."

Mu shook her head. On a certain level, Deng's explanation made a great deal of sense. How many threats had the man survived during his transformation from small-time gangster to one of China's wealthiest men?

Indeed, an assassination threat would throw most people into a panic, but Deng had barely batted an eyelash at Eumenides's note.

"In spite of all those who would relish the thought of killing me," Deng went on, "I am still very much alive. No matter the price on my head, I am not so easy to kill."

"Eumenides is not like the others," Mu countered. "In the past few days, he's killed three people right under the police's very noses! It didn't matter how watertight the police's defenses were, he broke right through them! He—"

Deng cut Mu off with a wave of his hand. "I know all about this man. He killed Ye Shaohong in the plaza in front of the Deye Building two days ago. Before sunrise this morning, he killed Peng Guangfu, the suspect from the Mount Twin Deer Park police slaying, inside a mining tunnel on the city outskirts. He also killed Xiong Yuan, the SPU captain who was guarding Peng. Apparently he's killed some dozen-odd criminals who were previously wanted by the police."

Mu was amazed. As far as she knew, none of these facts had been leaked to the media. Han had insisted on an airtight seal around the investigation—which was why she had been so surprised at his apparent leniency toward this little venture of hers. Yet Deng knew almost everything. Almost.

"I've been following this case ever since Eumenides made his first post online," Deng said with more than a hint of vanity. "I'm quite a bit more capable than you have assumed. As far as I'm concerned, the city's law enforcement system has no secrets from me."

"So you *are* aware of the first murder?" Mu asked. Leaning back in her seat, she allowed herself a satisfied smirk.

Deng raised a skeptical eyebrow. "You're referring to Ye Shaohong's death?"

With a feeling not unlike satisfaction, Mu told him about Zheng Haoming.

"He was a highly decorated sergeant, respected all over the city. And he was murdered in his own apartment."

Deng narrowed his eyes. It was the first sign of vulnerability Mu had seen him display.

"We can help keep you safe. This killer has made good on every one of his threats so far."

"Only because the police were too confident in their ability to protect the public. I won't make that same mistake. You've seen the kind of capable people I surround myself with—these men will be responsible for my safety today. If the police want to stick their noses into this, they'll only be allowed to do so if they play by my rules. I do not take orders. I give them. Once your people arrive here, they can contact my personal assistant Hua, and he'll tell you what you need to do."

Mu thought back to the rigorous security measures she had witnessed upon entering the building. Deng's confidence was more than an idle boast. Even if the police could protect him, despite their recent losses, how could they be more effective than the man's personal security team? The black-suited bodyguards had been hired and trained specifically to protect Deng. They could remain at his side day in and day out—a task that would be impossible for the police.

Deng simply had no reason to trust the police over his own staff in the wake of an assassination threat.

A gentle tapping against the door broke the silence within the office.

"Come in," Deng announced, his voice having lost none of its dignity.

Brother Hua entered the room. He walked with quick, firm steps, vigor radiating as he moved. When he looked at Deng his face shone with near reverence.

"Sir, the fax was sent from an imaging shop a few miles away, on Zhengtai Street. The employees there had no idea that anyone had used their fax machine. We did some digging and found a Trojan horse on their computer. It allowed someone to control the machine remotely. Whoever set it up did a clean job; it's untraceable. This is a pro we're dealing with."

"Yes. As expected." Deng turned to Mu. "So, Officer, I believe I've made myself quite clear. Right now, you can wait for your people down in the first-floor lobby. I still have a great deal of business to take care of."

Hua walked her out of the office. Once Mu had reached the hall, the bodyguard disappeared back into his employer's grand, shadowless office.

IIIII

Deng stared at a surveillance monitor on his desk. The cameras followed Mu as she walked down the hallway and entered the elevator.

"What do you think of her?" he asked Brother Hua.

"Intelligent. Extremely perceptive. If she's an ally, we should still keep a few things up our sleeves. If she's an enemy, she's going to give us a lot of trouble."

Deng gave a noncommittal nod. "We'll see about that. She's a member of the so-called '4/18 Task Force.' She also dragged up another case from eighteen years back—the famous drug bust of March sixteenth, and ascertained that Yuan Zhibang, one of the corpses from the explosion in the warehouse that year, had an ex-girlfriend named Bai Feifei who also happened to be Xue Dalin's administrative secretary."

Hua's eyes narrowed.

"She has an informant. This person may be aware of other things." Deng's voice darkened. "Find him."

Hua nodded.

"Begin your search immediately."

Deng did not need to say anything else. He knew of Hua's skills in investigation and combat well, and trusted him to be the equal of any law enforcement officer in the country. He also knew the level of Hua's loyalty, that he would even take a bullet for his boss. Deng had no cause to worry.

IIIII

A FEW MINUTES EARLIER
POLICE HEADQUARTERS, CONFERENCE ROOM

". . . And tell Deng to keep himself inside and safe. He is not to set foot outside. Am I clear? We will be there any minute." After waiting for Mu's response, Han hung up. He turned to the rest of the task force.

Moments after Zeng and Han had received a copy of the death notice sent to Deng Hua, Han had called an emergency meeting to order. The makeup of the team differed slightly from the last meeting. In addition to Mu's absence, which Han's phone call had provided an explanation for, Liu Song had replaced Captain Xiong as the team's SPU representative.

The tragic outcome at the mine left a dark cloud hanging over the team. Everyone had bloodshot eyes and puffy cheeks due to lack of sleep.

Liu was badly shaken and barely able to pay attention while

Han delivered the report. After presenting the new death notice, Han spent several minutes briefing the team on Deng Hua, Eumenides's next target. Due to Deng's prominent status, the new development had drawn the attention of Chengdu's highest-ranking law enforcement officials. The commissioner had already ordered Captain Han to ensure Deng's personal safety by any means necessary.

Once Han finished, he gave the team the opportunity to present their own opinions. Liu spoke up first.

"I have several questions for you, Yin," Liu said, his tone as blunt and cold as the side of a glacier.

The other members looked on in wonder as the newest of their team grilled the captain's assistant.

"What questions?" Yin did his best to keep his demeanor calm.

"Earlier at the mine tunnel, you, Captain Han, and I each pressed a different switch. How do you account for the long delay between our actions and yours?" Liu paused, as if to let the accusation sink in. "It was your second time going into the cavern. How did the captain find his switch before you found yours?"

"My flashlight broke," Yin said. "I had to use my lighter to find my way ahead. It was too dark in the cavern for me to move around easily. I ran into the captain as soon as I made it back into the tunnel with the bodies. He asked me the same question."

"A broken flashlight?" Liu sneered.

"That's right," Han broke in, nodding. "We've already had our equipment technicians look at Yin's flashlight. It was broken, no doubt about it."

"Fine. Then let me ask you something else, Yin. When we pressed the switches, Xiong didn't respond over the radio. The captain and I rushed to the tunnel entrance right away. We arrived at about the same time, and Captain Xiong was already fading fast. The two of us carried him into the back of the SUV.

Meanwhile, you went straight to the driver's seat and started the engine. Would I be correct in saying that you didn't lay a single hand on Captain Xiong during this time?"

Yin swallowed dryly. Seconds passed as the room held its collective breath.

"Yes, you would be correct."

Yin's heart skipped a beat as Liu asked his final query. "Then why did I find blood on the gearshift? You were the only person to drive the SUV. How did blood get on your fingers?"

As soon as the words left Liu's lips, everyone looked at Yin's hands on the table. There was not so much as a paper cut on them.

"I . . ." Yin froze.

He glanced helplessly at Han, as if pleading to the captain.

Han turned his attention to the SPU officer. "Liu, what exactly is the point of all these questions? Just speak plainly."

"There's no way that Captain Xiong could have been killed so easily!" Liu gritted his teeth. "He was completely focused on defending Peng. How could Eumenides possibly manage to cut his throat during such a short window of time? Unless . . . Unless the killer was someone he trusted. Someone he wouldn't think to defend himself against!"

As disturbing as the accusation sounded, Pei could follow its cold logic. By the time Han and Liu had reached the ends of their tunnels, Yin had still lagged behind. There could have been enough time for him to murder both Xiong and Peng Guangfu. The bloody print on the gearshift was worth considering.

"And Peng would have been the only witness," Pei mused.

Liu nodded. His unvoiced implication was clear.

"How can you be sure that it was Yin who left the blood on the gearshift? What if it was put there earlier?" Zeng asked.

"I drove the SUV to the mine," Liu said icily, "and there was no blood on the gearshift then."

"You have the facts all wrong!" Han barked.

The SPU officer snapped to attention at the sound of Han's commanding voice, and he reined himself in. Han continued.

"When we arrived at the hospital last night, Yin rushed to help us lift Xiong out of the back. He was in such a hurry that he jumped out of the driver's seat without shifting the car into *Park*. I noticed this a little later, and I put the vehicle in the right gear myself. So if there's any blood on the gearshift, it must have been from my hand."

Zeng let out a deep exhale. "See?" he said. "This was all a misunderstanding. Just take it easy, Liu."

Liu grunted, but remained silent and disciplined.

"Liu," Han said, "we're all grieving over Xiong's death. But that doesn't give you the right to throw suspicion on one of your colleagues without grounds. None of us here can deny that Captain Xiong was a brilliant officer, but this opponent of ours is smarter and deadlier than we could ever have imagined." The captain shut his eyes. "I didn't argue with Xiong when he volunteered to stay behind. If you want to talk about the losses we suffered in these last two operations, I'm the one who should be held responsible."

The sorrow in Han's words was contagious. Liu simply hung his head, and suppressed tears.

"I've already made my decision," Han continued. "Once we solve this case, I plan to resign from my post as police captain and end my career in law enforcement. But before that happens, I will find this scum. I will bring Eumenides down with my own two hands if I have to, and I'll see that he gets the punishment he deserves!"

As Han shouted, Yin and Liu raised their chins. Zeng grinned. Pei didn't alter his morose expression.

"A new battle awaits us. I believe that this is our chance to turn the tables on our adversary, and end this once and for all!" Han swept his eyes over the faces around the conference room table. "Here are your assignments: Liu Song, before we do anything else, you will lead an SPU detail to the Longyu Building. Protect Deng Hua. He's our objective. Captain Pei, you're to assist Liu as we begin our operation."

"Understood!" Liu exclaimed. Pei, on the other hand, remained silent.

"Captain Pei, is there something you'd like to share with us?"

Pei suddenly brought his attention back to the room. He glanced at Yin and Liu. "I'll do my best to help Officer Liu complete our mission."

"Excellent. You should get going now." Han turned to Zeng. "I want you to stay behind at headquarters. You're in charge of relaying information and intelligence."

"Sure thing." This decision did not come as a surprise to him; desk jockeys were rarely assigned to the field.

Finally, Han addressed the last member of the team. "Yin, you're going to stick with me. We're going to a separate meeting with the police to discuss our security measures in more detail. As soon as we're finished, we'll head to the scene to provide support."

Yin looked at the captain. A silent understanding seemed to pass between the two men.

||||

OCTOBER 25, 9:15 A.M.

EN ROUTE TO THE LONGYU BUILDING

Captain Pei sat beside Liu in the front of a police SUV. Behind them were six of the SPU officers who had participated in the operation at Deye Plaza. Their failure on that day and the recent loss of Xiong Yuan were more than enough motivation for them to carry out their duties.

Pei had had his misgivings during the meeting, but considering the tension in the room, he had kept those thoughts to himself. Now that he and Liu were alone, he saw no need to do so any longer.

"Liu Song, something's bothering me."

"What?" Liu said, turning his attention away from the wheel.

"Han said he touched the gearshift after he arrived at the hospital. You were in the vehicle then. Did you happen to notice this?"

Liu shook his head. "I don't remember, but I can't be sure. I wasn't thinking about anything other than picking up Captain Xiong's body. I wasn't paying attention to anyone else in the SUV."

Pei understood. The officer had been in a state of intense distress, which would have made him less perceptive.

Liu seemed to sense Pei's thoughts. "You think there's something odd about that too, don't you? Is Han protecting Yin?"

By now the captain knew how candid and straightforward Liu was, and so he made no attempt to guard his thoughts. He answered calmly. "I have to say it's very likely. It's hard to imagine that someone could have managed to cut Captain Xiong's throat without a struggle. But as suspicious as these circumstances are, we haven't found a single piece of evidence that stands up to scrutiny. That's why I didn't say anything during the meeting. At a crucial moment like this, a misunderstanding among anyone on the team could prove disastrous."

"I don't want there to be any problems inside the investigation either," Liu agreed.

Pei patted the officer's shoulder. "There's a way to verify what Captain Han told us. All I need is your help."

Liu brightened. "What are you going to do?"

"If Han was telling the truth, the blood on the gearshift should contain his fingerprints. If he was lying, then the fingerprints would be Yin's. It's simple logic. No one would be able to dispute it."

"I've already thought of that." Liu shook his head in disappointment. “It would be impossible for us to run any kind of test on those prints. Any request for a print analysis would have to go through Han. And it seems you’re the only person in the whole city who thinks my suspicions are worth looking into.”

“But we don’t need to analyze anything. All we need is to go check out that SUV together.”

“Check out what, exactly?”

“To see whether the fingerprints are still on the gearshift. If the fingerprints and blood are still there, then it would mean that no one is worried someone might investigate, and our suspicions are unfounded,” Pei said. He gave Liu a moment to process the idea. “But if the blood is gone, it would imply that in spite of the impending deadline Eumenides has given us, certain team members still chose to take the time to go wipe away fingerprints. If that’s true, then we have a serious problem.”

Liu looked at Pei with admiration. He took out his cell phone, and placed a call to Wei Tangyuan, an old high school friend who now managed the parking garage at the criminal police headquarters.

||||

Two men sat across from each other inside the police captain’s office. The air inside was so thick with tension, they felt they might choke on it.

“You know the truth, don’t you? You saw those bloodstains too.”

“That’s right.”

A pause.

“Thanks for helping me keep that quiet.”

“What good does thanking me do? I’m helping you, but I don’t even know if I’m doing the right thing or not.”

“Come on. Is everything really so black and white? It’s hard to tell with some things.”

"Why? Why are you doing this?"

"I don't have any other choice."

"Are you being forced to?"

"You could say that. I made one tiny mistake, one that created a big mistake . . . and then that led to a bigger one. Once you take your first step down the wrong path, there's no turning back."

"I don't want to be on this path."

"No! I can't stop now! I still have a chance. I'm going to personally end this."

"You can't take part in this operation. Make up an excuse. Find a way out."

"So what should we do about everything that's already happened?"

"I don't know. It's too much to take in at once. For all I know, I might end up guarding this secret until I die."

||||

OCTOBER 25, 9:30 A.M.
THE LONGYU BUILDING

When Captain Pei, Liu Song, and the SPU officers arrived, Mu was already waiting for them inside the first-floor lobby.

The security guards and receptionist blocked the police officers from moving beyond the front desk. Liu displayed his police credentials, but the employees refused to budge.

"How do you like your first taste of Mayor Deng's style?" Mu grimaced. "I had to go through this charade earlier. If you want to see him, the front desk needs to contact a certain 'Brother Hua' first."

"This is ridiculous," Liu said, frustrated. "We're here to protect Deng."

"Believe it or not," Pei said, "this is a good sign. If it's this hard for us to get to him, then it certainly won't be any easier for Eumenides."

Mu smirked. "You haven't even seen the security he has farther inside the building. He even built a metal detector into the door that leads to his office. This man could live out the rest of his days inside this building. Not even a laser-guided missile could touch him. Tonight, however, he plans to catch a plane to Beijing."

"When?" Liu asked.

"His flight departs at 8:40."

Pei nodded silently as he considered the information. *Eumenides must know this too. Why else would he have specified today's date on the notice?* The airport was public, and it was one of the few places that Deng could not avoid showing his face. A showdown was imminent, and Pei's intuition told him that it would happen there.

Liu's cell phone rang, and he stepped aside to answer it.

Pei took the opportunity to question Mu. "What are you doing here?"

"I'm following a lead," she said proudly.

Before Pei had time to react, Liu approached him.

"Pei, the blood is gone! They actually did it! They wiped the fingerprints away!"

Pei was tense. His suspicions were confirmed by the evidence, and it meant a new major obstacle on the road ahead.

"What should we do now?" Though he had only known the man for a matter of days, Liu felt a sense of camaraderie with the captain from Longzhou.

After a moment of contemplation, Pei decided to let Mu in on the plan as well. "We need to go over Han's head and bypass him in the chain of command. Do either of you have the connections to make that happen?"

"I can give it a try," Mu answered, despite her uncertainty as to what Pei meant. "But regardless, I hope you're going to fill me in on what's going on here first."

Before either man could answer, Brother Hua approached. Pei's shoulders stiffened and he shifted into a defensive posture.

"Pei Tao?" Hua said.

The captain shifted uneasily under the man's gaze. "Do you know me?"

"Mr. Deng is looking for you. I'm going to have to ask you to accompany me upstairs. As for your friends," he said, motioning over at Mu and Liu, "they can wait here in the lobby. Mr. Deng has specifically instructed me that he would like to meet privately with Captain Pei in order to discuss how to best coordinate our security efforts."

Mu had been prepared for this. Liu, on the other hand, fumed at the bodyguard. He grunted in anger, but knew that he still had to carry out the mission and there was no time for an outburst.

"I need five minutes. There are a few things I still need to discuss with my colleagues," Pei said to Hua.

"My employer wishes to speak to you about a very urgent matter, and I believe it would be preferable for you to take the time to see him now. You may continue your discussion when you return."

Behind Hua's diction lay a domineering force, which left no room for dissent. After considering his options, Pei decided that he had no reason not to meet with Deng before proceeding to other matters.

"I'm going upstairs," he told Liu. "Stay put for the moment. We'll go over everything when I get back. And please, don't do anything reckless. The truth won't be as simple as you think."

Liu nodded. After the events of the previous day, he saw no need to question the captain.

On their way up to the eighteenth floor, Hua radioed ahead to inform his boss of Pei's impending arrival. When Deng's voice crackled through the speaker, Pei could hear the impatience in his voice.

Pei was led to Deng's office, and he gasped at the room's broad extravagance and the sparkling adornments that covered its walls. The captain quickly collected himself, and sat down in the chair facing Deng's desk. Hua took his customary place at Deng's side.

"Officer Pei." After sizing up the man, Deng nodded slightly, as if making a courteous gesture. "A pleasure to meet you."

"Likewise." Pei mirrored Deng's nod.

"Let me get to the point. You're a police captain from Longzhou. What brings you here to Chengdu?" he demanded.

Pei didn't flinch. "I received a letter from Eumenides."

"Another one of his 'death notices'?" Deng asked, seemingly amused. "When's this character supposed to do you in, I wonder?"

"It wasn't a death notice," Pei clarified. "I received an actual letter."

"Why would Eumenides be interested in you?"

"I could ask you the same question."

Deng snorted to himself. He flashed Pei a smile as authentic as a plastic rose. "It would seem we have a few things in common. Both of us have received notes from Eumenides, and we were both close to people who received death notices eighteen years ago. For you, it was Yuan Zhibang. And myself? I counted Xue Dalin among my closest friends."

"Good friends?" Han had mentioned nothing about Deng's previous life during their briefing earlier. His jaw slightly agape, he asked, "What do you mean? Exactly how close were you to Xue Dalin?"

"You aren't familiar with the narcotics bust that took place eighteen years ago?"

"Of course," Pei replied without hesitation. "It's legendary around these parts. I was still studying at the provincial academy back then. Everyone majoring in criminal investigation was talking about that case. It's a classic example of how to work with a police informant."

Pei's description brought a sincere grin to Deng's face. He couldn't deny the satisfaction of hearing about his life's turning point from a police officer such as Pei.

"I was the insider. I'm Deng Yulong."

Pei was stunned. He never would have guessed that the man sitting before him was the "one-man army" that had become a legend among the Chengdu police force. Pei's mind raced—Xue Dalin had received a death notice eighteen years ago, and Deng Hua had just received one now. Both men had been involved in the same narcotics case eighteen years ago. Was it more than coincidence?

"Did you know Bai Feifei?" Deng asked.

"Bai Feifei?" The name seemed to ring a bell. Pei knitted his brows in thought. Finally, it came to him. "She used to date Yuan Zhibang. The offenses listed on Yuan's death notice included womanizing, which was in regard to her."

Deng had kept his eyes fixed on Pei this whole time. Now a look of relief came over him.

"Captain Pei, I believe our conversation is finished. It was a pleasure talking to you." Deng sounded relieved.

"Is that it?" Pei didn't follow, but something told him that a man like Deng wouldn't make this much of an effort to see him just to ask several random questions.

"Yes, it is." Deng glanced at his watch. "I need to hold a group-management meeting at ten. That's in five minutes. I'm needed in the meeting room next door."

Pei involuntarily checked his own wristwatch. "Your watch is fast. It's exactly 9:50 right now."

"A habit of mine. My time is always five minutes ahead of everyone else's. That way, even if I'm five minutes late, I'm still on time."

It wasn't a bad habit, Pei mused. But as a police officer, he always kept his personal clock aligned with the precise time.

Of course.

"Officer Pei," Hua said, taking a step forward, "you can go back downstairs now. Don't you still need to discuss something with your colleagues in the lobby?"

"Yes, I do!" Pei shot out of the chair and strode to the door, running out as soon as he could and even breaking into a jog.

Hua gaped after the officer. "What was that about? He can't be Mu's informant, can he?"

Deng offered a confused shake of his head. "No. There's one thing we can be sure of—he isn't the person we're looking for."

"Then the task before us is clear. Sheng and the others left half an hour ago. We should have some information coming in soon."

"You and Sheng have both proven your value in the past. I'm confident that I won't be disappointed. Besides, the person they're dealing with can barely walk. But there's no need for you to concern yourself with that at the moment," Deng said, rising from his seat. "Come with me to the conference room."

Hua followed his employer into the next room.

⁞⁞⁞⁞⁞

Downstairs, Pei stepped out of the elevator and into the first-floor lobby. As soon as they spotted him, Liu and Mu gathered close.

"That was fast. What did you two talk about?" Mu asked.

"Captain Pei," Liu blurted, "what are we going to do? Should we call the city department or provincial supervisors now?"

Pei suspected that Liu had already convinced himself that Yin was connected to Xiong's death, and wanted to arrest him as soon as possible. However, there were more urgent matters at hand. "No, there isn't enough time now," Pei said. "I have a situation, and I need to leave right away. You two stay here. Don't do anything until I get back."

"What's going on?" Mu asked. "This isn't like you."

"Then what do we do about Yin?" Liu was dumbfounded. "Are we just going to leave it alone?"

The captain's mind was racing, and he forced himself to focus. "Deng's plane leaves at 8:40 tonight. I'll be back before five, when we go to the airport. Nothing will go wrong as long as he doesn't leave this building. Do the both of you understand?" The two of them nodded. "Just remember what I said, and don't do anything until I'm back."

Pei couldn't bear to wait another second. He had finally seen through the paradox. The two-minute discrepancy, the eighteen-year wait. It all made sense.

There was just one question he needed to answer—*Why?*

||||

Twenty minutes later, Pei arrived at the Cockroach Nest. Once he had navigated the shabby alleyway, the dim apartment lay ahead of him. His blood ran cold.

He was already too late.

The door was wide open, but no one was there. Once inside, Pei saw that the home was far more cluttered than it had been during his last visit. The table and chairs had been overturned and the blanket had been torn apart. Huang's collection of miscellaneous trash was scattered all over the floor.

Someone had ransacked this apartment. Pei poked through the mess with his foot, trying to find some clue as to when Huang had left. It was impossible to tell. What interested him more was the suggestion that someone—or perhaps even more than one person—had come by this apartment in hopes of finding something.

Where had he gone? What had these other people been looking for? And had they already found it?

Questions swam through his mind like eels through a muddied river. He wracked his brain, but was unable to fit any of the pieces into a narrative that made sense.

Huang must have known that Pei would come. He had known ever since Pei had mentioned the two-minute discrepancy during his previous visit.

Perhaps he was hiding in some dark corner, chuckling to himself smugly. Pei stepped into the doorway of the apartment and peered in each direction. He clenched his fists, took a deep breath, and roared out into the alley.

An elderly woman poked her head out of a window in the opposite building and gaped at him. Pei turned and saw a pair of older men staring back at him as well. Both looked to be in their late fifties or sixties, and both wore dark faux-leather jackets.

"Where are you? Come out and face me!" he yelled.

||||

The burned man watched the apartment from his hidden spot. Beyond the alleyway, the sunlight streamed through the window of a nearby residential building, allowing for a clear view of the alley. However, the sunlight also rendered the man invisible to anyone at the apartment who might be looking for him.

Within the past hour he had seen a team of black-uniformed men enter his home. He knew who the men were, and why they had come.

The plan, his gambit, still had a real chance at success.

Originally, he hadn't even had the need to make such a move. But his opponent was extremely troublesome, and had forced the man's hand.

When they came to his apartment, it confirmed his hypothesis.

"It isn't that I don't want to face you. This simply isn't the appropriate place," he murmured, his voice ghostly. He descended the stairs one step at a time, hobbling against his cane.

It's time for this to end. Let's finish this last move together, he thought. *No matter how elegant the preceding movements were, the piece won't work unless it ends on just the right note.*

CHAPTER TEN

THE BIRTH OF EUMENIDES

OCTOBER 25, 11:03 A.M.
THE JADE GARDEN

The Jade Garden restaurant was located at the southern end of Xingcheng Road, right in the center of Chengdu's industrial development zone, an area packed with startups and up-and-coming businesses. The restaurant was relatively small, but its elegant interior design had turned it into a favorite destination among the local white-collar workforce. By 11:00 a.m., customers were already streaming through its doors. The restaurant staff went about their regular work, which was the well-organized chaos of any busy restaurant.

A man approached the restaurant. He was wearing a long trench coat with a broad hood that hung over the upper half of his face. He had concealed the rest of his features beneath a white air-pollution mask. While a mask like this was common, especially in China's larger cities, the combined effect of his outfit was odd, to say the least. With his head lowered, the man's entire body retreated into the trench coat, like a wounded animal taking shelter from a storm.

He leaned on his cane as he walked, his right leg trailing limply behind him. The man shambled into the restaurant one cautious step at a time.

In spite of the customer's appearance, the hostess greeted him with a warm and welcoming smile. "How many people are in your party, sir?"

Ignoring her, the man walked straight toward a table nestled in a corner of the restaurant. There were no windows nearby and few people had chosen to sit there.

He deliberately sat at the table closest to the juncture of the walls. From this cramped angle, he had a full view of the restaurant's interior.

A server handed the man a menu, but he gently pushed it away. "I'm not hungry," he said, his voice sounding as if it were trying to claw its way out from his lungs. "I'd like to speak to Ms. Guo."

"Is there something you'd like to speak to her about?" the server asked. The man's question had caught her off-guard. She tried to get a closer look at him, but he kept his head low. The mask obscured most of his face.

"I'm here to collect on a debt," he said.

"And your name?"

"Tell her that an old friend sent me."

Perplexed, the server walked away to fetch her boss.

The owner of the Jade Garden was a twenty-seven-year-old woman named Guo Meiran. Her rather attractive appearance was complemented by a spirited personality. Every day she would stop by the restaurant to check on the front counter and kitchen. After the server informed her of the man, she emerged from the kitchen and surveyed the situation. No matter how hard she searched her memory, she remembered nothing about a debt, and certainly not one to a man who looked like the one she saw sitting in the corner. She hesitated before walking over to the table. If she was startled by the man's appearance or his message, she did not show it.

"How may I help you, sir?"

The man tilted his head to look at her. "I'm here to collect on a debt."

"I heard. What exactly do you feel I owe you?" she asked, smiling.

The man finally lifted his head. His eyes were so blood-red that Guo had to fight the urge to shriek.

"You owe me nothing. I'm here on behalf of Xu Yunhua."

Her previously friendly tone was replaced by an icy chill. "Who are you?"

Rather than answer, the man reached out and seized Guo's left wrist. The owner felt a cold sensation upon her flesh. When she looked down, she saw a pair of handcuffs linking her wrist to his.

"Let go of me!" she demanded. She tried to wrench herself away, but the man held on with a strength that felt almost inhuman. Guo lost her balance, and as she staggered down the man yanked her onto the seat adjacent to his.

"What in the world is wrong with you?" Guo's fear overwhelmed all her other thoughts, and ignored the other customers around her. She raised her voice and cried out, "Call the police!"

Guo's cries stirred the server, who dashed into the kitchen. The customers inside the dining area, on the other hand, twisted around for a better look at the commotion.

Keeping a firm grip on Guo with his right hand, the man removed his hood. Then he slowly peeled off his mask and revealed his true face. A chorus of gasps filled the restaurant.

A ghastly face met their eyes, broken and twitching and covered with scars. The corners of his lips were split open to expose teeth that gleamed harsh white, forming a grotesque grin.

Guo let out a piercing cry. "Wh—who are you? Why are you doing this?"

At that moment, several employees burst through the kitchen doors into the dining area. At the front of the group was a pudgy man with a vicious look on his face and a broad cleaver in his hand. While the others stood frozen by the still swinging kitchen doors, he steeled himself and advanced. Brandishing the blade before him, he called out to the man.

"Hey! You heard what she said. Let Ms. Guo go!"

Rather than replying, the man at the table reached his left hand into a pocket of his trench coat.

The heavyset employee tensed, and held his cleaver before his chest. In a stern tone he demanded, "What's that you're reaching for? Put it down on the table right now!" He looked back and yelled, "Someone call the police!"

"I'm afraid I can't exactly put this down." The man lifted an object in his free hand.

"What the hell is that?" The employee swallowed, but his mouth was drier than sawdust.

"It's a detonator. To be more precise, it's a detonator for a bomb." He peeled open his coat as he spoke. There was a plastic box clipped to his waist, and a lead wire ran from the box to the device in his hand. "If I so much as loosen my grip, the bomb will explode."

Waves of panicked cries filled the restaurant, and people began scrambling over one another in an effort to run to the doors. The would-be hero holding the cleaver hesitated, but seconds later he joined the fleeing crowd.

It took less than half a minute for the restaurant to empty. Only Guo and the disfigured man remained inside, both nestled in the room's far corner. She was frightened beyond words, lacking even the strength to struggle with the man. All she could do was cry out while choking with sobs, "Help . . . Someone help me."

||||

While Guo Meiran shivered in fear, Captain Han was leading a team of police into the Longyu Building. One member of the investigation team, however, was not among them.

Officer Liu Song, head of the SPU team, scanned the new arrivals. "Where's Yin?" As far as he was concerned, finding Yin was just as important as carrying out the current operation.

"No idea," Han said. "I haven't seen him since the meeting, and he isn't answering his phone."

"He's on the run," Liu said, swelling with excitement. "This proves he's connected to Xiong's death! Why haven't you sent someone to arrest him?"

"It isn't up to you to decide if one of my officers is fleeing!" Han shouted. "Our primary task is to ensure Deng Hua's safety. This order comes straight from the top. If you can't get that through your head, I have full authorization to remove you from the task force."

Mu walked over to Liu and pulled him aside. "Control yourself," she whispered. Even though she didn't fully understand why Liu was so anxious, she was sure that this was no time for anyone to lose sight of their objective.

Liu Song took a deep, steadying breath. He was certain Han was covering up for Yin, but he had to focus on what Pei said before he left: *Don't do anything until I get back*.

In a way, Han was right—the most important mission was to protect Deng from being Eumenides's next victim. Liu refocused on the task at hand. They had to stop Eumenides now.

Brother Hua had also arrived at the first-floor lobby. He relayed Deng's earlier command to Han—the captain was to meet him inside the office, where they would discuss how to carry out their joint security arrangements.

Han's cell phone rang just as he was preparing to enter the elevator. The screen told him that the call was coming from police headquarters. He answered.

"Captain," said Zeng on the other line, "there's been a new development."

"Fill me in."

"There's a hostage situation at a restaurant called the Jade Garden on Xingcheng Road. The suspect is wearing an explosive, and he's handcuffed himself to the owner."

"Let the local police take care of it!" Han snapped. "You called to tell me that at a time like this? I don't want to hear about anything that isn't related to our case!"

"But it *is* related!" Zeng shouted. "The local officers stationed in the city's development zone are already at the scene, and they've even made initial contact with the suspect. He has demands. He wants to see three people in particular."

"Out with it, Zeng. Who does he want to see?"

"Mu, Pei, and Deng Hua," he listed. "There's more. The suspect . . . It's the lone survivor from the warehouse explosion eighteen years ago. Huang Shaoping."

After a tense few seconds of thought, Han replied with a new order. "Contact Mu and Pei immediately. Tell them to get to the restaurant as soon as possible."

"What about Deng?"

"Out of the question," Han replied without hesitation. "We're supposed to be devoting all our manpower to his personal safety. How could we even consider sending him into such a dangerous situation?"

"I'll go," Hua interrupted. He had been standing next to the captain the entire time. "I can represent Mr. Deng in this matter."

Somewhat annoyed at the man's acute hearing, Han studied the bodyguard closely. He had no objections to sending the man to the restaurant in Deng's stead, aware that Hua's employer was the key to unlocking the entire case. No matter what kinds of challenges might come up on the edges of this operation, he needed to protect Deng. His future depended on it.

IIIII

FIFTEEN MINUTES LATER

Pei squirmed against the police SUV's leather seat. Mu was sitting next to him, her eyes fixed on the storefronts flitting past the window outside. At the rear of the vehicle sat Deng Hua's head bodyguard, his features fixed in an inscrutable expression.

Needless to say, it was not an enjoyable ride.

When the police vehicle pulled up to the Jade Garden, its passengers saw that the local police had already secured the area surrounding the building. Because of the bomb threat, they had cordoned off a 100-meter radius around the restaurant. However, they could not stop all the curious onlookers from gathering behind the barrier, and the officers' repeated warnings had not persuaded most to leave. Reporters were also flooding into the area, each of them hurrying to claim a prime spot.

As the three of them exited the vehicle, a middle-aged police officer approached. He introduced himself as Sergeant Chen, the officer in charge of the scene.

"I'm ready to go inside the restaurant," Pei said grimly.

Sergeant Chen shook his head. "Not so fast. The suspect has demanded that Ms. Mu go inside first. Then Brother Hua and then Pei."

One of the local officers handed Mu a bulletproof vest. She slipped into the heavy piece of gear as if it were made of cardboard. The vest rose and fell with each breath she took. Her breathing was speeding up, Pei noticed.

"You don't have to do this, Mu," he told her.

"Yes, I do. And besides, it's not me that I'm worried about. Out of the three of us, you're in the most danger. You're the last one he wants to see."

Pei had nothing to say in reply, and Mu walked toward the restaurant. She reached the door and entered the dining area alone.

The disfigured man had not moved at all from his position at the table in the corner. For the police waiting outside, it was a blind spot. The only way to keep an eye on him was to enter.

Guo cowered at the man's side, shivering like a falling leaf. She looked up with weak hope when she heard Mu enter.

Raising his hand, the man called Mu over. "Hello, Mu!" He was calm, even a little friendly.

Mu approached the two individuals and sat across from them. "Huang, what are you doing?" she asked.

"I'm out of options," he said, squinting at Mu. "You're the only one who can help me."

"What do you mean?"

"I've already been found out. My life is in danger," he rasped. "I'm up against a powerful foe here. Too powerful for me to stand a chance against in an honest fight. The only way for me to stay alive is to hole up here and attract everyone's attention any way I can."

Mu could hardly believe it. Even if what he said was true, couldn't he have chosen a less drastic method? "We can't let you harm innocent people." She pointed to Guo Meiran. "Let her go before it's too late. I'm sure you can hear all those officers outside—do you honestly think they won't be able to protect you?"

At Mu's words, Guo turned her head toward Huang. "Please . . . ," she shuddered.

He shattered the trembling woman's hope with a firm shake of his head. "No." Turning to Mu, he said, "Besides you, there's no one I trust."

Mu wasn't sure if she should consider his trust an honor or a disgrace. After some thought, she said, "If that's true, you can let her go. Take me as your hostage. I'll stay here with you."

"That won't work. There are still important things that I need you to take care of. You need to find out as much as you can about the person pulling the strings here, and you need to do it as soon as possible. If you succeed, it may help me break free of the danger I'm facing. I've already told you that the 3/16 narcotics bust is the key."

"I've stayed true to my word—I haven't told anyone else about you. You're getting too anxious. I've already found a few leads; just give me some more time."

"No, I can't give you any more time. Although . . ." His voice was a hair louder than a whisper. "I can give you a final clue."

Mu perked up. "What kind of clue?"

He looked over at Guo. "Reach into my pocket and take out what you find." Her right hand shaking in fear, the hostage obediently reached into the man's coat. After fumbling inside, she extracted a sealed envelope and an opaque plastic bag that had been wrapped up tight and sealed with thick tape. "Hand the bag to the officer," he said, and she gave the package to Mu.

Mu felt something slim and rectangular inside the bag. Just as she was about to rip the tape off and open it, he stopped her.

"No," he said sharply. "You can only open the package after you leave, when you're alone. It's vital that no one else see what's inside."

What kind of secret could he possibly be hiding? "Does that mean that I should leave now?"

"Yes. Tell Deng's man to come in next." He focused his sight deeply on Mu. "Remember, how this game finally ends is up to you."

At the sight of that face staring at her, Mu repressed a shiver. She shook off her unease and left, just as he bid her to. She had a new lead, and the first thing she needed to do was to find out what was actually going on.

When Sergeant Chen saw that Mu had exited the restaurant, he rushed over.

"What happened in there? Does he have any new demands?" Chen asked.

"He wouldn't let the hostage go. He wants to see Brother Hua."

Mu took off the vest and hurried away from the crowd. She searched for an isolated area, but police officers and reporters had flooded the entire perimeter. She sprinted down the road and flagged a taxi, finally securing her escape from the horde of reporters behind her.

Hua watched Mu depart the scene, his eyes as sharp and focused as a sniper's.

"What the hell was that about?" Sergeant Chen asked, hiding his humiliation beneath a look of confusion.

Pei couldn't hide his puzzlement either. "I have no idea."

Hua donned a bulletproof vest, just as the psychologist had done, and prepared himself.

A minute later, he was sitting down at the corner table across from Huang and Guo. "Mr. Deng won't be coming to see you. Therefore, I've come as his proxy." Hua's speech was level and self-assured, despite the bomb mere feet in front of him.

"I never expected him to come. We're talking about a man who is worth more than his weight in gold, after all." A crafty gleam flashed in his eyes. "The fact that you came here personally, Brother Hua, is flattering enough."

"You know who I am?" Hua said, stone-faced.

"You were born Rao Donghua. Your parents died when you were very young, and you moved into an orphanage at the age of five. Mayor Deng took you in and paid for your education. He also paid for your training in close-quarters combat, driving, and firearms, to mention just a few fields. After all, as his bodyguard, you need to be as sharp as our best-trained police. Your gratitude for the man is so profound that you would follow him through hell if he asked."

"Well, now," Hua said with a chuckle, "I never imagined that anyone would take interest in a life as miserable as mine. One correction, though. I'm sharper than any cop."

Huang let out a sigh. "If you look at it a certain way, you and Deng aren't so different."

Hua had no desire to mince words. "Who are you?"

"I'm someone who knows things." Huang drew his lips back, and a touch of smugness crept into his voice. "Like all the secrets surrounding a certain narcotics seizure eighteen years ago."

"That's it?" Hua sneered. "That's ancient history. Deng's one of the most powerful men in the entire province. I don't care about these so-called secrets of yours. You're nothing but a cripple. A weakling."

"There's no denying the influence Deng holds. Next to you, I'm merely a speck of dust," Huang said. Brother Hua merely shrugged. "But there's something he's asked you to find. Something you just haven't been able to track down. Isn't there?"

Hua's eyes twitched, and his pupils dilated.

It was hard to tell through all the horrific scars, but Huang was smiling. "Yes. What about the tape? You know the one I mean. Wouldn't you say that tape holds a certain influence of its own? Such as the power to strike fear in the hearts of certain well-connected people . . ."

"Speak."

"I have a copy of the tape."

"In other words, you're throwing your own wretched life away." Hua's words were more frigid than an arctic winter.

Huang did not so much as flinch. Laughter hissed from inside his damaged chest. "I've been a cripple for quite a long time. Death would have been a much kinder fate than what I've been through these last eighteen years. The only reason I keep clinging to this miserable life is so that I can see the day when everyone knows the truth behind the famous 3/16 drug bust. I had all but lost hope, until recently. See, I've found someone I can trust. She's capable and determined, and she has the guts necessary to uncover the secrets that have stayed hidden all these years. I trust her. Even if I die, she'll be able to make this dream of mine a reality."

"Did you give it to her?" Hua shot him a stern look He thought back to Mu's encounter just moments earlier—and remembered the plastic bag that she carried out from the restaurant.

Huang snickered, but did not speak. *Sometimes silence says more than words,* he thought.

Hua jumped up from his chair. Glaring at the man, he said in a voice drained of all warmth, "You aren't just signing your own death warrant. You're signing hers, too."

Without another word, the bodyguard stormed outside, and dashed through the police barrier without so much as acknowledging Chen's questions. The sergeant watched helplessly as Hua ignored him. For the second time that day, he burned with humiliation.

As Hua emerged from the perimeter around the Jade Garden, several black-uniformed men broke away from the crowd. They converged upon his position in seconds. Hua addressed two particularly menacing-looking bodyguards. He pointed toward the intersection where Mu had last been seen. The two bodyguards nodded, and they disappeared into one of the three black Mercedes-Benzes parked alongside the road. The car sped off with a screech of rubber. Moments later, Hua and the rest of the bodyguards got inside the remaining two vehicles.

||||

Pei drew a sharp breath as he watched the luxury cars pull away. His turn to face the man had finally come. He declined the vest the officers offered him. There was no need for him to bother taking any excessive precautions. Even if he did, how much protection could a mere vest offer from a bomb in his face?

He walked alone into the empty restaurant.

Pei approached the far corner, and his gaze settled on the

man's tattered features. He searched his memory in an attempt to match the face to images from his past. Yet it proved impossible. The explosion had completely disfigured him, transforming a dashingly handsome young man into a bizarre gargoyle.

If not for the secret hidden within the discrepancy between the police files and his own memory, Pei never would have realized this man's true identity.

He reflected on the chain of logic that had led him to this unavoidable conclusion.

Despite the skepticism Mu had shown toward his theory about the two minutes missing from the eighteen-year-old police report, Pei was more convinced than ever that the error was concealing something much larger. It was the same hunch that had led him to hope that Meng had not perished in the explosion, but the dental cast at the evidence center had shattered it.

Pei was unable to stop thinking about the paradox. He had locked himself inside his room for hours last night, but no matter how he analyzed this contradiction, he had still been unable to unravel it. With no solution in sight, he began to suspect his own sense of time. He wondered whether the discrepancy even existed at all. These doubts had plagued him until this morning, when his interview with Deng had given him sudden clarity.

All those years ago, according to the clock in his room, he had lost Meng's signal on the walkie-talkie at precisely 4:15 p.m. But the police report stated the explosion was at 4:13.

There was one simple possibility that explained everything.

Someone had adjusted his clock.

Whoever manipulated his clock would have been certain their actions would remain undiscovered—he or she would have anticipated that the police would seal off Pei's room for investigation once they discovered Meng's note to him, and the death notice for Yuan. Likewise, this individual would have also expected Pei, as a person involved in the case, to be taken to police headquarters for a long period of questioning. With no one to wind the clock in his absence, the timepiece would already have stopped by the time Pei returned to his room, thus covering up the secret.

More questions immediately arose.

Why would someone make his clock run fast?

Who had the opportunity to do it?

The more Pei pondered, the harder it was for him to ignore the one name that kept rushing to the forefront of his thoughts.

Yuan Zhibang.

As his roommate, Yuan would have had multiple opportunities to adjust the clock. He would have been aware of Pei's fixation with precise timekeeping as well. Only he and Pei knew how exact the clock's time was—and that even an adjustment of several minutes would throw off Pei's sense of time.

But what could Yuan have hoped to achieve with this deception?

Pei reimagined the eighteenth of April in light of his new theory. He came to two conclusions: first, that Yuan most likely survived the explosion; and second, that the abrupt end of the transmission from Meng had been staged. According to his final conversation with Meng, Yuan had been about a meter away from her with a bomb strapped to his body. If that had been true, neither of them could have possibly survived an explosion.

It followed that there had in fact been two explosions. One had been real; the other faked. The staged explosion would have occurred when Pei lost the signal. It led him to mistakenly assume that both Yuan and Meng had died. But Yuan actually did still have a two-minute window in which he could subdue Meng and escape before the actual explosion.

Pei concluded that this was the reason Yuan must have adjusted the clock—to cover up the staged explosion, and give himself time to escape.

Yet the very existence of a time discrepancy brought new questions. Yuan must have been trying to eliminate doubt about the time, but how did he fail to execute his scheme properly?

The moment the staged explosion ended Pei's conversation with Meng, the hands on his clock indicated the time was 4:15. Yuan would have wanted Pei to believe that was when the explosion occurred. But the explosion happened at 4:13.

No one knew Yuan better than Pei, and no one was more aware of how meticulous a thinker and planner Yuan had been. If he had intended to detonate the bomb, then there was no way that its earlier detonation could have resulted from an oversight in planning.

Something had gone wrong inside the warehouse. Something that Yuan had been unable to prevent. Whatever it was, it had caused the real bomb to detonate early. Yuan, who Pei could only assume intended to emerge unscathed from the ashes of his own staged death, had been unable to escape in time. Instead he had emerged burned beyond recognition.

Pei walked through the evacuated restaurant, and stared at the changed creature sitting in the corner. Step by step, he drew closer to the man who had once been his closest friend. Two decades earlier, their relationship had been one of mutual respect and admiration. But in spite of their friendship, this man had plotted to murder the woman Pei had loved.

As he sat down, Pei kept his eyes fixed on the man's scarred features, as though he were attempting to pierce that ugly visage and see through to the answers to the questions in his own heart. Yet he saw nothing. The man's bloodshot eyes locked with his. Harsh features remained static, as though they consisted only of a layer of dead and hardened skin.

A long time passed before the man across from Pei finally spoke.

"Do you hate me, Pei?"

It was a question that Pei was not even sure how to answer. Yes, he had once hated the killer behind the explosion. He had hated him from the depths of his soul. But now that he knew the truth, "hate" was far too simple a word to describe what he felt.

Pei's mind was still reeling. He had no idea how to handle the emotions rushing through him—how was he supposed to reconcile four years of brotherhood with eighteen years of pain? After all this contemplation, only one word reached his lips.

"Zhibang . . ."

"You know me better than anyone else in the world, Pei. You should know that I'm not the monster you've been imagining."

"Not a monster?" Pei gritted his teeth. "Only a monster could do the things you've done."

Huang—Yuan—shook his head as though in disapproval of this accusation. "You've been a cop for eighteen years. The number of criminals you've put behind bars is higher than I can count. I'm sure by now you've realized that many criminals aren't actually bad people at all. They break the law simply because they don't see a better choice."

"But you chose her," Pei said, his voice trembling. "Why?"

"I needed a witness to prove that I was dead. That was the only way I could go through with my plan. Once I'd seen just how well-connected my foes were, and how weak I was in comparison, I made up my mind to carry on this fight to the bitter end. I realized that there was nothing left for me to remain attached to. Not even my own life. I know how much Meng meant to you, but once I took a step back and reexamined everything from a more objective point of view, I saw things differently."

"Your plan . . . It was all for your plan . . ." Pei looked at Yuan and shook his head in disbelief. "All to become this so-called Eumenides?"

"You think that I'm Eumenides?" Yuan laughed grimly. "You're wrong, Pei. After all, you and Meng were the ones who created Eumenides in the first place. You are Eumenides. As was she. You could say that there's a Eumenides inside many of us. People need Eumenides to exist."

Pei struck the table with his fist. "No. People need laws."

"The law doesn't bring justice. The powerful and influential can break rules however they please, and the law can't touch the people who hide in the shadows." An icy cruelty crept into his voice. "This is the reality I awoke to eighteen years ago. Are you telling me that after eighteen years on the force, you still can't see it? Or are you abandoning justice simply to refute my theory? All because you lost the girl that you loved?"

Pei was at a loss for words.

Meanwhile, stress had burned Guo Meiran's nerves to a crisp. She was catatonic. Raising his right hand, Yuan yanked the woman closer to him. She let out a weak shriek.

"Just look at this one. Once upon a time she was a server in this very restaurant. With the help of her youth and good looks, she seduced the owner and eventually convinced the sucker to abandon his wife and come running into her arms. And just like that, the former server became the boss's wife. Now she runs the shop."

Pei fixed his gaze on Guo. The young woman seemed both frightened and perplexed.

"I do love a good rags-to-riches story," Yuan continued. "But Guo here just couldn't bear it when her new husband's ex-wife took half the property in the divorce. Every day she would call the woman to harass her. She would say a few choice words—maybe tell her how she and her ex were getting along in the bedroom. The poor woman couldn't bear the humiliation. She began to suffer from depression. In the end, the ex-wife went and swallowed a bottleful of pills. Dead, just like that."

Pei just looked at Guo.

"It makes you angry, doesn't it? Guess what—the law won't touch people like her. She did every despicable thing she could, yet still she lives a comfortable life, pampered by her rich husband and squandering the rightful property of a dead woman. Can you tell me that, when faced with a crime like this one, some part of you doesn't hope for Eumenides to appear?"

Yuan turned to her. The young woman had turned ash-white.

"Open the letter," he commanded.

She dared not defy him. With meek and obedient movements, she opened the sealed envelope she had removed from his trench coat earlier. A slip of paper was inside, one that contained only five lines of precise, written script:

DEATH NOTICE

THE ACCUSED: Guo Meiran
CRIME: Second-degree murder
DATE OF PUNISHMENT: October 25
EXECUTIONER: Eumenides

Even through the fog of terror surrounding her, Guo understood the implication.

"No," she pleaded through sobs. "I'm so sorry! I'll never do anything like it again. Please, I'm begging you, both of you—forgive me, just this once—"

Yuan pulled Guo closer toward him. Pointing to Pei, he said, "Ask this police officer. Can the law forgive a killer who promises to change their ways after they've already committed a murder?"

A shiver shook Guo, and a pungent, sour smell reached Pei's nostrils. He heard a gentle trickling against the floor.

Wrinkling his nose, he forced himself to collect his thoughts and break loose from the path Yuan was attempting to lead him down.

"Eumenides . . . Someone who can reach beyond the limits of the law and punish those who commit crimes. Sure, we've all had fantasies about being a superhero or a vigilante, but—" Pei shook his head in frustration. "But no one in their right mind would actually try to apply this idea to real life! Even if Meng and I did create this character, we only did it to match wits through a few practical jokes. The idea of killing couldn't have been further from our minds."

"That's because neither of you ever faced the choice I did!" Yuan shouted, his voice like steel nails on concrete. "Everyone has crazed thoughts, but only a small number of people actually go mad. This isn't because most people are better than the rest, but simply because they lack the experiences to drive them insane! I have been through things no one else will ever understand!"

Rage deepened his voice, and he began recounting the painful history of his journey into madness nearly two decades earlier . . .

||||

It began on March 16, 1984, with the narcotics seizure that sent shockwaves through law enforcement circles throughout the province. In truth, there was far more to this case than most people would ever know.

Deng Hua—still known to the world as Deng Yulong—was barely twenty at the time but had already demonstrated extraordinary resourcefulness as well as a sharp mind. These traits would prove essential in making him an influential figure in the success of the narcotics bust. He emerged from its aftermath far richer and more powerful than anyone could have foreseen.

It was Deng who instigated the firefight with the gang members after the police surrounded them. He then ambushed both gangs, allowing the police to arrest Liu Hong's gang and the Southeast Asians. In the end, he claimed half of the drugs and money for himself.

Despite Deng's meticulous planning, Xue Dalin had seen right through him. The day following the raid, Xue called Deng into his office for questioning. However, perhaps out of reluctance to abandon the secret weapon that he had spent so much time and effort training—or maybe because he had no desire to cast a pall over his own shining reputation—the conflict between the two ended in mutually favorable terms. The silver-tongued Deng promised to destroy the drug cache he'd stolen if Vice Commissioner Xue would officially close his investigation. And in the interest of fairness, Xue took 50 percent of the drug money Deng had stashed away.

But the matter did not end with that meeting. Things became more complicated when another individual entered the picture: Xue's secretary, Bai Feifei.

The department had recently purchased a batch of imported state-of-the-art Japanese surveillance equipment. Xue had received his own set, which he left in the care of his secretary. The girl was curious about new gadgets like these, and she often entertained herself by toying with the devices while in Xue's office. Despite not having been present during Xue's secret conversation with Deng, Bai had heard and recorded the entire conversation through one of the office's new hidden microphones.

Bai was a young intern, and her experience with the harshness of the real world was meager. She snapped when she realized that the man she considered not only her superior but also a hero, had stooped so low as to make a deal with a criminal. She confronted Xue and confessed that she had overheard his conversation with Deng. She pleaded with him to rethink his actions. The deal he'd made with Deng, she told him, could ruin his career and even his life.

Xue was surprised at the young woman's heartfelt appeal, and used her naïveté to outwit her. Bai was the only person who had overheard the conversation; she had come to him before taking the time to share the incriminating tape with anyone else. Pretending to be persuaded by her plea and contrite, Xue told his secretary that he would hand all the stolen money and drugs over to his superiors. And he swore that Deng wouldn't get away with it. Bai was ecstatic to hear it—so much so that she even handed Xue the tape recording of his exchange with Deng.

Two nights later, Bai drowned in a river on the city outskirts, a short distance from the path that the girl took on her way home after work.

As Bai's supervisor, Xue publicly confirmed that the young woman's recent romantic misfortunes had caused her to fall into an unstable emotional state. According to his statement, she had even confided in him her suicidal thoughts on multiple occasions. Bai's former classmates corroborated his remarks about Bai's romantic life, and the investigation of the young secretary's death soon wrapped up as the police announced that she had committed suicide after enduring severe emotional stress.

Bai's ex-boyfriend, Yuan Zhibang, was blamed. But Yuan knew the truth. He had been framed.

Yuan had indeed been fond of young women. While his kind of serial but earnest romantic history might have raised far fewer eyebrows in twenty-first-century society, in the 1980s it had given him quite a scandalous reputation.

Yuan and Bai's relationship had gone through an initial period of tenderness, but as time went on their personalities grew to be incompatible. The abortion had been the breaking point, but the decision to go through with the procedure had been a mutual one. The two remained friends after their breakup, and they spoke in person at least once a week.

The investigation's conclusion that Bai Feifei's emotional problems had led to her suicide may have convinced everyone else, but it could not deceive Yuan. Ultimately, it took Yuan little effort to discover the truth behind Bai's death.

After confronting Xue, Bai had been thrilled at his apparent change of heart. She wanted to share this good news with someone, and Yuan was the first person she thought of. She told him the whole story from beginning to end. At the time, he had assumed that the matter was relatively cut-and-dry. Every student at the academy idolized Xue, and Yuan was proud of her for bringing their hero back from the brink.

Yuan never could have anticipated what happened next—Bai perished in a mysterious drowning, and Xue blamed her death on him. Yuan did not need to be a criminal-investigation genius to know there was more to these events than met the eye.

How was he supposed to handle such an abrupt twist of fate?

Even though he and Bai had severed their romantic ties long before her passing, that made little difference to Yuan. He vowed to avenge her death.

He had once promised Bai that he would always protect her. If anyone ever took advantage of her, he would find the person who had wronged her and make them pay.

As an academy student just weeks away from graduation, it was only natural for him to seek justice through the law. However, the only evidence supporting his story—the recording of Xue conspiring with Deng—was in Xue's hands. Furthermore, Xue and his allies had enough power and influence to silence Yuan if he pursued any legal action. Yuan realized that if he wanted to exact justice on Xue Dalin, he would have to act outside the law.

Torn between grief and anger, the young man who had spent years preparing to uphold the law began to harbor deep reservations about the very thing he was supposed to protect. He saw that villains could escape legal punishment, and that there were dark corners of society where the law would not reach.

Professor Yang, the academy's head of the criminal investigation department and one of the institution's most-admired instructors, often said that police officers and criminals were actually two sides of the same coin. Yuan now did something he had never imagined himself capable of.

He decided to use his skills and training to bring Xue and Deng to justice.

He knew that what he was considering could destroy his

chances of becoming an officer, his lifelong dream. Then, an idea came to him by way of two fellow students at the academy—his dear friend Pei; and Pei's girlfriend, Meng.

Eumenides, the vengeful trickster that had sprung from the depths of Meng's imagination, had been stirring up trouble at the academy. Pei and Meng may have been able to fool everyone else with their game, but not Yuan. He was as sharp as either of them, and even shared a room with Pei. Eumenides took on an entirely different meaning for Yuan, one more daring than anything Meng had ever conceived. In Yuan's mind, Eumenides transformed from a prankster into a true vigilante—one who could exact justice upon those whose crimes went unpunished.

In order to carry out his plan, Yuan had to set off down a path from which there was no return. His main goal: to kill Xue Dalin and Deng Yulong.

Four years at the academy had taught him to master the skills and knowledge that were mandatory for any officer on the force: explosives, lock-picking, combat, and the techniques and methodology that drive every police investigation.

Yuan knew that murdering Xue and Deng would not be easy. Deng's years of criminal experience had made him as crafty as a wolf. He maintained a high level of vigilance at all times, and had strong instincts that kept him alive. Yuan would have one shot to kill Deng. If his attempt failed, Deng would retaliate without mercy.

He was also aware that while his own skills would be invaluable in helping him accomplish these goals, they could also ultimately be his undoing. The province's police force was brimming with expert analysts and investigators. Anything could become a threat if it would lead the police straight to him. With such a large net spread out for him, where could he possibly hide?

After a long period of contemplation, Yuan knew that there was only one solution to this problem. Yuan Zhibang had to vanish. He had to become Eumenides.

Eumenides needed to be someone who had never existed. An individual without any records or files, someone whose very existence was untraceable. No matter who he went up against—whether they were a powerful criminal or the police—he would always remain out of their grasp.

Yuan needed to fake his own death. Only then could he become someone who no longer existed.

He could not do it alone. Yet at the same time, he could not reveal his plan to anyone else.

Only Pei and Meng could help him accomplish this task.

First, Yuan struck up an exchange with a nonexistent pen pal. His forged correspondence would substantiate his own supposed unfaithfulness, and disrupt the future police search for Eumenides.

Then, early on the morning of the eighteenth of April in 1984, Yuan slipped into Xue Dalin's residence with the help of his lock-picking kit while the vice commissioner slept. After he slid his razor blade across Xue's throat and set a death notice on the apartment's dining room table, Yuan located the drug money that Xue had hidden inside the apartment. The bundle of cash would eventually finance Yuan's life following his disappearance.

Yuan hid the money later that morning and made his final preparations to end his normal life. One by one, he severed each of his emotional attachments with the world.

He pretended to meet with his pen pal that afternoon. Before leaving the dormitory, he adjusted the room's clock to make it run two minutes fast, thus covering up any chronological holes in his plan. With that step complete, he left the next death notice—his own—in the stationery pouch on the door to his room. A grim sense of satisfaction flowed through him when he penned this particular notice.

Once he finished these preparations, Yuan left the dormitory. He ran across Meng outside, wanting her to believe that it was a chance meeting. He told her where he was going, and mentioned that Pei would be back in his room soon. Pei wanted Meng to wait for him inside their room, Yuan told her, and specifically asked her to bring her radio.

Yuan had already planted a disruptor inside the radio, so that he could kill the signal when necessary. Next to the disruptor, he had installed an additional countermeasure mechanism containing a small amount of gunpowder—essentially a tiny bomb. It would be strong enough to stun anyone who was holding the radio up near their face, rendering them unconscious long enough for Yuan to detonate that bomb's much larger, and deadly, brother.

Meng spotted the death notice as soon as she arrived at the room. Naturally, she had assumed that Pei had penned the immaculately inked characters. After leaving a note of her own in the room, she rushed to the location that Yuan had happened to mention during their encounter outside.

To her surprise, the location turned out to be an abandoned warehouse. Despite her reservations, she entered the building. Inside she found Yuan chained to the wall, with an explosive device strapped to his chest.

Yuan had already changed into the scrap collector's clothing by this time, but Meng's panic at seeing the explosive overshadowed any suspicious thoughts that might have otherwise occurred. Her immediate reaction was that he needed to get in touch with Pei, which was exactly what Yuan had planned for. As 4:13 drew closer, he prepared to trigger the signal disruptor inside Meng's walkie-talkie, cutting off the call.

As Meng struggled to disarm the bomb according to Pei's desperate instructions, Yuan thumbed the remote control stashed in his clothes. The disruptor killed the radio signal, and the tiny bomb exploded in Meng's hand. The blast stunned Meng, knocking her out as planned.

Back in his dorm room, Pei heard a short burst of static come from his radio . . . and then nothing. He glanced up at his clock at that very instant. Even as shock rooted his feet to the ground, he saw the time: 4:15.

Yuan moved quickly. He pulled Huang Shaoping, a beggar he had befriended in anticipation of this day, out from the cement tunnel the man called home. He handcuffed Meng and Huang together. After checking the time, he set the deadly bomb to detonate at 4:15, in two minutes. This would ensure that Pei's testimony would confirm the actual time of the explosion, and also give Yuan just enough time to escape the blast.

In 120 seconds, the man known as Yuan Zhibang would die bathed in flames. Eumenides, an individual without a single personal record or file, would emerge from the ashes of the demolished warehouse.

||||

It *had* been a brilliant plan, Pei admitted. He also knew, however, that something must have gone terribly awry.

Yuan's eyes were distant as he peered eighteen years into the past.

"It was Meng. I underestimated her. And she was the last person I should have underestimated." Pei heard a hint of admiration in Yuan's solemn words. "Both of us have matched wits with her. And in the end, both of us lost."

"What did she do?" Pei said, unable to keep his voice from shaking.

Yuan squinted, and continued to recount what had happened inside the warehouse.

||||

It was 4:13. Two minutes remained before the explosion.

Meng drifted back to consciousness. Her face was warm with

blood, her ears were ringing, but she was sharp, and her wits quickly returned to her.

Yuan was gone, and she was handcuffed to a stranger. The man's eyes were shut, and he was motionless. Meng couldn't tell whether he was dead or unconscious. Then she noticed the explosive device attached to the man's waist. The timer was counting down, second by second.

She quickly inspected the bomb, but she had no idea how to disarm it. Only a minute remained on the timer.

Meng looked up and frantically searched her surroundings. She spotted a figure retreating into the distance. Comprehension came to her. It was a trap.

"Yuan Zhibang!"

He stopped. Yuan turned around and met Meng's eyes. Time seemed to stop as guilt and sorrow darted over his features.

"I'm sorry," he said softly, before turning back around and walking toward the warehouse exit.

"You son of a bitch! Stop and look at me!"

A magnetic force emanated from her. Yuan, almost at the door, stopped again in sudden shock. He turned around to look at Meng. Even then, he was still confident that everything was under his control. She could do nothing to interfere with his plan.

Less than a minute until the bomb would detonate, but he only needed seconds to reach the exit. Just enough time for him to flee, but impossible for Meng to free herself. What would be the harm of delaying his escape by just a few seconds?

That was his mistake—he assumed that Meng *wanted* to save herself.

Glaring at Yuan, she grabbed the bomb's lead wire and yanked.

Yuan gaped in horror as he realized what she was doing. She had no intention of surviving. At once he leaped for the warehouse exit, but it was already too late. A wave of scorching heat lifted him up, and the world faded into fire and darkness.

||||

Pei's head felt like it was floating miles above the earth. Tears ran down his cheeks. Somehow, he was relieved.

"It wasn't because of me," he said.

With the realization that he was not the cause of Meng's death, the stone that had pressed down upon his heart for eighteen years finally lifted. Even stronger was the feeling of admiration he felt for his dead lover. He had never imagined that her death could have been so heroic.

Wiping his eyes, Pei stared at Yuan. "That was Meng, all right," he croaked. "Never one to admit defeat. She was unbeatable!"

"Yes," Yuan said, unmoved by Pei. "I wasn't able to beat her. Nor could I beat you. She took almost everything from me. Now, because of you, I can finally lay the remnants of my life to rest." He paused, as if suddenly reconsidering. "But even so . . . neither of you was able to defeat me. You'll understand soon enough. When this eighteen-year-long struggle of ours ends, it'll be easy to tell who wins."

Pei shook his head. "I've found you. It ends here."

"I wanted you to find me." Yuan laughed, painfully. "And I'm not Eumenides. Not anymore, at least. I stopped after your girlfriend burned me to a crisp."

Pei closed his eyes, ashamed of his own hubris. The explosion in the warehouse had crippled Yuan, but not his motivation. That was why he had waited eighteen years. He had to.

"There is another," Pei said, testing his new theory.

"Yes." Yuan nodded, and he tightened his grip on Guo.

Pei clenched his jaw. Yuan had needed time to train a successor, to teach someone the skills needed to carry out his mission of justice.

"I'm going to find him."

"No, you won't." Yuan smirked. "He has no records. Not

even a single photograph. Tell me, Pei, how do you find someone who doesn't exist?"

"Deng Hua!" Pei exclaimed, his enthusiasm not at all diminished. "That's how I'll find him. And I already know the location that's essential to your plan!"

Yuan's cracked face contorted into a grin, one that took Pei back two decades. The feeling was haunting beyond words.

"I like the way you've turned out, Pei."

Pei stiffened.

"Think back to eighteen years ago, before the explosion. Back when we were roommates—practically brothers—both fighting to prove that we were the top students at the academy. Did you ever think that one day we would end up like this? Here we are, on opposite sides, fire against ice. We do all we can to best the other, yet neither has the least assurance of victory."

Pei said nothing. His brow furrowed in concentration.

"I know that you've thought about this, just as I have," Yuan said. "We both crave challenge and excitement, yearning for a great enemy more than a good friend. I know that we've both fantasized about the same thing: standing face-to-face on the battlefield in a life-or-death struggle. Either you kill me, or I kill you."

Pei hissed through his teeth. Yuan laughed, but he sounded like a dying animal.

"I turned our fantasy into reality. You should be thanking me, really. I'm the one who wrote the letter that brought you here. I'm the one who invited you to join the game. And you haven't disappointed. To tell the truth, I'm jealous. You still have a chance to face off against an exceptional opponent."

Pei stared at Yuan for a long time before he finally shook his head. "You're insane."

"Insane?" Yuan sneered. "I may be insane in your eyes, but at least I am able to punish acts of injustice. I'm doing the work you and the rest of the police should be doing."

"But we would never murder someone who was innocent!" Pei roared in indignation.

"Come on, Pei. What does it really mean to be innocent?" Yuan shrugged. "Let me ask you something. If I hadn't killed Meng or Zheng Haoming—if I had only killed those who deserved to be punished for their crimes—would you arrest me?"

Pei barely needed any time to consider his response. "Of course I would."

"Fine. Now take another look at her." He tugged on Guo's arms, bringing the sobbing woman back into their frame of reference. "Pretend, for a moment, that I'm someone who has always been a good, law-abiding citizen. However, I find it impossible to stomach this woman's despicable actions, and now I want to kill her. Would you go as far as to shoot and kill me in order to stop me?"

"Yes, I would," Pei said resolutely.

"But you also detest this woman. You don't actually hate what I'm doing, but in spite of this, you still have to do whatever it takes to stop me. You would even kill me if you thought you had to. All because of your need to uphold your rules, and because you believe these rules protect the people."

"That's right," Pei said, nodding.

"I've done something that you want to do, but are unable to carry out. Yet you'd still shoot me. Now tell me: Would I be considered innocent?"

Pei merely shook his head.

"Why are you hesitating? Let me answer that for you. I wouldn't be innocent. You see, we're already on opposite sides of the battlefield. Even if we can sympathize with each other, even if we're pursuing the same brand of justice, we're doomed to fight to the death. We're both prepared to sacrifice ourselves in order to punish crime—all for the good of the public. No one is truly innocent." Yuan exhaled deeply before he went on. "Besides, with the exception of Meng, everyone I killed deserved it. Even the man I used as a decoy for my own death had done unforgivable things."

"But Zheng was innocent. Your successor killed him anyway."

"Zheng was too curious for his own good. I'm prepared to eliminate anyone who gets in my way."

Pei looked Yuan in the eyes. "Then why haven't you killed me?"

"Do you remember the 'catfish effect'?"

Pei thought back to those hours he had spent in the lecture hall. Professor Yang had taught that the term originated from an old Norwegian fable. Long ago, when Norway's fishing boats would sail out from the coast in search of sardines, the fishermen found that the valuable fish rarely survived the trip from sea to port. However, to the others' astonishment, one ship captain was able to bring home live sardines without fail. His secret was surprisingly simple: He would drop a catfish into the fish tank. As soon as the sardines spotted the predator, they would dart around the tank in an anxious effort to avoid it. This forced the sardines to grow strong, and to survive until the ship returned to harbor.

"You're the catfish," Yuan explained. "Your presence is what keeps Eumenides on his toes. That's why I won't kill you. I have nothing left to teach him. You, on the other hand, will become his greatest opponent in the days to come, and at the same time you will become his greatest teacher."

Pei wasn't sure whether Yuan intended the label as an insult or a compliment. Perhaps neither.

"You've lost it, Yuan. You're so wrapped up in your own lies that they've blinded you to the truth. You can't even see that your days of killing are coming to an end." Pei allowed himself a cold grin. "I'm looking forward to sinking my teeth into that sardine of yours."

Yuan licked his cracked lips. "You're really going to try to stop me from killing Deng?"

"Of course. Are you saying I can't?"

"Oh, I have no doubt that you can. You already know what kind of person Deng is. He's a criminal. He traffics in narcotics. He's neck-deep in blood. Is this really the kind of person you'd risk your own life to save?"

"The law judges by its own standards. Deng's crimes are one thing. For you to try to execute him through illegal means is another. The law doesn't permit you to carry out your own perverse brand of justice, and neither will I."

"Such nobility comes so easy to you." Yuan bared his bone-white teeth. "You only think this way because you've never had to face a more difficult choice. But soon enough you'll understand. There's no way out for you, either."

"What's that supposed to mean?"

"When Mu left this restaurant earlier," Yuan said, smiling, "she was carrying something that I'd given her. Your powers of observation have always been razor sharp. I'm sure that particular detail didn't slip past you."

Pei froze as he remembered the hurried manner in which Mu had rushed out from the Jade Garden and into a taxi. His jaw clenched. "What did you give her?"

"It doesn't matter *what* I gave her." Yuan's cheeks twitched. "But what does matter is what Deng believes she now has in her possession. The tape that Bai Feifei recorded all those years ago."

Pei's breath caught in his chest as he realized what this meant for Mu. Slamming his fist against the table, he leaped to his feet.

"You son of a bitch. You're going to get her killed!"

"*I* won't harm a single hair on her body. Deng wants her dead. Oh, and don't bother trying to convince his lapdog Hua that it's a trick. I've already told him that you'd do anything to save your teammate."

"You bastard . . ." Pei's rage was burning so fiercely that it charred away every other thought. He grabbed Yuan by the collar of his trench coat. The veins in his neck bulged as he demanded, "Why did you have to drag her into this?"

"This is your test," Yuan said slowly, enunciating each word carefully. "I needed to give you a difficult choice. I needed to see how you'd respond."

Pei's hands began to tremble, and he let go of Yuan. Taking out his phone, he frantically tapped for Mu's number. But there was no answer. Pei slammed his phone onto the table.

Yuan did not appear the least bit flustered. "It's time to go, Officer Pei. If you wait any longer, it'll be too late for you to have a choice."

Pei picked up his phone and walked toward the door.

Yuan called out from behind him.

"Wait."

Pei stopped, and looked back.

"Don't I even get a good-bye?" Yuan asked.

The two men looked at each other. Their entire history—from the friendship to the eighteen years of grief and longing and regret, and even the enmity and anger that defined today's encounter—coalesced into a single moment.

"I'd rather leave you in peace, before you go to hell," Pei hissed. Turning back, he ran out the door.

Yuan felt his life force ebbing with each pounding step that Pei took. He leaned back against his seat, as frail as a man on his deathbed.

"We've had a good run, Guo, haven't we?"

"That cop is right. You're insane," she hissed.

He draped an arm around her shivering shoulders. "Maybe I am. But the two of us won't have to worry about that for much longer."

Yuan had completed what he had set out to accomplish. He'd completed the mission that had consumed the latter half of his life, but he felt no joy.

All he had was loneliness.

||||

This was certainly the most miserable day in his entire law enforcement career, Sergeant Chen thought. It was bad enough that a hostage situation had sprung up in his jurisdiction, but it was even more infuriating that none of the individuals who had met with the hostage taker so far had stayed behind at the scene to debrief him in any way as to what was said, or what to do next.

However, when Pei left the restaurant, he at least had the courtesy to shout two words to the police: "Fall back!"

"Everyone, move back!" Sergeant Chen promptly yelled at his officers. While he was not sure what had happened, one look at Pei made him fear the worst.

A blast shook the ground, shattering the windows of several neighboring buildings. The Jade Garden collapsed into a pile of concrete and plumes of dust. The only sound Chen could hear was the deafening ringing within his ears.

Chaos engulfed the scene. People screaming in shock while others ran for cover, and others even pushed toward the rubble as if drawn by an awful curiosity.

Pei, meanwhile, had already crossed the barricade at the end of the street. He did not look back. When he reached the intersection, he looked in the direction Mu had taken. The roads in this area could lead anywhere, and he was not an expert in the local geography.

Just as he stood at the crossroads, his phone rang and he saw Mu's name on the display. He answered without a second thought. However, it was Zeng's voice.

"Hello? Captain Pei?"

"Zeng?" Unsure whether to expect good or bad news, Pei anxiously asked, "Where are you? What about Mu?"

"We're at the Number One People's Hospital. Mu ran into some trouble. Shit, I'm just lucky I got there before anything really bad happened!" He was fuming.

Pei needed to get moving. He scanned the crowd for the young officer that had driven him, Mu, and Hua. The man was nowhere to be seen. Frowning, he looked at Sergeant Chen, who was currently hurling orders at the officers swarming outside the restaurant. He could ask Chen to provide him with transportation to the hospital, but every one of his instincts told him that the sergeant would deny this request without a second's thought.

Turning his head, he spotted a row of taxis parked several dozen feet away. He sprinted over to the one in front and wrenched the passenger door open. The driver, who had been gaping at the destroyed restaurant, yelled in shock as Pei slid into the taxi.

"What the hell do you think you're doing?" he asked.

Pei showed the man his badge. "I need to get to the Number One People's Hospital as fast as humanly possible."

"Sure, sure," the driver said, finally calming down. He shifted the taxi into gear. "Anything you want," he said, eyeing the gun poking out of Pei's side holster.

Pei dialed Zeng's number. The younger officer immediately picked up, and Pei asked him to explain what had happened earlier.

"After Mu left for the Jade Garden," Zeng explained, "I couldn't put my mind at ease. I left the station and headed for Xingcheng Road, arriving outside the police barrier just in time to spot Mu entering a taxi. She was carrying a package. I got in another cab and followed her. After a while, Mu exited the car and entered some dilapidated alleyway. I wasn't sure why she went there, but judging from the way she carried herself, she didn't plan on being noticed. I waited outside the alley. Soon, two men entered. They were looking for something. I heard Mu cry out, and I rushed in!"

Pei exhaled in relief.

"I found her on the ground, deep in the alley," Zeng continued. "She was unconscious, but still breathing. One of the two men I spotted was keeping watch while the other searched her. The first guy saw me, and then rushed over. You should have seen me! I was about to kick his ass, but then the other guy whistled and they were both gone in a flash. I was too concerned with Mu to pursue. I hoisted her on my back and carried her to the first taxi I could find, and now we're here at the hospital."

"I'm almost there," Pei said. "What's her present situation?"

"The doctor told me later that she suffered a minor head injury. She's going to make a full recovery. She's awake now. We're in room 417 in the east wing."

The taxi pulled up to the hospital, and Pei leaped out. He ran to the entrance of the east wing and sprinted to the elevator. When he reached room 417, he found Mu resting on her cot and gazing out the window. Zeng was sitting by her side, rubbing the contents of a bottle of antiseptic ointment onto the bruises on his arm. His hair was tousled, and the cut over his eye would need a couple of stitches. He shot Pei a loopy grin.

"How is everything?" Pei asked.

The room's two occupants turned to him, and Zeng grinned.

"Nothing serious. Those thugs didn't know that they were going up against the academy's undefeated boxing champion."

Pei and Mu looked at each other, and saw the truth in one another's eyes—those "thugs" were Deng's men.

Without wasting any more time, Pei asked Mu, "What did Yuan Zhibang give you?"

"Who?" Mu squinted one eye at Pei.

"Huang Shaoping is Yuan Zhibang! I know it sounds crazy, but I'll explain everything later. Just tell me one thing! What did he give you?"

Pei hurried to the window as he spoke. He peered out the window, and immediately noticed several young men standing in front of the hospital. While some would assume that they were simply loitering, Pei could tell from their mannerisms that they were actually keeping watch over the building's entrances and exits. Deng's men were already here.

Pei stepped out into the hallway and called Liu Song. After explaining the situation as quickly as he could, he asked Liu Song to dispatch a security detail to Mu's room as soon as possible. The SPU officer agreed immediately.

When he returned to the room, Pei saw that Mu and Zeng were still attempting to process his revelation. Despite her initial doubts, Mu did appear to understand the seriousness of the matter. She removed a slip of paper from her pocket.

"He gave me this. It was inside an envelope . . . But what does it mean?"

Pei took the slip of paper. Only two words were written upon it. *I'm sorry.*

He rubbed his forehead and let out a long exhale.

I'm sorry.

Eighteen years ago, Yuan had said those words to Meng moments before she tore the wire from the bomb. Now he had done the same to Mu before casting her off to be pursued by Deng and his men.

Given what Yuan had led Deng to believe, there was no way that the kingpin would give up his pursuit of Mu. With the power he wielded in this city, he was fully capable of subduing his enemies. Eventually, Mu would be unable to escape his reach. Deng would interrogate her—quite possibly even torture her—until she gave up the location of the recording. Even though the recording did not exist.

Pei's mind worked quickly. Deng's web of influence was too vast. If he was to save Mu, there was only one option. He would have to sidestep the law and end Deng's life.

Pei would have to defy every principle that he had upheld his entire career.

Yuan had left him with a choice.

It was either Mu or Deng. He could only save one of them.

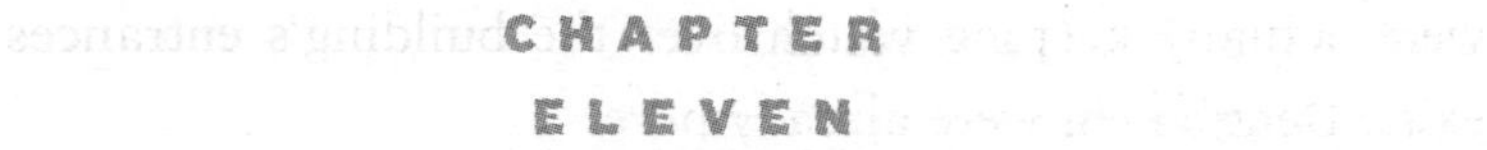

CHAPTER ELEVEN

LAST BLOOD

OCTOBER 25, 5:11 P.M.
THE LONGYU BUILDING

When Pei entered the lobby, he saw that the SPU officers taking part in the operation had already assembled there. Han was telling them his detailed strategy to keep Deng alive.

Liu Song spotted Pei approaching and immediately walked toward him, steering him away from the others.

"Any progress, Captain?" Liu Song asked anxiously. "What's our next move?"

"Nothing. There's nothing to do."

"What?" Liu's eyes widened in shock. "You told me to make preparations for tonight. I've already gotten in touch with my department's political commissar—he's waiting for my report as we speak. Anything we need to tell the higher-ups can go through him."

Pei considered his response. "That's no longer necessary. Let's just wait until we've made it through the night, and then we'll deal with Han and Yin." He studied the crowd. "Where's Yin?"

"Han said he hasn't seen him. He's definitely on the run!" Liu lowered his voice to a whisper. "If we don't take action now, it's going to be a hell of a lot harder for us to catch him."

There was so much new information to tell the officer, but right now he could say nothing. "I'll be straight with you," he said. "I'll give you an explanation for Xiong's death as soon as I can. I promise. But not yet."

"Understood," Liu said coldly.

The captain pointed to the crowd. "Let's join everyone else. Right now, the most important thing we can do is listen to the captain's battle plan."

As they approached the assembly of officers, Captain Han finally caught sight of the captain.

"Captain Pei!" Han called out. "What the hell happened over there?"

"Huang Shaoping is really Yuan Zhibang," Pei grimly informed the captain. "He's dead now."

Captain Han was speechless.

"Huang—I mean, Yuan—was the same person who called himself Eumenides in the three murders eighteen years ago," Pei continued. "But Eumenides's legacy still lives on. There is someone new."

Pei quickly gave a concise account of the situation, from the hostage situation to the restaurant's explosion and subsequent cleanup, although he was careful to omit several details that would be inconvenient to mention in front of the others. *Xue Dalin,* Pei thought to himself. *Deng Hua. Mu.*

"Shit," Han said. "There's a new Eumenides responsible for the recent string of murders—and we have no idea who he is?"

Pei nodded. "He is someone without any personal records. No paper trail. It's as if he doesn't exist."

"We'll wait for him," Han said through his teeth. "It's time for Eumenides to learn the true meaning of justice."

"Yes," Pei said.

"We need to focus on this operation now," Han ordered. "I'll get you up to speed, Pei."

Han explained that Deng had insisted his personal security detail consist solely of his own bodyguards. The police were to handle secondary security duties, and control all entrances and exits. At 6:30 Deng would depart from the Longyu Building and travel to the airport. He would then quickly board his 8:40 flight to Beijing. According to the arrangement Han and Deng had agreed upon, Liu would first leave the building with the SPU team in order to ensure that the path ahead was safe and unimpeded. Deng's fleet would then accompany a police motorcade led by Han. When they reached the airport, Deng would wait inside his bulletproof car while the police oversaw his boarding procedures. Once everything was in order, he would leave the vehicle and go directly to the security checkpoint, subsequently entering the departure lobby under the twofold protection of his bodyguards and the police.

Deng's route to his Beijing-bound plane had been designed to minimize contact with the outside world. He would enter his Bentley right at his building's entrance, and his chauffeur would drive directly to the airport's underground garage. When Deng emerged from the vehicle, he would be at the private VIP entrance to the airport. There, he would not only be under the protection of his fleet of personal bodyguards and the police but all civilians in the vicinity would be restricted from approaching him.

The security measures for the operation were airtight.

The one and only brief window of time in which Deng would be forced to be in public was when he entered the departure lobby. Not even the police had the authority to prevent other passengers from entering that area of the airport. However, as every traveler would already have passed through airport security, none of them would be able to carry anything even as small as a razor blade into the lobby.

Resourceful as Eumenides had proved himself, this was a different situation. With the additional protection of bodyguards and full police surveillance, he would never get close to Deng. The departure lobby was an isolated space. As soon as the police or Deng's bodyguards caught a whiff of anything suspicious, Eumenides would be trapped like a fish in a net.

Assassinating Deng Hua inside the airport would be simply impossible. Yet if Eumenides had proven anything, it was that he possessed an uncanny ability for achieving the impossible.

Everyone knew their role. Liu's SPU team left the building, while Pei waited inside the lobby with Han and the others. Pei had no doubts as to where the key to this operation lay. Eumenides would make his attempt inside the airport.

Pei looked over at Han and saw his tension. Veins bulged from the team leader's temples.

Han was also waiting for a crucial moment in their operation. He had already lost far too much—there was no turning back now.

I made one tiny mistake, one that created a big mistake . . . and then that led to a bigger one. Once you take your first step down the wrong path, there's no turning back.

The blood on the gearshift had nearly given him away.

Han thought back on how he had set out upon this path on an autumn night one year ago. He had been walking along it ever since.

IIIII

TWO NIGHTS EARLIER

POLICE HEADQUARTERS, CONFERENCE ROOM

"What is your name?"

"Peng Guangfu."

The instant Han saw that Peng was alive, his heart sank to the pit of his stomach. Eumenides knew. He had uncovered the truth about the Mount Twin Deer Park case. Each of the criminals featured in the other videos had been killed; he had kept only Peng alive. Eumenides was making his intentions crystal clear.

Han resisted the urge to look away from the screen. What if Mu or Pei noticed? They were the most perceptive members in the group, and with Mu's background in psychology, she was more likely than anyone to notice that something was wrong.

At the end of the recording, Eumenides sliced off Peng's tongue. *"I'm giving you an opportunity,"* the silhouette said. *"I only hope you can make the most of it."*

It was fair to assume these words were meant for Peng—or they might be another taunt aimed at the entire police department.

Likewise, everyone seemed to assume that Eumenides had cut out the man's tongue in order to prevent him from revealing any information about the killer. Han alone understood the true meaning of Eumenides's threat.

Even with his tongue cut out, Peng could still write. If the task force rescued him and brought him back to the station alive, Han had no doubt that he would reveal everything.

Han saw what was at stake, and his sharp instincts grasped the dark opportunity Eumenides offered.

Several minutes after the captain had returned to his office, his direct line rang. The voice that spoke was harsh and low, as though the speaker was trying to conceal his identity. It was identical to the voice in the videos. Eumenides.

"You should be thanking me for not revealing your secret."

Han locked the door and listened.

"The ball is in your court now. I'm sure you know what you should do to make the most of it.

"Don't worry, I will help you. Once you arrive at the location the transponder indicates, your window of opportunity will open up. It won't last for long, however. You must be decisive—you cannot hesitate, not even for a second."

Han clenched his teeth. So this is how it felt to be a puppet.

"What's wrong? Cat got your tongue? Allow me to describe what will happen if you refuse. Your shame will be public. You'll be a disgrace. An outcast. Peng will live on, despite his crimes. He won't have a tongue, but in the end he will win. He will watch your fall from grace, and he will do so with wicked happi-

ness. This is your fate, unless you act. You will have one chance. Kill Peng, or live with the consequences of your crimes. Do you understand?"

Han could not breathe.

"Follow my instructions, and they'll say Eumenides killed another victim. You will be free, if you can live with it. I will be watching. Once you've succeeded, I will destroy every remaining shred of evidence.

"These are the rules. If you don't play, you won't like how it ends."

The caller hung up without Han ever saying a word. He couldn't. He had no choice.

||||

Not a day went by that Han didn't relive what happened at Mount Twin Deer Park. The mistakes. The secrets. The guilt.

When he encountered Zhou Ming and Peng Guangfu in the rock garden that night, alcohol had numbed his senses. The adrenaline of the chase had sobered him up a little, but he was still drunk. He was sluggish, and he needed to shut one eye to keep track of the figures he was chasing. Han knew deep down that he was to blame for what happened next.

It was Han who first cornered the thieves down the park path. The two men tossed down their knives and Han made the mistake of relaxing. He was too slow when Zhou Ming pulled out a gun from his waistband and shot Han in the leg. Han immediately returned fire, but his aim was compromised.

Zou Xu leaped out from behind a boulder, at their left flank. He tackled the shooter. At the same time, Han aimed his gun at Zhou Ming and pulled the trigger.

Zuo Xu fell instantly. Han's bullet had pierced his chest.

Han's partner used his final breaths to pull Zhou Ming to the ground and seize his gun. Peng Guangfu fled the bloodbath.

Han approached, hobbled by the wound to his leg. He held his gun pointed at Zhou Ming while Zou Xu died. After letting out a ragged breath, the officer fell limp. A terrible mixture of dark emotions filled him. He looked upon his fallen partner, and bellowed up at the night sky.

Zhou Ming cowered against the rock, pleas for mercy spilling from his mouth. He had dropped his gun, and was holding his hands out in total submission. But Han was engulfed in rage. Han pressed the barrel of his sidearm against the man's chest and pulled the trigger.

Zhou Ming's blood spurted onto Han's face, and the officer's drunken haze finally began to lift.

He had made mistakes. And he had to make a decision.

There were three bullet casings at the scene. He had fired two bullets, killing his partner Zou Xu and the criminal Zhou Ming. Zhou had fired the bullet that wounded Han. This material evidence alone was enough for the police to extrapolate the truth behind the chaos that had just transpired.

He needed to change that.

Powering through his own injury, Han searched Zou's body for the bullet that had killed him. He quickly found it—it had passed through his partner's chest and was protruding through the skin of his back, right below his rib cage. Han wrenched the bullet out and slipped it into his pocket.

The gunfire did not go unnoticed. Sirens sounded outside the park within minutes. By the time the officers rushed onto the scene, Han had just placed the bullet from his partner's body where he had found the bullet that had killed Zhou Ming. When the officers questioned him, his shock was genuine. But his mind was spinning. On his way back to headquarters for questioning, he formulated a plan to cover up the evidence of his own actions. It wouldn't be easy. But if the truth came to light, things would be so much worse.

Over the next several days, Han rewrote history. He was the

only one to know who had really shot his partner and mercilessly executed a criminal. The only one—except for Peng.

Articles about the shootout in Mount Twin Deer Park dominated the media for days. Chengdu's criminal police department gave Han a medal for distinguished service, and eventually the promotion for which he and Zou Xu had competed for so long.

Han Hao was a hero.

The pain in Han's heart never ceased. Every day, he relived the moment when Zou Xu collapsed to the ground, and the feeling of Zhou Ming's hot blood staining his face when he shot him at point-blank range.

He needed to forget it all. Once he had decided to distort the truth, he was beyond the point of no return. He began the wild manhunt for Peng Guangfu, not just to apprehend the man and bring him to justice, but to put a bullet into him and silence the only other individual who knew the truth about what happened that night in Mount Twin Deer Park.

Despite all his efforts, he never found Peng, and Han's superiors ordered him to call off his hunt for personal vengeance. He had no choice but to let it go. From that day on, he harbored a secret hope that Peng would never fall into the hands of the police, and that his shameful secret would remain buried forever.

But Eumenides wasn't ready to let Han's past crimes stay buried and unpunished.

||||

In the early hours of October 25, with Peng Guangfu chained helplessly to the mine wall like a sacrificial animal, Han did what he had to do.

Eumenides's plan had lured three of the four officers away from Peng's side—the criminal was handcuffed to a scaffold—and down three separate tunnels. If only Xiong had obeyed Han's order to go with them, it would have been perfect. But the SPU captain refused.

It was the worst-case scenario. Han had anticipated it, however, and was prepared.

He had already sown the seeds of his fate long before.

A second step always follows the first.

Han had to kill a brother-in-arms. But this time it was no accident. He walked up to Xiong and guided his razor neatly through the man's throat. Blood spurted onto his flesh and dripped down his wrist. Peng's blood flowed next. It was becoming a familiar feeling.

Xiong crumpled to the ground, but he refused to succumb to his wounds. The deep gash across his throat left him incapable of uttering so much as a single syllable. Robbed of his ability to speak, he could only gape at Han in rage and betrayal.

Han's courage failed him. No matter how much he told himself that this was necessary, he couldn't finish the job. He sprinted into the depths of the tunnel as though fleeing from hell—or running into it.

The last look Xiong had given him chilled him to his core. Han stumbled through the tunnel in a trance. When Yin appeared, Han did not recognize the officer at first. Instinct made him lash out at the silhouette rushing toward him; in doing so he transferred Xiong's blood from his hand to Yin's, blood that would later appear on the gearshift.

Once they had rushed Xiong to the hospital, Yin noticed the blood on his hand under the building's fluorescent lights. His mind edged closer to the horrifying truth. It was a hypothesis he did not dare to believe, yet at the same time he could see no other explanation.

Yin kept his uncertainty buried deep inside his mind. Han was not only a leader to him—he was a mentor and a hero. To see his ideal of the man crumble before his eyes was more than Yin could bear. Faced with terrible reality, he saw no better choice than to hide from it.

But Liu insisted on dredging up the matter at the following meeting.

Han gave his alibi, saying he had put the blood on the gear-shift, and Yin still stayed silent. Han was not surprised. He had pushed Yin out of the way of a burglar's knife three years earlier. Since then, the young officer all but treated him like a second father. Yet Han could not remain quiet. He needed to tell Yin the truth.

Inside his office, Han told Yin everything. From the messy killings at Mount Twin Deer Park to the threatening phone call from Eumenides. Because of his loyalty to Han, Yin agreed to protect his secret. However, he demanded that Han resign from his position as investigation team leader immediately, so as to prevent him from becoming Eumenides's tool once more.

Han intended to do just that. But Eumenides would not let him off so easily.

Two hours before the task force met to discuss Deng Hua's death notice, Han received another call in his office.

||||

"You did well, Han. I'm watching the video from the mine again. Very compelling. You have a real talent for killing police! But the game isn't over yet, Captain. I have one more task for you. Complete it, and I will delete the video.

"Deng Hua will be surrounded by his bodyguards at the airport. No one will be able to get close to him without being caught. Don't worry. Do you honestly expect me to ask a police captain to kill someone in plain sight of everyone else?

"I will be at the departure lobby tonight. When I'm ready, you will cause a diversion where I tell you. This will be child's play for you. No one will suspect a thing.

"That's all I need you to do. I'll alert you via text message when it's time.

"Once the game ends, I'll destroy the video. You know I keep my word."

Every sentence left Han more of a nervous wreck. He was furious. Furious at himself for having made that mistake ten years earlier. Furious at his own helplessness now. Han was simply in no position to refuse Eumenides, and they both knew it.

However, Han wasn't naive enough to believe the promise of an enemy as devious as Eumenides. He would stay in the game, and he would bring it to an end. He had a plan of his own.

"I'm going," Han told Yin, as he prepared for the day's operation within his office.

"No, Captain. You can't."

"I'm going and that's final!"

"What are you doing, Captain? This has to stop." Insistent on stopping his captain from going down any further on this path, Yin grabbed at his shirt.

Han's face contorted with anger. He struck his assistant.

This first blow led to more. The more experienced Han subdued and knocked out the younger officer with a punch to the temple.

Han saw only one option now: to tie up Yin inside the locker room, and hope that by the time he woke up it would all be over with. If he succeeded tonight, or so Han told himself, everything could still be all right in the end.

||||

OCTOBER 25, 6:30 P.M.

THE LONGYU BUILDING

Within the citadel-like headquarters of his empire, business mogul Deng Hua was in an extremely disturbed state of mind.

He had never expected the case from eighteen years ago to leave such a bothersome trail. *Who is this dead cripple?* he wondered. *How was he connected to those murders from two decades ago?*

Was he close to Bai Feifei? How else could he have known about the narcotics bust?

Were the slayings of Xue Dalin and Yuan Zhibang meant to avenge her death?

How much did he tell those two officers?

What the hell is going on?!

The questions would not leave Deng's mind. But regardless of the situation, the answers didn't matter.

What mattered was that the man was already dead.

In his office, Deng had received the news from his men that the bomb at the Jade Garden restaurant had exploded, and the cripple was dead. Of course, even if the bomb hadn't gone off, Deng had taken precautions. He had arranged with certain officers at the scene that if the man showed his face, whether to surrender or to flee, a bullet from a police sharpshooter would end his life.

Despite everything, Deng enjoyed the irony that he owed Eumenides a debt of gratitude for murdering Vice Commissioner Xue Dalin all those years ago. That corrupt bastard had taught him so much, but he had gotten too greedy.

No one understood Deng better than Xue. When the officer had taken Deng out from lockup and started grooming the young man as his informant, Xue was essentially taking on a wild animal. Deng's raw but deadly instincts had shown themselves when he had turned on Liu Hong during the narcotics operation that brought Xue so much acclaim. Xue had seen an opportunity. He needed a wolf, a wild beast that he could control. And so he had stayed his trigger finger and allowed Deng to live. As they continued to work together, Xue kept an iron grip on the collar around young Deng's neck.

Then Eumenides murdered Xue, and Deng Yulong vanished into the wilderness never to submit to another master again. He reemerged as Deng Hua, powerful businessman, and began to forge a future of his own making.

As the last man standing, Deng swiftly established a firm hold on the province's resurging drug trafficking industry. His career as an informant had made him an expert on police habits, and also allowed him to amass a sea of connections. With these advantages, dodging investigations and legal sanctions simply became a matter of careful planning and execution.

Deng amassed massive capital, but was fully aware of the consequences of his kind of business. Trafficking in narcotics was a short-term venture at best. By the time the police launched their next crackdown, he had already stepped away from that industry. However much it baffled his colleagues at the time, their misgivings cleared when China's police forces launched a nationwide anti-drug campaign and narcotics squads began arresting drug dealers by the hundreds. Deng's empire continued to grow unfettered.

As China's economy boomed during the 1990s, Deng began investing in leisure and consumer industries. With the help of his far-reaching connections on both sides of the law, his businesses flourished more with each passing day. He then oversaw the construction of the most luxurious entertainment complex in the entire province, and with his new headquarters he was able to increase both his power and political connections.

Deng's prominence grew in commercial, criminal, and even governmental circles. No one was more gracious when it came to networking. When it came to confrontations, no one was more vicious. As his influence increased, so did his enemies.

Just as he had told Pei, more people wanted him dead than he could count. He barely batted an eyelid at the written death threat Eumenides had sent him. With Brother Hua at his side, and the police watching his back, Deng's mind was perfectly at ease.

He had lived his life under the threat of death—what was so special about this particular occasion?

Deng was more interested in deciding what to do with a certain female psychologist. If she really did have that tape recording, then he had a real problem.

I've weathered storms much worse than this, he thought. *After all I've accomplished, there's no way that one little problem from eighteen years ago is going to ruin me. I'm untouchable. No one will destroy my empire.*

Pity about the girl, though. There really is quite a bit worth admiring about her . . .

A knock came at the door.

"Come in," Deng said.

Sheng entered. He avoided looking directly at Deng. This meant that there was a problem.

"Sir, the two men we sent after Mu . . ."

"Did they find the tape?"

Sheng finally made eye contact with Deng. "There were . . . complications."

IIIII

Emerging from his secure office, Deng was on schedule to depart for the airport.

Captain Han was standing by in the lobby of the Longyu Building. He gave the order and officers sprung into action, clearing the vicinity of any unauthorized personnel. Deng's chauffeur guided his Bentley to the guest-reception platform in front of the entrance. Coordinating their actions with the other members of the operation, Liu's SPU team stood guard around the platform.

A dozen black-uniformed bodyguards streamed out through the building's doors with synchronized steps. They were all tall and wore black sunglasses, as if they had sprung from the same mold.

The bodyguards formed two lines, creating a safe path from the building to Deng's vehicle. Once his people were in place, Deng entered the lobby. An entourage of three men accompanied him—two bodyguards, and his trusted attendant.

Brother Hua stayed at Deng's side, matching him stride for stride. As they approached the Bentley he quickened his pace and opened the door for Deng. Despite the circumstances, Deng carried himself with assured ease, appearing totally unfazed. This was business as usual. Or so it appeared.

Pei watched from nearby, keeping himself apart from the other officers. Something wasn't adding up between Captain Han and Peng Guangfu. He hadn't figured out all the details yet, but what he already knew was troubling enough.

When he'd studied the ballistics report in the files on the police slaying at Mount Twin Deer Park, he learned that the bullet that killed Han's partner showed significant signs of wear and tear. But after entering Zou Xu's chest, its velocity would have been severely reduced, meaning that the tip of the bullet couldn't have struck the rock behind him with nearly as much force as it had appeared to, despite exiting through his back. The conclusion was irrefutable: the bullet evidence had been tampered with.

He was forming several hypotheses, but could not yet raise them in public. Doing so wouldn't just challenge a captain of the Chengdu criminal police force and the leader of the 4/18 Task Force—it would question the authority of Chengdu's entire law enforcement system.

The facts behind Xiong Yuan's murder had seemed clear enough—he had been ambushed by Eumenides. But with the revelation of Han's tampering with the evidence in the Mount Twin Deer Park murder—and the fact that Peng Guangfu had also been present at the mine—Pei saw a different picture. Xiong was renowned for his fighting skills, and the wound on his neck indicated his attacker came at him from the front. Pei was now certain that Xiong's attacker had been someone the SPU captain would never have thought to defend himself against. An ally.

Liu Song had suspected Yin. However, Pei could see no convincing motive for him, and he set his sights upon Han. If Pei was correct that something very bad had happened at Mount Twin Deer Park, then Han would have done anything to make sure that Peng Guangfu did not survive.

Pei had to get approval from Han's superiors to officially investigate his fears. He was confident that this move would checkmate Eumenides and cripple the scheme he was preparing to carry out, while simultaneously giving the police an opportunity to turn the tables on the killer.

But Eumenides had reacted too swiftly, presenting Pei with a major dilemma. If Pei stopped Eumenides, Deng would live but Mu would likely die. If he wanted to save Mu, the only way was to stay out of Eumenides's way and let Deng Hua die.

It was either Deng or Mu.

Pei watched Deng climb into the Bentley. Then Pei observed the captain, the central figure of Eumenides's scheme, standing nearby.

The Bentley's motor started with a purr. Deng's bodyguards entered their own vehicles, forming a protective phalanx that guarded the luxury vehicle from the front and rear. Han and his officers entered two police SUVs waiting ahead of and behind the formation.

Night had fallen. The city streets were radiant with light, and the sidewalks bustled with pedestrians. It was time to move.

They reached Chengdu Shuangliu International Airport at 7:17 p.m. Liu and the SPU officers were preparing their reception. Deng's driver pulled into the underground garage and up to the airport's VIP entrance, which was cleared for exclusive use during the operation. Once all bodyguards and law enforcement personnel were in position, Hua exited the vehicle's front seat and opened the door for Deng.

Before Deng exited his limousine, he donned a fedora, face mask, and sunglasses. By the time he stepped onto the pavement, he was masked from head to toe.

Pei exited his police SUV, and gritted his teeth at the performance. There was nothing inconspicuous about Deng's grand entrance.

Brother Hua remained at Deng's side, and the black-uniformed bodyguards crowded around. The police were responsible for clearing the way forward and remaining vigilant against any potential threat. Deng took the green path that had been exclusively opened for him, following it directly to the airport's security checkpoint, which led directly into the departure lobby. The officers leading the group showed their identification to airport security, and they were all permitted into the room.

Having already received orders from his superiors, the head of the airport police sub-branch was on hand to personally lend his cooperation to Deng Hua's security arrangements. When Deng and his entourage passed through the checkpoint, the chief of airport police approached Han. "Captain, you and your men can rest assured. You won't find a safer place in the world than this lobby. There's never been a single serious crime committed here in the history of this airport."

It was 7:35 p.m., and Deng's flight to Beijing was scheduled to depart on time. Deng would be able to board within the hour. The airport's staff had pulled the passenger manifest to compare it against Zeng's list of those matching the Eumenides profile, but there were no suspicious hits—no last-minute ticket purchases, no names linked to recently stolen IDs. A major politician would have a private car ready to receive Deng upon his arrival in Beijing. His safety in the capital was guaranteed by the government.

Deng found a spacious seat in the lobby and sat as his bodyguards gathered around him. They were anything but subtle, and they attracted many curious stares from other passengers.

Captain Han marshalled his officers, distributing them evenly throughout the terminal. Based on Eumenides's threats, he anticipated that the assassination attempt would occur in the lobby. If the security detail was impenetrable, then Eumenides would have to reach out to Han to ask for a clear path to Deng.

That was what Han was hoping for. He was ready for Eumenides.

Meanwhile, Pei kept an eye on both Han and Deng Hua. As Eumenides's target, Deng would be Pei's best chance to catch the killer. Having also concluded that Han was one of Eumenides's pawns in this round, Pei resolved to watch the captain closely for any abnormal actions until Deng was safely on board, and the plane was in the air.

Pei had made his decision. One that he hoped he could live with. If he allowed Eumenides's assassination of Deng to succeed, Mu could stay safe. Then he could seize this opportunity to bring both Eumenides and Captain Han to justice.

Pei was carefully scanning the lobby, as was Han. Even Deng was doing the same. All of them were searching for the same target: Eumenides.

IIIII

Eumenides tracked the police as they entered with Deng and his bodyguards. His lips curled as Captain Han Hao glanced anxiously around the airport lobby. Without looking at his phone, Eumenides sent the message he had already composed.

"I'm here. It's time."

Seconds later, Captain Han felt his mobile phone vibrate and slyly removed his phone from his pocket to see the display.

His left eye twitched, and he swept his gaze over the entire terminal. Han did not identify his target with any assurance, but he did pick out several candidates.

The man who had just exited the restroom looked in Han's direction before turning his attention to search for a place to sit.

Even though he was holding a newspaper, he flipped through the pages quickly. It was easy to tell that his attention was focused elsewhere.

There was a man using the computer terminal in the lobby's business services area. Dressed in a suit and leather shoes, he appeared to be a government employee. But why was he wearing sunglasses indoors?

Then there was the cleaner standing on the other side of the terminal window. Han had been watching him sweeping the ground there for some time. Could he be monitoring the lobby through the reflection in the window?

As much as he wished it weren't so, Han could not order any of his officers to question these individuals. Eumenides could not fall into the hands of the police. Instead, Han could only observe while he hurried to analyze the situation in silence.

At the same time, someone else was observing Han.

Han's eye twitched again—the phone in his hand had vibrated.

"There are two officers standing ten meters south of Deng. Move them somewhere else."

Han sucked in a deep breath. He saw the two members of his team. Why did Eumenides want them moved? Was he near them, or was he going to launch his assassination attempt from that direction?

He had no time to waste; he needed to show Eumenides that he was following his commands to the letter.

He quickly walked over to the two officers.

"The two of you need to check out the man at the terminal. He's wearing a suit and sunglasses."

The two officers walked away, and Han occupied the position they had just vacated. Moments later, he received another message.

"Very good. Once I've made my move, do not attempt to stop me."

He's here, the captain thought, gritting his teeth. *But where?*

His phone vibrated again.

"I'm standing among the bodyguards, wearing a red shirt."

Of course. Eumenides had already wormed his way into Deng's personal entourage. He had changed into the same black uniform and glasses that the bodyguards wore, but his last message indicated that he didn't have enough time to change out of all his original clothing. While the others wore white shirts underneath their uniforms, he was wearing a red shirt . . .

Every hair on Han's body prickled. He was standing mere steps away from Eumenides. He scanned the sleeves of the bodyguards' black uniforms. The shirt each man wore inside his uniform was exposed at the wrist. Each wore a white shirt—with one exception.

The red-shirted man stood right next to Brother Hua, and only a short distance from Deng. Other than the discrepancy in his attire, the way he carried himself also differed from the other bodyguards. Their eyes were focused outward as they vigilantly scanned their surroundings for any unusual activity. Unlike the others, this man's head was lowered and turned to the side, as if trying to evade the gazes of people nearby.

Han's heart began to race. The man had not noticed him. He navigated to the last text message sent to his phone.

He just had to be sure.

Replying to the message would leave a trail for the police to follow in their later investigation. Calling the number, on the other hand, was a different matter, and much harder to trace. He could use his own resources to delete the record of the call.

Eumenides needed to die. Any other problem was solvable. Any incriminating pieces of evidence could be destroyed. Even if anyone else suspected him, the argument for his innocence would be unshakeable.

Eumenides, and his own nightmare, would finally end.

Han was feigning cooperation for only one reason: to place a bullet between the man's eyes as soon as he had the chance.

He finally had the killer in his sights. He only needed to leave no doubt before taking action.

Han pressed the *Call* button.

The call went through. The man wearing the red T-shirt reached his hand into his pocket and drew out a cell phone. A second later, he pressed a button on the device and returned it to his pocket.

The ringing on Han's end ceased. A familiar recorded message played instead.

"*We're sorry. The caller you're trying to reach is currently unavailable . . .*"

Eumenides had finally slipped up.

Han had only seconds to act; hesitation was not an option. The bodyguards watched as he approached, suspicion registering on their shielded faces. Brother Hua turned his head toward Han. "Is there a problem, Captain Han?"

Unlike the others, Eumenides turned away, as if sensing the noose growing tight around his neck. Han was resolute. Raising his right hand, he leveled the barrel of his semiautomatic at the man.

The gunshot rang through the lobby with the force of a small explosion. Han had fired from a distance of only five feet. The bullet entered the side of the killer's skull just above his left ear. Eumenides fell flat against the floor, completely still.

The gunshot sucked all the sound out of the terminal. Only after a moment did anyone even think to react. The silence turned to screams.

Hua pounced savagely upon Han and pinned him to the floor. He kept both his hands tightly pressed against the police officer's gun. Several of the bodyguards clustered in confusion around the fallen man, while the rest swarmed to subdue Han.

The police sprang into action as well. Despite their uncertainty as to what had just transpired, their training kicked in and it was essential that they bring this chaos under control. One after another, they pulled out their guns and took aim at Hua, who was still straddling Captain Han.

"Drop your weapon!"

"On your feet right now!"

"Let go of me!" Han roared. "That's Eumenides! I just shot the killer!"

Two officers rushed forward and wrenched Hua away from his savage struggle with the captain.

Deng Hua finally stood up from his seat. He shakily removed his sunglasses and face mask. His eyes went from Han to the man now lying in a pool of blood. Shock and bewilderment filled his face.

Pei rushed over. He had gotten suspicious when he saw Han making a call, but he never would have imagined that the captain was planning to do anything like this. Everything had happened too quickly for him to stop Han in time. He looked at the face of the man who had removed his sunglasses and face mask, and his heart sank.

It was not Deng Hua.

Two of the bodyguards had just turned over the shot man lying motionless on the floor. They removed his sunglasses. Even though their eyes remained invisible, the horror in each of their expressions was palpable. The man that Han had shot had already taken his last breath, yet fierce eyes remained, as did a self-assured, dignified expression.

Han had killed Deng Hua.

Brother Hua lost all control. Desperation and rage turned his words into barely discernible screams. "Han, you bastard! I'll fucking kill you!"

In spite of the two burly officers restraining him with all their might, Brother Hua broke free and charged Han like a rabid animal. His fist was a blur, and landed with a solid *crack* as it connected with the side of Han's head. The captain stumbled back, shaking his head from side to side. A corporal grabbed Han and pinned him to the ground.

"Get ahold of yourself!" Pei yelled at Hua. "Isn't this enough chaos for you?" He turned and addressed the officers around him. "Seal every entrance and exit. Nobody leaves the terminal! Liu, if Captain Han moves, shoot him!"

Several officers looked questioningly at Pei, and then at Han, who lay immobilized on the ground. They didn't appear to understand this new change in the chain of command. "You heard the man," Liu shouted, gesturing to the SPU officers flanking him. "Arrest the captain!"

Han stared at Deng Hua's lifeless eyes. He had lost. He had fallen for Eumenides's scheme. With the killer pulling the strings, he had used his own weapon to shoot Deng dead.

Han let his gun fall from his hands to the floor. He didn't fight back when an SPU officer twisted his arms behind his back. Liu approached and handcuffed him, and the captain could only smile dumbly.

The remaining officers looked at one another in stunned silence.

"What are you staring at?" Han said. "Carry out Captain Pei's orders!" He was defeated. There was no doubt, but he could not let Eumenides escape. Maybe, just maybe, Eumenides's capture could salvage something from his ruin. The only hope he had left was that the captain from Longzhou could do what Han could not.

The SPU team swiftly sealed every entrance and exit in the terminal, effectively shutting down half the airport. The police rushed around, attempting to restore some semblance of order and cordoning off the murder scene.

"Where is he?" Pei asked.

With a grimace, Han shrugged and shook his head.

"Where is he?" Pei repeated, and he slapped Han across the face. "You were in touch with him just moments ago. He has to be nearby. Where the hell is he?"

Han's eyes suddenly widened in revelation. *Eumenides knew exactly what was going on in the terminal when he contacted me. He must be close!*

Fueled by desperate purpose, Han searched his surroundings. In seconds he had found his target.

"There!" he said, gesturing with his chin.

Pei, Hua, and Liu all followed the direction of Han's gaze.

The cleaner who had previously been sweeping outside the lobby window at floor level was now washing a window on the upper floor. He appeared to be calmly watching everything unfold inside the terminal. The light from one of the airplanes taxiing across the tarmac outside was shining directly upon the man's back; the intense backlight made it impossible for anyone to get a clear look at his face—but the silhouette emanated a strangely powerful presence.

"It's him! That's him right there!" Han trembled, as though the rage and pain inside him was tearing his throat apart.

Pei and Brother Hua were already in full sprint. They flew like twin blurs across the terminal floor. Liu immediately gave an order, and several SPU members followed closely behind. In moments, everyone else involved in the operation was rushing toward the exit.

The man outside the window did not show the slightest sign of panic. After observing the terminal for several more seconds, he turned almost lazily around. The men in pursuit still needed to cover a long distance before they could reach the terminal exit.

By the time everyone reached the other side of the window, Eumenides had vanished.

Deng's corpse lay still on the terminal floor, blood leaking from the wound in the back of his head. Deng Yulong had run from his past for eighteen years, changing his name and erecting one of the largest business empires in the entire province. In the end, it hadn't been enough. Deng's past had finally caught up with him.

EPILOGUE

The airport just a dot on the landscape behind him, he roamed across a desolate strip of wilderness. The bitter autumn wind whipped across his face, but cold meant nothing to him. His blood was still boiling.

He was sure that there were countless people trying to track down his whereabouts. Yet none of them knew who he was. They only knew what he allowed them to know. He was Eumenides.

He was a man without an identity.

Eighteen years earlier he had been a poor and lonely orphan roaming the streets, on the brink of vanishing into society's cruel and uncaring maw. It was at this time that he had met a man burned and scarred beyond recognition. Most thought him a freak.

The burned man helped him achieve something that he had never before dreamed of. Eventually, he had nothing but awe and reverence for the man who became his mentor.

He trained to be his apprentice, and his abilities and skills grew.

He was going to help people.

Three years ago, his mentor gave him a list containing the names of people whose grave crimes had gone unpunished. He began searching for these people. When he found them, he exacted upon them the harshest possible punishments. He was well trained. Those thieves, rapists, and murderers were like lambs lined up for the slaughter.

He was ready to end his apprenticeship, but his mentor would not allow it. Only once he killed a certain person would he be able to become a qualified executor of justice.

Deng Hua.

It was an impossible task, but his death was what his mentor demanded.

He spent nearly three years searching for a solution to this problem. He had almost nothing to show for his efforts. That is, until he seized the next quarry on his list—Peng Guangfu.

Peng had revealed the truth behind the homicide of the police officer at Mount Twin Deer Park. This was the crucial piece of information that illuminated how he would execute Deng.

His mentor approved of his plan, with one crucial addition. He was to murder Zheng Haoming, an old police officer of the original 4/18 Task Force, to ensure Han Hao's involvement in the subsequent investigation.

The order baffled him. Zheng Haoming was not one of the names on his teacher's list. If he did wish to involve Han Hao, there were far more expedient methods of doing so.

"You're going to become a true executor of justice. Therefore, you need to understand that you will always face two enemies. The first is the criminal whose name is written on your death notice. The second is the police. Never doubt the antagonistic relationship that binds you to the police. Given the opportunity, they will kill you without the slightest hesitation. You must be prepared to do the same to them. Kill this officer, Zheng Haoming, and you will be sure never to hesitate in any of your future dealings with law enforcement."

It was not long before he became convinced of the value of these instructions. When he began to orchestrate his plan, the death of Zheng Haoming was its prelude.

The task force re-formed, with Han as its leader. The first step was complete.

Ye Shaohong came next. Murdering her when she was surrounded by police was a rather risky endeavor. Nevertheless, his success achieved a twofold effect. First, it dominated the police inquiry; once Peng Guangfu's death notice was delivered, most people would not think to focus on the Mount Twin Deer Park case. Second, it showed off Eumenides's formidable strength. It worked: when Han killed Peng and subsequently covered up his actions, no one initially suspected that the murderer was one of their own.

His plan continued. Han murdered Peng, and Xiong Yuan was collateral damage. Then the threat of releasing video from the mine ensured that the captain both feared and further despised him, and would be driven to stop Eumenides no matter what the cost.

Exactly as he had planned.

Even though he had been unable to find an opportunity to assassinate Deng over the previous couple of years, he had turned up quite a great deal of information. Deng was rarely spotted at public events, and on the few occasions when his attendance was necessary he would always surround himself with a retinue of bodyguards. He would even use a decoy to ensure his own safety . . .

Therefore, Han assumed that the man disguised as a bodyguard was actually Eumenides. The last piece of the puzzle was simple—Eumenides exploited a common feature offered by Chinese mobile providers and rerouted his incoming calls to Deng's phone.

In the end, Han had killed Deng Hua. He had finally carried out the impossible task.

With the dream fulfilled, his late mentor could finally rest in peace.

He had completed his apprenticeship. He was justice's true executor.

No one in the world knew his true name, but he would make sure that everyone would learn the name Eumenides.

||||

Brother Hua raced through darkness. He could feel his lungs aching, but he was not yet ready to stop.

He would track the bastard down, even if he had to run to the ends of the earth.

No matter where, no matter how, he would do what it took to find the killer.

This he swore.

||||

Han Hao stood in the airport terminal. The handcuffs were rings of ice against his wrists. It was a sensation he had never felt before.

Once his initial shock and torment subsided, he finally forced himself to regain control of his thoughts. He knew the consequences he would soon face for his actions. But he wouldn't go down without a fight.

Han could not just give up and accept his defeat. He needed to find a glimmer of hope in the midst of his desperation.

He was going to turn the tables. He had allies, and he was going to find the bastard that had destroyed him. He was going to tear the man to pieces with his bare hands.

This he swore.

||||

Pei Tao stood on the upper floor, on the other side of the terminal window. The killer had stood in the exact same spot only minutes earlier, but had long since vanished.

However, Pei did not lose hope. At the very least, he had finally seen the man. He believed that regardless of what came next, he would be able to find Eumenides's trail.

It was time the bastard paid for *his* crimes.

This he swore.

END OF PART ONE

About the Translator

Zac Haluza is a freelance translator and writer from the United States. He currently lives in Shanghai.